Edgewise:

An Assignment To Remember

by

Darlene F. Wofford

Bloomington, IN Milton Keynes, UK

authorHOUSE®

AuthorHouse™
1663 Liberty Drive, Suite 200
Bloomington, IN 47403
www.authorhouse.com
Phone: 1-800-839-8640

AuthorHouse™ UK Ltd.
500 Avebury Boulevard
Central Milton Keynes, MK9 2BE
www.authorhouse.co.uk
Phone: 08001974150

First published by AuthorHouse 2/7/2007

ISBN: 978-1-4259-8299-7 (sc)

Library of Congress Control Number: 2006910943

Printed in the United States of America
Bloomington, Indiana

This book is printed on acid-free paper.

I Dedicate This Book With All My Love to The Following:

To my best friend and loving husband, Carl, for all our wonderful times, and for being there as my solid rock when life was crumbling around us. To our incredible sons, Kenny and Cory, for appreciating the importance of "family," and for encouraging their mom to go for it. To our son, Collin, our precious angel, who is forever in our hearts. To my parents, Jack and Ruth, my brothers, Jimmy, Bill, and Jerry, and my sister, Pat, for always making me feel special. And to God, for sending His love to me through the special people in my life, and for never giving up on me.

I'd like to acknowledge and give special thanks to my son, Cory, for using his creative talents in designing the front cover.

Table of Contents

PART I...1

Today's Question..3

Chapter II Rainbow In The Mist 21

Chapter III Who's In The Kitchen?...29

PART II...47

The First Man In My Life 49

Chapter II They Said It Was Haunted...62

Chapter III Get Us Out Of This Chicken Outfit 68

Chapter IV Little Miss Big Ears..76

Chapter V What Could Be A Better Place? 86

Chapter VI 230 Aggies And Cat-eyes 98

Friday, May 5th, 1984: Back At Oakwood Institute.................107

Chapter VII They Grew In Groves...112

Chapter VIII A Full-fledged Woman 119

Chapter IX That's Daddy's Chair! 129

Thursday, June 15, 1984: Chestnut, Georgia Dr. Robinson's
   Office, Oakwood Institute's Satellite Facility 136

Chapter X Hang On For The Big One! 141

Chapter XI First Degree Love..154

Chapter XII I'm A Bargain At Twice The Price Friday, May 27,
   1966: 8:00 P.m., Atlanta City Auditorium 160

Chapter XIII That's The Brakes, In Reverse 168

Chapter XIV The Lost Chapter 171

Tuesday, July 23, 1984: Chestnut, Georgia Dr. Robinson's
   Office, Oakwood Institute's Satellite Facility.....................184

Chapter XV Best Friends And Lovers.....................................191

Chapter XVI All Dressed Up And Nowhere To Go 199

Chapter XVII Halloween's Nightmare...................................209

Chapter XVIII Who Sent The Dead Roses?............................224

Chapter XIX Lock The Door And Throw Away The Key 234

Thursday Afternoon, September 6, 1984: Chestnut, Georgia Dr.
    Robinson's Office, Oakwood's Satellite Facility................245

Chapter XX The Stairway To Paradise 250

Chapter XXI $8.63 Included The Broom..............................257

Chapter XXII The Cement Block Palace 265

Chapter XXIII We'll Never Live This Time Again! 272

Chapter XXIV Invastion Of The Uninvited Visitors..............277

Chapter XXV Another Year Together And Deeper In Debt 280

Chapter XXVI The Very Best Christmas Gift Ever 286

Tuesday Afternoon, October 4, 1984: Chestnut, Georgia
    Dr. Robinson's Office, Oakwood's Satellite Facility...........293

Chapter XXVII Practice Parenthood? 295

Chapter XXIII The Man In The Window...............................304

Chapter XXIX The Six Week Late—three Day Early Birthday
    Present 314

Chapter XXX A St. Bernard And French Poodles 320

Chapter XXXI One Tenth Of A Century 327

Hand On My Shoulder November 22, 1984: Monday Morning
    Before Thanksgiving 338

PART I

TODAY'S QUESTION

April 1984: Thursday afternoon before Easter

Oakwood Institute: Cheatham, Georgia

    I was content enough to go right on sitting there in Dr. Robinson's office enjoying my candy, but I knew the inevitable was about to happen. The doctor always had to start talking, and around that place her northern accent stuck out like a glob of black paint on a white picket fence.

    "You look very nice today, Delaney. Your husband will be so pleased to see you dressed in regular clothes, and your hair brushed."

    It was the first time since the day I was brought to Oakwood that I was allowed to wear my own clothes, no more gowns and robe. Belts were prohibited, and my jeans fit much more loosely than when I last wore them, two months earlier. They sagged in the back, like a whole herd of cattle had moved out, but I just considered them more comfortable that way. I couldn't stop fidgeting because that damn under wire bra was pinching me in the most awkward places. I doubted I would ever get used to it again.

"It's such a gorgeous spring day. You're in for a beautiful ride home. The weather's supposed to be pretty all weekend..." She always went on and on in such a way. I wondered if I shouldn't be paid for having to listening to her jabbering away as if she were competing for the world record. Why should that afternoon be different? I supposed it was okay to let her go on like that, as long as she didn't expect me to participate—that is, more than I had agreed.

The doctor had made a deal with me after two miserable months there. If I'd answer one question a day, she'd let me go home for the long Easter weekend. So far, I had lived up to our deal.

Of course, until that afternoon they had all been simple questions, such as, "How are you feeling, Delaney?" "Is the medication helping you rest?" "Are you sleeping all right, Delaney?"

* * *

Delaney, Del-a-ney. It echoed again and again within my disjointed mind. Oh, I suppose it's a pretty enough name, and I recognized it to be mine, all right. However, when any one called me now I'd start to wonder, *Who is this 'Delaney,' really? What has she done that's so terrible? Why is she in this place, alongside all these others? Had a part of them been taken away, too? Is that the reason they've lost or misplaced their minds?*

It's not as if I couldn't remember anything at all about Delaney. I knew she was married and had a family. I even remembered what they looked like, and their names: Mama, Kyle, Keith, Craig... and...beyond that, my memories were jumbled and confused.

Dr. Robinson said I wrapped myself in a security blanket--at least that's what she called it. If she said it once, she said it dozens of times, "Delaney, you've gone through such trauma. It's common for the mind to create a security blanket and pull it up to cover the head, shutting out the rest of the world and painful memories. It feels safe and comfortable, but sooner or later we have to pull back

4

the blanket and expose those memories—talk about them so you can get better."

There's no way she could know how that security blanket did nothing to shelter me from the cold in my own heart. And those "painful memories?" They lurked in the darkest corners of my mind, just out of sight. But the pain was still very real. So I would never consider the blanket a safe and comfortable place, but rather a place of constant confusion. The warm part of my heart that felt love, caring emotion, and the will to live was no more. In its place was a cold void and the desire to fall into a deep, peaceful, never ending sleep—one without nightmares.

In my earlier days at Oakwood, prior to our deal, I couldn't answer her questions. They were too painful and unsettling, such as, "How did you feel when you saw...?" "Can you remember anything about their...? And "What went through your mind when you realized...?" She inquired and probed, repeatedly about times I obviously couldn't remember.

I loathed that damn place, and revulsion enraged my thoughts, *I hate all the damn questions! I despise her for asking them!*

That afternoon her question of the day was much too easy, "Is it good?" She was referring to the daily bribe.

I nodded, but then remembered the rules of the game, and answered aloud, "Yes, Terri, thank you." It was the smooth type, dark and solid. Its irresistible aroma grabbed my stomach and turned it into knots while my mouth watered in anticipation. It measured a full ten inches to the tips of its extended ears—until I started gobbling away at it, feet first. The voracious growl roaring from within the pit of my empty stomach announced my starvation to anyone within ten feet. The ultra-sweetness exploded inside my mouth, and my deprived taste buds were relieved, embraced by a sense of gratification. I was always ravenous by that time of the day, and that afternoon's candy was her best bribe yet.

She had given me candy every day for the past month. It was the game we played, but I always considered the chocolate a bribe, since she knew that was my favorite. When she offered it—usually M&Ms—she required that I say the words, "Yes, please Terri. Thank you very much." Those were the only words I had spoken for months, and she insisted I call her by her first name, Terri. I didn't exactly feel comfortable being so informal, but it was always worth it to get the chocolate—the only food in the place not contaminated by those filthy-bastard roaches.

Grinning, she seemed amused at a grown woman savagely gnawing on a defenseless little chocolate bunny. I didn't care what she thought, as I bit off another bite and another. I couldn't seem to swallow fast enough as I savored the sweetness, *Mm-m, solid chocolate.*

Her expression suddenly changed and took on a serious tone as she stared at me, gliding her finger the full length of her cheek, "Does Dr. Ford think you'll require plastic surgery?"

I silently accused her of cheating, thinking, *Another question? Wait a minute—no fair. That makes two...*

With no warning other than two loud thumps that sounded like thunder, the door swung wide open, and my thoughts of accusation were halted. Even with my eyes closed I knew it was Big Mo, as the heavy thud of her elephantine walk always gave her away. Without invitation or permission, she charged into the room with a sway of her wide hips and a swish-swish of her rapid stride. "Doc Terri? Don't mean to interrupt ya, but here's some forms ya gotta fill out." Glancing across at me she continued in that irritating, high-pitched babytalk, "so that Little Miss Delaney can go home for the weekend."

"Thanks, Mo. I'll have them back to you before her husband gets here."

"Okay, Ma'am." She proceeded to leave but stopped in mid-stride, "Just send Delaney over when ya finish. I'll be there to catch 'er."

The doctor nodded and Mo was on her way, but not before calling attention to my mouthful of chocolate. "Delaney, you don't have to eat all that today. You're going to get choked… I'll get Norma out front to bring you a Coke." There was a slight resemblance to that of a halo as the glow of the fluorescent lighting bounced off Mo's starched white cap atop her salt-'n-pepper hair. She smiled down at me, winked with a twinkle in her hazel eyes, and before I knew what hit me, one of her so-called gentle pats almost knocked me off my chair. Unaware of her own strength she sometimes got a little carried away, so pats translated into slaps on the receiving end.

Her name is Modene, but abbreviated to "Mo" on her name badge. The patients called her "Big Mo," but never to her face. She was as big as the building itself, and her white uniform gave her the appearance of a side-by-side refrigerator. As strong as a bull, she had that heavy walk and a voice to match, "I'll see *you* shortly, little girl. You do good for Doc Terri, ya hear me?"

Ha, "little girl," my mind mimicked. *The way she's always adjusting my clothes and wiping my face, anyone who didn't know better would think I _am_ a little girl. Indeed, I most assuredly am _not!_*

A few minutes after Mo left the room, Norma the secretary brought me a can of Coke which I grabbed from her without hesitating. After all, it was sealed, eliminating concerns about contamination. I had survived on canned drinks and those cartons of watered-down juices for the entire first month I was there. And I would've continued those same survival techniques if not for the doctor's daily chocolate bribes.

With both hands wrapped around the ice-cold can I turned it up. In between gulps I rubbed my sticky hands all around the can's outside, moistening them with its icy condensation. I only had to wipe them on my jeans once before the good doctor gave me a handful of paper towels. After quenching my thirst I continued to nibble on the bunny during our visit.

She rubbed me the wrong way and struck a nerve when she asked yet a *third* question…a question I was unable to answer. "Delaney,

I want you to try to focus on better times now. Can you recall your first pleasant memory of your childhood?"

Recalling any pleasantry at this point was like trying to bleed a turnip. It just wasn't there. Her question did trigger one memory. But it was far from pleasant.

It was my very first memory at less than two years of age. I was asleep in my baby bed over in the corner of my parents' bedroom. Lying there on my back, my small body jolted out of reflex when I was abruptly awakened by a loud noise overhead. My eyes popped open to see and feel the world crashing down on me. First there was a big, heavy chunk, then a million pieces falling on and around me. And there was a giant monster reaching toward me through the huge hole above.

The shadows cast by the monstrous sight intensified by a dim light coming from the opposite corner of the room. I was frightened and overcome by total helplessness. Surrounded by the bars on the bed's side rails, I was trapped—caged, so I couldn't get away.

I screamed and cried out the only word I knew, "Ma-ma!" Pandemonium reigned down all around until someone finally came to my rescue.

I didn't understand what had happened. I was so horrified. I wouldn't go to sleep in that baby crib, ever again. Mama and Daddy took me to sleep with them, but the nightmares continued in their bed and beyond for years to follow.

I wasn't sure whether those events were real or a horrible dream until several years later. I was always apprehensive and unsettled when I passed beneath or looked at the patched ceiling in the corner of that room.

When I finally mustered up enough nerve to ask Mama about it, she went on to explain, "Well, Sugar, your daddy almost fell through the ceiling one night when he was in the attic. He lost his balance and his foot slipped off the rafters. His leg tore right through the sheet-rock ceiling and was dangling right there above you in your little baby bed. It scared us all half to death; and you--poor little thing--you didn't know what in the world was going on. We thought we'd never get you back to sleep, so your daddy and I brought you to our bed."

I was relieved to know what had actually happened, however my newfound knowledge did not rid my nights of the alarming dreams. They continued throughout my adolescence.

That was my first and only memory and it definitely wasn't pleasant. So, in answer to Dr. Robinson's question, I shook my head repeatedly side-to-side. Any good memories I once possessed were completely consumed by nightmares.

The doctor became insistent, "Oh, come on now, Delaney. You know you've had some good times. Try to remember. Think hard about your childhood. I know you can remember something pleasant from when you were a little girl."

I should've known she couldn't resist pressuring me; she wouldn't stick to the simple questions. Agitated, I gritted my teeth, gripped the chair arm, and raised my voice, "No!" My back became rigid and I gnawed off a big mouthful of the chocolate bunny's ear as I thought, *I've never liked or trusted that doctor, with all of her probing questions. Ha! Doctor? She's so young—still in her twenties—and she's going to help me?*

She affixed her eyes on me in such an intimidating stare, I surprised myself when I leaned forward in my chair, stared right back at her and beat my fist on her desk. I repeated emphatically, "No!"

She was visibly shocked by my actions and to hear me speak in such a tone. Fact was I hadn't spoken more than a handful of words since the first day they brought me to Oakwood on that icy-cold day in February.

I remembered when I first saw Dr. Robinson, there in her pathetic excuse for an office. She was so young, I thought, *surely this woman is no more than a medical student in training or a doctor's aide. She can't possibly be a licensed doctor.* I took an immediate dislike to her, and I knew I didn't trust her. Unfair? Maybe, but as far as I was concerned, there was no fairness in the world. I was only following suit.

I wasn't even sure what kind of a doctor I was there to see in the first place. All morning Kyle and Mama kept saying, "Delaney, you have to get dressed to go to the doctor."

I was confused by the sign outside in front of that two-story, antebellum brick building—WELCOME TO OAKWOOD INSTITUTE.

Was it one of those medical institutes or colleges where the students treat the patients for reduced fees? The thought never occurred to me that it was a facility for the insane. And I certainly didn't think my own family would take me to a place like that and leave me with no warning.

That frigid afternoon was when my husband Kyle, Mama, my sister and brother left me there, without so much as a *Goodbye, We love you, or Go to hell*. I didn't see or hear from a soul in my family until a month later. When Kyle tried to convince me it was all part of the doctor's therapy, I didn't believe him. I couldn't trust anyone, not even my own husband. But if what Kyle claimed was true, then I hated that doctor even more.

In the two months that followed Dr. Robinson still never stopped trying to size me up and control me, "Alright, Delaney, calm down and settle back in your chair. You don't want me to call the nurses, do you?"

I receded like a trained animal at the crack of the whip. I wanted to gouge her eyes out of their sockets. But I settled for the bunny's pink candy eyes, tossed them into my mouth and washed them down with a big gulp of Coke.

The doctor was perched with all her authority behind her dilapidated green metal desk. Its Formica top chipped around the edge, it had a colossal-sized dent right in front, looking as if someone with a heavy foot and a hot temper had kicked it dead center. The worn out furniture suited this whole place perfectly, with its cold, black tile floors throughout, walls painted that putrid shade of green, pealing in places, and the unsightly water-stained ceilings. Oakwood was indicative of any underfinanced county facility. I was accustomed to an attractive home that was clean and nicely decorated. However, I considered Oakwood's aesthetic shortcomings trivial in comparison with the filthy roach infestation. It was beyond any exterminator's control.

I scoped the room to see if any of the hard-shelled bastards were scurrying about, while the doctor continued to lean back in her antiquated chair, swiveling side to side. She swept her long, straight, auburn hair away from her face with her hands, holding it at the base of her neck. That was a nervous habit of hers, and every time she did it, I was compelled to reach up and do the same with mine. But mine wasn't as long as hers. In fact, it was in that aggravating, in between stage: longer than I liked it but not long enough to pull back. Except for a wave dipping across my right brow, the only remnants of my natural curly hair as a child, mine was straight like hers. But I would never consider my plain, dark brown color nearly as pretty as hers. With its color and healthy sheen, hers reminded me of our neighbor's Irish setter Red. I wondered if it were natural or out of a bottle, and imagined myself mustering up enough gumption one day to ask her.

* * *

Leaning forward and propping her elbows on the desk, she sighed in a somewhat defeated manner and said, "Delaney, Delaney, tell me, how am I ever going to get through to you?" Her eyes resembled flawless emeralds as they penetrated deep into mine, searching, as if the answer were there waiting to be uncovered.

I turned to gaze out the window to my left and avoided eye contact. But she continued to stare, observing me as though I were an unknown oddity. My chair wobbled as I squirmed from right to left, left to right.

The room was completely silent except for our breathing and the squeak of her antiquated desk-chair. I wondered, *Is she waiting for me to respond? Does she think I know the answer?*

She reached into her top drawer and pulled out a yellow, legal-sized writing pad and a pencil. "Delaney, I've been sitting here thinking. You haven't said but a few words in the two months since you've been at Oakwood. I don't need the tests to tell me that you're highly intelligent and strong willed. I see it in your eyes. But I see pain and fear in there, too, along with some very deep thoughts. You've been through so much, it's only natural to become a little off-centered. I understand, and I'd like to help you through all this as your friend." She cleared her throat in an effort to regain my wandering attention, "You with me on this?"

I nodded, but then I saw tears welled in her eyes before she quickly dabbed them away with the tips of her fingers. I was puzzled, *Are those tears of a genuinely compassionate woman--concerned about me? But why? As a doctor she's supposed to help people get better, but she'll be paid whether they get well or not. So why does she care so much about me?*

"Now, about those thoughts. I presume a good many of them are about what happened. Some are painful. Frightening, maybe."

She paused, awaiting my response, but my attention was focused someplace other than that room—other than that planet. As I gazed out the window into space, my afternoon's nightmare took control of my thoughts.

My nightmares were always the same. In them, the area is devoid of even the slightest trace of light. I can see nothing, but I feel my skin—my cold, aching skin –and the walls that enclose me. Entombed in such a cramped space, unable to stand or sit, I'm forced to lie, curled up in a fetal position. Sounds amplify a hundred times—my heartbeats pound inside my head—throbbing—growing louder with each racing beat. My teeth chatter incessantly from the freezing cold, and my face cracks open in pain. Stiff like a mask. I stop breathing and become very still at that point when I hear a small child—crying like a baby—then screaming. Muffled at first, it crescendos into an ear-piercing volume, only to fade into the distance, far beyond my reach, "Mommy! Mom-my…!" I claw at the walls, yelling, "Let Me Out, Please! Somebody Help! But my pleas go unanswered and I'm unable to reach the child. No matter how hard I try, I can never break free of whatever holds me captive. I'm totally helpless. And the pain, pain of a wounded, tormented animal is such that I'm unsure if I'm human or a wild beast someone has captured, moaning, and sobbing, "No-o-o."

The torture of the nightmares always continues until I'm abruptly awakened. Rescued, usually by Big Mo. Thank God for Mo.

That afternoon in the doctor's office, numbed by the nightmare's residual effects of helplessness, I wondered, *Why am I so claustrophobic in such a large room? Why am I so cold when I'm directly in the sun's rays as they shine through the window.* My heart raced such that I was short of breath, exhausted.

The doctor was oblivious to my state of distress as she continued, determined to make her point. "Well, Delaney, if I can't figure a way to get those thoughts out into the open so they can be discussed and dealt with, they're going to fester inside of you. Eventually, they'll tear you apart and you'll be beyond helping."

Once again, she paused to await my reaction. She did that quite often.

Is this what doctors like her do—talk, going on and on—then pausing to await the patient's reaction? What kind of a reaction is the woman looking for? What am I supposed to say? Oh, please, please help me doctor? I can't make it without your help? I could care less if I ever get better. My strongest desires are to go to sleep forever and just get away.

When she realized I wasn't responding to her scare tactics, she took a softer approach, "You may not feel like it right now, but you have a very strong mind. I want you to use it to help yourself, and help me bring you back to your husband and children. You do want to be back with your family, don't you, Delaney?"

I nodded.

"Delaney, I'm changing my question for the day. My new question is: What are your deepest thoughts and feelings?" She got up, walked around the desk and stood behind me. Placing her hand on my right shoulder, she lowered her voice, as if telling me a secret, "Don't be afraid to go into that darkest part of your mind to give me your answer." Gently but firmly squeezing that part of my shoulder, as in reassurance, she added, "and Delaney, you don't have to speak a word."

Reaching around and over my shoulder she placed the writing tablet and pencil in my hand. "Here, write it down. That's all you have to do. Get them out into the open. Will you try that for me?"

I nodded but didn't have the foggiest notion where to begin. She stepped out of the office after saying, "I'll leave you to be alone with your thoughts for a few minutes. Just take your time."

I was alone with those terrifying thoughts for three months. I knew them inside and out, yet I didn't know how to explain or describe them. I scratched my chin and stared at the paper for what seemed like forever. There was a time when I enjoyed writing, but not now.

I began writing, then scribbled all over the page in a childish fit. I ripped the page off the pad, wadded it up in my fist and tossed it into the trash can. I started over a dozen more times, throwing each page aside. In no time I'd covered the floor around me with my failure.

I was aggravated with myself and the whole stupid idea of writing about my damnable thoughts. I gobbled half the remaining bunny while wishing I could crawl inside the "darkest part of my mind," as she'd called it.

I could take a knife and cut out all those terrifying thoughts and feelings, and then spread those horrendous demons across the top of her desk. Then she could see for herself—see first hand—a portion of the damnation I face every cursed minute. I'd like to see her reaction when she sees my hell and pan, up close and personal.

My hopes were raised when a sudden flickering glint caught my eye. The sun reflected off something shiny on the desk. A metallic key ring. The doctor had been more cautious since that incident just after I had first come to Oakwood. I should've known she wasn't foolish enough to leave another metal letter opener laying around for me to snatch.

All I'd wanted to do was take what belonged to me. It was none of their business. I would have done it, too, if that night nurse hadn't discovered the blood. A glance down at the scar on my left wrist made me shudder at my failure. The letter opener hadn't been sharp enough to do the job properly. All that blood but not an ounce of pain in my wrist. All the pain was in my heart, so I'd started digging to get the thing out of my chest. I only succeeded in making a mess. So I started on the wrist again, slashing and jabbing over and over. The nurse saw the blood and called for reinforcements, who strapped me down while they bandaged the gashes. When they changed the bed linens, that's when they found it—tucked underneath the mattress. Its slender, once shiny blade covered in blood.

That's when they jerked me up, strapped me in the chair and wheeled me away to the Silent Room downstairs in the main building. Every square inch of the place was covered in dingy, gray-white padding. The bright overhead light remained on the entire time, but even in all that brightness my world remained dark.

The roaches were breeding twice as fast in the warmth and darkness beneath those filthy mats. I could hear them. I can't say for certain how long I was kept there, sharing that space amidst that infestation of undesirables, but as far as I counted, Dr. Robinson came in four times. I usually didn't see her but once a day. She'd told me I could go back to my room, but only when I calmed down and was no longer any danger to myself.

The chaplain they'd sent to pay me a visit always wore the same black, pet hair covered suit and white shirt in need of an iron. The tie with its holes from cigarette burns confirmed the reason he always smelled like an ashtray. He intruded daily, barging in with his Bible thumping, holier-than-thou words of a hell and brimstone, indicative of a hard-core southern Baptist preacher. "You know, little lady, the Good Book right here says your soul will be condemned to eternal hell if you take your own life!" Then he'd read passage after passage from his "good book" and await my response. His penetrating eyes revealed how much he was disturbed by my nonchalant attitude. I turned a deaf ear to the old man while my mind raced, *If there really is a God who is all-seeing and all-knowing, as this so-called, man-of-the-cloth is claiming, then God understands. Get me out of the darkness, away from the demons.*

So now, with that whole ordeal fresh in mind, I wrote:

> Demons abound in the darkness and void of the loneliness within the walls of my mind.

My pen took off like a poet possessed, and I continued to write:

I'm so alone, though surrounded by others.
  This loneliness is like being in hell.
I've given up and lost all will to live,
  Caring less if I ever get well.
Nightmares cause so much pain in my life;
  There's too much for me to face.
My mind closed the door to the rest of the world,
  Now I'm alone…in this hell of a place.

* * *

I'm unsure how long Dr. Robinson left me there in her office. No matter how much longer she might have given me, I had expressed my thoughts as well as I could. As she re-entered the room she stopped beside me and asked, "Well, how did it go?"

I shrugged my shoulders.

She gestured to the wads of paper scattered on the floor around her desk and asked, "Did you do all this?" She assumed the obvious answer to her question and bent over to properly dispose of the papers, "Were you able to write something for me?"

I nodded and she looked pleased, as she took the writing pad and began reading my words, while slowly walking behind her desk.

She cleared her throat and read the poem once more before she sat down and laid the paper on the desk. Her face turned a brilliant crimson when she looked up to express her reaction. She took a deep breath and barely shook her head side-to-side. "Delaney, I don't know what to say. I had no idea you were so smart and talented— able to write so beautifully. The way you expressed these painful thoughts in such a profound way…you've left me speechless."

While she read my words once again, the room became silent except for that annoying pen-tapping habit of hers.

She leaned forward on her desk, enthusiasm in her voice, "Tell you what, Delaney. Your husband should be here soon, and you'll have the next four days in your own home. So I'm going to give you a weekend assignment. Okay?"

She looked away, disarming me of all arguments, "It's obviously easier for you to communicate through written words. So, now I want you to write about your first pleasant memory. When you bring it in on Tuesday we'll have something to talk about. Will you do that for me? Please."

Her face broadened with a smile when I nodded. Directing her attention to a folder with my name on the tab, she proceeded to complete the forms Mo brought.

* * *

While my taste buds absorbed the scrumptious chocolate flavor to the last drop, my eyes and thoughts were focused outside the building.

The grass and trees had begun to turn green, as they sprouted their tender new foliage. The pink and white blooms of the dogwood trees and azaleas were in their early stages of blossoming, while the landscape took on a delicate, laced effect from their scattered bursts of color. I enjoyed this view so much more than that of the building's opposite side. There the ragged remains of the landscape, left by the havoc of the prior week's tornado, gave the scenery the look of a war zone. The angry hand of the Almighty took a gargantuan comb and parted the giant pines on the hill. The winds of fury ripped trees and bushes out by their roots and tossed them to their demise.

It amazed me how the path of destruction and devastation from the tornado was confined to that one area, leaving the other side of the building unblemished. I had been originally roomed in that round, flying-saucer-like building across the lot. The damage was such that, along with all the other patients, I was transferred to the peaceful side—the one spared by the storm.

The view changes, depending on where you're standing and through which window you happen to be looking.

From one side the view was beautiful—alive—peaceful and heavenly. However, from the other side all was that of destruction—death—remnants of utter turmoil and hell.

I was somehow caught in the path of a tornado, and my life reluctantly drawn into its vortex. No matter how hard I tried, I couldn't find my way over to the side with the heavenly view. Effort of any degree would be futile without the presence of desire and hope, neither of which I possessed. They were far beneath the surface of my heart, buried among the fragments of my shattered soul. I lacked the strength and energy required to delve so deeply within and recover them.

I noticed the hearty, deep-rooted oak trees with their reputation for longevity, and imagined how it must feel to be them, regenerating every year—starting over—fresh, with every spring.

But then they shed their leaves in the fall, becoming lifeless and barren throughout the winter. They appeared so sad in those months and I wondered if they endured pain or a feeling of loss during that time. If so, did they mourn or cry out in their own way. And so I pondered, *If trees have feelings, can they sense their off-spring— their leaves—as they fall, scattered about on the ground to decay, surrounding the very roots that brought them nourishment? How could the oak trees bear the repetitious pains of such loss over the hundred years of their lives?*

Perhaps they just considered it part of life's cycle. Accepting the every year process of losing parts of themselves as simply the Almighty's cruel plan.

I wished I could express all that was going through my head—wished I could have told Dr. Robinson in such a way she would interpret my thoughts as normal.

Rather than say a word, however, I cleaned the sticky chocolate off my hands and remained quiet.

I can't afford to open up too much. If I do, I'd be exposing myself and she'll proclaim me totally insane. She has the power to destroy any chances of my ever getting out of Oakwood, and the coldness of that vision makes me shiver.

Unexpectedly I was touched by the sun's rays as they shone through her office window. It brought such a welcomed feeling of warmth, like a mother's loving embrace in the middle of a dark and cold winter's night.

The doctor completed her paperwork, closed my file, and interrupted the serenity of the moment, "I think we've really accomplished something here today. Don't you?"

She sounded awfully proud of herself, but I nodded thinking, *If she wants to feel that way, I guess there's no harm done.*

She walked around the desk and hugged me with the tenderness of a kitten, "I'm so proud of you. You're very brave—it took courage as well as talent to do what you did today. It tells me a lot about what's inside of you. And from what I've seen, I'm looking forward to becoming friends and helping you become the real Delaney again."

She quickly hugged me again, "Now, I want you to have a good weekend. And I can't wait to see you Tuesday and read what you've written." As I reached the door she said, "Have a happy Easter, Delaney."

* * *

Before going to my room, I walked through the gardens and gazed up at the row of second floor windows in an attempt to see Dr. Robinson in her office. I couldn't explain why, but my feelings toward her had changed though I doubted there would ever come a time when I'd be able to comply with her request and be friends. As far as I was concerned, she was just a doctor doing what she was paid to do.

Yet there was something about her. Maybe it was just because she said so many nice things about me back there in her office—that I was intelligent, had a good mind, so smart, and that she was proud of me. I wondered if she told all her patients that, and then again, I didn't care if she did or not. I liked it when she said those things— they made me feel good.

CHAPTER II
RAINBOW IN THE MIST

I was in no hurry to get back to my room; the concrete bench on the patio was enticing me to stop by and visit. Like a cozy bed calling out to a weary traveler on a winter night, the bench extended an irresistibly alluring invitation.

In a silent reverence it said, "Come over here Delaney, enjoy my flower garden. Sit and appreciate the splendor of my beautiful fuchsia, white and pastel pink azaleas, and the bordering lavender thrift. Allow the tranquility of the quiet moments to soak in as you bask in the sunshine's warmth. Observe my yellow-and-black monarchs, fluttering in freedom's formation. And look, the first hummingbird of the season has made a visit especially for you. Acknowledge their untiring grace among the splendor of the Almighty's creation."

I was compelled to accept the invitation, as though I had no choice in the matter. I sat on the bench amidst the garden, and pretended to blend in with the surrounding beauty. I tried to imagine what vibrant color I could be to achieve an existence of such harmony.

Would I be pastel pink or a deep rose, perhaps a brilliant red or a regal purple?

A slight breeze gently brushed across the tender petals of the azalea blooms, inciting a desire within me to touch them—to feel the tenderness of their delicate colors. I walked to the edge of the patio and reached down to caress one of the blossoms, expecting unmitigated softness at the touch. Instead the walls of the dimension barrier separating me from life and all things of beauty generated a sense of numbness. The distortion extended from the depths of my heart to the tips of my fingers, leaving me unable to feel anything whatsoever.

I was agitated, as if tricked—betrayed—though unsure by whom. The entire exhibit was nothing more than a cruel prank as the color of every bloom I touched suddenly faded to black, like the darkness within me.

I clinched my fist at the thought of such a tease, crushing the fragile cluster. I was a murderer. I opened my hand and watched the lifeless petals slip through my fingers. They fell, scattered around my feet, leaving no more than an empty stem in their place.

Beyond the darkness around me, I heard a loud whispering noise, *pssst...pssst...pssst*. The sound was coming from behind me. When I turned to investigate, my face met with a refreshing, light mist from the automatic lawn sprinkler. I realized it must be 5:00, as it was set to come on at that time every day.

My breath was suddenly caught in my chest, as I observed the awesome beauty of the most incredibly vivid rainbow. I was drawn toward that spectrum, compelled to bathe in the sheer mist surrounding it, to absorb the energy—the life—from its vibrant colors.

Entranced by such a peaceful promise of salvation, I approached the rainbow in the mist. But then, the sudden boisterous noise of Mo's irritating loud voice made me flinch.

"Delaney! Time to come on in. You're husband's here!"

I ignored her. But as I turned to continue toward my original destination, I could no longer see the rainbow—it had disappeared as magically as it appeared.

Once again I had fallen victim to a cruel prank by which I was teased with the promise and hope of renewed color in my life, only to be disappointed. My tormenting thoughts ran amuck.

First I was lured over by the bench, then the azalea blooms and now the rainbow. Am I crazy? I must be insane, for inanimate objects such as those would never talk to a sane person. And if they did, a person in their right mind would have ignored them.

I wasn't ready to see Kyle. I needed to be alone so I could have time to think about what had happened and determine who the prankster might be, but Mo wouldn't allow it.

Standing in the doorway, clapping her hands together, as if that would hasten my steps, she yelled, "Hurry up, little girl! Don't take all day!" Once I was within a few yards of her, she stopped yelling but she was still loud, "Delaney, Honey, your husband sure seems anxious to take you home for the weekend. Don't you go on keeping him waitin' now. He drove a long ways to get ya." She tucked my blouse inside my jeans again, adjusting my clothes in her annoying motherly way.

A heavy German accent would be expected to come from someone with the last name of Hindenburg, but Mo was like me—a native Georgian through and through—only she'd been one about twenty-five years longer. In that time she had mastered turning on the southern sweetness whenever she so desired, with her honey-dipped, sugar-n-molasses, down-home drawl, "Dawlin', I want ya to eat somethin' besides sweets and chocolate while you're at home, and let's see if we can't put some meat back on those bones of yours. Your clothes are damn near falling off ya 'cause ya ain't been eatin' enough to keep a baby bird alive."

Mo sure was different from that first time I'd laid eyes on her. It was my first night at Oakwood, though I didn't know where I was at the time. When I saw the roaches in my room and realized the door was locked, I went stark-raving wild.

First one, then a second nurse came in to quiet me, but I fought tooth-and-nail, thrashing and kicking them with all my strength.

They used leather restraints, strapping me down by my ankles and wrists. There I was in an unfamiliar place, on my back in a strange bed. Tied down, with my legs spread apart and my arms at my side—unable to move—I was trapped like a wild and dangerous animal.

The loud *swish-swish* coming through the doorway was from the stride of one of the biggest women I'd ever seen. It was Mo, and with her the first hypodermic that looked as huge as the woman herself. I was horrified of it and her initially. But then the serum in that sweet injection took me away to another place—a place of unmitigated sleep.

I grew to love Mo's bedtime visits and her shots of deliverance from the demons of the conscious world. So much so I threw tantrums and fits every night, just enough to require one of those wonderful injections. Whenever I tried doing the same thing during the daytime my only accomplishment was finding myself strapped down again. I soon learned to restrict my wild episodes to bedtime, so I could be rewarded by Mo and her beloved hypodermics.

"Lordy mercy, child. Would'ya look at that mess on your face." She reached down and grabbed up a portion of her white uniform's hem and moistened it with her tongue, then proceeded to wipe the chocolate from around my mouth. Nudging my chin with her index finger she positioned my face upward, enabling her to look me in the eye, but I turned away. Then she grabbed my jaws forcing my attention toward her, "Look here, Dawlin', and I want'ya to listen to me. That ole mark's gonna be gone before you know it."

She was always talking about that damn scar, as if I cared about it. Dr. Ford, the resident physician, tried to tell me, "Delaney, don't worry. One of my colleagues is the best plastic surgeon in Atlanta. He can make you good as new."

Ha, no one could do that. Not since that part of me was taken away. Any pains endured from the gash in my face paled in comparison to the emptiness within my heart.

A wide grin broadened the chubbiness of Mo's cheeks, as she instructed me in the most certain of terms, "Now, Little Girl, I expect you to put a smile on that pretty face for your man, and act like you're glad to see him."

I couldn't understand why she was always compelled to treat me like I was a child—babying me—as if I were incapable of taking care of myself. Then I wondered in a panic, *What will I do without her at night while I'm away? Without her injections? Who will take care of me while I'm at home? Home—at least there are no filthy roaches there.* With that thought, I took a deep breath of relief. However, I remained concerned about the absence of my injections and how I would get through the dark hours.

* * *

Kyle was sitting on the side of the bed when I entered the room. He stood up and hugged me like he hadn't seen me in years. "Sorry I'm late, baby. That *damn* car again. It was the alternator this time. I'd planned on leaving by 3:00, but they didn't have it ready."

Then he stared at me and with a radiating smile of approval, proclaimed, "You look great."

I suddenly left the ground, lifted up by his arms and swung around, as though I were a child. Before bringing me in for a landing he gave me a kiss that expressed his true abounding happiness. My husband was so alive and excited, I wished I could share his enthusiasm.

Truthfully I was jealous and wondered why he deserved to be so happy all the time when I was trapped in hell? *Could it be that my sanity and soul were stripped away from me because I alone had been standing in the tornado's path; yet he remains unblemished, spared, simply because he was on the peaceful side? It's not fair. I want to be like Kyle—I want to be happy. Hell, I'd be satisfied just to be normal.*

It never occurred to me how much Kyle's heart was aching, and the degree of difficulty my husband endured to present such an outstanding performance. After all, a part of him had also been taken away.

I attempted to smile, but it was far from genuine. The part of me that once felt those emotions was no longer functional. In its place was a dark, empty space.

He teased me about my baggy jeans, "Looks like we might need to fatten you up a little this weekend, Baby. Thought I might cook hamburgers out on the grill. How's that sound?" I nodded and forced another smile.

"Well, do you have everything you're goin' to need?" He opened all the drawers in my chest to double check, and when he satisfied himself, his voice developed a definite tone of excitement, "Ready to go?" His eyes were as bright as patches of the clear blue sky that spring day."

First he swung open the door. Then he bowed his tall, lean body at the waist, and waved his hand in a wide sweeping motion. A royal gesture, indicating I should pass through the door before him. "Let's get you home where you belong. The boys have been excited all week."

Before leaving we had to stop by the nurses' station and sign me out for the weekend. Mo was all smiles as she leaned across the counter to hand Kyle a piece of paper. "Here ya go, Mr. Rutherford. There's two prescriptions here—one to keep her calmed down and one to help her sleep." She winked as she lowered her voice, "And I don't have to tell ya to keep 'em out of her reach."

Kyle nodded, "I understand. And thank you, nurse. I really appreciate how great you've all been to her."

The walls seemed to vibrate from her boisterous laughter as she responded, "She ain't been no trouble—at least, not like some of 'em. That's a mighty fine little girl ya got there, and we aim to help her get better. Ya'll go on now, and have a good weekend."

Kyle put a hand on my shoulder. "We're planning on it. Aren't we, Delaney? You have a nice weekend, too, nurse."

We almost reached the door, when a *swish-thud-swish-thud* came from behind us, "Oh Mr. Rutherford, Sir? Wait! Will you see that she gets plenty to eat? I mean good hot food, that is."

"Sure will. In fact, we're grilling out tonight as soon as we get home."

"Mmm-mm, sounds mighty good to me. Come here an' give me a hug, little girl." After she squeezed me with a bear hug, she couldn't rest until she gave me final instructions, "Now you behave yourself and have a good time. See ya Tuesday."

And with that, we were out the door.

I was more than a little agitated. *She calls him "Sir" and "Mr. Rutherford," and all she can ever call me is "Little Girl." And what's all that about keeping the damn prescriptions out of my reach? And telling him to make sure I eat—talking about me like I'm no where around.* I sighed out of relief and reassurance when I remembered the prescriptions—that I wouldn't have to get through the dark hours all by myself. Then I wondered if they had the same sweet ingredients as Mo's wonderful injections? I could only hope it to be so.

Kyle carried my blue overnight case as we walked to the car. I hesitated for a moment when I saw the light blue Mercedes in the parking lot. A sudden rush of nausea came over me at the sight of the sedan.

My pounding heart was deafening inside my head. I swallowed hard, choking back the fear as we continued forward.

When Kyle opened the trunk lid for the case, I stepped back several feet, acquiring a safer distance from the threats of its ominous, gaping jaws. I was about to faint right on the spot. It was unseasonably warm for April in the mid-eighties however, I was overcome by extremely cold chills and nausea. Unaware at the time, those feelings were reminiscent of a violent memory my subconscious had locked away—a time in my life my conscious mind would not allow me to face.

Jolted by the airtight sound of the trunk's lid slamming shut, claustrophobia rushed through me, even though I was outside in the wide open parking lot.

Raking my fingers through my hair, I took a deep breath as I fought back the anxiety and slid onto the front seat of the car. Even if it was an older model car, it was immaculate inside and out. But the leather's aroma I had always loved was overpowered by an unexplainable sense of fear. When Kyle closed the door behind me, it was as though he'd enclosed me in a tomb with windows.

I was suffocating, so I quickly reached over to open the sunroof. *Ah, that's better,* I thought, breathing deeply as Kyle instructed me to fasten my seatbelt. When we drove away, I noticed the white wooden sign that read WELCOME TO OAKWOOD INSTITUTE was badly damaged in the tornado. A forlorn sight with its broken frame still where the winds had left it—lying on its side.

Only a few miles down the road from Oakwood, we passed another sign that read:

YOU ARE NOW LEAVING THE CITY OF CHEATHAM.
HURRY BACK!

Wishing I never had to see that awful place again, I was relieved I didn't have to go back… until Tuesday.

CHAPTER III
WHO'S IN THE KITCHEN?

Kyle tried to keep the conversation upbeat during the ride home, but he was running out of topics. It was an hour-long trip, and he'd never been much of a talker. "The damn oil light's on again. Baby, we're gonna have to do something with this car. I don't care if it is a Mercedes; any car's gonna start needing some work when it gets this old, and with this many miles on it."

I totally agreed, but I didn't see or feel the need to respond, so he continued. "There's always something-- $300 here, $500 there. We just can't afford it, especially with you not working."

I supposed there was nothing wrong with letting him get it all out of his system as he apparently had more to say on the subject, "I know how much you've always loved it, but what do you think about trading in for a newer, American car?"

I remembered a few weeks earlier, I'd overheard as Kyle told the doctor, "Sgt. Brady called to say as far as the car's concerned they've completed that part of the investigation. I'm not sure how she feels about the damn thing since all that's happened. But I can't see a real reason to keep it. So, should I get rid of it?"

I jumped, a little startled when he patted my leg and cleared his throat, as he repeated, "I said, what do you think, Baby?"

I shrugged my shoulders, indicating I didn't know or I didn't care, leaving him to interpret my body language.

I gazed out the window, watching the passing countryside that seemed to go on forever.

Two hawks in the air caught my attention as they glided effortlessly against the blue sky. I wondered if one of them was the one I saw when they'd brought me to Oakwood. If they were a male and a female, maybe they had a family of babies somewhere.

The sun was so warm shining through the window as I became relaxed. Laying my head back on the headrest, I tried to connect my thoughts with the two hawks. I wished I could've traded places with them if just for a little while, as I said under my breath, "It feels so good to fly."

Kyle asked what I'd said but I didn't answer; instead I continued to watch the show, thinking, *I've flown before—in my dreams, that is—but it felt so real.* I vaguely recalled my father telling me when I was a little girl, "Special people who dream they can fly can do anything they set their minds to." And I truly believed it because I always felt so invincible when I awoke from those dreams.

I've always wished I could fly for real. I would've soared up to the heavens, reclaimed that lost part of me and brought it back where it belonged. Then I could be complete again—once I regained my soul.

* * *

We passed the subdivision's entrance sign: Magnolia Landing Estates. The place looked quite different from when I'd last seen it.

That day back in February, Mama had pointed out, "Look, doll-baby, it looks just like white diamonds scattered all over the ground and rooftops." She was referring to the sun reflecting off the last remaining patches of ice and snow from January's winter storm. What she perceived as beautiful was merely a cold and frigid sight that made me shiver.

A little more than two months had passed and Kyle was pointing out that April had brought its usual green lawns and colorful blooms. He drew my attention to the refreshing scent pouring through the opened sunroof, "Mm-m, baby, smell the freshly mown grass. Spring is definitely in the air."

I sneezed and silently damned the pollen for stirring up my hay fever.

We lived in Magnolia Landing the entire eleven years since it was built in '73. Shortly after we moved there I started my interior design business. A number of the neighbors played a big part in it getting off the ground, as I decorated for some while advising others. My fees were nominal and over the years I developed a reputation for decorating on a shoestring budget, so my income was limited because of the obvious clientele.

I supposed I was never destined to become independently wealthy by decorating homes. Even though the business was struggling, I found renewed hope when I acquired several commercial accounts in January. 1984 was going to be "my year" and I was on my way to real success. Right after that was when everything in my life went straight to hell and my mind went right along with it. I'd accepted that to be the story of my life, and 1984 to be a year I definitely could do without.

I sighed, remembering I had my assistant Angie to take care of the business in my absence. At least she was someone on whom I could depend—she would never abandon me.

There were only a half dozen floor plans in Magnolia Landing, all of which were three-bedroom/two-bath layouts. They were either split level with drive under garage or traditional brick ranch with double carport. Ours was the latter of the two.

Through the years I'd watched the young, newly planted shrubs grow to maturity, just as the children grew to bike-riding age. The neighborhood always had its share of kids—mostly boys.

It seemed that all of them were riding their bikes in the street that afternoon, as Kyle slowed down to avoid an accident. "Hey, Mrs. Rutherford—Welcome Home!" Waving as if they knew me.

But they only thought they knew me.

When we rounded the corner at the bottom of the hill I could see the sign. Lord knows, it was big enough—WELCOME HOME MOM—in bold black and red letters. Kyle stopped in front of the house so I could get a good look at the sign that stretched across the entire double carport opening. "Well, what do you think?" There was a definite tone of pride in his voice.

I nodded, to acknowledge I saw the sign.

He blew the horn as we pulled in the driveway. Before we were completely parked, the boys ran out to the car. "Welcome home, Mom. Did you like the sign? Keith drew the letters and I colored 'em in…It's big, ain't it? Do you like it?" Clay wasn't any less anxious than any other ten year old boy would be who hadn't seen his mom in two months.

I remembered my manners and instead of just nodding, I said, "Yes, thank you."

Keith was always big for his age so he was expected to act more mature. Though only thirteen, he could sense I was feeling a little awkward, so he proceeded with a degree of caution and more contained enthusiasm. "We really missed you, Mom. I'm sure glad you're home," as he helped me out of the car. Once I was standing, both feet on the ground, he added, "Mom…can I hug you?"

I nodded and he gave me a very gentle hug, one so tender and warm it could have melted the most frozen of icicles at a touch. Unfortunately I was far colder from the heart out than any icicle.

Clay's eyes were wide with apprehension. Stepping forward with only a trace of hesitation he wrapped his arms around my neck for a hug so lengthy, his dad had to intervene. He kissed me on the cheek and then gave me another quick hug before saying, "I really missed you, Mom...I love you so much." He added one simple plea: "Don't go away again."

I knew I was supposed to be feeling something other than emptiness within. I vaguely recalled being in my right mind and having those kinds of normal feelings.

Once we were inside and settled, Kyle said, "Baby, I need to run up to the pharmacy and get your prescriptions filled. Will you be all right while I'm gone?"

I nodded, and he said, "Why don't you go lie down across the bed. I won't be long. The boys will be here to keep you company." After gently placing a kiss on my forehead he was out the door, leaving me alone with my sons.

Clay came in and lay next to me on the bed. Keith, already the size of a man, opted to sit on the bench at the foot of the four post bed.

Clay was all excited to bring me up to date, "I made all A's on my report card. And my book won second place in the county. Wanna see 'em?"

It was awkward—as though I were listening to someone else's son and trying to become enthused. Clay resembled his father, with the same vivid blue eyes and I read excitement and pride in them as he awaited my response.

When I nodded and said, "Yes, please," he was off the bed and out of the room in a flash.

Keith cleared his throat, as if trying to think of something to say that might interest me. "I---I didn't make all A's...but I didn't get any F's. Mostly C's and a B in English." Before I had a chance to respond, he sat straight up on the bench and his big, brown eyes became even bigger. "Oh yeah...our soccer team hasn't lost a game this season. So far we're division champs—and I'm the goalie. If we win the title, Coach Brannon said we'll have a cookout over at his house."

I wasn't as good an actor as their father, but I smiled and said, "That's great."

Clay was showing me his award-winning book and prized report card when Kyle came in. "Okay, boys. Let Mom rest a while. Come and help me start up the grill."

Before going outside, Kyle handed me a glass of water and placed a beautiful bluebird in my hand, one of my keep-me-calm pills, robin's egg blue.

I had been given bluebirds regularly since my first day at Oakwood. Blue had become one of my favorite colors. The bluebirds didn't make me sleep—they never did—however, I did begin to feel a bit calmer.

According to the clock it was 7:30, but it was still daylight. It seemed like it should've been much later.

Kyle opened the den door that led out to the screened back porch and stuck his head inside to say, "Delaney, the hamburgers are ready. It's so pretty, I thought you might enjoy eating outside on the porch."

When I went through the doorway and approached the porch, a sick feeling overtook me in such a way I became weak at the knees. He rushed to catch me saying, "Okay, Baby, you don't have to go out there if you're not ready."

He made sure the back door was closed and the window shade was pulled the remainder of the weekend.

After he helped me back to the bedroom he brought our hamburgers inside, and the four of us ate in there on T.V. trays. Had I been myself, food of any kind in the bedroom would have been taboo, much less eating the entire meal there.

I gobbled the burger like a starved dog would gnaw on a T-bone steak. The boys stared but didn't comment. They were probably thinking about the times when I had chastised them for doing the same thing.

After dinner I took my time in a relaxing, hot shower. I was exhausted so I went straight to bed. The boys came in to kiss me goodnight, and Kyle brought in a tall glass of ice water. "Here you go, Baby. Hope this helps you sleep." He placed a bright, canary-yellow pill in my hand.

It didn't have quite the same effect as Mo's sweet serum, but it did the job. Although I'd never really been very fond of yellow, it quickly began to grow on me. Blue and yellow—yellow and blue. Blue birds to calm me down, and yellow birds to fly me away to the land of sleep.

* * *

I slept the majority of the next day, something Oakwood never allowed, and I never realized how much I missed my independence.

* * *

Kyle took us all to the movie on Saturday afternoon. I don't remember which movie—I didn't even know what movie it was at the time we were there watching it. The movie theater was a regular form of weekend entertainment for the Rutherfords. The popcorn and Coke were good but we didn't get any candy. Kyle said we didn't need it and there'd be more than enough candy the next morning. Easter morning.

That night after the boys were in bed, Kyle suggested, "Delaney, why don't you go tuck the boys in and kiss them goodnight. I know they've missed their mom doing that."

I did what he asked, wishing I was really their mom—the woman they seemed to love so. Something didn't seem to make sense to me. I couldn't understand why they were both sleeping in the room across from ours, when their bedrooms were downstairs.

When I went back into the den, Kyle had drug out the box of photos, trying to jog my memory of some good times. "Dr. Robinson told me about your assignment to take back on Tuesday. Maybe we'll come across some pictures in here that will help you remember something happy to write about."

"I don't want to look at those. There's nothing…"

"Please Baby. Try," he pleaded. "I'll help you remember…I'll even help you write it. Okay?"

He was so anxious for me to be that woman he loved, and I wanted so to be that person as I sat beside him, looking and trying my best to remember. But the pictures were all of someone else… someone who was smiling and happy. It just wasn't working, so I left him there in the den with pictures spread all around him on the sofa.

I went to bed and pulled the covers up over my head. I wasn't going back to that hell-place until Tuesday, but I was worried about coming up with something to write about. Though unsure of the reason, I didn't want to disappoint the doctor—she had bragged on me so.

Kyle gave me my yellowbird before he jumped in the shower, and when he came to bed I pretended I was already asleep. After standing next to the bed gazing down at me, he leaned over, gently kissed me on the cheek and whispered, "Good-night Baby. That's right, get some good rest—you got a big day tomorrow."

We both needed our rest, as Sunday was sure to be an *extremely* long day with relatives coming that afternoon for the traditional gargantuan Easter feast.

* * *

"Hey, Dad, you mean we're not going to church?" Because of Clay's question, I assumed staying home on Sunday morning wasn't part of the regular weekend routine.

Kyle and the boys were in the back part of the house getting dressed and I was still in my gown. I sat in the den watching T.V., thinking how nice it was to see the whole screen without having to look around Bobby, like I had to do back at Oakwood. No matter where I would sit in the group room, he'd get up there between me and the television, as if it were the only place in the room to stand.

I became entranced by the church music on one of the channels as I listened to the members of Roswell Street Baptist Church singing familiar songs—songs I had sung all my life and I knew the words, all too well. Words praising God for His graciousness and love. Then the pastor led the congregation in prayer.

It wasn't so long ago I did that, pray and sing—*believe*—and where had it gotten me? I wondered, *What terrible thing have I done to deserve God's damnation of me? What kind of God would turn His back on and condemn one of His followers to another dimension?* A dimension where I could see, hear and touch the people I loved, but only in a distorted way. Unsure at times, whether they could see and hear me at all. I could *see* them touch me but the actual *feel* of their touch seemed to be hindered or muffled by that dimensional barrier, as though separated by a thick sheet of plastic.

It was probably out of habit more than anything else but I suddenly found myself thinking, *Dear Lord, if you really do exist, have mercy and forgive me for my sins. Release me from the pain and fear of this hell and restore my soul."* Then sobbing, *"Please, God, it just hurts so much…like someone took a knife and carved a hole in my heart. I feel so empty inside since you took that part of me."*

My deep thoughts were interrupted by the sounds of someone outside tapping three times on a car horn. I seemed to be the only one who heard the noise, so I dried my eyes with the sleeve of my robe and went to investigate.

By the time I reached the kitchen they were knocking on the carport door. When I opened it, there stood the petite figure of a woman loaded down with bags of groceries—loaded down in such a way I could barely see her face. But her shiny, silver-gray hair gave her away, that combined with my mother's soft voice, "Happy Easter!"

Her husband was much older and remained in the car until someone could assist him. They came early so Mama could cook dinner for the rest of the crew, who would be there after church.

Kyle came down the hall just as she stepped into the kitchen, so he hurried to relieve her of her load.

As soon as her arms were free, she turned to look at me and in the perkiest of voices said, "How's my little Doll-baby feeling? You look so *sweet!*   Come here and give me a hug!" I'd probably be her little Doll-baby until I was a hundred and she always told me I looked sweet even when I knew I looked like hell, but that was just her way.

First she hugged me so tightly it hindered my breathing as I gasped. But then she lightened up on the squeeze and gave me her trademark three firm pats on my upper back. Before ending the embrace completely, she kissed me on the cheek and, holding me by my shoulders, she stepped back to take a better look at me. Her face was red and moist from the tears streaming down from her big, darkest-of-brown eyes.

While wiping her eyes with the backs of her hands, she said, "Okay, Doll-baby, you go on back and get dressed. I'll get everything under control in here."

Kyle headed outside to help John out of the car, and I went back to the bedroom to get dressed so I would look as normal as possible by the time my family arrived.

* * *

After church services, the house was filled with my entire family: three brothers and their wives, my sister, her husband, all my nieces and nephews, and Aunt Maisie. I knew Aunt Maisie was in the house before I laid eyes on her by the *clop clop* of her brown, hard-leather orthopedic shoes and spit cup for her disgusting snuff dipping habit. A total of 27 people were in our house that day.

Initially it was only a three-bedroom, brick ranch but we had finished off five more rooms downstairs and enlarged it to a total size of about 4,000 square feet. At that time it was the largest house in our family; however, after less than an hour I was convinced it wasn't *nearly* big enough.

They didn't think I overheard Aunt Maisie quizzing Mama in the kitchen, "Ruth, Honey, tell me, what do the doctors say?"

Mama replied, "Oh, she's healing all right, except for that gash where they hit her up the side of the face—it left a pretty deep scar. But, it's her mind we're all worried about..."

"Well, do they think she's ever gonna be normal in the head again? Course, what she's gone through is enough to drive *anybody* slap crazy. Poor thing, what with all that happening only a couple weeks after finding little Chris the way she did. I got the willies just seeing her car out front. Why in the name of hell ain't they got rid of that damn thing, anyway? And did the police find those bastards?"

The proverbial pin could be heard hitting the floor as a silent hush fell over the room when I walked in. Bluebirds were foremost on my mind as I wondered how much longer I had to wait for another one, but then I thought, *Hell, just give me the whole bottle.*

* * *

Mama suggested we have the Easter egg hunt in the front yard, so everyone poured outside. Of course, we had to record yet another holiday get-together, so before the hunt began we all gathered in front of the giant pink azalea bushes for the traditional family Polaroids. As usual, Aunt Maisie was the designated photographer, so with camera in hand she waddled out, faced the group and said, "Okay, everybody, stand up straight and smile—say Happy Easter Bunny!" Snap, went the camera. Snap and snap again.

At last everyone could exhale. "Whew," my brothers sighed so heavily afterward, as though it exhausted them physically to smile. Actually the strain of holding in their full bellies after overindulging in the afternoon feast was the more probable cause for their difficulty.

One of my nephews brought a new girlfriend, someone he'd only dated once or twice. She said, "Gee, it'd be nice if the cover was off the pool in the backyard. It's hot enough out here to go swimming."

Kyle overheard and flinched at her statement then watched for my reaction. He noticed the color drain from my face and I was extremely jittery, biting my bottom lip like I do when I get nervous. Much to my relief, he realized what time it was as he brought me a glass of tea and one of my sweet little bluebirds.

My nephew whispered something in the girlfriend's ear and she glanced over at me with a look of remorse. I read her lips though I didn't grasp what she meant, "I'm so sorry. I didn't know!"

* * *

After dinner some of the neighbors came over thinking I was going back to Oakwood the next day, not realizing I had until Tuesday. They talked about trivialities, about anything and everything other than me or my problem.

They talked around me as though I wasn't there. I wondered if I had become invisible again, so I walked over and thumbed through the afternoon's snapshots. I was there alright. In the center of the back row, the only face without a smile.

I had the feeling that everyone including my family just wanted to see what a crazy person looked like up close and in person.

Later that afternoon when the crowd began to thin, Angie, my business assistant, came to bring her depressing tidings of woe. "Delaney, I wanted to tell you in person. I didn't want you to find out from someone else. Please don't be upset with me—but I've taken another job. I had to."

She paused and nervously stared at me while she studied my silent reaction, as if she expected me to go completely wild and stab her with a butcher knife. Then she began explaining, "I told Kyle weeks ago. I'm not trained like you are, and the clients want you. When the news came about—you know—well, they all canceled. I know you've been struggling for a long time, but I'm sorry. I just hope we can still be friends." Tears were rolling down her face.

The medication allowed me to remain emotionless. I didn't say anything, but I just sat there and let her hug me so she'd feel better. Truth was I didn't blame her. The company had been on the brink of bankruptcy since November. I would've jumped ship, too. Besides, I couldn't care less if that damned business went straight to hell, which I felt was its probable destiny anyway.

* * *

I was so exhausted. I couldn't wait until the circus had all gone so I could go to bed and pull the covers up over my head. I didn't want to be bothered with Kyle or the boys, so I went to bed early, before it was even dark. And I took my Easter basket with me.

It was loaded with chocolate candy and my favorite was the milk-chocolate bunny with the pink candy eyes. I didn't realize I had bitten off his head until after I did it. It looked so sad without a head, and it was all hollow inside—empty.

* * *

When Kyle came to bed he snuggled up close, gently laying his arm across me and quietly pulling the covers off my face. He kissed me, first on the neck, then the cheek and finally the lips. "Delaney, are you awake?" He kissed me again, trying to arouse some sign of mutual desire. "Baby, it's so nice to feel you next to me. It's been so long since…"

I pulled the covers back over my face and rolled over onto my side, facing the opposite direction.

He obviously got the message, as he dropped the pursuit and rolled over. Before my yellowbird flew me away to paradise, I heard Kyle sniffling into his pillow. I wondered if he might've been coming down with a cold. It had never occurred to me that my husband also endured his painful moments of loneliness and tears.

* * *

I had no problem drifting off, until the nightmare invaded my dreamland. The every-night invasion had become routine, always the same. However, that particular night's dream was different.

In it I was back at Oakwood, locked up in the Silent Room. The light was off and I was in total darkness. I heard thousands of the hard-shelled demons scurrying within the walls, and breeding beneath the matting. I couldn't find the door, so I clawed at the padded walls, screaming, "Somebody, help me, please!" It was forever before my pleas were answered, and in the interim I paced back and forth repeatedly. I had to keep moving around or the roaches crawled up my legs. I continuously swatted about my head as they were dropping on me from the ceiling.

In my dream the overhead light finally came on and the demons scurried into the darkness behind the mats. The door swung open with a thud and there stood faithful Mo, once again rescuing me from the evils of the darkness. She stood with one hand behind her and in the other one was my beloved hypodermic. "Delaney, calm down in here, dawlin'. Don't worry, Mo knows what her little girl needs."

From behind her back she pulled out a jar. In it there were dozens of the filthy, hard-shelled bastards and their larvae. "Let Mo fill her hypodermic with ya favorite sweet serum. The one ya love so much." She unscrewed the lid, reached in and plucked out one of the demon's larva, then drew the fluid out of it and was about to inject me...

I could only whimper in fear. I don't know where I found the strength, but I fought her and knocked the needle out of her hand. It flew against the padded wall and when she waddled over to pick it up, I put my foot to her rear end. When she fell, my feet sensed the floor's vibration.

I was almost out the door, when some one grabbed my hair from behind.

Abruptly awakened by my own yell, I sat straight up in the bed. I was soaking wet with perspiration and completely disoriented at first, *Where am I?* The streetlight outside the house lit the room just enough so a quick scope confirmed I was indeed still at home... where there were no roaches.

That nightmare had totally unnerved me. Oakwood was supposed to be the place that was helping me get better. And Mo was my friend, at least that's what I had grown to believe. But that dream led me to think, *That just shows me I can't trust anyone. Damn, I have to go back there day after tomorrow. What if my dream is for real? Or an omen?* It didn't make any sense, yet it made all the sense in the world. No wonder the roaches ruled that place; they were being bred for the serum. *Ugh, and they've been pumping me full of their larvae.* I felt nauseous, imagining the disgusting things hatching within me.

The thought of going back to that hell-place sent a chill rushing up my spine. *I can't go back there. I have to do something!* That's when I remembered the knives in the kitchen drawer.

I leaned over to make certain Kyle was asleep and as I got closer I could hear the rhythmic buzz of his light snore.

I moved with the silence of a cat as I slipped out of the bed and went into the bathroom. Standing before the sink's mirror, I was repulsed by my own reflection. With a closer look at that hideous scar, I was all the more determined my final destination would be the drawer next to the kitchen sink—the cutlery drawer...

I imagined the sight of myself lying on the kitchen floor in a pool of my own blood, and I shuddered. *What am I thinking? I can't do that here. What if one of the boys finds me?* I didn't want that to happen. *I know. I'll slip one of those steak knives back into Oakwood when I go back on Tuesday. I'll wrap a paper towel around it and place it in the bottom of my tennis shoe. No one will think to check there. And if I wait and do it at Oakwood, I won't have to worry about any one but Mo or the others finding me.*

The first thing I did when I reached the kitchen was get a drink of cold water. Then I opened the cutlery drawer. *What the...? Where are all the knives? Damn! The doctor must've told Kyle about the letter opener stunt.* I damned God, whom I doubted really existed. I damned the doctor for warning Kyle, and I damned Kyle for being so damn cautious. I'd just have to think of another way.

I turned up the glass to drain the last bit of water, and that's when I saw it—there on the counter—like an amber-colored plastic beacon. I couldn't believe my over-tired eyes. Maybe Kyle's exhaustion from the day made him forget to be cautious.

I grabbed it and read the label, "Nembutal, take one at bedtime. Do not drive or operate machinery." I removed the cap and gazed inside. Staring back at me were my sweet little canaries. There were enough yellowbirds left in the bottle to fly me away...forever. I smiled at the thought, *Maybe there's a God, after all.* I'd just down them all and go to bed. No bloody mess and no fuss—I just wouldn't wake up.

I poured some more water and raised the bottle of pills, as in a toast, "God, if you're up there and you arranged all this, here's to ya." I turned the bottle upside-down in the palm of my hand, but I froze in my tracks when I heard someone giggling.

I became very still, straining to hear above my heart's rapid pounding. "Clay, is that you?" No answer. "Keith? Kyle?" When there was still no answer, I was puzzled, *Who's in here besides me? Who else is awake?*

The sound came again, clearer this time. It was the voice of a child. A little girl!

My heart was racing. I not only *heard* her, but the image of her and a man with her became so vivid they were almost real to the touch. Their eyes reflected the love between them as she sat there on the man's lap and he stroked her flowing, chestnut brown ringlets.

Of all things, she was spelling—spelling a long word—a word you wouldn't hear everyday, and yet I recognized it right away. And when she finished spelling the word, the man gave her a big kiss on the cheek, praising her for being so smart.

Her genuine happiness was contagious. I smiled and even laughed aloud, totally captivated by the energetic child.

I sensed her emotions in such a way they became my own. They *were* my own. The child in my vision was me as a little girl, and the man with the kind eyes my daddy. The memories unfolded and became so clear as though I stepped back in time, actually reliving them as they happened. I didn't want to wait until morning, fearing I might forget some of the details. With the thought of getting back to the pills later, I put them back in their place. I eagerly entered the vision alongside the images of Daddy and myself where I felt right at home, as I grabbed a tablet and pen and began to write.

I had no way of knowing that over the next several months I was destined to progress through a lifetime of memories. But those beginning pages of the assignment would never have been written if it weren't for the ones who saved me from myself that night—the man and his little girl with cascading curls and brown eyes filled with life.

PART II

THE FIRST MAN IN MY LIFE

"C—O—N—S—T—A—N—T—I—N—O—P—L—E spells *Con-tan-dinoble*," I recited confidently. Daddy's round cheeks were red with a glow of pride in his five-year-old little sweetheart.

"Okay, now spell encyclopedia," he encouraged me to continue, as he stroked my long, naturally curly hair.

"E—N—C—Y—C—L—O—P—E—D—I—A spells *cy-glo-peda*."

"Ah-h, that's my Delaney. That's Daddy's smart little Sweetpea." His gentle squeeze, a tender kiss on my forehead and his deep-bellied chuckle made me giggle and smile so big it exposed my missing bottom front tooth.

* * *

My vision was so vivid; I felt the warmth of my father's loving arms in his embrace. I could almost reach out and touch the pink, soft cotton dress I was wearing.

The familiar fragrance of Daddy's Old Spice aftershave filled the air as his contagious smile and periwinkle blue eyes lit up my world. I'll never forget the touch of his smooth, clean-shaven face in contrast with the roughness of his hands, overworked and splintered.

Born ten years after the rest of the brood and the youngest daughter, I was Daddy's Sweetpea—his pride and joy.

My dad really liked to show me off to others. I had a good memory and I was easy to teach. He spent a good deal of time working with me to develop those talents. I don't know who received the greater pleasure when the others responded to my performance with, "She is *so smart*..." I only know my feeling of excitement when he asked me to spell for friends and relatives.

Every summer Uncle Joel and Aunt Janie drove to Atlanta from Jacksonville, Florida. In preparation for their visit my daddy would say, "Okay, Delaney, go get your blackboard. You need to learn some fresh new words."

I was the youngest of all my cousins until their daughter Jolene came along three years later—then of course *she* was the youngest. That was good, and that was bad. Good because when she was in town, my older cousins left me alone and sometimes even allowed me to join them in ganging up to aggravate her. Bad in that since she was the youngest and so cute, she got most of the attention.

As if she weren't already cute enough, to make matters worse, her parents had enrolled her in dance lessons as she was coming out of the womb. She was only three or four and sang with a bit of a lisp. Everyone's applause followed as they would exclaim, "Oh! How *cute!*"

I on the other hand always thought, *Oh! How spoiled,* wishing I could take that big bow out of her pretty baby doll curls and stuff it down her cute little throat. I always observed from the corner of the room, arms tightly folded across my chest and gritting my teeth during her entire performance. Even though I'll admit I may have been a little bit spoiled too, I truly don't believe I was ever jealous of her. Okay, so there may have been a slight trace of jealousy, but for the most part, I was just anxious for *my* turn to show off.

I had a good many cousins and they all took piano or dance lessons. After performances on the piano by Melinda then Diana and whoever else who had a talent, whereby their parents had paid for lessons…then it was finally my time to shine. I may not have had a talent, but at least I had a brain.

Then *I* smiled big to show off *my* dimples when I was asked to spell—usually long words that my daddy and later my brothers and sisters would find in the D—I—C—T—I—O—N—A—R—Y. That spells '*dish-on-ary*.'

* * *

As a worker in a local ironworks factory Daddy never had an abundance of money. The fondest memories I have of him however, did not involve spending a great deal of money. He made me laugh and I had fun and enjoyed even the simplest things when I was with him.

Golden highlights danced about his thinning brown hair as I pretended to wash and brush it while he lay on the sofa or sat on the front porch swing.

I was his sidekick. He took me everywhere with him—to the barber shop, the shoe shop, the drug store.

My favorite place was the Custard Girl Grill. It was there that I remember tasting soft ice cream in a cone for the first time. I looked forward to Saturdays as that was a regular stop for us, that and Brown's drug store for a Cherry Coke.

We spent many days and nights on the front porch, where we sat on the glider swing and bet from which direction the next car would come. Or what color it would be. Other times we chose directions, right or left, and bet a Coke on who would have more cars come from their side. We earned extra points at night for every popeye, a car with only one headlight working. When we first started playing the betting game Mama said, "Jack, I wish you wouldn't teach her to gamble like that."

He always shrugged and teased, "Aw Ruth, for God's sake, *life's* a gamble. Besides, it's just a game and it's a good way to teach her to count."

* * *

Trixie was just a little brown-spotted mutt, but she was smart—like me. She couldn't spell, but she could speak in "barking" language of course. Daddy taught her to do that along with some simple tricks such as roll over or stand on her hind legs and spin around. She followed me everywhere except in the house. She wasn't allowed in there. She was a really good little doggie. I loved to dress her in my baby doll clothes. I remember smiling at Daddy's Brownie camera when he took a picture of us on the back porch. I looked like Annie Oakley with my new red cowboy hat with guns and holster from Santa. I held her by her paws while she stood on her back legs. I told her to, "Smile, Trixie." Daddy assured me she smiled real pretty, but looking down from my angle I only saw her tongue hanging out.

One afternoon I yelled, "Here, Trixie," but she didn't come. I looked out the kitchen window and saw Daddy and my brothers, Jerry and Bud, in the back yard digging a hole beside the fig tree. Jerry was holding something in his arms. It was wrapped up in an old red plaid flannel shirt. He laid it in the hole and Daddy covered it with dirt and then packed it down with the back of the shovel. Bud placed a big rock there with black letters painted on it. I couldn't make out the whole word, only the first few letters "T" and "R."

They were all so sad-faced, but Mama wouldn't let me go out there with them.

When they came inside, I asked, "Daddy, what were you doing? Have you seen Trixie?"

"She's gone to heaven, Delaney."

"When's she coming back?"

"She won't be back, sweetheart. She's gone to be with the other little doggies and Jesus."

I cried because I didn't understand about heaven or how far away it was. And I didn't know why Trixie wanted to go and be with Jesus.

I kept imagining I heard her barking, and there were times I thought I saw her on the driveway chasing after the neighbor's cat. But Daddy was right; she never came back. And I missed my little friend.

* * *

Easter Sunday wasn't too long after that and it was my favorite holiday, next to Christmas.

I always got a pretty, frilly dress. A lot of my frilly little dresses came from my sister. I loved when she took me downtown and bought things for me at Kessler's, the department store where she worked.

Easter morning we always went to the little Baptist church. Afterward all my aunts and uncles and cousins came over to our house for a family feast. The only cousins near my age were Melinda and Joe, only a couple of years older. We compared our Easter baskets filled with candy and our stuffed animals left by the Easter Bunny.

Aunt Maisie was Mama's aunt and the only woman in our family who dipped snuff. I asked her a few times, "Aunt Maisie, how come you put that stuff in your mouth and spit like that?"

She rolled it to the side of her jaw, brought the tin can to her mouth and spit in it, then dabbed the knuckle of her index finger to the corner of her mouth to catch the drool. "Hm-m, I dunno child. It's good, I reckon. I been dippin' since I was nine years old. Don't remember when I warn't dippin'. But don't you ever start. It's a nasty habit."

She never had to worry about me dipping snuff, and she was right—it was nasty.

Mama said Aunt Maisie had polio as a child. That's why she walked with a cane and always wore brown or black hard-soled, leather orthopedic shoes. In the summer when I was barefoot, that cane or one of those shoes of hers always found my toes.

I thought Aunt Maisie was rich because she had a watch with diamonds around the face, a big opal and diamond ring and she was the first in the family to own a television. For a long time she was the only one with a Brownie camera, deeming her the family photographer. She insisted we pose by category, first the children alone, then the girls by themselves and so on.

Finally came the group pictures, adults on the back row and children on the front, with our Easter baskets at our sides. Aunt Maisie loved our pink dogwood trees in the front yard. That's where we stood for every photograph, facing the sun so she could get a good shot of our faces. "Smile and say Happy Easter Bunny!"... *Click...click*, and *click* again. Unfortunately she often delayed before clicking, so we were no longer smiling, and our faces were always scrunched up from the bright sun.

Following the feast and the photographs was the traditional egg hunt.

The Easter bunny always left me some real live baby chicks that had been dipped in purple, pink, green, blue, or bright yellow-colored dye. They were bought that way, not dyed at home like the Easter eggs were. They were cute and sweet and ever so cuddly. So much so, they were held and cuddled to the point that they got sick, and eventually "went to be with Trixie and Jesus," as Daddy told me.

I never developed a taste for those individually plastic-wrapped colored Easter eggs with the white centers. I normally loved anything sweet—the sweeter the better—but those were too much for even my sweet tooth to handle. They lasted a long time after Easter, mainly because I didn't like them, but I did get some enjoyment from them. For several days after Easter I'd put all the eggs in a brown paper lunch bag and go out to the backyard. I'd swirl around and around with my eyes closed as the eggs flew out the open end of the bag and were tossed and scattered all over the yard. I would have my very own private Easter egg hunt all by myself. I didn't need any grownups to hide them and I didn't need any other kids to hunt them with me.

Sometimes they were hidden so well I couldn't find all of them, but they'd turn up eventually, usually underneath Daddy's lawnmower the next time he cut the grass.

* * *

Initially we didn't have a bathroom inside our house like my aunts and uncles had at their houses. Thanks to my little blue-flowered, porcelain potty I never had to go to the outhouse. But I remember my brothers beating on the door and yelling at each other to hurry up and get out. The sounds echoed such that the neighbors ran outside to investigate the commotion. *Bam! Bam!* "Hurry up! Somebody else has gotta get in there too, y'know!"

One day Mama dressed me in my new sailor dress, all white with navy blue trim and a red tie. I was wearing my Easter shoes, black patent leather with straps with lace-trimmed white socks. She said, "You look so sweet! Now don't get dirty, your aunt and uncle are going to be here any minute."

Even though I was only three or so, I understood her instructions. It was such a warm day the back door was open to let air in the house. I got excited when I saw our neighbors, Sally and Sam, picking muscadines in their back yard just on the other side of our fence. I couldn't wait for them to see my new dress, so I sneaked out when Mama wasn't looking.

With my head held high, knowing I outshined even Shirley Temple that day, I showed off my recently developed skill of skipping. Then it happened—I slipped and fell into a big mud puddle! Sally came running and helped me up, "Are you alright, sweetie?" When I began to cry she consoled me and put her arm around my mud-covered shoulder. Sam and Sally didn't have any children of their own, so they always treated me like a daughter.

Mama came running outside in a panic, "Are you okay, Sugar?" She checked me over from head-to-toe for bruises or cuts, but I wasn't hurt. Just muddy. "Delaney James, you know you weren't supposed to come outside. Now look what you've done. You've ruined your new dress. That mud'll never come out!" She began scolding me there in front of Sally and continued until we were back on the porch, "I better get it in the sink to soak right now."

She jerked the dress off over my head, yanked off my socks and shoes, and put me into a big gray metal washtub on the back porch to bathe me. That's where she bathed me when it was pretty weather, and normally I enjoyed it.

That day was different, however. Strange men I didn't know were in and out of our house through the back door. Even at that age I felt uncomfortable and embarrassed for those men I didn't know to see me without any clothes. They were building what would later become another bedroom, and a bathroom that was inside! A bathroom where I would hear my brothers and sister, parents, and later myself all standing outside of, knocking on the door yelling, "Hurry up! Somebody else has to get in there, too, y'know!"

* * *

My whole world revolved around my family: Mama, Daddy, my sister and brothers.

My older sister's name was Trish but I called her Sissy. I slept with her until that man named Bryan came along when she was eighteen and took her away that evening.

They had gotten married that afternoon but I was only four years old and didn't understand what the big deal was all about. When they told me they were going away that evening, moving to a place way up north, I felt as if my heart was breaking.

My best friend in the whole world was going away, and I was sure she'd never come back. That's why I couldn't stop the tears. I was crying because I didn't want to be by myself in that big bed and in that dark room, left to sleep alone. Didn't Sissy know I was afraid to be alone?

They thought the big black-and-white teddy bear they gave me would take her place beside me in the bed. And so it did, but only because it had to. I had no other choice.

Bryan turned out to be a real okay kind of guy after all. When he played with me he'd swing me around in the air like an airplane. I decided he was good to have around and he also brought Sissy home from time to time, although not often enough.

I didn't know exactly where they lived. When I wanted Daddy to take me to see her he said, "Sweetpea, I'm sorry but they're all the way up in Minnesota. It would take us a couple of days to drive all the way up there."

I thought, *Whew! Minnesota? Couple of days? They must really live a very, very long, long ways away.* I hated that she lived so far away, and as a four-year-old I was unable to understand why they would need to live anywhere else but home.

* * *

When the first day of school rolled around I hadn't planned on Mama leaving me there with all those kids I didn't know. All the others were crying, so I wasn't the only one.

Through my tears I watched as a woman approached. She knelt beside me and placed her hand around my waist. She was pretty like Sissy with dark hair and a nice smile. "Hi there. My name is Miss Johnston and I'm your teacher. What's your name?"

I dried my eyes with the hem of my blue dotted Swiss dress for a better look before answering, "De-lane-y."

"Delaney? My, what a pretty name. Just like you."

She seemed nice enough and I warmed up to her right away. "I can spell. Do you want me to spell for you? I can read and write and count, too. Do you want me to show you?"

Daddy had taught me to write a few simple sentences and then he taught me to read them. I suppose it was more like memorizing; nonetheless, she was impressed, "Why Delaney, you are so smart!" I already knew that. That's what everybody always said after I performed for them.

Her warm smile and words of praise made me forget all about crying as I thought, *Hmm, maybe this place ain't so bad, after all.*

* * *

I looked forward to recesses. We had two a day, one in the morning and one in the afternoon. I spent my time climbing on the monkey bars and hanging upside-down. Though I can't explain why, that was one of my favorite pastimes, whether on the monkey bars on the school's playground, or at home on my swing set. I was fascinated by how different everything looked from that angle.

But there were two problems with my favorite pastime. One was in the fact that my hair was naturally curly and unusually long, tumbling down to the back of my knees. My mother never knew what she'd find in my hair at the end of the day when she brushed the tangles out before bed. There might be leaves, pine straw, or God knows what.

She developed a tone of aggravation in her voice at hair brushing time, "Come on now, Delaney…hold still!"

"Ow, Mama! Ow-w-w!" My screaming alerted the entire neighborhood as to when Mama was brushing my hair. I don't even want to talk about when it came time for the comb.

The other problem with a girl hanging upside down was that my panties would show, ruffles and all. I didn't like Miss Johnston anymore when she said, "Delaney, Honey, nice girls don't hang on the monkey bars like that."

"Why not?"

"Let's just say you mustn't do that anymore...it's not ladylike."

I cried and pouted and then cried some more when I got home that afternoon. The teacher had written a note for me to give to Mama informing her of our discussion. All along I thought she'd be on my side and go tell that teacher a thing or two. I was wrong. "Well, Sugar, if that's what the teacher says, then I guess you shouldn't do that anymore."

I was convinced it was a conspiracy. Of course, at that time, I had never heard the word "conspiracy" or knew what it meant, but I'm sure that's what I would have called it. I never said I wanted to be a lady and I decided I didn't want to go to school and she couldn't make me. It wasn't fun anymore.

I decided I would rebel by giving my Mama a hard time in the mornings when it came time to get up and dressed.

Then I had the bright idea to go to someone I knew would help me with my exasperating dilemma...my Daddy.

He told Mama to write a note to the teacher and the principal asking permission to allow me to wear long pants under my dress in cool weather to avoid catching a chill. They agreed and it was the solution to my problem.

It wasn't exactly an attractive fashion statement, and at first the other kids made fun of me, calling me a monkey. After only a few weeks though the look caught on and almost every girl in my class was following suit.

* * *

Once I had settled in with the routine I was excited to be going to school like my friend Margaret Brinson, who lived across the street. Her father was the school bus driver and everyone in the community called him Uncle Buddy.

My mother or brother would walk me across the street to their house every weekday morning where I stayed until time to leave for school. I was lucky to be the first one on the bus because Uncle Buddy always let me ride shotgun. That was the front seat right behind him and the best seat on the bus.

I was so impressed that Margaret's house always had a refrigerator full of Coca-Colas. I always envied her so, as I sat and watched her drink one every morning with her breakfast. Mama always made me drink juice or milk for breakfast. In fact we rarely ever had Cokes in our house. Mama said they weren't good for us, but the main reason was that we couldn't afford them at a nickel a bottle. I always considered our neighbors the Brinsons to be rich because they owned the bus, they had nice cars, and they always had plenty of Cokes in the house!

The first week of October, the teacher gave all the students discount coupons for tickets to the Southeastern Fair. When the other kids asked me when my parents were taking me, I said, "I don't know yet."

Truth of the matter was I didn't even know what a Southeastern Fair was. I heard all the other kids talking about it, and they made it sound like as much fun as the circus we went to see that last year. I knew I had to go!

I couldn't wait to get off the bus and run inside the house to tell Mama about it. She listened intently but then said, "You'll have to wait until your daddy gets home."

I thought I'd never hear his car pulling onto the gravel driveway.

"Daddy's home!" I shrilled, after what seemed like eternity. I greeted him before he ever even got out of the car. I ran into his arms, hugged him and started kissing him all over his cheeks. "Daddy!" I proclaimed, "I love you so-o much!"

"Well, I love you too, Sweetpea." He began that deep-bellied chuckle as though I were tickling him. "But what's this all about?"

I sneaked another quick bear hug to assure myself of his complete attention. As I attempted to reduce him to mere putty in my hands I turned on the charm. I looked up at his glowing face and in that flirty little girl way, I smiled and batted my brown eyes, going in for the kill, "Daddy, can we…"

"Tell Daddy—where'd you get those big brown eyes?"

I didn't want to change the subject and lose my level of control in the situation. However, the infamous question about the origin of my eyes could work to my favor, so I answered, "The moo-o-o cow over there in the pasture."

He just laughed that jolly laugh of his and gave me a big squeeze, "That's Daddy's little Sweetpea." He smiled and his brightest of blue eyes widened so the glow in his face outshined the sun, "Now, what was it you wanted to ask me? Can we do what?"

"Can we go to the Fair? It has rides and games and all my friends are going—everybody's going—can we go? *P-l-eeease.*"

CHAPTER II
THEY SAID IT WAS HAUNTED

My father was never one to say "no" to anything when it concerned me, especially when I wanted so much to go to the Fair.

The following Saturday afternoon found us in Lakewood, standing in a mile-long line at the front gate of the Southeastern Fairgrounds. I'd never before seen so many people waiting to get into a place.

There were nine of us: Mama, Daddy, my aunts Gracie and Emma, my uncles Clyde and Clarence, and my cousins Melinda and Joe.

I was so excited I couldn't stand still as I jumped up and down on my tip-toes, straining to see over the tall, canvas draped fences. Suddenly my entire being jolted as Mama reached out and grabbed me by the shoulder of my sweater, sternly pulling me closer to her side, "Delaney, get back over here and be still!" Her sisters giggled when she glanced at them and, out of the side of her mouth she said, "I swear…acts like she's got ants in 'er pants."

Once we were through the gates I was all eyes. I'd never seen so many rides. There were big ones, not so big ones, a beautiful Merry-go-round and a huge Ferris Wheel. Each ride produced a musical sound of its own, blaring through the speaker as it pumped familiar tunes.

Music was everywhere. A mixture of screams and laughter, and loud voices of the crowd as they pushed and shoved. I was frightened when some husky man bumped into me and my hand slipped out of Mama's grasp. I was pulled away from my family and into the sea of people. "Mama! Daddy!"

"Delaney, stay there, I'll get you!"

I searched the crowd but I couldn't see either of their faces. There were too many people and I could barely see above the armpits of all the grownups. I began to panic.

"Mama!"

Suddenly, I felt Mama's familiar hand in mine as she snatched me toward her, "Delaney, don't ever pull away from me again!"

"But Mama, I didn't pull..." Bone-chilling screams of sheer horror grabbed my attention. They grew louder as we approached a gigantic, gray wooden structure. At first glance it just looked like a bunch of boards haphazardly nailed together. There were pretty little blinking lights chasing along the outline of its enormous silhouette, but up close I could see the paint peeling. I was awe-stricken by the size of the thing. It must have reached a mile into the sky. My cousins pointed at it and said, "Look Delaney, there's the Greyhound!" (The Greyhound was one of the oldest and largest wooden roller coasters in the country.)

The Greyhound? Hum-m-m, I'd heard all about the Greyhound... that was what all the kids at school were talking about. They said it was haunted; that people, especially children were killed on that ride and that monsters and ghosts lived underneath and ate the bodies.

I believed it all, after seeing that thing and hearing all the screams. When I realized my daddy was headed over to ride the thing with my uncles, I jumped in front of him and stretched to clasp my arms around his waist, "No, Daddy, please don't ride it. It's a monster."

He uncoiled my arms and held my hand tightly, "Ruth, come get your daughter."

As she pulled me to her side I cried, "No Daddy. Daddy!" But he turned away from me and proceeded to get in line. Once they got on it, I couldn't see them, but I could hear them screaming. It took them high against the sky and back down again so fast I feared their heads might suddenly snap off at their necks, like an ear of corn is snatched from its stalk. While I waited for them to get off I stared at the area beneath the giant gray creature, and I believed there were indeed monsters living in that dark pit of a ravine.

I imagined it was a live monster, with its creaks, groans and moans of the wooden planks, and its passengers' haunting screams of terror. I ran and hugged Daddy's legs when he finally came down the ramp to rejoin us.

As we walked away hand-in-hand leaving the giant monstrosity behind us, I pleaded, "Daddy, please don't ride that again, okay?"

He leaned over and kissed my forehead while squeezing my hand reassuringly, "Sweetpea, don't worry, it's just a ride."

"But it has monsters. They'll kill you and eat you."

He scooped me up in his arms and hugged me, "Delaney, there's no such thing as monsters…and don't worry, nothin's gonna happen to me. I'm never gonna leave you—I promise." He nuzzled my forehead, and the colorful lights reflected in his eyes when he smiled, "and Daddy always keeps his promises to his little girl, doesn't he? Now give me a kiss…and look over there."

He was directing my attention to the rows of colorful game tents where we could win things by tossing rings around bowling pins, throwing a basketball, or tossing pennies onto a plate sitting atop a stuffed animal's head. He won a pink-and-white teddy bear, a tinted-glass piggy bank, and a pinwheel, one of those little things on a stick that spins when it catches the wind or if someone blows into it.

I was fascinated by my pinwheel, and I wondered what made it work and how it created all the pretty colors. It didn't have to be wound and it didn't need batteries. It was just a simple toy, but to me it was magical.

Of all the rides there, I only rode the small ones, always with Daddy or Mama—never alone.

The Merry-go-round was beautiful and it was my favorite. Mama and Daddy stood on either side of me while I rode one of the carousel's big white horses. As we went around and around, I held up my pinwheel, first in front of me, and then out to my side. It was fun watching the breeze make it spin, creating those pretty colors in a magical sort of way.

* * *

I was curious about those shows. Some had freaky, strange looking people, others had snakes and lizards. Then there were those with women strutting around to music outside on a stage. A man out front was yelling, "Step right up, ladies and gentlemen!" The women looked all painted up like nothing I'd ever seen before. They all had long red fingernails and bright red lipstick, and they wore floor-length capes. The real show was inside, but of course I didn't know that.

We didn't go in that show. In fact, Mama always took my head and turned it toward her when we walked by, "Turn your head, Delaney, and don't look at that! It's nasty!"

That made me strain my neck even more to see it. Mama was unaware that I had caught a glimpse of my daddy and uncles going in there. We girls and Joe got some cotton candy and candied apples and waited for the men to rejoin us.

The air was full of excitement, but it also carried a combination of smells and odors. It all depended on where we were standing. Toward the middle and down the hill the smell of corndogs and popcorn were prevalent. The sugar-sweet aromas of cotton candy and candied apples were such that the air alone could rot a tooth or two.

Further up the hill I wrinkled my nose when I caught a whiff of the livestock exhibit, "Whew! That stinks—like the pasture at home."

* * *

There was another girlie show at the very back edge of the fairgrounds, but it was different. There wasn't a white woman in the bunch. It was the same as the other except for that. Also the music seemed to be faster, louder and with more horns. Mostly colored people were standing around outside, but there were a few white men, three of which were my daddy and uncles. My mother thought she covered my eyes before I saw them. I never knew if they actually went in or not, as I headed in the opposite direction along with Mama and my aunts.

During my visit to the Fair I had been shoved and lost in the crowd, bumped into and spilled grape snow cone down the front of my blouse, and stepped into a glob of pink bubblegum, "Yuk, it's sticky on my sneakers, Mama. Hurry and get it off!"

All day long I had stepped in a variety of food spills and endured the sticky surface of the concrete, or sank down in the smooshy, smelly sawdust. But it was the best darn time I'd ever had, as I squeezed Daddy's hand and smiled up at him, "Wow, I really love the Fair! Don't you?"

By the end of the day I was exhausted. Daddy carried me on his shoulders as we made our way over to the grandstand to get a good seat for the fireworks. All of a sudden there was a loud *'Pow! Pow!'* as the sky lit up and exploded in every color of the rainbow. There were a million lights as the entire display reflected in the lake waters in front of the grandstands.

After the fireworks show was over, it was a mad rush for everyone to get out of the park. It was officially closed for the day and they would soon be turning off the lights.

We made our way through the crowd to get to the exit and we passed the Greyhound. This time the pretty lights outlining the silhouette weren't on. The thing was even scarier with the void beneath even darker than before. The very sight of it made me shudder, "Brr-rr, I'm never gonna get on that thing." Perched atop Daddy's shoulder, I almost choked his neck. I wanted to hurry and get out of there.

In the car on the way home I sat on Mama's lap hugging my teddy bear. She kissed my forehead and gave me a squeeze, "Did my little Dollbaby have a good time?

Just before dozing off to sleep in her arms, I responded in an exhausted little voice, "Yes ma'am. Daddy, can we go back to the Fair sometime?"

He reached across the front seat and lovingly patted my leg, "Sure, Sweetpea, we'll go again next year."

I smiled and closed my eyes. That was the answer I wanted to hear.

* * *

October was one of my favorite months because of my birthday, Halloween and the Southeastern Fair.

We went to the Fair that next year just as he'd promised. Daddy gave his word, and he always kept his promises.

CHAPTER III
GET US OUT OF THIS
CHICKEN OUTFIT

Family ties were important to us, and we never missed the annual Simpson reunion here in Georgia. There I would see all my relatives on Mama's side of the family. It was usually held at Granddaddy's brother's house in Snellville. My grandparents always came up from Jacksonville around that time of the year. They took turns staying with us part of the time and the rest with Aunt Gracie and Aunt Emma.

I was fascinated by Granddaddy's hearing aid. One time he took it off and let me listen through it. "Granddaddy, you got great big ears, so how come you can't hear so good?"

He laughed, "Well, Sugar, the size of my ears don't got nothin' to do with my hearing. That comes from way down inside my ear holes." He slid his wire-rimmed glasses to the tip of his nose and looked down at me, "Besides, my big ears and nose are what holds my glasses on my head so they won't fall off. " His smile could light up a baseball stadium.

He was a big baseball fan and one of his favorite teams was the Atlanta Crackers. He played with me a lot but I had to be quiet while he listened to the games on the radio. He always had the same response to the sounds of their bats cracking and the fans roaring, "I gotta go see my Crackers play at least one game while I'm here." And so the Ponce de Leon Ballpark was one sure-fire stopping point during his Atlanta visits.

He was amazed and puzzled as to how I always beat him at cards, proclaiming to Gramama, "I'll swear, Era, our little girl's a natural." He was such a good sport about losing I could never bring myself to tell him how I saw a clear reflection of his cards in his glasses.

Gramama was always nearby and I was sure she saw me cheating, but she never turned me in. She just continued crocheting quietly. Occasionally she'd look over her glasses at me and grunt or clear her throat. That always prompted me to ask, "Gramama, are you thirsty? You want me to go get ya somethin' cold to drink?"

"No, Sugar, but you're a mighty sweet girl to ask."

* * *

The reunions were held in the middle of summer as Daddy always complained, "Damn it, Ruth, your family plans these get-togethers on the hottest damn day of the year."

Driving to Snellville wasn't easy back then as the highway wasn't paved out that far, so we were in for a long and bumpy ride in all that heat and dust. Snellville was out beyond Stone Mountain, another place we went as a family for picnics. I always knew we were close to our destination when I saw the mountain. I became engrossed by the way the huge mass of granite seemed to move from one side of the road to the other. "How's it do that, Daddy?"

"It goes underground and pops back up on the other side of the road, but nobody knows how. Watch and see if you can figure out how it does it."

I should've known he was teasing me, but I believed him and tried my best to solve the puzzle. It was the summer before I turned six years old, I figured out it was the road twisting and turning, and the mountain wasn't moving at all. "That's right, Sweetpea. How'd ya figure it out so fast?"

* * *

One year the reunion was held in August in celebration of my great Uncle Dewey's birthday. He looked to be about 200 years old, but he was probably more like sixty. All I knew was that he sure was old.

When it started raining everyone ran to take shelter inside the little wooden house or out on the porch. The floor in the kitchen began to sag from the weight, so Uncle Walt said, "We need to give this here floor a rest. Some of ya'll need ta run on out yonder to the barn till it slacks off a bit. Y'all will stay dry out there. It's just one of them summer showers—it'll be over before ya know it."

Daddy grabbed me in his arms as if I was a toy, and he ran as fast as he could to the barn. The barn to which my uncle referred was actually the chicken house.

Alongside a dozen others we squeezed inside that little chicken house—in the rain—on that steamy August day. It was hot and the stench was so awful, I'd never been that miserable in all of my six years.

The rain began around lunchtime and didn't let up the entire afternoon. After a while I shook Daddy's pants leg and when he leaned down, I whispered in his ear, "I have to go the bathroom." Mama was still in the main house with the others, so once again he scooped me up and ran to the outhouse.

I hated going to my Uncle Dewey's when it came to that part of the trip. The stench was more awful than the chicken house and I had to hold my nose the entire time I was in there. I was always afraid of spiders, or that I was going to fall into the hole and be eaten by snakes, or that a snake was curled up beneath the seat, just waiting to strike.

There came a time in the late afternoon when the rain looked as if it were set in for the night. Daddy said, "All right, let's go get your mother and get out of this chicken outfit." It was the best idea I'd heard all day.

We bid our farewells to all the huggers, kissers, and cheek-pinchers as we three climbed into the car, headed back to Atlanta. It was just the three of us, as my brothers were smart that time and old enough to have other things to do.

It was raining so that we could hardly see where we were going.

The road wasn't paved and the car kept sliding all over in the mud, from one side to the other. Mama kept screaming, "Oooh! Jack! Look out!"

Daddy, screamed back "I know what I'm doing!"

I just sat there hoping he was right.

The car began weaving, and then it slid off the road and got stuck in a ditch. Daddy got out of the car and told Mama to mash the gas peddle when he told her to. He went around to the back where he was pushing the car when he yelled, "Okay, Ruth, *now!*"

Mama didn't know how to drive a car and didn't know the gas peddle from the brake or the clutch. After a few minutes of grunting from the rear, Daddy trudged in the mud around to the driver's side and asked in a loud, agitated voice, "What are you doing? I said mash the gas!"

Mama started crying, "I thought I was!" But she had been mashing the brakes all along, so Daddy showed her which one was the gas peddle, then he showed her the clutch and the gear knob.

After he had given her a quick lesson on shifting the gears and mashing the gas, he asked, "You think you can do it now?"

Mama nodded and with the rain pouring harder than ever, Daddy went back in position to the rear of the car. He pushed and yelled to Mama, "Now!" The wheels were spinning but the car didn't budge, so he pushed and yelled again, *"Now!"* It just got deeper and deeper in the mud. Mama kept right on trying though, grinding those gears such that the car was vibrating beneath us and making an awful racket. It sounded and felt as if the car were tearing up, right where we sat.

I was afraid we would have to spend the night out there. Even though it was still daylight, I knew that lonely stretch of road would be dark before long. And it always got dark earlier when it stormed. I was beginning to get really uncomfortable, not only about our predicament, but I had to go the bathroom again. However, I sensed it wasn't a good time to bring it up, so I just sat quietly.

Daddy gave up trying to push the car out of the ditch when he slid down covering his clothes in mud to the point that I couldn't tell what colors they were anymore.

I could tell he was really mad, as he pulled himself up out of the mud and tromped around to the driver's side then slung open the door with such a force the car shook.

"This is not working. Stay here and I'll walk up the road a piece for help. I think there's a house in about another mile or two."

Mama said, "All right, but be careful!"

I really began to worry, and I told Mama I didn't know if I could wait to go the bathroom. She lowered the window and yelled to Daddy before he got out of hearing distance, "Jack! Jack, come back! Delaney has to go to the bathroom!"

"Tell her she'll just have to hold it!"

"But she has to go real bad!"

When I saw he was ignoring her pleas I started crying, begging her to tell him to come back and get me. At first she didn't, but then she started blowing the horn and flashing the lights. Daddy thought we were in trouble so he turned around and started back.

He was only a few feet in front of the car when he stepped into a mud puddle. It was so deep the mud sucked his shoe right off of his foot!

He fished around for it, but after a while he gave up and came back to the car. He jerked the door wide open, "What's wrong for @#*%'s sake?"

"Jack, calm down. Delaney says she really has to go to the bathroom."

Daddy yelled, using language that made my ears burn, "@#@*#!!! I said she'll have to hold it!"

I started crying, and so did Mama. That was more than Daddy could stand, "Oh, all right. Come on—come to Daddy."

Still crying, Mama said, "You're not going to leave me out here alone, are you? It's getting dark!"

"Oh, #@*%! For God's sake, Ruth, stop blubberin'. Nobody's gonna get you! Nobody's stupid enough to get out in this—except for us! But she wouldn't stop crying so he finally gave in, picked her up and took her to a less muddy part of the road. Then he came back for me. He carried me in his arms until we came to a little house.

I wasn't sure how far we had walked but the car lights had long faded into the distance.

I was sure glad to get there—to their outhouse—and the thought of snakes or spiders never entered my mind.

The people who lived there were real nice. The old man got his big tractor and took Daddy back to the car to pull it out of the mud.

They were back soon on the tractor without the car. The car battery was dead because the headlights had been left on from when Mama had signaled Daddy. I was certain that if we ever got out of there, Daddy would never let Mama forget...all the way home and then some.

There wasn't a dry thread in our clothes, so Mama pulled off my dress and socks and the nice lady handed her a quilt to wrap around me. I was exhausted, after such an eventful day so I fell asleep on Mama's lap.

They got the car started during the night, and I was awakened by my mother's soft voice, "Delaney, sugar, wake up. Time to go home."

Home. The sweetest sounding word I'd heard all day.

I thought I'd never again hear the crunching sound of our driveway's gravel beneath our tires, but when I did it was like music to my ears. It meant I could crawl under the covers, lay my head on the big fluffy pillow, and go to sleep in my own bed. It meant I was home—where I belonged.

* * *

I must have gone to dozens of family reunions and picnics at places like Stone Mountain, Joy Lake, and Grant Park. The park had a big merry-go-round and a huge swimming pool with an enormous sliding board. Everything seemed bigger than life.

Grant Park went on forever, as we walked from the reptile house with snakes and alligators to the monkey houses to the lions and then over to the elephants. *Whew!* The smells were worse than any outhouse.

One time when we were at the park it was so hot and I was thirsty. I ran over to get a drink from the water fountain and I heard Mama yelling, "No, Delaney, not *that* one!" She took my hand and led me away from it, "Always use the one that says WHITES ONLY," as she pointed to the sign posted on the water fountain. "Never use the other one," gesturing toward the sign that read "COLORED ONLY."

The same went for restrooms, except it was even more confusing: aside from whether or not the sign read "WHITE" or "COLORED," I had to make sure it read "LADIES" instead of "MEN." It seemed like an awful lot to keep up with, when all I wanted was a drink of water or to go to the bathroom.

I shrugged and wondered, *I don't know what all the goin'-on's about. A water fountain's a water fountain, and a bathroom's a bathroom, ain't it?* But then I nodded, indicating that I did understand, just to satisfy Mama.

After a while I grew accustomed to looking for those signs. That was just the way it was, no different than the fact that the back of the bus was "saved for the coloreds." That's what Mama always told me when I wanted to sit on the back seat so I could look behind us out the big rear window.

I wondered why they had their own separate restrooms and water fountains, and why they were always given the best seat on the bus.

CHAPTER IV
LITTLE MISS BIG EARS

Christmas was my most favorite time of the year. It was exciting when the entire family went shopping with Daddy for the perfect Christmas tree. We always bought the most beautiful one on the lot.

Untangling and testing the strands of tree lights was an every year ritual. If only one bulb were blown, none of the others on the strand would work. So then came the task of detecting the rotten one.

Daddy invariably reached a point of frustration when he'd grit his teeth ad say every nasty word he could think of.

One raised eyebrow and a hard stare from Mom's dark-brown eyes meant she was serious when she reminded him, "Jack, watch your mouth. Remember Little Miss Big Ears."

He'd try his best to substitute mere grunts for the bad words. However, the grunts couldn't adequately express his level of aggravation and another "#%$%#!" was destined to slip out, sooner or later.

The kitchen was Mama's solution to get me out of hearing distance. "Delaney, sugar, let's go get you some cookies and milk."

I don't believe Daddy used those kinds of words or expressions any other time of the year—unless he smooshed his finger with the hammer, or tried to assemble something that had missing parts, or the lawnmower wouldn't crank, or the car wouldn't start. Come to think of it, he used those kinds of words and expressions pretty much year round.

Nonetheless each year's tree was the most beautiful of all, as I'd fall asleep in his lap while squinting my eyes to make pretty colored halos around the lights. The Christmas tree's glow always lent a feeling of true warmth to the cold, damp December evenings.

On Christmas Eve day I always loved to sit at Daddy's feet there on the rug in front of the big gas heater in the living room. While he rocked in his favorite chair and cracked pecans for the ambrosia, he shared them with me. They went great with the chocolate cream drops and tangerines. A cup of hot chocolate with marshmallow topped things off just right, and made me sleepy while we watched Christmas movies on our black-and-white television.

We tried that so-called colored TV kit we ordered from Howdy Doody and Buffalo Bob on television. The "kit", which amounted to a sheet of colored plastic, was supposed to change our black-and-white picture to color on our TV screen, and it did—it turned it red all over! The neighbors ordered one and theirs was green, and the one my cousin ordered was blue. We'd swap off from time to time, but Daddy said he'd rather look at the plain old black-and-white picture, so that's what we did.

My favorite movie was the one with Shirley Temple as Heidi, but I felt so sorry for her, without a real mama and daddy—only her grandfather. When I cried at the sad parts, Daddy scooped me up onto his lap and rocked me until I fell asleep.

* * *

Daddy had a great sense of humor, always telling jokes and making others laugh, including me. I walked into the kitchen one evening when Daddy was telling a joke, but I only heard the punchline, "So, he said, Get up and get your own damned water!" I didn't get it, but Daddy and our neighbor Sam were laughing so hard their bellies shook.

The next day in my second grade class at school we had Show and Tell day, when we all brought our favorite toys to show or we told a joke or a story. The girl who went before me stood in front of the room at the big, green chalk-board and recited:

"Brush your teeth with Pepsodent

And you'll wonder where the yellow went.

 Now I have no teeth at all,

 'Cause I brushed my teeth with Oxydol."

The entire class broke into hysteria, while I thought it was cute, but certainly not that funny. Not to be out-done, I had to come up with something to top her, so I recited the one-line joke I had overheard my daddy tell, "So he said, 'Get up and get your own damned water.'"

First a hush of silence fell over the room. Then hands covered mouths and "Ooohs" and "Uh-oh" were heard throughout. Miss Wood raised her eyebrow, placed her hands on her hips and shook her head. Her bewildered sigh of disapproval quickly transformed into the sternest of voices, as she said, "Delaney, sit down! That will be all!"

That afternoon Miss Wood gave me a note to take home to my parents. I didn't know what it said because it was in grownup writing rather than printing. I looked forward to the day when I could read and write like grownups.

Mama handed the note over to Daddy for him to read, "Here, Jack. I think *you* ought to see this."

After he glanced at it, he chuckled under his breath then cleared his throat. "Sweetpea, the teacher says here that you said "Damn" today. Is that true?"

"Yessir."

"Well, you shouldn't say that word, you know. It's not nice."

I pleaded, "But I had to say it, Daddy. That's the way the joke went."

He cocked his head a little. "What joke?"

"The one I told at Show and Tell today. The one you told Sam last night about the glass of water."

"Glass of water?" His face suddenly took on a red glow as he realized the joke to which his six-year-old daughter was referring. "You told that at school?"

"Yeah, but nobody laughed. Why didn't anyone laugh, Daddy?"

He tried to explain how, "Well, you see, Sweetpea, it's like this. That's a grownup's joke, so kids just wouldn't understand it."

Mama's eyes were shooting daggers at Daddy as she said, "Well, Jack, what do you have to say for yourself? I've warned you about Little Miss Big Ears. This is all your fault, y'know."

Daddy threw up his hands in exasperation and as he turned to walk away, I heard him chuckle and say under his breath, "*Damn*, I guess it's my fault she's a chip off the old block, too."

* * *

Besides recess and lunch, my favorite part of the school day was art time. Sometimes we drew with crayons or watercolor paints, but one Tuesday in the third grade my teacher, Mrs. Johnson said, "Boys and girls, this afternoon I'd like you to use these colored charcoals," as she placed the box on the table then instructed us to form a line. "Look out the window and draw a picture of what you see. Now, do a good job. They'll be displayed at tonight's PTA Open House."

Most of the class drew the forest with tall brown trees, green leaves, and birds flying against the blue sky with a yellow sun. I was the last in line and by the time I reached the box all the good colors were taken. So I took a different approach, using the colors which were left over.

But what could I draw with gray, black and red? She specifically instructed us to draw the view from our window; so, as a joke, I imagined what it would look like after a big forest fire. In my picture the trees were all lying on their sides, colored black because they were scorched. I made some squiggly lines against the gray sky above them to look like smoke rising from the singed wood. One lonely redbird hung upside down on a charred limb where it smoked with the rest of the remains.

I thought it looked funny, but the others said it was ugly and called me stupid for drawing it that way. Sue Ellen said, "You're weird, Delaney. Nobody likes your old picture."

That Sue Ellen was so prissy. She was always saying something mean to somebody.

Once the good colors has been returned to the box I had intended to draw another one for the night's display, but the bell rang and I had to run in order to catch the bus.

When I got home I didn't mention the PTA meeting, hoping my parents had forgotten all about it, but during supper Mama said, "Jack, I've laid out your good suit and tie for tonight."

"What's tonight?" he asked, mouth full of food.

"Remember? We're going to Delaney's school for PTA Open House."

"Is that tonight?" Daddy then turned to me and said, "Oh boy, I can't wait to hear your teacher tell us how smart you are…again." He rolled his eyes and winked at me, "Is my Sweetpea's picture gonna knock our socks off like last year's?"

A sick feeling came over me when I thought of my ugly picture, and I grabbed my stomach, "Ooooh, I don't feel so good."

Mama placed the back of her hand to my forehead, "You don't have a fever. Tell Mama where you don't feel good."

"My tummy hurts."

Daddy said, "Oh, she's just got the jitters about tonight. She's gonna be all right." He looked at me and smiled "You'll feel better, once everybody's braggin' on ya. Now, go get dressed. Don't wanna be late."

The other parents just gawked at my picture and made comments such as, "How odd," "Now that's different," "Whatd'ya make of that?" or "Wonder which little girl is Delaney James?"

At first glance, Mama looked a little puzzled then she shook her head and took a deep sigh, "Delaney, I declare. What on earth?" But when Daddy nudged her with his elbow, she cleared her throat in midquestion, and in a proud tone of voice she said, "Delaney, I declare. I just can't get over how artistic you are. Why...it's the prettiest picture here."

"Really, Mama? Do you think so—really?"

Daddy chimed in to say, "Sweetpea, you've made us proud. Why, just look how it stands out from the rest. You'd have to be really smart and a true artist to be able to draw something such as this."

I felt so embarrassed and ashamed for anyone to see my picture. Even though I knew it was meant to be a joke, no one else knew it. They thought it was just a stupid old, ugly, makeshift attempt at art and figured I couldn't draw any better than that. But Mama and Daddy's praises made my face light up in a proud smile and I truly believed that picture was beautiful. I thought, *Aw, heck! If they think THAT's good, just wait till they see the one I'm gonna draw for 'em tomorrow!*

I never told them I had no other choice but use the leftover colors—the colors no one else wanted.

* * *

I stood with my parents while Mrs. Johnson talked with them, mostly about me. "Mr. and Mrs. James, your daughter is so smart. She's one of the brightest students in the class." Daddy looked down at me and winded as she continued. "Delaney has such a vivid imagination and she's so talented." She gave Daddy a folder and said, "Here are some of the short stories she's written and illustrated. You'll notice she earned an 'A' on every one…"

My attention suddenly drifted toward the art-wall when I noticed a girl, a little smaller than me. She was standing before my picture—just staring at it. I knew who it was without seeing her face. She was wearing the same red sweater she'd worn every day since that first day of school, and her hair was a long, tangled mess. It was Mary Elizabeth Wade. The "freak." The ugliest girl in my class.

No one wanted to sit next to her on the bus or in the lunchroom. She smelled bad because she wore the same dirty clothes day after day, and she never washed her hair. That old ugly wrinkled-up scar on her neck and side of her face extended down her right arm and onto the back of her hand. I didn't want her looking at my picture, so I marched over and stood in front of it so she couldn't see. "Mary Elizabeth, you go away and look at somebody else's picture. Go look at your own."

Her eyes widened as she explained, "But mine's not pretty like yours. Yours is the best one. I could never draw as good as you."

"Well, maybe not as good as me, but…which one's yours?"

She pointed to the one at the very end on the bottom row.

I stated, "That's not what Mrs. Johnson told us to draw. That's not what you see when you look outside the window. Who's that supposed to be, anyway?"

"That's my mama and my papa and my baby brother, Seth. And that's me there in the middle." The one in the middle was wearing a red sweater, too.

They were pictured holding hands, with big smiles on their faces.

"Are they here?" I asked. "Show them to me and I'll tell you if they look like the picture."

"They're not here—just Granny." She pointed to an older, gray-haired lady. She was wearing a flour sack looking, blue-and-white print cotton dress. Her hands were rough looking, like my daddy's, and her hair was pulled back in the bun at the base of her neck.

"How come ya mama and daddy ain't here?"

Her expression saddened, and her voice weakened, "They're with Jesus. Ever since last Christmas Eve when our house burnt down, Mama, Papa and Seth been with Jesus."

"You mean you ain't seen them since then?" I was puzzled.

"No. Once somebody goes with Jesus, they don't come back. It's just me and Granny, now."

"Oh yeah, I know what you mean. My dog, Trixie went there and never came back, either. Where do you live if your house burnt down?"

She answered matter-of-factly, "We live in her trailer over in the park."

"You live in Grant Park?"

"No," she chuckled, "the trailer park on Jonesboro Road."

"Oh, yuck—you live there? That's not far from my house. Must be awful, living in a place like that. Mama says 'ain't nothin' but drunks and no'counts live there.'"

Prissy Sue Ellen Whirter came out of nowhere to knock into Mary Elizabeth and sassed, "Delaney, what are you doing talking to her? You trying to get cooties?"

I just leered at her. "Just go on and leave us along. Nobody asked you to butt in."

She commented on how Mary Elizabeth was stinking dirty and as ugly as my picture. So I let her have it, all over her pastel yellow lace dress with the ruffled crinolines.

"There! Now who's dirty? Grape punch won't come out!" I howled.

Before I knew it, my fists were balled up and I put a live punch to her jaw...

"All right, break it up!" The teacher grabbed Sue Ellen and Daddy pulled me away to the other side of the room.

"Delaney, what's gotten into you?" Mama reminded me, "Little ladies don't fight."

"She was saying mean things to Mary Elizabeth, that's what. If she does it again, I'm really gonna let her have it!"

The gray-haired lady approached me and said, "That was nice of you...takin' up for my grandbaby like that. Mrs. James, I'm Emma Lou Wade, Mary Elizabeth's granny. Got yourself a mighty sweet little girl, there." As they walked away, hand in hand, Mary Elizabeth glanced back over her shoulder at me and waved, "Bye, Delaney. See you tomorrow."

I threw up my hand and thought, *She ain't so bad as she looks.* I felt sad for her. She reminded me of Heidi in the movie—without a mama and a daddy—living with her granny like that. I was lucky not to be like her, and I was glad Mama and Daddy weren't with Jesus.

* * *

The next day she wore the same clothes, including the red sweater. At recess we were hanging upside down on the monkey bars and I laughed, "In that sweater of yours, you look like the redbird in my picture."

She only chuckled once then I saw tears well up when she said, "Ever since last Christmas Eve, my tummy feels like I'm hanging upside down all the time."

* * *

Mary Elizabeth and I became good friends—not best friends—but good ones. Mama boxed up some clothes for her. Clothes I had outgrown, and when she opened them she wouldn't stop hugging me. Mama cut her hair and gave her a perm. It was a little on the frizzy side, but it looked better than it did, and at least it was clean.

Some of the blouses and dresses were long-sleeved, so she didn't have to wear that old sweater to cover the scars.

* * *

One afternoon in the following weeks, our art project was Joseph and the Coat of Many Colors from the Bible story. That day I forced my way to the front of the crayon line, determined I wasn't going to settle for the leftover colors again. I didn't want to present my parents with a rendering of Joseph and the Coat of Black and Gray to adorn the refrigerator.

I grabbed up the good color crayons, then shared them with Mary Elizabeth and taught her to draw…almost as good as me.

CHAPTER V
WHAT COULD BE A
BETTER PLACE?

My family moved to our house when I was six months old. It only had two bedrooms, so it certainly wasn't big enough for seven people. My parents' room was actually the dining room, with no doors separating them from the rest of the house. My crib was in their room until I was almost three years old when I began sleeping with my sister.

A little while after Sissy and Bryan moved away my oldest brother, Gene, brought his wife, Jackie, and their new baby daughter to live with us. When they took over my bed, I moved back into Mama and Daddy's room and slept on a twin bed.

Relatives came to see the new baby and asked me, "How does it feel to have your very own niece living with you?" I wanted so much to say, "Why don't you take her with you and see for yourself?" Whenever anyone proclaimed her such a precious, pretty little baby girl, my only thoughts were *Big Deal!* I didn't like her being there and I didn't like sharing Daddy's attention with her.

* * *

That afternoon in April I rode the school bus home with Julie and Linda Fowler and stayed for dinner. Julie was seven years old like me, and we were best friends, so we always had a great time together.

It was unusually quiet around their dinner table that evening. "Delaney, would you like the last little bit of apple cobbler?" I thought that was strange because Mrs. Fowler never offered seconds on dessert.

Julie and Linda were even polite, "Yeah, Delaney, go ahead... you eat it."

Mrs. Fowler had tears in her eyes, but she explained how the onions made them water.

I declined the cobbler and said, "I know. Mama's eyes do that, too. So do Daddy's when he's peeling onions for the potato salad."

It was so late when my brother Gene, his wife, and Mama came for me. I didn't understand why they came instead of Daddy, nor did I understand why they were so quiet.

"Where's Daddy?" I asked.

Gene said, "Let's go, Delaney. Get your things together."

"But where's Daddy?"

He still didn't answer my question. "Let's go and let the Fowlers go to bed."

Julie and Linda both hugged me, and of all things, told me they loved me. They'd never done that before, but I told them I loved them, too.

Mrs. Fowler walked with us through the kitchen to the back door. She hugged me first, then my mother, "Ruth, if I can do anything at all, just let me know."

Mama's eyes began to water, so I asked, "Are the onions making you cry, too?"

* * *

I was excited when we arrived home to find so many of our neighbors there, as I saw this as an opportunity to stay up late, even on a school night. The only thing missing from this picture was the talking…only quiet whispers.

Of all people, I didn't expect Preacher Reynolds to be there. He asked me to join him on the front porch on the glider swing. His voice was very sad, "I'm so sorry, Delaney. Your father died of a heart attack this afternoon while he was at work and now he's in heaven. Do you understand?"

When I shrugged and shook my head, he placed his hand on my shoulder and squeezed firmly, as he reassured me, "Don't worry. He's gone to a better place. Jesus called him home to be with Him."

Was that supposed to make it all clear to me? I remembered when I stayed with Sam and Sally one afternoon while Mama and Daddy went to Snellville. I asked them why I couldn't go and Daddy said, "Your Mama's Uncle Grady has gone to be with Jesus…you remember, like Trixie and the baby chicks?" I couldn't place Uncle Grady, but I remembered when Trixie and the baby chicks went to be with that Jesus. They never came back, but I didn't know why. And then there was Mary Elizabeth Wade's mama and papa and baby brother—all of them—went with Jesus and never came back.

A million questions raced through my mind. *But what could be a better place? What does the preacher mean?* I didn't understand why Daddy would leave me. *Doesn't he want to stay with me? Doesn't he love me anymore? Am I being punished for something I did?* I couldn't imagine doing anything so bad that would make him go away. *Daddy told me he would never leave me…he promised.*

* * *

I didn't believe he was gone—I refused to believe it.

When I saw him lying there in that place, he looked the same, as if he were sleeping. I touched his face and it was cold, but his hair felt the same.

I was convinced he was just sleeping.

As the confusion in my mind was stirring up so many emotions at once, I asked myself and others, "Why are all these people around?" "Who are they?" I'd never seen most of them before. "Why is everyone crying?" "I'm sure he's gonna wake up—he *has* to wake up. He *always* wakes up."

I wondered, *Who is this Jesus—really?* We sang about him in Sunday School. "Jesus loves the little children, all the children of the world..." And "Jesus loves me this I know, for the Bible tells me so..."

I directed my next questions to my brother Jerry, but he couldn't answer me. "If Jesus loves children so much, why is he being so mean to me? Why won't he let my daddy wake up?"

I hated that mean old Jesus.

* * *

Those questions and more continued over the next couple of days, and then came that afternoon when everyone was the saddest of all. "Why are they lowering that box in the ground? The box where Daddy is?" I asked my brother, as a rush of panic ran throughout me. I wanted to scream, but I didn't know why. I didn't understand the awful feeling inside my chest and deep within my stomach. It was as if I were hanging upside down, or that the whole world was that way, but it wasn't the same as when I was playing—not like that at all. I wanted to get right-side-up again.

I thought he was going to be with Jesus at Jesus' house. That's what everybody had been telling me. *They lied. He's not. They're pushing dirt into the hole where he is.* The very thought made the inside of my chest feel the way it did when I fell down on the playground, and the breath was knocked out of me. I wanted to jump in there with him and dig the dirt away with my bare hands. "No! Daddy! I want my Daddy!" I began crying so I felt as though I might never stop.

Mama hugged and kissed me, trying to tell me "Everything's gonna be all right, Baby." I could barely understand her, she was crying so hard.

Everyone came back to our house afterward. Different people had brought in food—lots of food. They all stood and sat around, talking, eating, and eating some more, and some were even laughing—laughing aloud.

I wondered, *How can everyone be so different than they were just awhile ago? How can they all sit around eating and laughing at a time like this—a time so terrible?*

Don't they realize that my Daddy is gone to be with that Jesus, like Trixie and the baby chicks? And they never came back! And neither is he.

The feeling was like a slap in the face and I was sick. Sick in my heart. I couldn't eat or laugh or play.

I saw my aunts insisting that Mama eat something before she got sick. I thought they should just leave her alone as I went up and hugged her around the neck, "Mama, I love you."

She kissed me and said, "I love you, too, Baby," but then she began crying again, harder than before. I felt bad. I didn't mean to make her cry.

* * *

I quietly withdrew to gather my thoughts. *I miss him something awful. He hasn't played with me for three days. I only remember him lying there in that box—so still. No more jokes—no more smiles—no more hugs. Oh Daddy! I miss you so much!*

I wished he were there to scoop me up in his arms, swing me around and sing his special song for me, "Goodnight, Del-a-ney, Goodnight Delaney. I'll see you in my dreams, Delaney, so

Goodnight Del-a-ney." I always thought he had written it for me until I heard the original version on the radio. The words were actually "Goodnight Irene," but that didn't matter. It would always be my special song from Daddy.

Remembering how he never liked to see me cry, I thought, *Oh Daddy! I do love you so much! I'm so sorry, but all the others are so sad, I can't help it—I can't stop crying.*

* * *

For a long time afterward, every time I heard a car driving up, I ran to see if it was Daddy, or I imagined I heard him laughing on the front porch. Sometimes, I closed my eyes and pretended he was sitting on the side of the bed next to me, as I imagined I could smell the scent of his Old Spice aftershave, and feel his soft kiss on my forehead. Tears filled my eyes as I opened them to the reality of no one there.

In those months, I felt Mama trying to make up for Daddy's absence. She began sharing her bed with me, and I slept in his place. Somehow I felt much closer to love there.

* * *

I came home from school one afternoon to discover we had new drapes and furniture for the living room and bedrooms. And Mama was so excited and proud of her new electric Singer sewing machine. We even had a new Zenith TV! It had the clearest black-and-white picture I ever saw, and it didn't roll continuously like the old Motorola. *But where did all the money come from to buy all these things?* I didn't know. I was just glad to see Mama smile again instead of being so sad all the time.

* * *

That summer my brother Jerry joined the Navy and went away, just like my sister, except he went away all by himself.

The afternoon he told me he was leaving, I thought my heart was going to break wide open. It was still aching so for Daddy, but then to find out Jerry was going away too? As I sat there next to him on the step and the walkway's edge I said, "It's just not fair—I don't want *you* to leave, too!"

He put his arm around me, squeezing me closer to him. As he brushed my curls back away from my tear-filled eyes he said, "Don't cry, baby sister. I promise I'll be home again before you know it."

I quickly responded, "Promises don't mean anything! Daddy promised he'd never leave me, but he did and never came back!"

"Well, I promise I'm not going away like Daddy. I'm coming back—wait and see. And when I do, I'll bring you something pretty."

Dabbing my wet eyes with the hem of my dress, I asked, "Well—what'll ya bring me?"

"It won't be a surprise if I tell you, now, would it?"

"Well then, when ya comin' back?" I continued.

"I'll be back before you can learn to stand on your head and stack greased b-b's." He always knew how to make me smile.

It would be another sad, sad day when we drove Jerry to the Greyhound bus station in Atlanta. I cried so because I didn't want my brother to leave me, too. It seemed that everyone I cared about was going away.

* * *

With all three gone, Daddy, Sissy, and Jerry, the house was so lonely. Gene, Jackie, and the baby continued living there for while, and Bud was still around to aggravate the living heck out of me. So there wasn't much spare time to feel the loneliness, except at night—always in the dark hours of the night.

* * *

A few days before that Christmas, I came home one afternoon to find a bushy, misshapen, poor excuse of a Christmas tree Mama had brought home from the grocery store.

I flew into fits, proclaiming, "Daddy would never have picked that one! I don't want it here—it's so ugly—take it back!" I broke into tears and stormed out of the room.

From the next room I heard Mama crying and Bud fussing about me, "Mama, why don't you just slap her? Don't let that little brat upset you. What she needs is a good spankin'…"

I didn't mean to make her cry. I didn't know what was wrong with me, but it seemed like every time I turned around I got her upset, and she'd start balling her eyes out. Heck, for that matter, my eyes filled up with tears at the drop of a hat, too—over nothing. And sometimes a restless feeling came over me, such that I wanted to lash out at somebody. Anybody. And Mama just happened to be the only one around. I didn't mean anything by it, and it wasn't that I didn't love her anymore.

I heard her tell Bud, "Delaney's going through a hard time right now. We all are. But she's lost a father who was her world. The sun rose and set in him as far as she was concerned. What she needs is love and understanding, not a spanking every time her emotions flare up."

Instead of punishing me, she purchased one of those artificial aluminum trees with the colored revolving light stand. She paid seven dollars for it and used that same tree for the next twenty years. It was pretty enough, I suppose, but I could never imagine Christmas to be the same again. Ever.

* * *

I learned to ride my cousin, Melinda's red bike by practicing on her driveway and the street in front of her house when we went there to visit. I couldn't wait to have a bicycle of my very own.

Daddy had promised me that Santa would bring it that Christmas if I learned to ride my cousin's bike well enough.

Christmas morning when I awoke, I fully expected to see Daddy sitting there next to the tree. That's what I had asked Santa to bring me when I saw him at the Rich's department store.

I sprang out of bed and rushed to the tree, but Daddy wasn't there. I was on the brink of tears from my disappointment, but then...

"There it is!" Santa had left a beautiful new bicycle! "Oh, Mama, look! It's just what I wanted—just like Daddy promised!" It was shiny royal blue and exactly the right size.

I rolled it down the hallway and into my brother's room. "Bud, wake up! Look at my new bike! It's got a horn!" *Honk-honk.* "And a bell on the front!" *Brrr-ring!* "And I can carry my doll in the basket! See?"

Bud was a little startled by all the racket, but then he yawned and stretched, attempting to look awake and excited that early in the morning. "Yeah, I see. That's real nice. If you'll let me go back to sleep I'll watch you ride it when I get up."

I was accustomed to the paved street at Melinda's and our driveway was gravel and mud holes, so it was difficult to keep from getting off balance. I fell a few times, scraping my knees and legs on the rock's sharp edges.

One time when I fell I noticed some of my bike's blue paint had scraped off, and underneath there was red showing. I cried and ran into the house screaming, "Mama, I broke my bike and it has blood on it!"

Gene went out to check and told me, "Don't worry, Delaney, by tomorrow morning it'll be as good as new."

I believed him and sure enough, the next morning there was no more red showing.

I never wanted to leave it, but the next day we went to Melinda's to see what Santa brought them. Melinda had a brand new bike, too! It was blue, the same exact color as mine, except hers was a lot bigger—too big for me to ride.

94

I wanted to ride her red bike while she rode her new one, but she explained, "Santa's elves took it away when they left my new one."

I asked her why, but she didn't know. I just shrugged my shoulders and watched her ride, looking forward to the time when I was big enough to ride a big bike like that.

A couple of months later I was plundering in Daddy's tool chest on the back porch, when I ran across a can of blue paint. It was exactly the same color as my bike, perfect for touching up the nicks and scratches where red was showing through. I was so proud of my discovery as I thought, *Wow, I sure am lucky.*

Gene helped me touch up the many scratches and, once again, it was almost as good as new.

* * *

I always hated Christmas when all of us weren't together as a family—*our* family. As long as Jerry was God knows where with the Navy, I don't remember more than one or two holidays when he was at home with us. I thought, *Families should be together, especially at special times like Christmas, Thanksgiving and Easter. It was meant to be that way.*

* * *

All my other friends had both their parents and I felt like a second class child because I didn't have a daddy like them. Sometimes I was jealous and other times I even resented the smiles and laughs they shared with their fathers. *Why does everything have to be so unfair?*

For a couple of years after Daddy went with Jesus I only attended church on Sunday because I had no choice—Mama made me go. It was a while before I sang those songs and didn't feel betrayed and angry. Angry at Jesus for calling my daddy away, and betrayed by Daddy that he left me.

* * *

Betty became my best friend at church and at school. I envied her and her older brother. They were like the families on television. The perfect family with a mother and a father. I wished I lived in their two-story brick home with cozy carpeted floors. It was so much nicer than mine, where my feet darn near froze during the cold months on those black hard tile floors in that old cement block house. In the most frigid weather we had ice formations on the inside of the walls and windows so we hovered around the gas heater in the living room or the tiny bathroom heater, the only sources of heat in the house. Mama would sometimes turn on the gas oven in the kitchen and leave its door open to let out a little heat. Otherwise, the kitchen was unbearably cold.

When I stayed overnight at Betty's her parents made me feel right at home. Like a part of their family. I even joined them during "family altar," for their nightly hour of Bible study.

Her father called me his "Daughter Number Two," and sometimes I pretended I really was. Betty and I could pass for sisters, and sometimes we dressed alike, so people who met us for the first time weren't the wiser. Her dad let me call him "Pops." It wouldn't have felt right calling him Daddy, like Betty did. It was all right to make believe, but I knew there would never be another Daddy in my life.

* * *

The television became my past-time, companion and my new best friend when I wasn't with Betty. It occupied my mind with thoughts other than loneliness, and it was there for me at the flip of a switch. But it never asked me to spell one word or told me how proud it was of me. It couldn't reach out to hug and kiss me or say, "I love you, Sweetpea."

Mama tried so hard, and my brothers Gene and Bud stepped in to help her. But no one could ever take the place of that special man in my life. The first man in my life. The one with the periwinkle blue eyes and smile that lit up my world.

Good-night, Daddy. I'll see you in my dreams.

CHAPTER VI
230 AGGIES AND CAT-EYES

Since Daddy was gone Mama had to go to work, so she took a job as a salesclerk at Rich's department store in downtown Atlanta. I hated the fact that she wasn't there in the afternoons when I got home from school. I never realized how much she did for me, or just how much I'd miss her company, until she wasn't there.

Each week it seemed as if Sunday took forever to roll around. That was the only time she was at home with me all day. She never worked then because at that time there was a law against stores opening on Sunday. I never knew why it was called the Blue Law, but I didn't care what color it was, I liked it because it meant Mama didn't have to go to work.

On the weekday afternoons I could hardly wait to hear the approaching clatter of the bus roaring down the hill. With its brakes screeching to a halt, it stopped at the bottom of the hill right in front of our house, and its bi-fold doors flip-flopped open, then Mama stepped off.

She didn't get home until after dark and sometimes she was too tired to cook a big dinner. More often than not, frozen chicken pot-pies or fish sticks, hamburgers or hot dogs took the place of home-cooked meals. I really didn't mind because I usually ate dinner with one of the neighbors. I guess I was one of the original latch-key kids.

As far as neighbors go, ours were the greatest. They all rallied to our family when we needed them most. Between the Vincents and the Echols, I had two other sets of parents who somewhat adopted me while Mama was at work.

The Echols' house was right next door. When I stayed with them Mrs. Echols read to me and I helped her do jigsaw puzzles. She never treated me like a little child, and I enjoyed the time we spent together. As I grew older I read to her and she helped me do jigsaw puzzles. They didn't have any children my age but their daughter Merriann always treated me as if I were her little sister. She was closer to Sissy's age and they were best friends growing up.

Mrs. Echols was a woman of few words and when she wasn't hanging clothes out to dry, shucking corn or snapping peas, I rarely saw her without a book or newspaper in hand. She read a lot and kept abreast of the news, so her knowledge of current events was helpful whenever I had homework. I learned a great deal from her.

Mr. Echols was an avid fisherman, so there was always an abundance of fresh bass or trout in their freezer, our freezer, and everyone else's freezer in the neighborhood. It seemed as if Mrs. Echols cooked fish every other night of the week. Whenever I ate dinner with them they always had fish and hushpuppies, mashed potatoes, corn-on-the-cob, and spinach.

Mr. Echols was as hairy as he was big and burly, with a deep, baritone voice when he spoke, which was seldom. He talked even less than Mrs. Echols. The inflections in his grunts normally sufficed as an adequate enough form of communication. However, the few times I remember him using actual words when he spoke were directed to me at the dinner table. His voice was so loud and deep, "Little Girl, if you want to grow up to be big and strong like me! Eat up, now…it'll put hair on your chest."

To which I'd respond, "Hair on my chest? I'm a girl! I don't want hair on my chest!" I mastered the art of eating around the spinach on my plate.

* * *

The Vincents, Sam and Sally, were an older couple who lived behind us. They raised chickens and sold the eggs to Mrs. Pear's corner store up the street. I always wondered if their roosters crowed at the sun early in the morning for the same reason Mr. Echols' hunting dogs howled at the moon so late at night.

Every year Mama warned me not to do it, not to become so attached to the Vincents' little baby pigs. "Delaney, it's all right to pet and feed 'em, but I wish you wouldn't go so far as to name 'em the way you do. You know they don't stay babies forever and you know what's gonna happen to 'em when they grow into hogs." She was right. I was always devastated when fall rolled around and it came time for them to be slaughtered.

I sure loved the crackling cornbread Mama made at that time of the year, but I probably wouldn't have if I had known they came from my friends, the hogs.

Georgia's heat and humidity in summer and early fall intensified the combined odors from the Vincents' chickens and pigs, with the stench from the cows and horses boarded in the pasture next to our house.

Sam and Sally used the manures to fertilize their gardens that ran alongside the properly line, only a few hundred feet or so from our house. There were no words awful enough to adequately describe the smell.

Sam and Sally taught me about growing vegetables, and about how the soil had to be tilled to prepare for the planting season.

They couldn't afford a tractor, or even a mule or horse, so they took turns wearing the harness and pulling the plow, while the other steered from behind. She wasn't quite five feet tall and petite in size, so it was pretty amazing to see such a little woman like Sally taking the place of a beast of burden.

The day finally came when they bought that bright red Ford tractor. Perched up there on the seat, head erect, wearing her broad-rimmed straw hat, she tilled the big garden all by herself and barely broke a sweat. She looked and acted as if she were a woman of leisure.

We always had fresh vegetables, thanks to the Vincents, for which I was far from grateful.

Even after I saw firsthand how much hard work goes into growing vegetables, I didn't like the taste of them, except for corn or yams. I wouldn't touch a bean or okra because I didn't like the way they looked. I didn't like the sound of the words squash or cabbage. And collard greens look too much like spinach. I shivered at the thought of having to eat any of those foods. *Yuck.* Furthermore, I didn't want any of those foods touching my good tasting other foods on the plate. Nonetheless, Mama always managed to have them touching when she fixed my plate. So, like I did with the spinach, I took my fork, separated them as best I could and ate the rest.

Determined I wouldn't grow up without eating everything on my plate, she gave me the proverbial speech, "Delaney, you should be ashamed. Think of all the starving children in China."

I never understood how cleaning my plate could prevent someone on the other side of the world from starving. "Why don't you just send them what I don't want? Here, send 'em these vegetables," to which she never replied.

She insisted I sit there until I ate every morsel. Mama was stubborn, but so was I. Sometimes I sat there until almost bedtime, and the food was so cold and hardened it wasn't fit to eat.

When I got older she asked me if I had homework. If my answer was yes, she brought my books to the table and said, "There, now you can do your homework while you finish your supper." I did my homework, but I left the food on my plate untouched.

When she finally gave in—which she always did—she told me to go take my bath and get ready for bed. While she forced me to sit for so long there at the kitchen table, I thought she was being mean and didn't love me.

I hated when she did that, but the bad feelings always went away once she gave in to me. I supposed that was just the way mothers were, but I thought, *I'm not gonna be that way when I'm a mother! No sir, I'm gonna let my children eat what they like and leave the rest. And another thing, I'll never fix their plates where the foods touch one another!*

* * *

One of my favorite places to climb and hide was the Vincents' apple trees that grew alongside the driveway. Those were the best green apples ever—crisp, tart, and oh so juicy. And those apple pies and cobblers, Mama made them the way God Himself intended. Heavenly as anything on earth could possibly be, my mouth watered as the aroma floated throughout the entire house when one was in the oven.

* * *

I always had someone watching out for me even when mama wasn't around. I really felt as if I was a part of our neighbors' families. They made me feel loved as though I were one of their own.

When they had family get-togethers or reunions at their houses, I was always there. Not because I was invited, or anything so formal as that. I just felt as if I belonged there. Their family reunions were always fun, and one good thing was if I stopped having fun there, I could just walk home. Unlike our own family reunions where I was stuck, no matter how mad I got at my cousins or how tired I became.

* * *

One day in May, when I was ten years old, I stayed with Sam and Sally while Mama was at work. That afternoon we went for a ride to a place I'd never been. It was a long drive and the couple's solemn silence made it seem even farther. I thought we'd never get there, but even at such a young age, I sensed it was better that I remain quiet and not ask the obvious question, *Are we there yet?*

We finally turned off from the main highway. The winding dirt road crossed a narrow creek by way of a rickety wooden bridge. There was an air of serenity about the place as we approached an opening.

The landscape's two small mounds were overgrown with dandelions and high weeds. Even the tallest of weeds couldn't conceal the masonry headstones, marking the unkempt gravesites of the strangers buried there.

Sally clutched a brown paper lunch bag, while Sam opened the trunk and pulled out a small bag of sand, then he instructed us to walk behind him. "I'll stomp down the weeds and make a path." We proceeded up the hill until we came to a stopping place in the shade, at the base of a big tree—an apple tree.

There was a small tombstone inscribed:

Samuel Edward Vincent, Jr
May 15, 1938 – July 4, 1940
Our Little Angel is in Heaven with Jesus

The gravesite was completely weed-free and the area that extended in front of the monument had been framed with bricks and filled in with sand. Within the sandy bed marbles had been embedded inside a colorful border, created by the bottoms of various bottles than lined the brick outer frame.

"Who's buried here?" I asked, as I leaned over to pick up a pretty blue, cat-eye marble. I was startled when Sam reached over and stopped my hand. I reassured him, "I don't want to keep it. I just want to look at it. Whose are they?"

"Most of the aggies were mine when I was a little boy. And the others...well, I bought 'em through the years. All of 'em would have belonged to our son, Sam, Jr. They do belong to him—this is his grave."

"But I thought you never had..."

He continued, "Yeah, we had a son. Today would've been his twenty-first birthday. He would've been a fine young man starting a family of his own..."

The sight of Sally carefully placing the tiny, colorful glass balls in the sand aroused tears in him, while she remained quiet and seemed to be emotionless.

He counted, "One, two, three, four, five..." until he counted twenty-one marbles positioned in their new resting place of white sand. "...twenty-one...a marble for each year. That makes a total of two hundred and thirty aggies and cat-eyes for my boy." May 15th of every year they placed the number of marbles to coincide with his birthday. They had planted that apple tree the year he died and maintained it ever since.

Sally's wide-brimmed hat obscured my view of her face, but what I could see was expressionless. She always wore a big hat to shade her eyes because she was sensitive to bright sunlight and nearly blind in one eye.

She broke her silence only to say, "Sam, why don't you take Delaney down to see the creek?"

Sam never hesitated to follow his wife's instructions, so he took my hand and led me to the foot of the hill.

After I threw several pebbles into the trickling water, I joined him where he sat on a rock. "I didn't know y'all had any kids."

He tried to smile, "We don't talk about 'im. It's too painful for Sally to remember."

"How old was he?"

"He'd just turned two in May when he died in July."

"What happened? How did he die?" I asked.

"He got the pox."

"I had the chicken pox but I didn't die. I itched to death...but I didn't die."

Sam put his arm around me and squeezed me closer to him in a firm, consoling manner. "No, sugar, it wasn't the chicken pox. It was the black smallpox disease what killed him."

"Why don't Sally wanna talk about him?" I asked.

"It's too painful. It makes her too sad. She blames herself, y'know."

"Why'd she blame herself? She didn't kill him...did she?"

He shook his head. "Sally caught the pox and give it to Sam, Jr. Where hers just blinded her in that one eye, it wasn't so bad as his. He took real sick and died in her arms. The doctor and everybody told her there wasn't nothing' she could've done to save him, but..."

His voice began to break and I leaned over to look up into his eyes as he continued. "She ain't never got over it." The tears rolled down his cheeks in such a way, he was forced to remove his glasses.

I stretched my little arm as far as it could reach around him and said, "But Sam, it's going on twenty years since your little boy died. Why ain't she over it yet?"

"Sugar, I hope you never fully understand how it feels to bury a child of your own, but a mama never gets over it. Heck, for that matter, neither does a papa."

I could hear a wailing sound from the hillside behind us. I glanced over my shoulder to observe Sally on her knees, sobbing as she hummed what sounded like the Happy Birthday song.

I turned back to Sam, "You think we ought to go up there with her?"

He nodded and took my hand, leading me to her side. It was one of those rare times when I found myself at a loss for words. I allowed my actions to speak for me as I quietly wrapped my arms around her in a gentle hug of compassion.

She responded, "My goodness, Sugar, you're almost as tall as ole Sally." She looked down at me and for the first time I could see the sunlight reflecting off her tear-covered face.

I didn't know what to say, except, "I'm really sorry about your little boy...I love you."

With the hem of her apron she wiped away her tears, and then mine. Then she returned the hug and whispered, "I love you too, Sugar."

When we returned to their house, she pulled out an old photo album and wiped away the dust. "This is my baby boy...this is our little Sammy."

I commented how pretty he was.

When she began to cry again, I tried to comfort her but Sam placed his hand on my shoulder and said, "It's best to leave her alone and let her get it outta her system."

My heart broke for that little woman who was still so sad and mourning a child who had been dead for so many years. *A mama never gets over burying her own child.* The thought made me shudder and my attempt to fight back the tears was futile.

I was crying for several reasons. Of course I felt sad for Sam and Sally. I prayed for the day to come when Sally could talk about her little boy, and that she could stop feeling guilty about something that was beyond her control.

Sammy was never again discussed after that afternoon.

The emotions from that afternoon also reminded me of the emptiness within my own heart since Daddy died. I wondered how long it would take for me to stop missing him...or if I ever would.

FRIDAY, MAY 5TH, 1984: BACK AT OAKWOOD INSTITUTE

The weather was so nice, Dr. Robinson and I had been having our sessions outside on the grounds at Oakwood. The free feeling of the wide open spaces was a nice relief from the stuffiness of her office. Our favorite place to sit was beneath a sprawling mimosa tree that was far to the edge of the property, next to the chain link fence.

I definitely preferred the outdoor sessions, however, I would have been satisfied to meet inside on that particular afternoon. My eyes were irritated by the bright sunlight.

The doctor had read the most recent pages of my assignment, but prior to our discussion, she asked a question to which the answer was obvious, "Delaney, have you been crying?"

I shrugged, trying to contain my emotions that were about the surface again, and erupt in the form of tears—tears I had been unable to shed for almost four months. I supposed my tear glands were making up for lost time, because I was crying when I went to sleep the night before, and again that morning when I awoke.

"Do you want to talk about it?"

I hesitated for a moment, then I responded, "Poor Sally and Sam."

"Yes, it's truly devastating to lose a child."

For some reason I was angered by that comment and my sarcastic tone lashed out at here, "How would you know, *Doctor*? You don't have any children. Hell, you're not even married."

"You're right. I'm not like you. I've never been married and I don't have children. But I plan to one day and I know I could never even begin to imagine the pain and heartache of losing a child. It's every mother's nightmare—but it does happen in real life, Delaney. It *does* happen."

I was still so frustrated. "But Sally shouldn't have felt guilty. It wasn't her fault. It's not like she was negligent, or wasn't watching him and didn't know where he was."

She started, "Accidents happen, too..."

A hummingbird caught my eye as it flew from the branch overhead, flitted around my face, then floated over to the vine of wild flowers on the barbed wire atop the metal mesh fence. Then it went about its way to freedom beyond the chain link boundary. However, my eyes remained affixed on the fence. It was the first time I had noticed—really noticed—that the fence was taller than eight feet, including the barbed wire, and surrounded the entire Oakwood property. I so envied the freedom of that hummingbird and wished I could fly. Fly away to freedom.

The doctor tapped the back of my hand and cleared her throat, interrupting my thoughts of freedom. "Where did you go? Have you heard anything I said?"

My glazed stare silently answered her question, so she reminded me, "You were talking about Sally's guilt. I said we accept the high probability that we'll outlive our parents. We understand it's a fifty-fifty chance we'll survive our spouse or siblings. But our minds reject the possibility of outliving our children. Instead we develop the notion that that only happens to other families—not us."

She paused for my response but I had none, so she continued, "Because of this, our minds often go into a conscious state of shock, and denial becomes ever present whenever a parent loses a child."

"But I still don't know why Sally felt guilty when he died of smallpox," I spoke without looking at her, "It wasn't her fault. It wasn't as though she hadn't been a good mother and let him run outside without watching him. It wasn't like that at all."

The warm breeze sent a sudden eerie chill up my spine to the base of my neck. I clasped my arms as the tears began to flow, "It's getting cold out here. Let's go back inside."

I was about to stand, but she grabbed my arm, "Delaney, I want you to listen to me. A mother's mind is programmed to love and protect here child from harm. Whether the child is newborn or an adult, whether the cause is illness or an accident, its death triggers the guilt mechanism. Her mind strikes out to blame whoever dropped the ball—or the protective guard—that someone being herself. That's a normal reaction. It's wrong, but normal. Don't you see?"

I didn't feel the question deserved an answer, so I blocked it out and began rocking back and forth, repeatedly shaking my head and moaning aloud. Wailing and carrying on, just like Sally on the hillside.

"I don't want to talk about Sally and her baby *anymore...ever!*" To prevent my heart from imploding I felt the sudden need to change the subject. "My heart feels like it's breaking for that little girl."

"What little girl?"

"You know, the one whose daddy died. She was only seven. That's too young to deal with death. She didn't understand."

She took a deep breath. "Delaney, you *do* realize that little girl was you...don't you?"

I nodded, thinking, *Of course, I know she was me at that age. It's just easier to talk about it if I call her "that little girl." Over the past several weeks I've been entertained by "that little girl's" antics and impish ways. I can't wait to see what mischief she gets into next.*

I felt so sorry for her when her little dog died. But it was different with her daddy...a daddy she obviously loved more than life, itself!

As I wondered how in the world she got through it, the tears erupted again from within me, like an exploding volcano.

I'd always been embarrassed to have anyone see me cry. I'd much rather talk about the funny and more pleasant times, but the doctor gave me one of her tender, kitten-like hugs while she kept encouraging me, "It's okay, Delaney. Let it all out." Continuing to embrace me, she patted me on the back in a comforting, reassuring way, and I cried even harder. I wept there in her arms until the session ended. Similar to a dam that had burst, I couldn't seem to control the flow. So rather than fight the futile battle, I chose to let the river run its course.

Ordinarily I would have felt uncomfortable, as I didn't like anyone to get that close to me. *After all, it's not like she's my friend.* But then, I supposed that one time wouldn't hurt anything. Just until I found a way to plug the dam.

* * *

During upcoming sessions when the doctor tried to bring up the subject of Sally I would immediately change the topic of discussion. Over the past couple of weeks I had become an expert at topic-changing.

I never mentioned the fact that recently Sally was often present in my nightmares, where I saw her on the hillside, standing over her son's grave. I even heard her sobs of morbid wailing.

Always in my dreams, when I approached her, she knelt and began digging. Digging up the remains of her son.

As I tried to stop her, I suddenly heard the haunting voice of a child crying out *Mommy!* The apple tree was suddenly hit by a bolt of lightning, severing one of its limbs and tossing it with such force it knocked me to the ground.

Sally disappeared and I was left there alone with the child's unanswered calls. I was driven to scoop it into my arms, and when I pulled the soiled and filthy blanket from its body I was sickened by the sight. Insects were crawling about the decayed skin that was falling from its bones.

It was all too real and I cried aloud for help while clutching the infant's remains to my chest. Sally was no where to be found and somehow *I* had taken her place. I was feeling the gut-wrenching void she must have felt in her heart, together with her incomprehensible pain and sense of loss.

In my nightmares, Sally's horrifying feeling of grief always became my own, as did her tears.

When I was growing up Mama always told me, "Delaney, don't dwell on bad dreams or they could come true." She said, "Put them out of your mind." I supposed her to be right and it was better that I didn't dwell on them—discuss them with anyone, including the doctor.

CHAPTER VII
THEY GREW IN GROVES

Mama always claimed our driveway was quicksand, because, no matter how much gravel was dumped there in the fall, all of it disappeared by the next summer. The horseshoe-shaped, one lane dirt road was shared by four other families, and when it rained, it became a muddy mess.

The Thomas' and Patricks moved into the houses at the very back of the horseshoe about a year after Daddy went to be with Jesus. There were two girls and a boy, all younger than I was, but at least they were someone to play with me.

The branch is what we called the creek that ran alongside their property and eventually poured into the South River. I wasn't allowed to follow the creek to the river by myself, but I had been there with Daddy and Bud when they went to fish.

That June after the Patricks moved in they had a dump-tuck load of white sand brought in for the banks of the branch beside their house.

My eyes popped wide open when I saw all the clean, white sand, "Wow! This is great—just like a beach!"

An idea suddenly hit me right between the eyes, "I know. We'll charge a nickel a person to come here. We'll call it White Sands Beach." In that it was my idea, I figured it only fair that I should get 3 pennies of every nickel. "And I'll make lemonade and sell it for 3 pennies a cup."

I could see it all—rich beyond my wildest dreams, and before I was even ten years old!

That vision was soon to be clouded. Despite the big sign we made and leaned against the telephone pole at the street, no one came to our beautiful new beach, except the three of them and me. And they couldn't understand why they should pay to play in their own branch.

So be it. I would simply make my fortune with the lemonade stand. However, I wasn't prepared for the *drink now—pay later* plan that I fell into with my so-called friends. One would say, "I'll pay ya tomorrow," while the others would say, "I'll pay ya next week." I soon discovered that tomorrow and next week never came.

I had planned on that money to replace the lemons and sugar before Mama discovered them gone.

My Sunday School teacher Mrs. Pear was the sweet little old, gray-haired lady who owned the corner store. I found 3 empty bottles on the back porch—one Coca Cola, one Sunkist orange and one Bireley's chocolate. I turned them in at the store and received a penny for each, but three cents wasn't enough. I asked Mrs. Pear to please let me pay for the sugar and lemons later, but she said, "No, Delaney. I'm not in a position to offer you credit."

"But I don't want any credit. I just need the lemons and sugar."

"When a store lets a customer have the merchandise and pay for it later—that's called credit." Her sad face and dark eyes expressed her regret in letting me down as she continued, "But I just can't afford to do business in that way. I'm sorry."

"That's okay. I'll think of something." I walked home, knowing Mama would find the biggest switch on the bush for this one, as I thought, *Hmmm, if I'd known about credit a few days ago, I wouldn't be in all this trouble.* I pretended the time had been rolled back and envisioned a different scene from the original. Whey they said, "I'll pay ya next week," I imagined myself saying, "I'm sorry, I'm not set up for credit. I can't afford to do business that way."

Unfortunately, that wasn't the way it had happened and I was in major trouble when Mama got home. I wished I could dig up all the switch bushes in our yard and wished even more that I could get even with those bill-dodging deadbeats.

* * *

That next afternoon Mama didn't have to work, so one of my friends, Julie, came over to spend the day.

While waiting for one of those summer afternoon rain showers to subside, Mama treated us to ice cold milk and Oreo cookies. We licked the creamy white filling from the centers and stacked the chocolate outer cookies on the kitchen table.

I'm sure lights and exclamation points could be seen dancing around my whole person when the idea popped into my head. I jumped up from the table, grabbed a spoon and ran outside to a mud puddle. I scooped up some mud and spread it onto one of the outer cookies then with another one I made a cookie sandwich. "Look, Julie! It looks like an Oreo with chocolate insides." We carefully placed them into a brown paper lunch bag and snickered while we imagined the expressions on their faces when they bit into them.

They didn't suspect the devilment behind my smile and apologetic offerings of good will, "Mama made me bring 'em to you and tell you I'm sorry I acted so mean…but, she said I better get back home before supper. So I gotta go."

Julie and I hid behind the end of their house and watched as, first, the baby brother and then the grandfather slid the cookies from the bag. Neither of them had many teeth at all, so they had to gum the Oreo look-alikes.

Mud drooled down their chins while their upper lips curled from the awful taste. I thought I would burst wide open before I reached a place beyond distance so I could laugh and bask in the satisfaction of sweet revenge. "Ha! That'll teach 'em."

As Julie and I reached the back door, we heard the phone ringing. Mama was outside at the clothesline, so I answered it, "Hello."

"DELANEY! Let me talk to your mother—NOW!"

I recognized it as Mrs. Patrick, so I told her, "O-okay."

I placed my hand over the mouthpiece, and then proceeded to impersonate my mother, "Hello?"

She was on to me immediately, and soon Mama was on to me, too—with another switch from the switch-bush. Switch-buses grew in groves around our house and Mama was always the one to spank me or take a switch to my legs, even before Daddy went with Jesus. She made me go outside and get my own torturing twig, so I made sure it was really thin and I took my time, hoping she'd forgotten about my misdeed. But she didn't forget that easily. In fact, I got additional whacking for taking so long.

She plucked all the leaves except on the very tip and she had a way of snapping the thing, such that its popping strike was twice as painful. The more I jumped around and tried to get away, the faster she snapped the switch. As I got older I learned the skinnier the switch, the sharper the sting.

* * *

The Patrick kids and I never stayed mad at one another for long. But Mrs. Patrick seemed to call Mama every other day, "Mrs. James, we need to have a talk about Delaney."

I was older than the girls, and I took full advantage of the fact every chance I got. One afternoon, we were playing in their yard on their swing set. That was one of those days a mean streak came over me, and I *nonchalantly* let it slip that I overheard the Vincent talking about it being a shame the little boy was only one of the three Patrick kids that wasn't adopted.

The girls fell for it, hook, line, and sinker, and they started yelling that it was a lie and for me to take it back.

I just pumped the swing to go higher and higher, explaining that, "I probably shouldn't have repeated something I overheard grown-ups talking about. Don't tell anybody I told you 'cause I'll get in trouble."

That set them off. Both of them completely shattered, believing what I had said was the gospel truth they ran into the house, crying to their mother.

I didn't wait around for the fireworks. I jumped off the swing and high-tailed it on home. But I was too late. I heard the phone ringing when I entered the back door and I overheard Mama saying, "Yes, Mrs. Patrick. I certainly will have a talk with her!"

I turned right around and went back outside to the switch bush. I was hoping if I went to her with switch in hand, looking pitiful and proclaiming how very sorry I was, she would forgive me, forget all about it and forego the switching. Once again I was proven wrong. Mama wasn't naïve, and she didn't forget easily, especially when it came to punishment.

I would rather have taken and out-and-out beating than do what Mama made me do next. Not only did I get the switching, but I had to go back down there and apologize to Mrs. Patrick and the girls, admitting that I had made up the whole thing.

It's a wonder they every allowed me to come back after some of the stunts I played, but they did. After all, we were the only kids in our neighborhood, so we couldn't afford to stay mad.

* * *

The Patricks had the biggest old weeping willow tree in the back yard. One afternoon, they all got so excited about an envelope they received in the mail. They danced around beneath the tree exclaiming, "The check came! Now we can go on vacation!"

I didn't understand why they were so excited just because they got a measly check, as I bragged, "I don't know why getting a check is such a big deal. My mama gets those in the mail almost every day. She gets so many, she's getting tired of getting them, In fact, when she gets one she always groans and says, "Not another one—what am I gonna do with all of 'em?"

At that time, of course I had no way of knowing the difference between a check and a bill.

* * *

The Patrick kids and I were all tomboys and we played cowboys and Indians, marbles, or we just hung upside-down together on their swing-set. When we weren't doing any of those things we played with our dolls.

When we played school I had to be the teacher or nothing at all. As I got older, I had to be the principal, or I wouldn't play. It only made sense that I would be promoted.

If I had known there was such a person as Superintendent of Schools, I would have promoted myself to that position.

* * *

Our house was situated next to a huge field, in which the owners boarded cows and horses. There were also bulls—big bulls—on the property. I always reasoned that the electric barbed-wire fencing was there to keep the animals in, certainly not to keep us out! Otherwise, why would the owners allow wild blackberries to grow in the field, if they didn't intend for us to pick them.

There was nothing better than freshly picked blackberries, except, maybe, one of Mama's blackberry cobblers with a scoop of homemade vanilla ice cream on top.

The local snakes seemed to love those blackberry bushes, too, as snake-holes were all around. I was never bitten by a snake, but one time little John Patrick was and they had to rush him to the hospital. He didn't die from it, but he sure had some wicked-looking snake-bite marks on his ankle.

I stepped on plenty of sticker-briars in the woods, and stumped my toes or bruised my heels on the gravel in our driveway. I fell out of trees and off the swing-set, I was shocked by the barbed-wire electric fence, and stung by bees, but I never experienced a single broken bone in my body.

Whenever I got stung by a bee, Mama always rubbed Brooton's snuff on the stung spot and spread it all around. It was really yucky but seemed to do the trick, along with a cookie and glass of cold milk. She always made sure any bystanders knew that the snuff was only in the house for medicinal purposes.

One steamy, summer day, I bought a frozen fudgesicle from the neighborhood ice cream man. I took a big lick of my favorite ice cream on a stick, but when I pulled away, my tongue remained connected as if it were permanently adhered to the thing.

The more I pulled on the fudgesicle, the more it hurt. I panicked because I just knew I was doomed to go through the rest of my days with my tongue stuck to the frozen piece of horror!

Mrs. Echols instructed me, "Calm down, Delaney. Just let it melt and it'll come lose all by itself."

I always thought she was smart and knew a lot about everything, but after that afternoon I felt as though I owed that woman my life!

CHAPTER VIII
A FULL-FLEDGED WOMAN

Mama cried when Gene and his family moved out of our house.

I on the other hand was happy. After all, that was the day I had been waiting for since they moved in. However, I had not counted on my niece, Jeanie, growing on me the way she did. I had tolerated her crying at all hours and the foul smelling diapers, and she just laid there most of the time, no more fun than a sack of potatoes.

When she finally got to the size so that I could actually hold her, dress her up and play with her, they took her away. I really hated to admit it but I really missed having the little munchkin around.

With Gene's family gone, that just left Mama, Bud, and me—alone in the house. At least I didn't have to compete anymore with the baby for Mama's attention, and the house smelled so much better. It was a lot quieter, too…sometimes a little too quiet.

When Bud was home, I never had to worry about the place being too quiet. He always had the television or radio blaring, or he was in the back yard working on his souped up '52 Oldsmobile. With the hood raised, it took on the appearance of a shiny, aqua-blue-colored dragon with its jaws gaped wide open. When he raced the engine it sounded as though the beast was enraged, roaring to cause such a thunderous rack, it could have knocked the birds right out of the trees.

I always loved it when he dropped me off, or picked me up at the skating rink or swimming pool. All my girlfriends thought my brother was the cutest and his car was so *tough*.

They thought he was cuter than Wally on one of my favorite T.V. shows, Leave It to Beaver, even if Bud was eighteen and a good ten years older than us. However, in the presence of grown-ups, most of us at that age wouldn't acknowledge boys as members of the human species.

If my friends had lived with my brother, the appeal would have worn thin. After I watched him lift weights, I had to sit on his feet while he did sit-ups, then he struck poses in front of the mirror while flexing his muscles, as if he were God's gift to women.

When he caught me staring at him while he was admiring his own reflection, he said, "What are you looking at? Come over here and feel these muscles!" So I'd go over and feel, then I'd roll my eyes while bragging on his hard muscles. I then had to listen to how he got them that way; i.e., how many times he works out, how many sit-ups he does, getting the right exercise, eating the right foods, etc.

I wondered if the carton of milk and stack of a dozen or so slices of bread at one sitting were the kinds of right foods to which he always referred. I thought, *If it's exercise he wants, why doesn't he get up out of the chair and get his own milk, ice tea, bread, or whatever else he always wants me to fetch?* I never actually verbalized those thoughts. Instead, I got whatever he requested. After all, as my big brother—emphasis on *big*—he was bigger than me.

* * *

One Friday afternoon I went home after school with my friend, Joanie. We went skating at the big roller rink in Lakewood then I stayed the night at her house. I always thought Joanie was older than the rest of us. She seemed more mature than ten years old in a lot of ways.

We undressed and changed into our pajamas for bed, when I was curious about the strange contraption she wore across her chest and over her shoulders. "What's that funny looking thing?"

"It's a brassiere. Ain't you ever seen one before?"

"No, what's it for?"

She laughed, "Women wear 'em to hold their boobies. Don't your mama wear one?"

"If she does, I've never seen it. But why are you wearing one? You're not a woman yet."

"My mama says I need one 'cause I already got boobies."

I never heard of such. Mama was always careful not to allow us to see her unless she was in a robe or fully clothed. I gazed down at my chest. It was as flat as a pancake and I could see straight to my toes without looking over bumps of any size. She giggled and said, "When I was a little girl I used to be flat as a flitter, just like you. That's before I grew boobies."

She was the same age as me, but she could've passed for thirteen—at least. I felt downright self-conscious and sat with my arms folded across my flat chest the rest of the night wondering, *How can I get Mama to buy one of those bray-zeers for me?* When she wasn't looking I tried on one of Joanie's and it felt so awkward. It was as if trying to put a size ten men's shoes on a two-year-old child. I read the label inside, "32B." That ten-year-old girl was already a size 32B cup and I was still a size NBAA—that's for *No Boobies At All*.

She continued to tease me and made me feel underdeveloped compared to her. But Joanie was the one who was different, because none of my other friends had boobies yet either.

* * *

I learned a lot through my association with Joanie.

We were plundering through some boxes in her attic and ran across a stack of her older brother's Playboy magazines. I was amazed at what I saw, and couldn't believe I would ever look like the women on those pages. They were so beautiful with make-up on their faces, long wavy hair, pretty legs that went on forever, and boobies—all shapes and sizes, but mostly big ones. And they were all naked!

We read an article in one of the magazines that had pictures of women with different shapes of breasts. It stated that the kinds of foods they ate as little girls determined how their breasts developed. The printed interviews beneath the pictures asked each woman what favorite foods she had eaten that attributed to the shaping of here own prize-winning breasts. The one whose were huge and blimp-shaped stated she liked watermelons. The woman who liked bananas had really long, skinny ones, and the one who liked apples had big—but not huge—rounded ones.

It made me stop and think, *Hmm, I like and eat all those foods, but my very favorite has always been little green grapes, and I eat more of those than anything else.* I worried that I may have eaten too many in my life and wondered if my boobies would be little-green-grape-sized and shaped when I grew up.

* * *

Joanie's parents owned the local Grill in Lakewood Heights. Whenever I spent time at her house, we went to South Bend swimming pool and walked to the restaurant afterward.

The skating rink was also within walking distance of the restaurant, and so was the Southeastern Fair when it was in town every Fall.

That October I was lucky because I got to go to the Fair twice— once with Gene and Jackie, and again with Joanie and her older brothers. I especially looked forward to that Saturday at the Fair, because Joanie had moved to East Point, in another school district, and I didn't get to spend as much time with her.

We had grown particularly close, primarily over the telephone. During that summer Joanie's mother had died of a heart attack, just like Daddy, so we understood one another's sadness. We rarely discussed Daddy or her mother, except when we talked about how much we missed them. When she cried I could honestly say, "I know how you feel." And whenever I cried, I was comforted when she said, "I understand," as I knew she truly did.

Her brothers were teen-agers and I had a mad crush on one of them. Since I was only eleven, he ignored me and acted as if he didn't know I existed. The only communication we had that day was when he said, "Beat it," and "Meet us at the front gate at closing time."

Joanie wasn't like me. She was really brave because she wasn't afraid to ride the grown-up rides. Besides being brave, she was extremely persuasive, and despite my fears, I found myself on them, sitting right next to her. We rode the Giant Ferris Wheel, the Double Ferris Wheel, the Whip and the Octopus. Then we came face to face with—the Greyhound.

I hesitated and swallowed hard, as I sat next to her in the giant roller coaster's car. My mind was suddenly invaded by all the things I had ever heard about that thing, and screaming just came natural—but we hadn't even started moving yet!

The nice man who ran the Greyhound let me get off because I was crying. Joanie just called me a big chicken and a cry-baby, while she stayed on for the ride of her life.

When she came down the ramp afterward, her face was all red, and her hair was standing up in all directions as she yelled, "Wow! What a ride! Boy, you sure missed it! What happened? Why'd ya get off?"

Embarrassed, I replied in a low voice, "I just got scared. I'll ride it next time." She never mentioned it again.

After several hours we were tired, so we sat down across from one of the girlie shows to eat a hot dog.

I was intrigued by the long, beautifully colored velvet capes the women on stage wore. Ever so often they flashed their legs in the open, revealing the black nylon stockings and their long beautiful legs. Sometimes they gave the onlookers a glance at what was hidden beneath the capes. From where we sat it looked as if they were wearing little or nothing! I kept hearing Mama's voice as I imagined her saying, *Turn your head and don't look at that—it's nasty!*

But I didn't want to turn my head. For some inexplicable reason I was excited by that, even if it was "nasty" as Mama called it. The men outside around the stage reacted to the women by whistling and clapping, and yelling all kinds of things. And the music—even it was naughty sounding.

Joanie asked, "Do you wanna go inside the show and see what they do in there?"

I quickly responded, "We better not," unaware they wouldn't have sold us tickets, anyway.

She went on to tell me, "I've been inside one before, y'know. I sneaked in under the tent last year, but nobody saw me. The women danced around on the stage while they took off all their clothes and got completely naked!"

"Completely naked? You mean no clothes at all? Like in the magazines?"

"Yeah, when they took off their brassieres they had tassel-like things on their boobies and they would spin 'em around and round like pinwheels. The men went crazy-wild, yellin' and goin' on!"

I never knew if she was telling the truth about going inside one before—but I believed her. She was awfully convincing.

I wished I could be more like Joanie. She was so worldly and knew so much.

When I looked at those women I thought, *Now, that's what I want to look like when I grow up.   I wonder what kinds of foods they ate when they were little girls?*

* * *

The next day at her house we were outside playing in the garage when some of the neighborhood boys came over. They were older—twelve to thirteen years old—and they weren't too bad looking. Since they went to a different school, I only knew them through my visits with Joanie.

Joanie had a great idea, "Let's play Girlie Show! We'll charge the boys to see us, so we'll have money to go to the movies!"

With much apprehension, I said, "Okay, but how?"

There was a clothesline strung in the garage, over which we threw a bedspread and created a stage curtain. She used an extension cord to hook up the record player for the music, though the song 'Johnny Angel' wasn't exactly naughty sounding.

She was braver than I was, wearing only her underwear—panties and brassiere. I wouldn't do that, so she let me wear one of her swimsuits. I stuffed toiled paper in the cups to make it look like I filled it out. We draped blankets around us and pretended they were velvet capes, as we proceeded on stage. I collected a nickel from each of the five boys and Joanie began dancing.

I couldn't believe my eyes! Joanie was taking off *all* her clothes! And the boys were going wild!

Then came my time. I danced and danced some more. I flashed my legs in the open a few times like the women at the Fair, and I even sang a little before I finally dropped the blanket. The boys began to yell, "Take it off! Come on, Delaney. Take it off!" I enjoyed the rush I felt for a few seconds…

But then I panicked as I thought, *They want me to take off the swimsuit—now what am I gonna do?* I'd always liked performing and being the center of attention. And it felt a little nasty, naughty and exciting, all at once. But I wasn't like Joanie—I wasn't brave. I didn't know if I had enough nerve to get naked in front of all those boys. Heck, even if there was only one boy there I wasn't sure I could do it.

I couldn't stop thinking about how they were all going to laugh at me when the wads of pink toilet paper fell out of my front and onto the floor. *I can't take off all my clothes...they'll laugh!*

I'd like to think I had more scruples than to strip completely, like Joanie did, even if it was for money. But, in truth, the toilet paper was the primary reason I kept my clothes on and my reputation in tact that afternoon. That and the fact that, after hearing all the commotion coming from the garage, Joanie's brother came out to investigate.

I was sure glad I didn't get completely naked like Joanie, as he charged through the door and yelled, "What's goin' on in here?"

All the boys scattered in five different directions. Joanie was grounded for a month, and I was taken home.

I'm unsure if they ever told Mama, but I grew apart from Joanie and only talked to her on the phone or occasionally at the skating rink.

I later heard that she had grown to be very wild as a teenager, and became pregnant and dropped out of school by the time she was fifteen. According to rumors, she and her baby continued living with her father but they moved to another state. I lost contact with her by the time we entered high school and I never heard from her again.

* * *

The spelling background from when Daddy trained me as a little girl helped me go on to represent Hoover Elementary school in the Atlanta city-wide spelling competition.

My spelling bee career was brief, confined to the sixth and seventh grades, but I imagined Daddy saying, "Sweetpea, I'm so proud of you!"

* * *

Since the sixth grade class was studying the Civil War, our destination for that afternoon's fieldtrip was the Cyclorama building at Grant Park.

I had been in the Cyclorama before, in the third grade, but I didn't understand the full impact of the war at that time. I was just fascinated by all the little doll figures they had placed around in different positions, alongside the miniature canons, horses, and houses, etc.. I thought the whole set-up was pretty.

After having studied all about it in class, I listened to the narrator that afternoon and thought about how much our country had changed over the past century—even since I was a little girl. The *Colored Only* signs had been removed from the water fountains and public restrooms, but an uneasy racial tension filled the streets of Atlanta, with the six-o'clock Evening News and our country's headlines jam packed with sit-ins, marches and violent demonstrations. Colored people were no longer restricted to the back of the bus, yet they seemed to automatically migrate there. Mama said it was because they were most comfortable there because that's where they had always sat.

* * *

My seventh grade class was to perform for the PTA Christmas musical, in which I was to have a lead solo with a front row position. All the girls were asked to wear black skirts, white blouses, dark shoes, and nylon hose.

The skirt, blouse, and shoes were no big deal. It was the nylon hose I anguished over.

Every time the subject was brought up, Mama had always discouraged me from shaving my legs, "Once you start, you'll have to continue the task for the rest of your life—'til your dying day!"

My legs were as hairy as an old grizzly bear's.

Sissy was visiting from out of state, and literally saved my life when she came to my defense and reasoned with Mama. She didn't have to say a lot because the best argument of all was to allow me to put the hose on my legs. The unsightliness of smooshed hairs underneath the nylons was convincing enough.

Mama agreed and I was plagued with the task for the rest of my days.

It was worth it, not to have the look and feel of ingrown mohair knee socks that evening. I smiled with confidence from the front row, and I looked as nice as anyone in my black skirt, white blouse, dark shoes, and—yes—nylon hose.

* * *

That Christmas Mama gave me my very first training bra.

I had my own bra and I was shaving my legs. Combined, that meant that I was a full-fledged woman...or so I thought.

CHAPTER IX
THAT'S DADDY'S CHAIR!

It was five-fifteen by the clock on the wall inside at the South Bend Pool's concession stand. I was fuming mad, while I sat there waiting for Mama, as I thought, *Where is she? She's late!* She told me to be out of the swimming pool and dressed, waiting for her at five-o'clock, which I was. I had been sitting there on that bench for fifteen minutes, long enough for the slats to make their imprints across my bottom and the backs of my legs. I couldn't wait until I was sixteen and could get my driver's license...only four more years.

I kept my eyes pealed for her light-green, '52 Plymouth, but my attention was suddenly drawn to the direction of a car-horn. It came from a sleek and shiny new, baby-blue, '62 Cadillac. Its horn had a sleek sound to match, with the smoothness of a saxophone. The car was so long, it reminded me of a giant, blue whale moving in slow motion, as it pulled into the parking lot. Every head at the pool was turned to see who was driving.

The sun's glare on the windshield prevented a clear view of the driver, but I recognized Mama's voice from the passenger side as she yelled, "Delaney, get your things and come on!"

I wanted everyone to know *I* was Delaney, so I waved my arms and yelled back, "Here I am, Mama! I'm over here"

A quick scope of the pool area confirmed I had been seen and heard by all, so I gathered my things and ran down the hill to the car. The closer I got to it the more beautiful it was. I expected the driver to be Mama's Uncle Clarence because he always had a new car of some sort, but he never had a Cadillac before.

I opened the door and as I slid onto the back seat, I rubbed my hand across the soft, cool leather and though, *Hmm, it's even got air-conditioning.* I said, "Wow! This is your best car yet, Uncle Clar--" That's when I realized the man driving wasn't Uncle Clarence. I didn't know who he was until Mama introduced him, "Delaney, sugar, I want you to meet my friend, Mr. Johnson."

He turned around in the seat and, of all things, reached across to shake my hand. "My, oh-my, Delaney. You're as pretty as your pictures. It's nice to finally meet you, Little Lady. You can call me Arthur."

I wondered what he meant by "finally." And where has he seen my pictures? Where did he get off calling me *his* Delaney? And why would I want to call him *anything?* I didn't know that man, and after I gave him the once-over, I asked, "Who are you, anyway? What are you doing with my mama?"

Both their faces turned as red as beets and Mama said, "Delaney! Be nice to Mr. Johnson. He's my friend."

I didn't like her tone of voice and I developed an immediate dislike for Mr. Johnson, especially when he kissed Mama on the cheek and said, "That's okay, Ruth. Just give her time."

We drove away with everyone at the pool gawking at the car.

I stared at the back of his head and the exposed scalp in a bald spot there about the size of my hand. "Did you know you've got big old, ugly freckles on the back of your head?"

His face, neck, and even his scalp changed to a glowing red.

Mama snapped, "Delaney! Apologize to Mr. Johnson, right now!"

"For what, Mama? Don't you see 'em? Right there where he's bald—where there's not any gray hair."

She just sighed and made excuses, "I declare, Arthur. She's not usually like this."

He said, "Give her time, Ruth. Just give her time." He reached up and touched the bare skin of his scalp, and before changing the subject he cleared his throat, "Okay, Little Lady, what's your favorite ice cream?"

"It depends."

"Depends on what?" he smiled.

"Whether it's soft or regular. It it's soft, then chocolate, but it it's regular I like Miss Georgia buttered pecan."

We stopped by Miss Georgia's ice cream parlor and he said, "Okay, Little Lady. Why don't you come inside with me and make sure I get the right kind?"

We came out with a big container of buttered pecan ice cream. He sat it beside me on the back seat and said, "Think that'll be enough to hold you for a while?"

The ice cream was for dessert, but I smiled in anticipation of its cold, sweet taste, *Hmm, buttered pecan—my favorite.*

* * *

The delicious aroma of pot roast in the oven floated through the air from the kitchen to welcome us as we opened the front door. Mama said, "Delaney, why don't you show Arthur some of your drawings while I put the biscuits in and finish up supper?"

"Yeah, Little Lady. I hear you're quite the artist."

Mama had saved every picture I had even drawn. She kept them in the cedar chest at the back hallway, next to the kitchen. When I came back into the living room and saw where he was sitting, I didn't hesitate to tell him, "That's Daddy's chair!"

He continued to rock and said, "Well, Little Lady, your daddy sure had a wonderful chair."

"No! You don't understand. I said that's my daddy's chair. Mama and me, or my brothers—we're the only ones who sit there!"

Mama called from the kitchen, "Okay, supper's almost ready. Go wash your hands."

He sat next to Mama at the table and I got a good look at the lines around his eyes and mouth, and the wrinkles in his rubbery-skinned, turkey-looking neck. His light-blue seer-sucker suit made his eyes appear bluer than they actually were.

The horseshoe-shaped, diamond ring on his pinkie finger caught my eye, and I noticed the gold wristwatch. Even it had diamonds on the face. All those diamonds and the Cadillac prompted me to ask, "Are you rich?"

When he laughed and smiled, his teeth were so white they didn't look real. "Well, Little Lady, I wouldn't say I'm rich. Let's just say my contracting company does all right for itself and I'm comfortable."

As he patted Mama's hand he smiled even wider when he said, "And since I met this pretty little lady I'm happier that I've been in a mighty long time."

I thought, *If he calls me "Little Lady" one more time I'll scream!* I didn't like the look in his eyes when he touched Mama's hand and I cringed when he kissed her forehead.

"Are you as old as my granddaddy?"

Mama sat straight up and snapped, "Delaney! Mind your manners!'

"Well, how old is he, anyway? His hands are all wrinkled like Granddaddy's."

Mr. Johnson cleared his throat and changed the subject again, "Are you ready for some good-ole buttered pecan ice cream for dessert, Little Lady?"

I refrained from screaming. Instead, I replied, "Yes, but I'll get my own...and *please* don't call me Little Lady again."

* * *

Our church's Fall Festival was the first Friday night in October. Mr. Johnson arrived early, and when I opened the door I was stunned when he yelled, "Happy Birthday, Delaney!"

"Birthday? It's not my birthday 'til next week!"

"Well, then I guess this would be what you might call an early birthday present."

He handed me a package wrapped in birthday paper, and Mama walked in the living room about that time, "Delaney, thank Mr. Johnson for the nice present."

Before I thanked him for anything I wanted to see what it was. While I tore into the paper, he embraced Mama and kissed her…in the mouth. Then he said, "Delaney, you sure have a pretty little lady here for a mother."

I felt anger toward Mama for letting him kiss her like that—like Daddy used to do. With the present opened, I exclaimed, "A *doll*? You gave me a *doll*? I'm gonna be thirteen next week—teenagers don't play with dolls!"

Mama gritted her teeth when she said, "Delaney, thank Mr. Johnson for the nice gift."

I offered a reluctant, "Thank you," and Mama went to the back of the house to get her coat.

Mr. Johnson started to sit in Daddy's chair again, but I ran and sat there first. While he waited for Mama, I rocked and thought, *I need to set him straight about a few things.* "Look, Mr. Johhnson, Mama's only dating you because you're rich. All the flowers and candy, and ice cream and dolls—and money you have will never buy your way into this family." I leaned forward in the chair and looked him square in the eyes, "You're not my Daddy—and you never will be."

* * *

That Sunday after church, Mr. Johnson took us to a nice restaurant in Atlanta. The chill in the air between that old man and me was such that it could have been cut with a knife.

It was apparent that Friday night's discussion went in one ear and out the other when Mr. Johnson pulled a small velvet box from his jacket pocket and said, "Delaney, I wanted you to be with your mama and me on this special occasion."

He looked into Mama's eyes and said, "Ruth, you know how I feel about you. There's not a minute in the day I don't think of you, and I want to spend the rest of my life with you."

I couldn't believe my ears when he placed the velvet box in her hand and said, "I love you, Ruth. Will you marry me?"

The expression on Mama's face when she opened the box sent a feeling of nausea rushing over me. I held my breath as I waited for her answer. I never knew how a few seconds could seem like an eternity until she finally answered, "Oh, Arthur. I love you, too…"

"Mama! You're not serious! You're not going to marry him?"

The look in her eyes answered my question, and the very thought of sitting there to hear her say "yes" to his proposal sent me running to the restroom in tears.

She followed me and when I saw the tears in her eyes, I felt bad for acting that way, but a lump in my throat prevented me from saying I'm sorry.

Instead, she was the one who apologized. "I'm sorry, Baby. I'm sorry you feel the way you do about Arthur. But I love him and he loves me. We could move to his house. He has a beautiful home in Sandy Springs—and I could quit working and be home for you."

"You mean you'd be home for *him*!"

"I mean home for *both* of you. I don't want to spend the rest of my life alone."

I pleaded, "But Mama. You're not alone. I'm with you. I'll always be with you. We don't need that old man. I hate him!"

"Delaney…"

I wouldn't have it. "If you marry him I—I'll run away! And I mean it!"

* * *

Mama declined Mr. Johnson's proposal, but their friendship continued and they dated on her days off. He never stopped sending her flowers and bringing her candy and gifts, and occasionally, he brought a present for me—none of which were dolls.

It didn't happen overnight, but eventually, Mr. Johnson and I became friends—not best of friends—but friends, just the same.

THURSDAY, JUNE 15, 1984: CHESTNUT, GEORGIA DR. ROBINSON'S OFFICE, OAKWOOD INSTITUTE'S SATELLITE FACILITY

The past months seemed to fly. I was allowed to spend weekends at home the remainder of April, and released from Oakwood in Cheatham on May 12th—the Friday before Mother's Day.

A warm sense of freedom chases up my spine, as I recall the fresh air and brilliant blue sky on that sunny day. We drove out the long, winding driveway through the thicket of green pine giants, and I lowered the car window for a distortion-free view. I admired the scattered bursts of color from the delicate pink and white Dogwood blooms, as they provided a touch of grace and elegance to the setting.

I enjoyed the show, as we moved along the path approaching the main road. If was as though God Himself were bidding me farewell with His special laser spectacular. The sounds of the birds singing provided perfect background music, while the rays of sunlight danced in constant rhythm, spotlighting the scenery as we departed the enchanted forest.

How could such beauty and serenity exist only yards away from the ugliness of that hell-place called Oakwood Institute?

A few miles down the road we passed that sign:

YOU ARE NOW LEAVING CHEATHAM…HURRY BACK!

I prayed I was leaving that place for the last time—never to return--and Oakwood Institute in Cheatham, Georgia would remain forever in my past, nothing more than memories.

With the opening of the new county satellite office in Chestnut, only fifteen minutes away from my home, it was so much more convenient. I could live at home while attending therapy sessions twice weekly on an outpatient basis—for as long as my memory was progressing and I continued to show improvement.

* * *

I could read Dr. Robinson's mind as I observed her reaction while she read the last chapter of my assignment. A few grins, a giggle or two, but mostly that raised eyebrow of disapproval at my rude treatment of Mama and her poor little rich friend, Mr. Johnson.

I said it before she had a chance to say, "What a brat."

She glanced up at me and said, "What did you say?"

"I said she sure was a brat, wasn't she?"

"If, when you're referring the *she*, you're talking about *yourself* in this last chapter, then yes, you could say that."

I scoffed, "I just did. She was a spoiled brat that needed more than her mama's switching. I thought it was bad when she put mud in the cookies and the way she treated the neighbor-kids."

"How do you feel about all that now, Delaney?"

I shrugged my shoulders, "I really don't think about it all that much. To tell you the truth, the memories make me smile. Is it perverted of me to smile at the part about the girlie show in Joanie's garage? Or should I be ashamed?"

"Hmm," she said, "I think you should feel the way you feel and don't force yourself to feel any other way. So if you feel like smiling—that's good. If you feel ashamed—that could be considered normal, too, to a certain extent."

I thought, *Sounds like a bunch of psychological mumbo-jumbo, doubletalk to me.* I glanced down at my ample chest packed into my D cup bra and laughed, "Well, it's obvious the little green grapes didn't affect them."

She agreed and laughed along with me, then she suddenly got serious again. "Back to this last chapter. Mr. Johnson seemed like a nice enough man."

"Oh, he *was* nice."

"Then why do you think you reacted to him that way?"

I grinned, "Because I was a spoiled brat?"

"No, I believe it goes much deeper than that."

Why did I know she was going to say that?

"Delaney, I believe you considered him an intruder, someone who was taking your mother's love and attention—love and attention you felt were meant for you, not some strange man. It's difficult for a child to accept someone who threatens to take their only parent away."

"But he wasn't taking her anywhere," I explained. "He just wanted to marry her."

"True, he wasn't physically taking her away. But, however unintentional it may have been on his part, he was interrupting the level of emotional bond between you and your mother. The normal reaction is to strike out at the intruder and protect your territory—the territory of your mother's love."

That made sense so I nodded and she continued, "How do you feel about the way in which you treated him and your mother?"

I thought hard and answered, "I wish I could turn the clock back and act differently—more understanding and co-operative. If she had married him, her life—our lives—would have been so much easier, financially. She could have quit work and traveled, and had nice things…and not worry about the bills."

She asked, "So you're saying the only thing her marriage to Mr. Johnson would have meant was financial security?"

"Yeah. I mean no—I mean—and she wouldn't have been so lonely. I knew she was lonesome because I could hear her crying at night."

"How did it make you feel when you overheard your mother crying?"

"Sad. Sick. Guilty. It was all my fault she was alone—if only I hadn't interfered. I'm responsible for ruining her chances at happiness."

The doctor nodded, "Delaney, I believe you. I believe you are sorry for your actions. But you can't turn back the clock, so the very best you can do is acknowledge your mistakes and go forward. Have you ever discussed Mr. Johnson with your mother?"

I shook my head, "No. They continued seeing each other as friends, but his name never came up in conversation, except a few years ago when she told me he died."

"What was your reaction?" she asked.

"I hugged her and told her I was sorry he died. I told her I thought he was a nice man—and doctor—I meant it. He was a nice man."

"Did you and she go to the funeral?"

I answered, "She did, but I really didn't see the need of my going to see a dead man. He wouldn't have known I was there."

"But your mother would have known, Delaney. Funerals have never been for the dead. They're for the living—the loved ones left behind."

I snorted, "I guess you can just make a note of that for my file— one more thing Delaney did wrong in her life."

"Don't be so down on yourself," she added. "Writing about it is the first step, but when you reach a point where you can tell your mother that you're sorry for the way you acted then do it. I'm sure she's already forgiven you and you're carrying around all that guilt unnecessarily."

I studied that for a minute or two before I said, 'Well, if she's already forgiven me, why should I bring it all up again? It'll only upset her and make her cry."

The doctor responded, "Sometimes it's good to cry. And it's always good to get guilt off your chest. Try it. It will bring closure and I guarantee you'll feel better after you clear the air."

* * *

The doctor had a way of making me feel better about things. But after all, that's what she was paid to do.

If only she could've found a way to rid me of the nightmares.

At times I scratched so incessantly, I drew prominent whelps and sometimes blood. When she asked me why I scratched so, I told her plain and simply, "Because I itch."

She blamed it on nerves, but I wasn't so sure. I wondered if my nightmares about the roaches weren't nightmares at all. *If roach eggs were really implanted in my bloodstream, were they hatching and crawling around in there?* She would've itched and scratched, too, if the things were inside her. But I couldn't take the chance of telling her of my suspicions. She would've sent me right back to Oakwood in Cheatham, and that's where the filthy things were bred. I wanted to continue living at home, where I hadn't seen the first roach, other than in those bad dreams.

I suddenly shivered at the thought, *If the roach nightmares really happened, then the other, more horrible dreams could be reality, too.* I wished I could trust the doctor enough to discuss my concerns, but I decided to keep quiet. Like Mama said, "Mustn't dwell on bad dreams."

CHAPTER X
HANG ON FOR THE BIG ONE!

I was always active in sports—cheerleading, softball, tennis, basketball, and even backyard football.

I had dreamed of being a majorette since I was seven years old when Santa Claus brought my first baton. I practiced and practiced. Eventually I learned how to twirl two at a time, tossing them high in the air and catching them as I did flips. Mama couldn't afford lessons, but I was pretty good for someone who was self-taught.

In order to become a majorette, I was required to play a band instrument, so I chose the clarinet. However, time would prove me to have absolutely no talent in that area. I kept breaking the reeds with my tongue and blowing spit into the instrument, making a horrible racket that sounded like a wounded rhinoceros.

The teacher was very nice about it when he talked to my mother, "That's why we encourage renting the instruments for beginners, Mrs. James. You're lucky you can return it and get your deposit refunded."

My heart was broken, and my dreams of becoming a majorette were shattered.

My brother, Jerry, was home on leave from the Navy. He told me that majorettes were conceited, and that cheerleaders were far more popular, anyway. Recognizing that he was someone who would know about those kinds of things, I abandoned my aspirations toward majorette, and directed my talents toward cheerleading. After all, I had been a cheerleader for the past three years in elementary school—so I knew all the tricks of the trade.

The strenuous twists, jumps, and splits I performed led Mama to warn me, "Delaney, you're gonna split yourself right up the middle and cause yourself to hemorrhage!"

Those films and books about the Facts of Life didn't make a dime's worth of sense to me. What did frogs, rabbits and the birds and bees have to do with human beings, anyway?

Mama was too embarrassed to discuss those kinds of things with me. It's no wonder, at age thirteen, I thought I had actually split myself open to hemorrhage that winter day at cheerleading practice, when the back of my slacks were spotted with blood.

I rushed home and called Mama at work. Through tears of hysteria I told her what happened. Very calmly, she directed me, "Look in the right-hand corner of the cedar chest in the hall. You'll find everything you need wrapped up in a pink towel."

However, no instructions were included, so I spent the next 45 minutes attempting to determine just how the apparatus—sanitary belt and pad—all fit together.

I was frustrated, confused and panic-stricken, overcome by the total fear that I was dying—and Mama had been expecting it all along. Otherwise, why would she have been so calm and have the preparations in the cedar chest for my final days?

Obviously, I didn't die, but as Mama told me when she got home, "All young women experience the same thing," and I was doomed to face the period curse every month for the rest of most of my life. I thought, *And she called shaving my legs a task?*

She told me it was called menstruation and it would happen every month, but when I asked, "Why?" she handed me a book to read.

In so doing, I learned terminology such as: cycle and pre-menstrual discomfort. The book said it would happen once a month—in thirty day cycles—and that the regularity of the cycles would be interrupted only in time of pregnancy.

I had been familiarized with the word *pregnant* at an early age. When I was five I told the ice-cream man, "Jackie's not fat—she's gonna have a baby."

Jackie's face turned red of embarrassment, and her tone of voice told me she was upset with me, "Delaney! I believe the man knows I'm pregnant without you telling him."

She grabbed my hand and as we walked back to the house I asked, "What's preg-ant mean?"

"It means I'm gonna have a baby! And the word is *pregnant*!"

Since that time Jackie had been pregnant almost every year until she and Gene had five children. For the longest time I thought she just swelled up like that when spring or summer rolled around.

* * *

A few weeks after my initial visit by the period curse, I would have the night of my dreams—my first prom date, which would also serve as my first date ever! I had met and skated with boys at the skating rink, but this was the real thing.

I took a trip to the beauty shop, where Mrs. Echols' daughter MerriAnn styled my hair in a stylish bouffant coiffeur in which she placed a rhinestone tiara. The dress was a strapless white, ballerina-length formal, with layered lace, and a hoop skirt. We didn't have the money to buy a new one, so I borrowed one from my Aunt Gracie, who had sewn it for Melinda. The dress was beautiful. However, as Melinda was about 3-4 inches shorter than me, the dress fell a little shorter than ballerina length, and hit me about mid-calf.

That was a fact I didn't realize until we saw the pictures afterward, so for that night, I felt like a true princess.

Imagine, me, the tomboy, with my tiara and long, white gloves—all decked out like Miss America on television. The V-neck suntan mark where my T-shirt neckline stopped was the only evidence of my less than prima donna past times.

Thank goodness for the stays sewn into the ribcage of that dress. Without them, my underdeveloped bust-line would have failed to keep up the front.

Jimmy, a childhood sweetheart, was my date. We doubled with Ronald and his girlfriend. Ronald's mom picked us up and Jimmy's mom brought us home.

The hoop skirt of my dress was so big that Jimmy sat in the back seat with the other couple on the way home, leaving his mom, my dress, and me in the front. It was too hot to be so crowded.

It was only natural for Jimmy to walk me to the door. He said, "Gosh, you really looked great tonight." He then leaned over and kissed me—in the mouth!

That was my first kiss—I mean *real* kiss—by a boy, in the mouth!

I was sure I was pregnant by that kiss when, for nine months, I failed to have another period.

The book showed pictures, and said the development period for a human was approximately nine months. I kept reading the part about the regularity of the periods being interrupted *only* in time of pregnancy. I kept hoping I'd read something between the lines--something I had missed before.

The anguish I felt was incomprehensible as the months rolled along. I examined my abdomen for changes every day, looking for swelling like in the pictures awaiting the birth of an infant—a real, live baby.

How was I going to explain it to Mama and my family? Worse still, what was I going to do with it? Where would I keep it? I thought, *I'm too young for this—I'm only a baby myself!*

Words cannot express my relief the day the period curse was finally with me again. I was told later by the doctor that young girls who are active in sports sometimes experience irregular periods. It sure would have saved me a lot of distress if the book had mentioned that fact.

I considered initiation into womanhood to be more that I expected, but at last, now—finally, I was a grownup woman…or was I?

* * *

One afternoon, a friend by the name of Linda pointed out the unsightliness of my bushy eyebrows. And she was right! My brows appeared as though two black fuzzy caterpillars had crawled above my eyes and taken root.

That was too unbecoming for a young woman such as myself, so I agreed to let her arch my eyebrows. She plucked out each follicle, one by one. "Ouch!" An experience of pain that I was sure would be unequaled by anything else!

Mama had a genuine fit, once again, pointing out that, "This is something else you're gonna have to do 'til your dying day!"

It was worth it, to no longer have the appearance of Groucho Marx.

In addition to plucking my eyebrows, I committed myself to my very first diet to lose ten pounds. I wore a bra, I was shaving my legs and wearing nylon hose, I was visited by the period curse on a regular basis, *and* I had been kissed by a boy—in the mouth.

What more could there be to womanhood?

* * *

When October rolled around, I went to the Fair with a group of friends. There were six of us in all—three girls and three boys. Thomas was the closest thing I had to a boyfriend, as we had talked on the phone a good bit and met at the skating rink.

We were having a great time, going through the haunted house, and all the shows, except the girlie shows. We rode all the rides, some twice and three times. Our favorite was the house of mirrors, where we laughed ourselves silly at each other's distorted reflection. For some reason, we always laughed the most at each other's reflection in the one that made us look fat.

The boys suddenly yelled, "The last one in line for the Greyhound's a chicken!"

The other girls scrambled to get in line, but I hesitated, so I was the last in line.

All the others started making clucking noises and calling me names, "Delaney is a chicken--*cluck, cluck, cluck!*"

If they only knew how much I didn't want to ride that thing, but I thought, *Okay, this time I have to go through with it, or be the laughing stock for being such a big baby.*

I took my seat next to Thomas in the roller coaster's car and swallowed hard, trying to block out all my childhood fears of the thing.

I gripped the safety bar so hard that my knuckles were already turning white, and we hadn't even moved an inch!

I tried not to think about the thing being a giant gray monster that killed people, as I told myself, *There's no such things as monsters.* The rumbling sound as the motor started made my blood feel colder than ice, and the sick feeling that was in my stomach overcame my entire body.

I tried not to think about how unsafe it felt, as the sounds of the old rickety, wooden tracks shook and creaked with every movement of the car. The rumors kept pushing to the front of my mind that "it had been closed down for a while after some teenagers were thrown from the track and killed." Those rumors triggered anxieties that made me think, *Being called a big baby wouldn't be so bad,* and I wished I was still on the ground, watching the others ride. I prayed, *God, please let me make it off this thing alive,* as we approached the first crest.

We were on top, and then…*down-n-n*, in an instant. Even though it seemed as if we'd never reach the bottom, that had been a pretty low crest and the break wasn't so bad. But that was only the first of many. I closed my eyes as we approached, rode and conquered each of the remaining ups and downs of the tracks.

The sound was deafening, and no matter how loud I screamed, it just blended into the other blood-curdling screams.

I felt the track level out and I opened my eyes, while I took a deep breath of relief. I thought we were close to the end and within safety's reach.

It was then I realized we weren't at the end at all, but quite the contrary. We were on a stretch of track that plateaus at a point where it towered over all. The view of the lighted park and Atlanta in the distance, was absolutely breathtaking.

The height alone was overwhelming. Thomas then leaned over and said, "Hang on for the Big One!" He was talking about the Giant Crest—the mother of all roller coaster crests!

Before I had time to close my eyes we were there, atop the Giant Crest, approaching the Break-Of-All-Breaks, headed *D-O-W-N-n-n*! The break that jerked me in such a way I felt my head becoming detached, while my heart stopped and jumped out of my throat at the same time. The earth had been pulled completely out from under us, and there was the horrifying sensation that we were no longer attached to the track.

My breathing stopped in mid-breath, and the air had solidified, forever caught in my throat! Sheer fright overcame me, as I yelled, "Ma-Ma!' with every ounce of energy I could conjure up.

I didn't care if I looked like a baby, crying and yelling for my mama. I just wanted God to let me live through that hell-of-a-ride and get back on the ground.

Once we conquered the Break in the Giant Crest, we were on our way to safety, with only a few short yards of track remaining.

The ride had finally come to an end.

I walked down the ramp with Thomas' help and there was such a sense of relief that surged through my body, I wanted to bend down and kiss the ground. *Thank you, God, for letting me live. I promise I'll never be stupid enough to get on that thing again!*

I couldn't believe my ears when the gang all yelled, "Wow! That was great! Let's go again!"

I thought, *Again? Are they crazy?*

They all rode it again. But I stayed true to my promise to God in that I never rode the Greyhound again!

* * *

No other roller coaster has ever frightened me in the same way as that damnable thing.

Years later, they closed down the old wooden roller coaster, permanently, after a car was thrown from the tracks and killed all the passengers.

The old dinosaur was demolished as part of a stunt in one of the "Smoky and the Bandit" movies. The old gray monster was huge and fell hard, with a blaring roar, as it caved in with a domino effect. The Greyhound—last of the dinosaurs.

I watched it fall in that movie, while I remembered how terrified I was that evening at the Fair. I felt relieved, knowing I would never have to endure that feeling again in my life. The Greyhound was gone—forever!

* * *

It was the summer before my sixteenth birthday and it would be my first real date, at night, in a car, without parents. Of course, it would be a double date.

He was eighteen years old, his name was Larry, and the knockout-of-a-guy who worked as the produce boy at the local grocery store in Warner Robbins, where my sister did her shopping. I had met him earlier that year when I visited my sister, and I couldn't get him out of my mind. But he was much older, and I never had any hopes of anything beyond friendship.

I rode the Nancy Hanks train from Atlanta and Sis picked me up at the station there in Warner Robbins. She couldn't wait to tell me about the date she had arranged for me with Larry. She was as excited about my first date as I was.

After all, it would have been every girl's dream to go out with a handsome hunk like Larry, especially to the Air Force Base Gala.

The dress was pastel pink, a Jonathan Logan original, at twenty-five dollars, high heels dyed to match, bouffant hairstyle, and, of course, pink lipstick. Sis covered the cost for that evening's attire and that just confirmed her as the best sister in the whole world.

I had worked hard to lose the fifteen pounds that had somehow slipped back on, in order to get into that size five dress.

I would have been the envy of all the girls back home, if they could have been there to see me.

Larry looked drop-dead handsome in his tuxedo with the bright red cummerbund. When he told me how great I looked, I was embarrassed and felt a little awkward, as I replied, "You look nice, too. I almost didn't recognize you without your apron." I thought, *At least I don't have to wonder anymore about what my first stupid statement's gonna be.*

Before we left, he told my sister he would have me home by eleven-o'clock. I wondered if he was already counting the minutes before he could get rid of me.

His black '54 Ford was bulging at the seams, as it was actually a double date times two, qualifying it as a group date. In fact, the word group understates the number. There were four couples— that's eight people in the car that night—with no air conditioning! A light mist of rain prevented the windows from being lowered, and I was thankful God had invented deodorant!

I was the youngest in the group, and didn't know anyone there but Larry, and I really didn't know him. At first, I was a little self-conscious, but we all became friends throughout the evening.

I couldn't believe it. He took everyone else home before me! Then he asked me to go to the lake the next day! I was so excited! With my sister's permission, I went with him, and we had several more dates before I went back to Atlanta.

It was one of the best vacations I ever spent at my sister's! He said he'd come to Atlanta to visit me, and I couldn't wait to see him again.

That evening, and the dates with him over the next several weeks at my sister's was a real step into womanhood.

After all, Mama had said, "Absolutely no dates until your sixteenth birthday," and I had the jump on my dating era by two whole months.

* * *

In my sophomore year's biology class we shared, two to a microscope. I was amazed one afternoon while viewing slides, and I commented to my lab partner, "Boy, it sure looks different than in real life."

Doc Cambridge was one of those older teachers with gray hair and skin to match, and a stone face so solemn it would've cracked if ever he smiled. His proper British accent was as thick as London's fog, and usually rolled out with the smoothness of fine velvet. However, I almost dropped the slide when the velvet suddenly changed to a foghorn-of-a-voice and blasted me off my stool, "And Miss James, would you like to tell the class where you've seen one in real life?" He pushed his black rimmed glassed down to the tip of his red, bulbous nose, folded his arms across his skeleton-thin chest, and leaned back against the desk, as he awaited my answer.

"In the woods, Sir."

He was visibly shocked by my response, but then his bushy eyebrows met in the center, indicating his puzzlement, as he looked over his glasses and glared at me, "Please go on, Miss James, tell us what it looked like in the woods."

"Well," I explained, "it was long, and green...and sort of feathery."

He repeated, "Long? And green? And sort of feathery?"

"Yessir," I said, as the others in the classroom were about to fall off their stools in laughter—the reason for which I had no clue.

He cleared his throat and in the sternest of voices, he said, "Miss James, see me after class."

I remained in my seat as the classroom emptied, and I soon discovered why everyone was laughing. I had understood him to say we were looking at a fern specimen through the microscope, when, he actually said it was a *sperm* specimen.

I felt my face turn crimson from the embarrassment. All I could think of to say was, "Well, a fern *is* long, and green, and sort of feathery, Sir."

I was one of the rare individuals who witnessed a smile on the old stone face, and contrary to belief, it didn't crack.

* * *

A wiener roast over an open fire, homemade fudge brownies, and ice cream, topped off with a bowl of buttered popcorn, Coke, and group of girls gathered around the television for a late-night, chilling thriller-of-a-horror movie. Those were the necessary ingredients for a successful pajama party.

Besides eating, talking and laughing, we listened to the record player, danced, and made prank phone calls at random.

After we plundered through the bag belonging to the girl with the largest brassiere, we snatched it without her knowledge and, before we stuck it in the freezer, we filled the cups with water. The next morning the chosen victim awoke to frozen cupsicles. I never worried about being the victim, myself, as Melissa was by far the front-runner in the large bra department.

After we reached driving age, we sneaked out through the bedroom window, sometimes in our pajamas and robes. Sweet revenge was a few eggs tossed at an old boyfriend's house or car, or a couple rolls of toilet paper strewn in the trees and yard of the girl who came between one of us and a boy.

Our parents always wondered why their egg and toilet paper supply was depleted the morning after the group of girls stayed over.

We always began the evening pledging to stay awake all night, but two-thirty or three-o'clock was usually the limit. I tried to keep at least one other person awake to keep me company. I knew I would make at least a dozen trips to the bathroom during the night, especially after all the Coke and Kool-Aid.

My floor pallet was usually farthest from the bathroom, so I was forced to step over, around and in between all those bodies to get there.

Betty's house was the worst place of all to be found in that situation. Her room was up seventeen steps and right above her parents' room. I knew there were seventeen steps because I had to count them in the dark to make sure I was at the bottom of the enclosed staircase.

Betty was my best friend throughout most of my childhood and teenage years. We shared summer vacations, cheerleading, and clothes, while we supported one another through the trials and tribulations of dating and the quest for the perfect boyfriend.

Going steady was the only way to go, because we were assured of a date on the weekend nights. We always had a steady boyfriend and each time we were sure it was the real thing. But we went steady so many times our parents couldn't keep up with us; in fact, there were times we couldn't keep up with ourselves.

Betty and I shared material things such as clothes, but more importantly, she shared her Dad with me. He made me feel as though I really was his number two daughter.

I always felt I was missing so much, not having Daddy during those years.

I felt so different from my friends, but none of them would've understood if I had told them. That even when I was surrounded by them at school, football and basketball games, or pajama parties—I felt alone. The feeling wasn't there all the time, but when it was, an invisible barrier separated me from the rest of the world. It usually happened when I thought of Daddy, and I'd think of him at the damnedest times. And when I did, I was reminded of how much I missed having a father's love—a love that Mama couldn't replace, no matter how hard she tried.

CHAPTER XI
FIRST DEGREE LOVE

My sixteenth birthday finally arrived and with it came the traditional surprise party, where in front of all my friends—boys and girls—I received my most embarrassing gift from Aunt Maisie. My face flashed all shades of red when I opened those knee-length pantaloons covered in a million two-inch, multi-colored polka dots. I couldn't remember a more awkward moment, except for the time when I was at Donna's birthday party. I was eleven and it was the first party I had attended where there were boys and girls. I was already embarrassed to take a present that Mama had wrapped in Sunday Comics, but the ultimate was when Donna opened the box and held up my present—nylon panties.

I felt like crawling under the table at Donna's party, but I wanted to out-and-out die at my own, as I plopped the lid back on my aunt's gift before anyone saw them. But I wasn't fast enough and the nickname Miss Polka Dots made me cringe for months afterward.

* * *

Even though I was finally of driving age, I had no real driving ambitions to get my license. I didn't see the immediate need because I could usually get a ride to most anywhere I wanted to go. All my friends either had their own cars or had access to their parents'.

Marilyn had a black '51 Chevy, and all of us girls would pool our money for gasoline. There were times when our combined funds totaled no more that fifty or seventy-five cents. Fortunately, in the sixties that afforded us enough gas for an afternoon of joyriding, or at least it got us to one of the local hamburger joints. One such place was downtown near the Georgia Tech campus—the world famous Varsity—home of the chili dog and frosted orange, where our food was brought to our car by colored carhops called 'Red-caps' because they wore red caps, of course. Another hangout was the Burger Chef on Moreland Avenue, and later, a new kid on the block in the burger business by the name of McDonald's.

It happened at the Burger Chef that evening in the spring of '64. That was where and when I met Richard.

He was a gorgeous 6'3" blond with blue eyes, and he drove the toughest of cars. Tough meant it was really fine looking and fast. We judged—and in most cases pre-judged—the boys by the kind of cars they drove. His was a red '61 Chevy Impala with red, leather, rolled-and-pleated interior—and mag wheels. Mag wheels were a must in order for a car to be really tough, like Richard's.

He seemed so mature compared to the others. He always opened the door for me and was so polite; neat and clean shaven, with the scent of good smelling after-shave at any time of the day. Mama had a way of describing him, "He always looks like he just stepped out of a band box." I never understood what she meant by that description, but by her pleasant smile and tone in her voice, I assumed she meant it to be flattering.

My description of him would simply be that he was irresistible—everything I was looking for in a boyfriend. And he didn't smoke—I wouldn't consider dating anyone who smoked. It always repulsed me that anyone would want to put that filth in their mouth. I abhorred the smell and the taste killed any desire I might have had to kiss them. Richard didn't drink, either—another vice I couldn't justify or tolerate.

Drinking and smoking were considered all right for boys to do, but if a girl were to be seen doing either, she would immediately be marked as a cheap tramp.

There was a good reason he seemed so mature, as I later discovered he was twenty-one years old. I kept that bit of information from Mama for several months; after all, what she didn't know wouldn't hurt her.

When we kissed there was a sensation that rushed all over me. A brand new feeling of excitement that made me all warm and tingly throughout, and I wished the moment never had to end.

He was so gentle and loving, and influenced me in so many ways as I approached womanhood.

However, possibly because of our age difference, our relationship would lead to certain pressures—pressures for which I wasn't prepared, and ultimately could not handle successfully.

One Sunday afternoon we went to Grant Park and then back to his house. His family had gone to South Georgia for the day and not expected home until late that evening, so we were alone.

We had been going steady for several months, and the love we shared for one another had grown stronger than anyone could imagine. Our emotions had become more and more difficult to control, and when he took my hand and lead me into his bedroom that afternoon, we had full intentions of consummating our love.

His room was always neat and tidy, just like Richard. That particular afternoon a yellow chenille bedspread was meticulously draped across his double-sized bed. In every detail, down to the pattern of rows and swirls of soft fluff, it was exactly like the yellow spread on Mama's bed. It even had the same clean and fresh scent of Tide detergent and sunshine.

We became lost in our embraces and kisses of unmitigated passion, while our emotions ran rampant. Mama's image suddenly popped into my mind and I pulled away, "This is not right…"

"What d'ya mean?"

I shook my head, "I'm sorry. It's just not right."

"What's wrong? Don't you love me?"

My answer was without hesitation, "Of course I love you! But— I'm not ready." It was obvious that he truly loved me, and I really wanted to be with him in that way, but my inexperience made me nervous and scared.

We had gone pretty far into the process and I understood his extreme frustration. But then he showed a side of himself I never knew existed. He became so angry he put his fist through the wall behind the door in his bedroom! "Damn it, Delaney!"

He frightened me and I began to cry. I begged him to calm down, but my pleas were in vain, so I said, "All right. If that's what I have to do to convince you how much I love you, then, come on—let's do it—right now! Hurry up, before I change my mind!" I was crying and shaking so hard, he knew my heart wasn't in it.

He calmed down, came back to the side of the bed, put his arms around me, and kissed me on the top of my head. He then did something that made me respect him so much, I forgot all about how afraid I was a few minutes earlier.

Tender sincerity was in his words of apology, "I'm sorry I went off like that. I've never loved *anyone* the way I love you. I want to be with you so much—it makes me crazy. But, you'll know when it's right, and I'm man enough to wait. I respect you enough to wait."

He gently kissed my cheek, and as he placed a tissue in my hand he said, "Here, dry your eyes and get dressed."

I loved him even more after that afternoon.

Over the next year, we became as close as two people in love could be. It was as though we were already married, in that we were only separated while I was in school and he was at work. He came over every afternoon before he went home from work, and we spent the rest of the day and evening together.

* * *

I was crushed when the day came that interrupted our plans for a blissful future together. Richard received his draft papers from the Army in the fall of '65. He served boot camp in Fort Benning, Georgia then he was transferred to Texas for additional training in preparation for Viet Nam.

As much as I loved him, I turned down his marriage proposal when he came home on leave because I had promised Mama and Daddy I would graduate from high school. I couldn't bear to see Mama's disappointment if I didn't get my diploma. She was so proud of me and I would be the only one of their five children to graduate with the class.

Texas was so far away, and I had so many social events in school that required my having a date; after all, it was my senior year.

We finally agreed that I should date others while he was in the service, which I did. Unfortunately, his jealousy and pride were such that our relationship came to an end a few months later.

I felt as though my heart were going to explode; the feeling of sadness familiar to anyone who has experienced a love ended.

My letters went unanswered, but several months down the road I discovered my prayers were being answered. Richard was being discharged from the Army and coming home! It was for medical reasons, though I didn't know what kind.

Even though he was back home, it wasn't the same between us. His jealous accusations drove me half-crazy, so we decided to give ourselves space.

I continued to date other guys, but no one meant quite the same as Richard. I wondered if I would ever find anyone with whom to experience those same tender feelings of closeness that we had once shared. It seemed doubtful.

All the other boys seemed as if they were only out for a good time, and they lacked Richard's maturity and level of sensitivity. For those reasons, I couldn't feel for them anything but a way to pass the time—someone to take me places and fill my evenings. I was still blinded by love—the love I had for Richard.

My frustration was incomprehensible, only to be intensified with time. I still dreamed about him and pretended I was with him—in his arms—even when I was with others. No one could compare.

Richard's family had always made me feel as though I was a part of them, and I had grown to love both his parents, as if they were my own. If Richard and I couldn't resolve our differences, I would not only lose him, but the loving relationship with his family—a fact that always left me feeling a sad sense of regret.

Our pride wouldn't allow us to patch things up between us, and sadly enough, Richard became a chapter in my past—a very important chapter.

* * *

I'll never forget the raging flames of my first love. All its tenderness and excitement made it a very special relationship. But it also introduced me to the hurt that comes from the burn of first degree love, when its dying embers are all that remain.

CHAPTER XII
I'M A BARGAIN AT TWICE THE PRICE

FRIDAY, MAY 27, 1966: 8:00 P.M., ATLANTA CITY AUDITORIUM

I was beaming all over with pride as I marched down the aisle and took my seat on the stage among Forrester High's graduating class. I gazed across the massive room at the sea of faces, occasionally making out those of friends or relatives. The countless others were there to see sons or daughters, sisters, brothers, relatives, or friends on one of the most important evenings of their lives.

I was disappointed when I didn't see Richard, even though I was meeting someone else for the senior dance, afterward.

While the principal read his welcome speech, I sat up straight and tried my best to look interested. I glanced around our class, with the girls in white caps and gowns, the boys in red. We were all wearing smiles and looked sharp to perfection, once our eyes adjusted to the bright stage lights and we stopped squinting.

We were an "all white class," for which everyone told me how lucky I was. We weren't a segregated school, anymore. It just happened that all the students in our class were Caucasian.

That thought reminded me of that September morning in '64 when the police escort drove up in front of Forrester High and Claudette Bradley entered our doors for the first time. It was in all the newspapers and television that ours was one of the first schools in Atlanta to be integrated. The smartest student from her school, Claudette was being transferred to Forrester in her junior year—bussed in from another area, since she didn't live in our part of town.

She was in my second period, Mr. Zorbina's Spanish class. Every morning, we were all expected to introduce ourselves to the teacher by saying our name and "How are you?" in Spanish—"Como esta usted, Señor Zorbina?"

Everyone snickered when it was Claudette's turn. "*Co-mo East-ah You-stead, seen your Zor been ah.*" With her combination colored drawl and southern accent it seemed as if it took her forever to say those few little words.

I don't recall any trouble. Nonetheless, I felt sorry for her being in a potentially hostile environment. As her blue-uniformed entourage accompanied her from class to class, her sad, dark eyes were directed toward the floor at all times. She ate lunch alone, and she went home alone in the afternoons—except for the police escort.

One morning when we were leaving Spanish, our eyes met, and for that split second I recognized her as a person, just like me, except her skin was a different color. The next morning, when I was sure no one else could see or hear me, I smiled and spoke to her in a low whisper, "Hi."

She responded with a smile, and that was the beginning of a very quiet and secret friendship, limited only to an occasional smile or greeting. I always looked around to make sure no one saw our exchange of smiles or contact. I didn't want to be called a *nigger-*

161

lover, as that's exactly what the others might have called me, crude as that may be.

I didn't know her well enough to like her. In fact, no one really knew her at all, and so we didn't know whether we liked or hated her as a person. We only knew that she was different, in that she was *colored*, the word used at that time when referring to someone other than Caucasian, Hispanic, or Asian. Throughout our lives we were taught to stay away from the *coloreds*, "They're mean and nothing but troublemakers!"

Grownups said, "That damn Martin Luther King and Malcom X. Just look at all the people getting hurt and killed in those protest marches and riots they're stirring up. Why can't they just leave well enough alone?"

The Civil Rights movement and the NAACP were kicking into high gear and no one in the country expected, nor were they prepared for the resulting changes in our society. Segregation was pronounced illegal and the Afro-Americans, as they wanted to be called, no longer sat at the back of the bus. They could sit anywhere they so desired, and eat in any restaurant. They drank from the same water fountains, used the same restrooms, and went to the same schools as everyone else.

I couldn't imagine being pulled away from all my friends—especially in my junior year! Sent to a school where I didn't know a soul, to graduate with a class full of people I didn't know anything about, except that they hated me, for no other reason that the color of my skin.

I glanced around at my class, thankful I wasn't colored, and subjected to all the ridicule and hatred that Claudette faced. As we stood for the pledge to the flag and Superintendent of Schools, Mrs. Whirter, led us in prayer, I was glad to be white, and that *white* was considered the right color to be.

My thoughts continued to wander during the valedictorian's speech. It seemed like such a long time ago when I cried so, that day Mama left me there at Hoover Elementary on the first day of school.

That was also the first time I met Clark Ponder. "Don't cry," he said, as she patted me on the shoulder. "I'll be your friend." And so he was throughout our school years.

Clark was on the front row of the stage that night. He was such a natural-born showoff, always making people laugh. He had been called "sissy" and a "queer" in grade school, but it never seemed to bother him.

Rosemary and Arnold were so fat they almost filled out their graduation robes, and the left side where they sat seemed a couple inches lower than the rest of the stage. Through the years they were the brunt of so many fat-jokes, and like Claudette, they were avoided because of the way they looked—left to eat alone, and go home alone in the afternoons.

I looked around and saw those I wished I had gotten to know better. I noticed the ones who were the most popular—some with whom I'd been on cheerleading, and the others who were active in sports. They always looked confident, and that night was no different.

However, the bookworms and the shy, quiet ones who kept to themselves seemed every bit as confident. Everyone was equal that evening and sharing something in common. There for the same purpose, we had obtained the same goal at the same time in life. We were receiving our diplomas—graduating. We'd had a lot of good times together, and I was going to miss seeing them everyday.

I suddenly heard the echoing voice over the auditorium's loud speaker, "Susan Delaney James." I smiled at the sound of my name as I thought, *That's me.* I stood erect with shoulders back as I stepped forward and reached out to accept that piece of paper Mama wanted so much for me. I swelled with pride and happiness, while a shadow of sadness clouded my sunshine with the fact that Daddy wasn't there to see his baby girl. I imagined him smiling down from heaven and winking at me when I was recognized among the top ten percent of the class. I smiled at the thought of him poking God with his elbow and bragging, "That's my Sweetpea."

The guest speaker that evening was the Mayor of Atlanta. In his speech he stated, "This night closes one episode of your lives, as you embark on an exciting future as bright your men and women. Man will walk on the moon and conquer space during your lifetime, and your future is destined to be a most interesting one. Together with the responsibilities of adulthood, may you have much happiness, success and prosperity.

* * *

The following Monday, June 2nd, I got a head start on prosperity when I began my secretarial career, with my first day on the job at the state's new mental institution. I had the responsibilities, and performed the duties of two secretarial positions—one in counseling and one in evaluation. I researched and typed case histories part of the day and worked with the progress reports for the remainder.

I was only seventeen and neither professionally trained nor prepared to work with emotionally handicapped or mentally disturbed people. My training was limited to the clerical field; however, I couldn't avoid becoming interested and involved to the point of caring about those poor people.

I had access to their background files, as well as case histories and I recognized them as individuals who came from similar backgrounds as myself.

They were everyday people who had become unbalanced and lost their way emotionally. They reminded me of laboratory mice in their own imaginary mazes—their own faraway world—wandering endlessly. Some drug their feet in a slow shuffle at a snail's pace, while others raced at such a fast pace as though they were running to catch a train. Still others would simply sit and stare into space, responding to nothing or no one. Their expressionless faces were as if they were molded of clay.

The background files revealed some of them were that way because they were victims of life's cruelty. Many were products of unstable family lives, while others had been beaten by lovers or parents, raped by strangers, or witnessed the same happening to someone they loved. The saddest were those who just couldn't cope with the death of a close loved one.

* * *

I learned that "paranoid" described someone who imagined themselves being plotted against by others, or talked about behind their backs—often brought on by self-persecution. "Neurosis" was a psychiatric disorder. "Schizophrenic" was someone with more than one personality, while "manic depressive" described someone suffering from acute depression. Most of the patients there showed symptoms of at least one or more of those conditions.

On the designated days they were visited by their families and friends who could only imagine the hell in which they were trapped.

* * *

The Institution was divided into *Unit I* in the main building, and *Cottages A, B,* and *C,* all connected to the main building by underground tunnels. *Unit I* housed the more severe cases, and the newer patients were usually assigned there. As progress was realized, the patients would be reassigned to one of the cottages. There they were able to enjoy television, music, and game privileges, together with participating in a vocational rehabilitation program. Out-patient status was the last phase, which meant they would live at home and report in on a regular basis.

So there was encouragement, in that their basis of residency in the institution did not have to be permanent.

I couldn't stop the feeling, *There but the grace of God go I.* I frequently took them home with me at night—in my heart and thoughts. There were many nights I had nightmares, being so caught up in their lives. My dreams and fears were always of myself, being locked behind those same doors, or experiencing the same ill fates.

My nightmares introduced me to their senses of confusion, frustration, hate, anger, sadness, and total fear. Fear of others, of myself, fear of life's known as well as the unknown.

When I awoke the next morning after one of those bad dreams I thanked God my life was free of complications. I prayed, God forbid that, if ever I was confronted with similar situations as theirs, I would be able to deal with them.

* * *

One July morning I was left in the Evaluation department with a group of patients from *Cottage A.* The boy from the mailroom ran in for my assistance, "Delaney, quick! We need help!" One of the female patients had stolen a metal letter opener from Rehabilitation's clerical department, and sharpened it in wood shop. She sneaked into the mailroom and was holding an employee around the shoulders, the letter opener pressed to his throat.

The patient recognized me as her friend, "Hey Miss Delaney! What are you doing here?"

I persuaded her to release the hostage and hand over the letter opener.

She laughed, half-crazed and starry eyed, jerking as if waves of electrical shock flowed through her body. She fell to the floor and I knelt beside her so I could hear what she was whispering. She then pointed to the mail-boy, "I really scared him! I really scared you, too, didn't I?"

Then she laughed and said, "You really took me serious, didn't you? You think I'm crazy, don't you?" Her unsettling voice and that distant look in her eyes burned into my memory, and I connected with the intense fear and confusion she was feeling within.

The orderly and his assistant soon came to take her away to the safe room, where she couldn't hurt herself or anyone else.

* * *

After less than two months my boss said, "Delaney, you're doing a fine job." I received a raise amounting to approximately double my original salary. Several months later I would discover I received that raise only because I was doing work that should have been divided up among several positions and filled by several people. It's no wonder I got a raise, but even at twice the price I was a real bargain.

CHAPTER XIII
THAT'S THE BRAKES,
IN REVERSE

There soon came the time when the need arose to have my own car, since I often worked later than my ride.

So it would be easier to learn, Bud taught me to drive his '65 Mustang with the automatic transmission. Boyfriends had tried to teach me in the past, but I was simply too uncoordinated to master the clutch and gear shifting.

Mama's white '60 Rambler had an automatic transmission with a push-button gear changer on the dash next to the radio. It was simple enough, but based on the few times I had gone out with her to learn, I didn't consider it worth all the anguish.

Friday morning, August 17th, 1966, Bud drove me over to take the driving test. It was essential I pass the test that morning, as I was to pick up my brand new beautiful '66 Mustang at six that evening. My brother-in-law, Bryan, had taken me to every car lot in the city until I found the car of my dreams—midnight navy blue metallic with light-blue, vinyl interior, sporty wheel covers, and 289 V-8 engine—all for two-thousand six-hundred dollars. I scrounged and saved five-hundred dollars to pay down and my monthly payments were sixty-six dollars.

Mama worried that I was getting in over my head. "I don't know, Delaney, that's an awful lot of money. Hope you know what you're doing.

I reassured her, "Don't worry, Mama.," but all the while I was thinking, *I'm not a child anymore. I'm almost eighteen, for crying out loud. I know what I can afford.*

However, my more immediate concern was passing that driver's test.

The written part of the exam was first, which I passed with flying colors. All I had to do was pass the driving part, and I would be home free, ready for my own tough new wheels.

Along with several others, my brother stood at the top of the hill overlooking the driver's testing course, observing as if they were spectators. A concession stand would've gone over in a big way— Cokes, peanuts, popcorn, cotton candy, anyone?

After the handsome examiner opened the door, he got inside, fastened his seatbelt, and said, "I'm ready when you are."

I was a nervous wreck as I placed the car's gear shifter into "R" and accelerated. We'd already gone several feet before I realized we were going in the wrong direction, and he scared the living daylights out of me when he yelled, "Stop!" I slammed on the brakes and put us both over on our heads.

He was as patient as he was cute, as he cleared his throat, took a deep sigh, and in a somewhat shaken voice, he said, "Okay, now… proceed, but this time in the forward direction, please." Underneath his breath, he made a sarcastic remark, "At least we know the brakes work in reverse."

The remainder of the test went downhill from there. I knocked down two of the five orange cones on the obstacle course, ran up on the curb and smashed into both front and rear cones during the parallel parking segment, and I stood him on his head while braking at a mock railroad crossing.

He said, "Whew, Miss James—it *is* Miss, isn't it?" A glance at my application confirmed his assumption correct, as he continued in a more relaxed tone, "Delaney, I'm really sorry, but you'll need to repeat the driving portion next week…"

"But…I have to get it *today*! I'm getting my new car tonight!" I really laid my soul out on the table, and he finally gave in—with two provisions:

Number one: If ever I saw a white, '65 Mercury convertible on the road, I would pull over to the side and let him pass.

Number two: That I go out with him, to which I agreed.

The next weekend we went to a fancy restaurant downtown and a movie afterward. Of course, we went in his car, and he drove.

I felt a wild rush of excitement that evening as I drove away from Harry White Ford in my gorgeous, brand new car. I was a genuine, bona fide citizen of working America, with my very own car-note!

I was on Cloud Nine, as I turned the radio to full volume and felt the power, both underneath the hood and within myself.

Womanhood—I have truly arrived—driving up in style!

CHAPTER XIV
THE LOST CHAPTER

Late August is typically one of the hottest times of the year in Georgia, but that particular Sunday was sweltering as I sat in my church's evening service. I wondered why God didn't provide air-conditioning in His house of worship. The very least He could have done was arrange for a much-needed rain shower to cool things off a bit.

I had practically grown up in that little Baptist church, and it had been an important part of my life since I'd been about eight years old, right after Daddy left us. A lot of young people my age went there, and it was like one big happy family.

I was thankful for so many things. I was happier than I had been in a long time. Everything was perfect in my life!

I tried to concentrate on the sermon, but I was preoccupied with the time, and glanced at my watch every few minutes. I had a date for later that evening after services, and the boy was to meet me at the street in front of the church.

It was my first date with Tommy and I was particularly excited about going out with him, because he had been so popular as an all-star football player for Forrester. He remained popular with all the girls, even though he graduated several years earlier. When I asked him about the rumors about his and Mary Beth's engagement to get married, he smirked and said, "No way—her and me?" I was glad to hear that, even though Mary Beth was the sister of one of my closest friends.

Since I had to work the next day I needed to be home by eleven-thirty, at the latest, so we planned to simply run by the Varsity and then take in a movie downtown.

I was pixie-petite in my favorite dress—the straight, white eyelet one that buttoned all the way up the front. My red heels and handbag matched the red belt, and my short, dark hair framed my oval face. I normally had a good tan by that time of the summer, but I was especially dark because I had just returned from several days in Daytona.

After church, I rushed down to the street, only to be disappointed because he was late. His loud, souped-up, toughest of cars drew attention in our direction, as he drove right up to me and came to a screeching halt, then raced his engine. With the radio blaring, he reached across the seat, threw open the door and said, "Hurry up and get in!"

I was utterly embarrassed and agitated by his crude display of behavior, but I excused him because of who he was. I jumped in, per his instructions, and slid all the way over next to him. I was surprised his car didn't have bucket seats with a console in the center like most of the other tough cars.

After he glanced over and gave me the once over, he grinned and said, "Man, you're looking tougher than hell tonight."

I responded. "Thank you."

We took off like a rocket, leaving tire marks on the pavement in front of the church. I didn't approve of his disrespect, but I remained quiet. I didn't want him to get mad at me or think I was square. The truth was, his car really did impress me.

He turned the radio down a few decibels before he said, "Hey, you know...it'd be closer and hell of a lot less trouble if we just went to the drive-in. What d'ya say?"

I thought, *Well, we could get something to eat and see a movie at the same time, eliminating the long drive downtown to the Varsity.* I agreed, so we went to the Star-Lite Drive-Inn theatre.

I wasn't born yesterday. I was fully aware that making out and heavy petting went on at the drive-inn. I'd been there many times with Richard, so I wasn't surprised when Tommy made his move.

However, I wasn't prepared for his crudeness as he reached behind the seat and pulled a beer out of a cooler that was in the back floorboard. He took a big gulp and burped, "Here. Want one?"

"No, thanks."

"Suit ya'self." He threw his head back and took a few more gulps. He guzzled one right after the other and tossed the empty cans out the window.

I had always detested the smell of beer, but I was trying to tolerate it—just that one night.

He was as smooth as glass but I could see right through his next move when he put his arm around me. He rubbed my upper arm with long, sensual strokes, up and over the shoulder and down to the elbow, brushing against the outside of my breast in a most obvious way. He was so handsome, strong, and forceful. No wonder he was so popular. I found him extremely exciting, if only he wasn't drinking so much!

He leaned over and kissed me on the ear, working his way around to my lips. He definitely knew his way around. I didn't know until that night, when he told me he had been drafted and would soon be leaving for boot camp. "Yeah, I leave next Sunday. Man, I really wish I'd called you sooner," as he started sliding his hand up my dress.

I pushed his hand away, and he said, "Okay, but come on, loosen up--take off that belt—it looks uncomfortable."

He was right. It was uncomfortable, so like a fool, I took it off.

He pulled me closer to him in such a way it felt awkward. He blew in my ear, and in a soft, sensual voice just a above a whisper, "You know how much you turn me on, don't you? I've had my eye on your tough little ass ever since the first time I saw you in your cheerleading uniform at a pep rally."

It excited me to hear someone like him say those things about me—to me—and I really felt sad that he was going away.

The beer smell seemed to dissipate as we were kissing and I got so aroused. He was sliding his hand up under my dress, again, and I felt inside as though I would explode! I knew what I was feeling wasn't love, but the chemistry between us made my hormones go crazy!

I suddenly came to my senses, "Don't. Stop."

"Okay. I won't stop."

"No! I mean it. Stop!"

He became angry, and his voice intensified, "You're nothing but a tease. Don't try to pull that innocent little virgin act on me!" He was getting rough.

"Please, don't…"

"What d'ya take me for? I know you went steady with that guy for a long time—don't try to convince me you haven't been putting out!"

His strength was scaring me as I pleaded, "Don't!"

"Aw, come on Baby, you know you want it. I can tell you're horny."

That's when I slapped him right across the side of his face. "I said *no*! And I used every ounce of my strength to push him off me.

"If you won't do it—I'll just take your ass home!"

That was music to my ears as I replied, "Fine!" Those awful things he said to me made me feel so cheap and like such a fool. I just wanted to get out of there and away from him. He was so drunk I was concerned, "Are you all right to drive?"

"Just shut up, Bitch, I can handle it!" He snapped with such a belligerent tone, I didn't say another word.

I was so ashamed. Was that the only reason he asked me out? I had been fooling myself, and I suppose protecting myself from the heartaches of love, since my breakup with Richard. I only dated boys with whom I felt safe—boys who were too good of buddies to even consider sex.

Boy, is this creep overrated, was my primary thought as he raced out of the drive-inn, throwing gravel from the spinning tires. It was suddenly amazing just how little the car impressed me. I would be thankful when I was back home, and that entire night was behind me.

But I noticed we weren't going home. "Where are we going?" He didn't answer.

He drove to the other part of town in an unfamiliar neighborhood. It seemed to be a big, dark park. We passed other cars parked there, where couples were making out.

"What are we doing here?

"What do you think we're doing here, bitch?" he snapped, as he pulled to a more secluded spot and parked the car. He turned out the headlights, and turned the radio to full blast.

"What are you doing?" The sound was ear-piercing so I reached across to turn the radio down.

He grabbed my arm, and before I could scream, he placed his other foul smelling hand over my mouth and held it there, pushing so hard he was hurting my jaw. "Now, go ahead and scream," he gritted, "Nobody'll hear you over the radio."

He then pushed his disgusting tasting mouth onto mine, as he grabbed my legs and pulled them around him, tearing my dress in the process.

The buttons down the front of my dress were ripped away, as he tore it open to expose my bra. Then he sucked on the exposed top part of my breasts, and bit them so hard, I thought I was bleeding. I pushed and fought, but I couldn't get a good swing at him. If I could just get a knee in his groin, but no matter how hard I tried, he was just too strong!

He tore my panties away from the elastic leg-band and shoved his hand up my dress and inside of me! He was hurting me. "Stop it!" I tried to push him off, but he was too powerful.

He forced himself inside me, penetrating in such a way that I cried out from the pain.

I felt cheap, and used—dirty and ashamed—but mostly afraid. He was so much bigger than me. The painful penetration lead to his immediate ejaculation, as he said, "God damn you—you'll learn—you don't get me all hot without doing it, you bitch!"

The stench and sticky mess was disgusting. Along with the pain and humiliation, I kept thinking, *Oh God! What would Mama say? Can Daddy see me?*

I cried afterward and he yelled, "Shut up, bitch! You know you wanted it as much as I did! I could tell!" He laughed at me. "You just wanted me to take it! Didn't you? That's what you like, ain't it?" He pulled a towel out from under his seat and threw it at me, "Here! Hurry up, clean up that mess—and get it off the leather before it dries!"

The tires squealed as we peeled out of the park and flew down the road headed home…finally.

He reached in the back and pulled out another beer. He was already so drunk the car weaved from one side of the road to the other.

I didn't say anything. I couldn't say anything. I was in shock. I never knew anything could be so painful…and humiliating!

The car jolted as we came to an abrupt, screeching halt in the driveway at the front of my house. Without a word, he reached across me, unlocked the door, and threw it open for me to get out. Just before the door closed, as if an afterthought, he said, "Oh yeah, thanks, Baby. You were great! We'll have to do it again, sometime."

I almost vomited on the driveway.

I didn't say goodnight or goodbye. He didn't offer to walk me to the door. I didn't want him to walk me to the door. One of the rocks grazed my ankle when the tires slung gravel as he backed out.

I was bruised on my legs, arms, and hips, my lip was busted, my breasts were aching, and I smelled badly. My clothes reeked of that awful odor, and I could still taste the beer from his mouth being on mine. I pulled together the front of my button-less dress the best I could, and I sneaked through the back door to avoid waking Mama.

Mama had gone to bed but she was till awake. Since Bud had married and moved out several years earlier, she and I lived there alone, so she never went to sleep until I was safely home, "Delaney, is that you?"

"Yes, ma'am."

"Don't forget to lock the back door."

I kept the calm in my voice, "Okay, Mama. Go on to sleep."

I went straight to the bathroom and turned on the radio, so she couldn't hear me vomiting in the toilet. I brushed my teeth over and over—several times—to get the taste of him out of my mouth. After I dropped my clothes to the floor, I stepped into the shower. The hot water was soothing and it felt so good to my bruises, as it ran down my back, even though it stung a little on my busted lip. It didn't matter what amount of soap I used or how much I scrubbed and rinsed, I couldn't wash away the filth—it was embedded in my mind. When I washed between my legs I saw blood in the water going down the drain and I thought,

No, it's not time for my period.

I couldn't stop crying. I was afraid he had done permanent damage or that I was hemorrhaging. I was so confused, I didn't know who to go to, or where to turn.

I got out of the shower, put on some fresh clothes, and slipped out the back door. I drove to a long stretch of road with a heavy growth of bushes and vines—a perfect place to dispose of all my torn, soiled clothes.

Then I just drove—anywhere, and yet no where. I drove over and sat in front of Richard's house, trying to get up the enough nerve to go to the door. It was after midnight.

Out of sheer desperation, I finally walked up to the door and knocked, but I couldn't explain to Richard as to why I was crying. He held me in his arms and tried to comfort me, but after a while, he became agitated, angry that I wouldn't confide in him. I wanted to tell him, but it was all too humiliating!

I broke away from his arms and said, "I'm sorry I bothered you." I didn't look back as I ran to my car and drove away.

My God, I'm so ashamed! I thought. *How could I let this happen?* I couldn't tell anyone. My brothers would surely have killed him, not that he deserved to live. I couldn't tell my sister or my mother because they would be so ashamed of me; besides, I always felt that I needed to protect Mama. I didn't know how she would react. It could cause her to have a heart attack—like Daddy—and I couldn't take losing her, too.

I couldn't go to the police. When they found out we'd been to the drive-inn first, and he told them his version of the evening, he'd make me look like a willing tramp.

No, I couldn't tell anyone.

And so I went home to the safety of my own bed.

I told my mother I had gone up the street to a friend's house, as an explanation of where I went so late that night.

I cried myself to sleep, completely exhausted. I explained the busted lip by saying that I ran into the door during the night.

* * *

The next morning I was relieved to discover the bleeding had stopped, eliminating the concern that I was hemorrhaging.

I went to work a few hours late. I told them I overslept. That morning I convinced myself that it was all just a horrible nightmare.

My co-workers and friends were very perceptive that day, as they commented that I wasn't myself. I avoided going to the cafeteria at lunchtime because that was when we always discussed our weekend dates. I had been so excited all that past week about my date with Tommy, so I knew they would want to hear all about it. For reasons, obvious only to myself, I surely didn't want to discuss it.

I was nervous, quiet, and kept to myself—and they were right— that wasn't at all like me.

When I got home from work that evening, Mama told me Tommy had called and he would call back later.

I wouldn't answer the phone that night, for fear it might be him. Though I didn't know what I was afraid of. He couldn't hurt me anymore than he already had, and he certainly wouldn't do anything to me over the phone.

When he called later that night, I told Mama to tell him I wasn't there and she didn't know when to expect me home. When she hung up, she asked, "Wasn't that the young boy you went out with last night? Why don't you want to talk to him?"

"Oh, I don't know. I guess I just didn't like him."

He continued to call over the next two nights, and I continued to be unavailable. I was thankful Mama was there to screen the calls. When he called her a "lying bitch," and slammed the phone down in her ear, she said, "Delaney, I think you're right in not wanting to talk to that guy—he's not very nice."

I thought that was quite an understatement, but I didn't say anything. I just shook my head in agreement and apologized for his rudeness.

* * *

That Thursday night I was talking on the phone to a girlfriend from work, when I heard a car in the driveway. I knew it wasn't Mama, since she was working until nine-o'clock that night, and not expected home for at least three more hours. I supposed it to be one of the neighbors.

Since it was still so hot, I left the front door open, thinking the screened porch was locked.

It was too late when I discovered I was wrong. I heard the squeak of the hinges as the door slowly opened. I really didn't think much about it. *It's probably one of my brothers. Besides, it's still daylight outside. Who would be fool enough to break into a house in broad daylight?*

It wasn't one of my brothers, and before I knew it, Tommy was standing in my living room. Startled at his sight, I asked, "What are you doing here?"

"Now, is that the way to greet somebody, after the other night?"

I didn't want my friend to hear, so I told her I'd call her later, and hung up the phone.

When I told him to "Get out of my house!" he acted as though he didn't hear me. Instead, he started walking through the house, asking questions, "Where is your sweet mother? Don't tell me she's not here. I was really looking forward to meeting the lying old bitch!"

He paced back and forth, like a hungry lion sizing up his prey. "I know you've been here every night I've called. Why wouldn't you answer my calls? I told you I'm leaving this Sunday. We don't have that much time to spend together."

He walked toward the bedroom that was just off the living room and said, "Is this your room? Is this where you and Richard always did it—when your mother was gone and you had the house to yourselves?"

God, how I hated him. I wished I had my neighbor's gun. His eyes belonged to the devil himself when he turned and reached for me, "Well, looks like we've got the house all to ourselves now. Let's go in there and do it right this time."

I backed away from him as he started toward me. "If you touch me I'll call the police!"

He picked up the phone and said, "Call the police? With what? You'll have to take it away from me, first! Come on over here and try to get it! Let's play rough, again."

I started to run out the front door, but he grabbed my arm and pulled me back to him, "You're not going *anywhere*! *Nobody* tells *me* no!"

He grabbed me by my hair and started kissing me on the neck, "Umm, you smell good, Baby. I'm gonna miss your little ass. Ya gonna miss *me*?"

I thought, *Is he crazy? We haven't dated but one time, and look what he did to me!* "NO! I'm not going to miss you! Are you crazy? I wish you were dead!"

He laughed and then he pulled my hair at the base of my neck, "You're lying! You know you want it again!"

I couldn't fight back the tears. He was hurting me.

"Now, get in there and..."

We heard the back door slam and a man's voice, "Delaney, are you in here?"

Thank God! It was my brother, Bud!

Tommy let me go and jumped back about three feet away from me, quietly instructing me to dry my eyes.

When Bud entered the room he could tell I had been crying, and I was more than a little shaken, "What's wrong?"

Tommy quickly stepped over close to me and put his arm around me, "Oh, she's just upset because I've been drafted and I'm leaving for boot camp this Sunday. She doesn't want me to go, but it's like I told her, 'I have to go and fight for my country.' That's the right thing to do. She's just gonna miss me, that's all. Ain't that right, Delaney?"

Bud said, "Oh, okay, well now, Delaney, he's right. He has to go if he's been drafted." I couldn't believe Bud started talking so casually to that bastard about his car, "Is that your Chevy out front? What is it, a '57?"

They talked about cars for ten minutes or so. Then Bud said, "I just came over to fix the toilet so I guess I'd better get started."

When he realized that Bud was likely to be there for a while, Tommy asked me, very nicely, "Delaney, would you like to run down to the Varsity with me?"

Trying to do so in such a way that Bud wouldn't detect anything was wrong, I replied, "No, thanks. I'm not feeling very well, and I need to wash my hair."

Then he asked me to go out with him the next night, which was Friday. I told him I already had a date but he was persistent, "How 'bout Saturday?"

I told him I had a date that night, too.

He reminded me, in front of my brother, "Baby, have you forgotten I'm leaving Sunday?"

I flashed him a defiant smile, "I'm sorry but I already promised those nights."

He then put his arm around me again, "Delaney, aren't you going to kiss me goodbye?" As he leaned over to kiss me, I turned my head the other way, and he kissed me on the cheek. My jaw was still sore from the other night, and I felt sick at the thought of him touching me. He waved as he backed out of the driveway and pulled away, "I'll call ya tomorrow!"

Bud commented, "He seems like a nice guy. How long have ya'll been dating?"

I told him we had only dated once. He shrugged and muttered, "Hmmm, seemed like there was more to it than just one date," as he turned and walked away.

I didn't respond. I felt nauseous as I went into the bathroom, to be sick in the toilet.

Bud heard me through the door and told me, "You'd better watch it—there's an early flu bug going around."

I was so thankful Bud came in when he did. The Lord only knows what would have happened, but that's probably why he sent Bud in the first place.

Tommy called several more times, and the last time he called, which was Sunday morning about nine-o'clock, he told Mama, "I'm sorry I ain't met ya yet. Delaney really wanted me to, but it'll have to wait 'til I come home on leave. Tell her I'll write and give her my mailing address."

A few days later I received a letter from him, but I threw it away, unopened.

* * *

I felt so relieved to know he was gone. The next morning I went to work feeling as though a big weight had been lifted off my shoulders.

I decided the best thing to do was pretend nothing had ever happened.

I wondered if some of those men and women I saw everyday at the Institute were patients in that place because of such nightmares. Nightmares that seemed so real they couldn't separate them from reality. Mama always told me not to dwell on bad dreams because they could come true, and I sure didn't want that one to come true. That's all it was—a horrible nightmare, that really didn't happen at all.

I did such a convincing job on myself—pretending it away—I consciously lost that night and the entire episode with Tommy.

I pushed that time into the darkest corner of my subconscious, as if it were a skeleton locked away in an attic's old trunk—where it would become a lost chapter in my life.

TUESDAY, JULY 23, 1984: CHESTNUT, GEORGIA DR. ROBINSON'S OFFICE, OAKWOOD INSTITUTE'S SATELLITE FACILITY

Dr. Robinson told me I was her favorite patient and one of the smartest women she'd ever known, to remember and write about things the way I did. I supposed she probably told all her patients the same things—just something she learned in Psychology 101.

Mama and Sis alternated driving me to my sessions with the doctor, so Kyle wouldn't lose time from work. I kept to myself and never went outside the house alone. Even on the Fourth of July when the family circus came up for the cookout and pool party, I stayed in my room, pulled the shades, turned the TV's volume to capacity, and watched a Three Stooges movie marathon on Channel 14. Mama tried to get me to come out and be with everyone, but Kyle said, "It's okay, Baby, if you're not ready."

He then brought lunch to the room and ate in there with me.

* * *

I didn't feel much safer inside, but it was as if I were less threatened there for some unknown reason.

I was compelled to change the looks of my indoor surroundings, so I stripped the paper from the walls and replaced the wallpaper throughout the main level of the house and part of the downstairs. I had to concentrate on hanging it straight and to align the edges so the patterns matched, and that was a good thing. My mind was focused on smoothing out the bubbles and wrinkles that formed underneath, but the wallpapering took a back seat to my assignment.

Whenever memories surfaced, I was drawn into them and the assignment became my obsession. I was compelled to remember and write.

I only wanted to remember the good times because they made me feel good and I enjoyed writing about them. But my memory had a mind of its own and forced me to face painful and sad times before rewarding me with more good ones.

Since April and the first pages of the assignment, a little girl had grown and developed into a young woman before my very eyes. I smiled and came close to laughing aloud at the times when she...I mistakenly thought I had reached womanhood. I was proud to write about the memories of that young person...until that last chapter. Pride was overthrown by shame.

Even though my memory allowed me to clearly see that she... that I was helpless against that bastard, I was unable to separate the things I saw from her feelings—my feelings. I despised that filthy bastard. He had taken a part of me to which he had no right. He was vile and evil to do so such a despicable thing, and I felt as though I had been raped by the very devil himself!

The painful sense of violation, along with the disgusting taste and smell of his hands and mouth on mine incorporated themselves into my nightmares, like a puzzle's missing pieces.

I was plagued by the questions, *Is this why I've lost my right mind? Have I repressed the memories of my encounter with the devil until now? Why did I repress them this long? And who opened the attic's truck—where I had locked them all away?* I decided that *my bad dreams must be caused by those things that happened such a long time ago.*

But I couldn't determine why, in my nightmares over these past months, I was always naked and frozen…and why was I in such a cramped space in my dreams? And who was the child I always heard screaming for his mama? Then I thought, *Maybe it was Sally's little boy. Maybe my sub-conscience had conjured him up in my dreams because of my sympathy and compassion for Sally and Sam through the years. But is it possible for the sub-conscience to do that?*

I was confused. There were still missing pieces to the puzzle.

* * *

Dr. Robinson read my latest addition and, after placing it on her desk, she asked, "Would you like to talk about it? Tell me how you feel about all this?"

I hesitated, "I—I really didn't want to bring it. I almost didn't. I was going to tell you I was sick and couldn't remember anything this week."

"Why?" she asked.

"Isn't it obvious? Because, I'm so ashamed." I answered. "She never told anyone about that night or Tommy. She—I mean I—I locked it all away. At least, I thought I did."

The doctor was concerned about how I kept referring to myself as "she" or "her," in our discussions. I didn't understand why she saw such a problem with that, as long as it made it easier for me to talk about things. I supposed she didn't care if it was hard or easy for me, as long as we continued our sessions twice a week and she got paid.

"But don't you see, Delaney? You can't just pretend something like that never happened."

"Why not?" I scoffed. "It's worked so far. I had forgotten all about it over all these years—until now. Now I feel guilty and ashamed all over again!"

"Why would you feel guilty and ashamed? It looked as if you were helpless and had no control over him. He was bigger and stronger than you."

"Yeah. I know, but…"

She continued, "So why should *you* have any guilt or shame?"

"I should never have gone to the drive-inn with him. I didn't know him that well, and I shouldn't have been so attracted to him in the first place."

"Let's talk about Tommy for a minute." She leaned forward. "It's been eighteen years since that happened. How do you feel about him today? What would you do if he were here right now? What would you say to him?

My answer came quickly. "I hate him so much—if I had a gun, I'd shoot him in the groin and then I'd blow the bastard's brains all over the floor and take pleasure watching him die. Just before he took his last breath, I'd spit in his face and say, 'There, you son-of-a-bitch…go back to hell where you belong!' Maybe if I could send his soul back to hell in exchange for my own, I'd be in my right mind again."

"Those feelings are perfectly normal, Delaney," she said, "and it's all right to talk about it and get the anger out of your system like this. But you know you would never carry those thoughts out…"

"Yes, I would—without blinking an eye! But I just want to lock all that away again, and forget I ever remembered. If I don't have the memories, there won't be any pain."

I needed to change the subject so I wouldn't have to talk about it anymore, and the painted walls in her office made a good enough deterrent, "Now *this* is *drab*—really boring."

"What are you talking about?" she asked.

"The walls. I'm talking about the walls. Why is it that all government building offices are painted this putrid color of baby's green-pea-spit-up green?"

She went along with this subject change. "Well, Delaney, it's obvious you're changing the subject and I have no idea as to how to answer your question, so why don't you tell me? After all, you're the decorator. What did you have in mind?"

I sized up the room. "First of all, I'd trim out the entire room with chair-rail molding. Then I'd wallpaper beneath the molding with a solid berry weave, and complement with a tasteful berry, navy and cream stripe above it."

"Sounds nice." She allowed me to continue rambling on.

"You have to be very careful with stripes, though. Don't want to be too hard on the eyes. Change the carpet to a nice cream or ivory—yeah ivory—that'd be nice. And finish out with a ceiling border—yeah a border. I see a simple pattern though. No, wait a minute. How about hunter green and berry? That'd be good, too…"

"Delaney, calm down. You're getting a little carried away. It all sounds beautiful, but you and I both know this office will always be county property, and so these green walls will probably never change. Now, let's get back to Tommy."

"I *told* you, *doctor.* I want to lock all of it away again, and forget I ever remembered this chapter! Here, let me have it back and I'll tear it up and throw it away." I reached across to take it off her desk.

"That's all right, Delaney. If you feel that strongly, I'll tear it up and throw it away for you." She placed it out of my reach. "We'll discuss it when you're ready."

I trusted her at her word, but I had no way of knowing at the time that she wouldn't tear it up, nor throw it away. She simply placed it in my folder and locked it in her file cabinet. I suppose she figured I've never find out about it, and what I didn't know wouldn't hurt me.

Nonetheless, I became more relaxed with her after that afternoon. The fact that she didn't push the issue and preach about how it was part of my past, and how I had to face it, led me to think, *Maybe she's beginning to understand me, after all.*

* * *

It was 3:00 and the session had ended so I stood up and was almost to the door when the doctor said, "Oh, wait a minute, Delaney. I have a card here for you. It's from Mo."

She handed me a lavender envelope and I noticed the return address was New York City, New York. Inside was a card from Mo and a photograph of her holding a baby. There was a younger, attractive, dark-haired woman sitting next to her. Mo was smiling bigger than I could ever describe, and the baby looked to be a healthy-sized newborn in a pink gown and booties.

The note on the card read:

Dear Delaney,

How do you like my beautiful new granddaughter? At 10 lb 4 oz, she was the biggest baby in New York General. My daughter named her Linda Delaney. I hope you don't mind us borrowing your name. I always thought it was so pretty, just like you. Speaking of which, Doc Terri tells me you're going in for plastic surgery next week. I just know they're going fix you up and you'll be just like new. I wish I could be there and see you when you get that old ugly scar gone.

Since I hadn't never taken no vacation in my twenty years with the county, I'm going to stay up here till the end of the year and help Marlene with the baby. Marlene's my daughter. Did I ever tell you how much you remind me of her? That's her in the picture with me and Little Delaney. If you're ever up this way, stop by and see us. There's nothing but Yankees up here in New York, and they sure talk funny—you know, like Doc Terri. Take care of yourself, and I'll be praying for the surgery to be a success.

Love, Mo

I smiled at the difference in the sizes of Big Mo and little Delaney, though the baby wasn't exactly tiny at that birth weight. But I would've expected any grandbaby of Big Mo's to be bigger than life.

A warm feeling came over me as I placed the card back in its envelope. I thought about her and all the times she called me "Little Girl," and doted over me, treating me like such a baby during those months while I was in Oakwood. I always got aggravated at her when she did that, but I felt as if she were the only kind person in the place, and seeing her picture made me miss her.

I even found myself envying little Delaney, as I thought, *Hmmm, now Big Mo has a real little baby girl to dote over.*

CHAPTER XV
BEST FRIENDS AND LOVERS

When mid-September rolled around it meant there was only one more week of summer. But that year, Mother Nature relentlessly squeezed every ounce of unbearable heat and humidity out of the season's last remaining days. That Monday afternoon it was so hot in Atlanta, I could have fried an egg on the sidewalk.

I didn't have to work late so I left the office at the regular time of five-thirty. All day I had frozen half to death in the office from the air conditioning, but it felt as if I opened the door to a blast furnace when I left the building, and my car was like an oven. The Mustang had everything—everything but air conditioning, so after working in a nice, cool place all day, the heat really got to me on the way home in the steamy afternoons.

I stopped by McDonald's on the way home for an ice cold Coke, and as I was leaving the parking lot I heard a horn blow. It was coming from the little maroon Corvair behind me. I glanced in the rear view mirror and the two guys in the car waved. I recognized the one of the passenger side to be Paul, the fiancé of a girl I knew from school, so I smiled and waved.

I pulled onto the street and turned right, heading for K-Mart. So did they. And they continued to follow me all the way into the store's parking lot.

After parking several spaces away, they got out and approached me while I was still inside my car.

I laughed at the one on the right, when he almost stepped on the flattened out remains of a cat, who by its appearance and odor, had met its Maker there on the pavement a few days earlier.

We all began to laugh about that, and as they came closer, I realized I had made a mistake! Neither of them was Paul; in fact, neither looked even vaguely similar to Paul! The one I mistook for him and the one who had the close call with the cat were one in the same. His name was Kyle, and the closer he got, the better he looked.

I apologized and explained about the mistaken identity. His friend, Jake, went in the store and left Kyle outside with me. I remained in the car.

After only a few minutes with Kyle, his sense of humor was revealed in such a way I forgot the reason I had gone to K-Mart in the first place.

The evening's golden sunset danced off the highlights in his dark hair and reflected in his bluer-than-blue, periwinkle eyes, while it burned an unforgettable image in my mind that made direct contact with my heart. He was tall, but not too tall, slender, but not too, and I was captivated by his smile. His teeth were so white the American Dental Association would have applauded their perfection.

My heart raced out of excitement when he asked for my phone number. However, I was disappointed when he explained, "Oh, I— I'm not asking for myself. I—I'm asking for Jake. He wants your number, but he's too shy to ask for it."

I smiled, "I don't give my phone number to just anybody, y'know."

"Yeah, but Jake…he's all right. He's just bashful. I guarantee you, if I wasn't going steady, I'd be asking for myself and to heck with Jake."

I may have been a little crazy, but Kyle impressed me as a nice guy—the kind I'd like to know better. Besides, he was irresistibly cute, and his jokes made me laugh, so I gave him my number.

On the other hand, Jake didn't appeal to me at all. He didn't have the wit and personality to compare to Kyle, not to mention he had an awfully long neck with an oversized Adam's apple…and he smoked.

* * *

Later that evening, I was pleasantly surprised to receive a phone call, but not from the right one. The call was from Jake, and he asked me to go to a birthday party that Friday night. I accepted the date for the lack of anything else better to do.

While we were talking, Kyle came into Jake's room and got on the phone to tell me another joke. I never knew anyone with such a sense of humor and so many funny stories.

He made me laugh so hard Mama came in to make sure I was all right. My side ached the next morning from laughing so much during the two-hour-long phone conversation with that nut.

* * *

Kyle developed the habit of calling me every evening that week. He asked me out for that Friday night to go to the first East Atlanta High football game of the season, and then to a party afterward. Before thinking, I said, "Sure!"

Well, what was a girl to do? It just wasn't fair, to be plagued with two dates for the same evening, with boys who were each other's best friend. Besides, Kyle knew I already had a date with Jake for that night. It wasn't fair of him to put me in that position.

After much soul searching I decided to do the right thing—the only thing—what any red-blooded American girl with the same problem would do. I told Jake a little white lie—something about baby sitting—and I went out with Kyle.

Kyle was there promptly at six-thirty, a quality I simply despised in a man since I was never ready on time. After all, it takes time for a girl to become picture perfect.

He was driving a nice, fairly new-looking, little white foreign car. It wasn't exactly tough but it was cute.

We arrived at the game, where we sat behind who I later discovered to be Jake's sister. I'll always believe Kyle planned that.

After the game we drove over to that party. Little did I know it was the same birthday party I had cancelled out on with Jake. My jaw dropped when I saw him there. I felt like the proverbial cat that swallowed the canary.

Kyle reassured me it was all right so we went on to enjoy the party.

I mentioned I hadn't eaten dinner yet, so Kyle suggested, "Wanna go grab a hamburger or something?" I later discovered the "or something" was what he had in mind.

We excused ourselves and went upstairs to get my things.

He walked over to help me with my jacket, and before I knew what hit me, he wrapped his arms around me and I found myself in his embrace. I couldn't catch my breath as our eyes met and he moved even closer. His lips were soft and moist, with a warmth and tenderness about them. I closed my eyes and took it all in, while a sensual force of energy raced throughout every inch of my body, from the top of my head to the bottoms of my feet. I floated off the floor by at least two feet, during the longest and most perfect kiss I had ever encountered. I never wanted it to end! He was passionate, and yet so gentle and sensitive. We'd known each other less than a week and kissed only that once, but I felt as though we were meant to be together.

Afterward, we just looked into one another's eyes—speechless. There was no need to say anything. We had generated enough electricity between us to supply the entire city of Atlanta.

I felt safe and comfortable with Kyle, as if we had known each other forever. It wasn't at all like the way I felt about the boys that I knew were just friends. I was genuinely attracted to this guy. I told myself, *Delaney, look out for this one. You could fall hard and be hurt all over again. For God's sake, take it slow!*

We left the party, but by the time we reached McDonald's it was after eleven and they were closed. So we went to the nearby Huddle House, where I ordered the most expensive thing on the menu—filet mignon. It wasn't a meal to write home about but, then of course, waffles were their specialty, not steak. Kyle claimed he had already eaten and so he only ordered a Coke. I had no way of knowing at the time that he couldn't afford to feed us both—not with my expensive taste. My meal, alone, probably set him back about three-fifty, and that wasn't including the tip.

From there we went to a quiet place, where we parked the car and sat there until three-thirty in the morning. We just talked about anything and everything. When he tried to kiss me I avoided the subject by encouraging his jokes and funny stories, and by utilizing my specialty—talking ninety miles an hour about nothing at all.

The truth was, I was avoiding falling for the guy. I didn't need to get serious, but what I did need was a good time and a best friend who could make me laugh. Kyle fit the bill, and in the interim he helped me forget about Richard.

When he asked me out for the next evening, I told him he would need to come inside the house and explain to my mother why we were three-o'clock getting home.

Mama didn't like my being out that late—not even a little bit. "Delaney James, where in the world have you been 'til this hour of the morning?"

I didn't have a chance to answer before Kyle spoke up, "Mrs. James, I'm sorry we were out so late. The time just got away. I give you my word, it will never happen again. Please don't stay mad at us."

"All right, but I think it's time to call it a day—or night—don't you?" He really impressed her by being such a man and coming inside to apologize in that way. And he really scored points when he asked, "Mrs. James, may I have permission to take Delaney out tomorrow night?"

* * *

Saturday evening he was there early, again. Lord how I hated that. He would simply have to learn the hard way. When we set a date for seven, don't be there before seven-fifteen, or he would just have to sit and wait for me to get ready!

That evening I was really impressed by his tough little MG Midget sports car, as I thought, *Now this is more like it.* But "Where's the little white foreign car?"

"Oh, that's my mom's car."

We had a great time at Harold's Bar B Que. He remembered I had said it was my favorite BBQ place. Afterward, we just rode around, talked, and, of course, laughed.

He asked me out again for that next afternoon. "You wanna go for seafood tomorrow after church?"

He had my number, all right. He knew he could get my attention by mentioning good food. "Sure, seafood's my favorite."

* * *

Sunday he drove up in a '61 Ford Star-liner and explained, "The MG's my sister's. This is *my* car."

I would never criticize his car, but a simple description should provide a clear enough picture. It was red, (using the word loosely, as it was the faded color the sun turns a five year old red car of any kind, especially one that had never been garaged at night, nor felt a drop of wax). There was a slight tear in the interior on the passenger side, strategically placed so that to avoid sitting on the tear, I had to move to the center, right up next to Kyle.

The dash appeared as though it had exploded, so I asked, "What happened?"

"Aw, every now and then the damn radio won't come on so I have to hit the dash with my fist. I guess it was too cold one morning last winter and I hit it so hard it cracked. I know it doesn't look very good—but the radio still has a good sound."

I thought, *Surely this good-looking, easy-going, crazy, witty, fun-to-be-with guy doesn't have a temper!*

After a turn of the ignition key to fire up the engine, the ominous, sputtering sound beneath the hood evolved into a gun-shot-sounding cough, and a blast of black smoke bellowed from the rear. Once that was out of its system and the car's idle settled down to normal, Kyle reassured me, "Does that sometimes…just needs a tune-up."

Then with a routine punch of the dash, the radio blared and Kyle sang along with Jim Croce, "If I could save time in a bottle…the first thing that I'd like to do…is save every day like a treasure and then…again…I could spend them with you." His voice blended right in with Jim's, and he smiled when I commented, "I love that song."

I smiled, "Yeah, me too."

He put the car in reverse and his forearm brushed against my shoulder when he laid his arm on the back of my seat. His slightest touch and the smell of his cologne set goose pimples all over me. "What kind of aftershave are you wearing?"

"English Leather." He leaned in closer to give me a better smell.

I should have recognized it because that's what Richard always wore, but I never remembered it smelling so good.

As we backed out and drove away, we left Mama standing on the front screened porch, waving goodbye with one hand and covering her mouth with the other. She almost disappeared, coughing her way through the heavy cloud of black smoke from the car. We nicknamed that car the '007 car,' in that it left a smoke-screen behind us wherever we went.

It was that very afternoon that confirmed what I had suspected all along. I knew, right then, without a shadow of a doubt—Kyle's the one. That was a fact, and even if I wanted to fight it, I was powerless to the truth.

He was the one I would dream about at night—the one I had *always* dreamed about—as I imagined sharing life's everything with him. I was in love with him, for himself alone, and I knew it was the real thing this time because I was certainly not influenced by his car. It was a completely new experience in that he stirred up new emotions in me I never knew existed.

I had only known Kyle for one week, but the feelings filled my heart in such a way there was no room left to miss Richard. He was exactly what the doctor ordered, as this new man in my life enabled me to forget the past. I looked forward to sharing a future with him as I loved him more than I had ever loved anyone—ever! And he loved me, too. He just wasn't totally aware of that fact…yet.

It seemed odd how we didn't need to be kissing or touching one another to feel the electricity. When I saw his smile and looked into his periwinkle blue eyes, or simply heard his voice over the phone it would create sparks and light up my world.

I had never been happier. My life was perfect!

I was certain the flames of first degree love were destined to burn forever, and we would become best friends and lovers for life.

CHAPTER XVI
ALL DRESSED UP AND
NOWHERE TO GO

Lunch with my friends where I worked and a crisp and clear sunny afternoon made the twelfth day of October and my eighteenth birthday absolutely perfect. I was thrilled when I received a record album by the Mamas and the Papas from my bosses and was told to go home a couple of hours early.

I cleared my desk and was about to leave when the florist delivered the most gorgeous flowers. I plucked the card from its plastic holder and smiled as I thought, *They're beautiful, but Kyle didn't have to do this.* The card read: "Happy Birthday to the best looking eighteen-year-old woman I know. I got two tickets to see Georgia and Alabama play this Saturday over in Athens. Hope you can go. Love, Brad."

Brad? I've never even dated him. He was the aide for Unit A and one of the guys I ate lunch with every day. I couldn't believe he waited all those months before asking me out. I thought he was cute and I had a secret crush on him since the first time I saw him. Under different circumstances I would've been jumping up and down. But

I was going with Kyle, and Brad knew that. After all, that's all I had talked about for a month.

On the way out I stopped by to thank him for the flowers and decline his invitation to the game. He said, "I know you think you've met Mr. Perfect, but you can't blame a guy for trying."

His words echoed in my mind as I thought, *Can't blame a guy for trying? Why the heck did he wait so long to try? Huh, they always want the ones who aren't available.* Over the months I had seen Brad's thirst for challenge where girls were concerned, but he would have to quench his thirst with someone else. I had taken myself off the market since Kyle was in my life.

* * *

Kyle hadn't mentioned anything about going out, so I figured he would just come over and we would spend time together at my house. I couldn't help wondering what he had bought for my birthday present...*a ring, maybe*? We had only dated a month, but I had no doubt he was the one for me, so I didn't consider it unusual to hope for such a gift.

I fought the afternoon traffic, dodging in and out of lanes to rush home in time to get dressed. For a change, I would be ready when Kyle arrived.

My mother was working that night, so she wasn't there to cook dinner. Scrambled eggs, grilled cheese sandwiches and tomato soup were the only things I knew how to cook, so I planned that Kyle and I would grab a hamburger at McDonald's.

I glanced at the clock and began to worry, *It's 6:00 and I haven't heard a word from him since this morning's phone call. I wonder what's keeping him?*

I felt relieved when I heard a car outside and then a knock of the door. *Ah, there he is.*

But I was mistaken.

It was one of my closest friends, Randy. He greeted me as he usually did with a brotherly squeeze and a peck on the cheek. "Happy Birthday, babe. Feel any different?"

Before he gave me a chance to answer he embraced me again, but in a less brotherly fashion. I was shocked when he rubbed his hands up my back and down around my bottom, finishing off with a firm pat on my rump, "You feel great to me! Here's a little something I picked up for you." His gift for me wasn't wrapped, but rather in a brown paper sack from Western Auto.

"Thanks, Randy, but you shouldn't have." I reached in the sack and pulled out a flat, round can. "Oh, gee..Turtle Wax." I hoped the disappointment didn't show, as that wasn't exactly the sort of gift that made me light up and get overly excited. "Thanks, I—I really need this."

I hugged his neck and went to give him a thank-you kiss on the cheek, but I was surprised when he turned his head and kissed me dead center—not just *on* the mouth but *in* the mouth! We had never kissed like that before! We were just friends, and friends weren't supposed to use tongues when they kissed. It felt so awkward, as if I had kissed my own brother in the mouth. I pushed him away, "Randy! Good grief! What'd you go and do that for?"

"I—I've always wanted to, and, well, you're eighteen now. It wasn't that bad, was it?"

The way I wiped my mouth with the back of my hand answered his question adequately enough. Embarrassment exploded in a brilliant crimson all over his face and it was the first time I ever saw his stutter. "It—it's your birthday. It—it was just a birthday kiss. Don't get all fr—freaked out over it."

He looked at his watch and asked, "Wanna go to Pizza Inn?"

I could tell he wanted to change the subject, "Gee, I can't. I'm waiting for Kyle."

"Oh yeah. I forgot about him. Maybe some other time."

I smiled, "Sure, but thanks for asking."

I had never seen him so uncomfortable around me, but he was mature—five years older than me—so he understood. After all, we were only friends. Actually, Randy was more like a big brother, only better, because we got along so well—all the time. We never argued or disagreed about anything.

He went to the bathroom, and when he came out he made a phone call. I was nervous, thinking Kyle might be trying to call. I tossed the can of wax up in the air and caught it a few times then I read the label, "Turtle Wax for a lustrous shine." I wondered, *Is this the best he could do for my birthday?*

I supposed the gift was the type of thing a guy might give a girl when there were no further intentions, other than close friendship.

I thought about how close we were and remembered the previous summer, when we were taking his boat to the lake with a group of friends. He invited me to stay overnight since we were leaving so early the next morning. It was all very innocent, but when I told Mama I was staying with a friend, I didn't specify which friend. She wouldn't have understood, nor approved. For that matter, neither would anyone else in my family. The plans were for me to sleep in the guest room. Besides, I was sleeping in shorts and T-shirt.

During the night, out of nowhere came unexpected, high winds, thunder and lightning, and heavy rains typical of summer storms in the South. Typical or not, I was frightened, and my fright intensified when lightning struck a nearby transformer and the power went out and I screamed, "*Randy!*"

"Stay where you are, Delaney. I'm coming." I soon saw the beam from his flashlight rounding the corner, "Come on back to my room. You can sleep in there with me."

"Okay." I knew I'd be completely safe with my friend, so I didn't hesitate to follow him. I slid next to him in bed, pulled up the covers and stretched them tightly, all the way to my chin. He kissed me on the forehead and whispered, "Okay, now relax and think about what a good time we're going to have tomorrow."

I rolled over on my side, facing the opposite direction, and fell asleep with his arm draped over me, as if to protect me from anything that might go bump in the night.

That next morning at his house, I awoke to beautiful sunshine and the smell of bacon frying in the kitchen. Randy had showered, dressed, and was cooking breakfast so it would be ready when the rest of the group arrived.

He stuck his head inside the bedroom door and said, "Wake up, sleepy-head. Better get up and get ready before the gang gets here. I left a washcloth and some towels on the bench outside the bathroom.

He had already set the table by the time everyone arrived, and he acted as if I had only been there a few minutes. He never let on that we had spent the night together, much less slept in the same bed, even though we both knew nothing happened between us that night.

* * *

I thought about all the nights Randy and I talked about my last date, or my heartache for Richard, and most recently, how I had met and fallen in love with Kyle. Over the past several years I had talked to him about all sorts of things…the kinds of things you talk about with your closest friend. He was always there to cheer me up when I was down, and he knew he could count on me, too.

I smiled when I remembered all the times Randy and I went to the drive-inn and sat on the hood of the car, leaning back on the windshield while we watched the movie and ate popcorn or hot dogs and fries. I always laughed when he acted as if he was coming on to me, but should I have taken him more seriously?

* * *

203

Now, here it was approaching six-thirty on the night of my eighteenth birthday and Randy was tying up the phone so Kyle couldn't get through if he was trying to call me. I thought he would never get off the phone and when he did, I thanked him again for thinking of me, and invited him over on Saturday to help me try out my new car wax. Then I kissed him on the cheek, gave him a big hug, and rushed him out the door. After waving goodbye I stepped back inside the house and closed the door, thinking, *I sure am lucky to have such a great best friend...even though his taste in gifts leaves a lot to be desired.*

* * *

Now it was after 6:30 and still no word from Kyle. I didn't want to wait around all night, so I was forced to do the unthinkable—the unforgivable.

Phoning a boy for a date was considered unladylike in those days. However, a woman had to do what a woman had to do, especially a newly arrived eighteen-year-old woman who couldn't afford to tarnish her image by staying home alone on her birthday.

So I picked up the receiver and called him. When the line was busy I dialed and redialed for five minutes straight, until it finally rang and his brother Howard answered.

"Hello, may I please speak to Kyle?" I asked, trying not to sound too eager.

It seemed forever before Kyle said, "Hello."

"Hi. It's Delaney. I—I just wanted to know what you're doing."

"Well, I—I..."

I noticed a sound of hesitation in his voice, so I just blurted it out, "Aren't you coming to see me on my birthday?" The few seconds of silence that followed seemed like hours, as I thought, *My God, what have I done? I've overstepped my boundaries. That's what I've done...*

But then he responded, "Sure I am. When is your birthday?"

My immediate thoughts were, *Wait just a minute, here! I'm certain he knows today's my birthday. I've told him so many times, he couldn't have forgotten! Could he?*

Rather than snap at the thought of his forgetting, I maintained my cool, "You're just messing around with me, right? You know today's my birthday." Then I thought, *It doesn't matter,* as I suggested, "Since you're not busy, you can come on over now."

He hesitated and stammered until he got up the nerve to say, "I can't. I—I already have a date."

"What?" My cool, ladylike behavior suddenly turned into a fit of anger, as the green-eyed monster saw red and I turned into a raging bull. "Well, cancel it and be over here by seven-thirty or I never want to see you again!" *Oh shoot. I didn't mean that...*

Just as I was about to apologize, he said, "Okay, let me make a phone call and I'm on my way."

I really hated to be that way, but it was my eighteenth birthday, and that only comes around once in a lifetime.

I hung up the phone feeling pretty proud of myself for standing my ground.

* * *

I knew we'd go in the Mustang and there were some files in the back floorboard, so around seven-fifteen I went outside to clean it out. I was leaning into the back seat when I heard a blaring radio and a car raced up the driveway, slinging gravel in all directions. Before I could turn around to see who it was the car came to a screeching stop next to me. "Surprise, Baby. Did you miss me?"

Why would a bastard like Tommy think I'd miss him, after what he did to me? I kept my composure, "What are you doing here?"

"I'm home on leave. I told you boot camp only lasted six weeks." He got out of his car and when he slammed the door of that white '57 Chevy and walked around the front of it, I wondered how I could ever have been so impressed by him and that car.

He sauntered toward me with his arms open, "Aren't you gonna give me a welcome home kiss?"

I took my car-door and pushed it into his chest, then I started to run but he grabbed me by the shoulder of my sweater, jerked me back and threw me against the car.

He just laughed. "Is that a way to treat a man in uniform?"

When he forced his mouth on mine I bit down on his bottom lip and raised my knee between his legs, but he was too close and I wasn't tall enough to get a good shot at his crotch.

"You want it rough again?" he shouted.

Mr. Echols' hunting dogs were barking and making all kinds of racket. I wished they could've jumped their pen's fence just that once.

"Stop, Tommy. Please! I don't want..."

The ground rumbled and echoed when a shotgun went off—*Pow! Pow!* And a man's deep voice blasted, "Get away from her, boy!" Mr. Echols stood there in all his brawn and glory, shotgun in one hand while he held his hunting dogs back by their leashes in the other. They were all chomping at the bit to sink their teeth into Tommy. And so was Mr. Echols, "Go on now, I said, 'Get away from her!'"

Tommy held his hands in the air and backed away from me, but when I ran onto the back porch and inside the house, he put his hands down and said, "Why don't you mind your own business, old man? You wouldn't shoot a man in uniform—that's shipping out to Vietnam in another month—would you?"

"Damn Straight I would. Now get on outta here," and he shot into the air again, *Pow!*

Tommy hurried back around to get into his car. Before he got in, he beat the Chevy with his bare fist. *Bam! Bam!* "This is YOU, Bitch! Every time I hit it, it's YOU!" *Bam!* He pounded it with such force he made three dents in the hood, and that made him even madder.

Mr. Echols shot once again and bellowed, "Boy, if you don't want this gun up your ass you'll be gettin' on outta here! And if I ever see you around here again, I'm callin' the police!"

Tommy jumped into his car, slammed the door and raced his engine before he put the car in reverse.

I heard Kyle drive up, so I yelled "Thanks, Mr. Echols! Thank you so much!"

I straightened my clothes and hair before I ran to greet Kyle at the front door.

* * *

Kyle entered the living room and asked, "Whose car is that outside?"

Tommy blew the horn on his way out of the driveway, and Kyle thought I had just rushed a secret lover out the back door while he was coming through the front. And I let him go right on thinking it—it served him right—as I felt a perverted sense of pleasure watching his blue eyes turn that funny shade of green. I was so glad to see him and feel his arms around me; I wanted our embrace to last forever.

He apologized for not bringing a gift, promising to make it up to me. We spent a quiet night together, as we went out to dinner and to a movie afterward. Little did he know, as far as I was concerned spending the evening with him was as good, if not better than any birthday gift all the money in the world could have bought.

* * *

More pleasant thoughts took over from there, *So this is what it feels like to be eighteen years old!* I had wanted to be eighteen ever since I could remember. It felt great and I was unbelievably happy and in love.

Since I had met Kyle, it seemed as though my life was becoming even more perfect with each passing day.

If the past month with him had all been a dream, I asked God to please turn off my alarm—or unplug my clock—so I would never have to wake up.

CHAPTER XVII
HALLOWEEN'S NIGHTMARE

The Friday night after my birthday we went to the Southeastern Fair. The assorted concession stands with candied apples, corndogs, popcorn and cotton candy became the main events, as we stopped by all of them. We also went into both the white and black girlie shows. Since I had never been in one at all, either was a novelty to me. Joanie was right. They do take off all their clothes. I was embarrassed, so I asked Kyle to take me back outside, but I guess I had no one to blame but myself.

I was relieved that Kyle had no desire to ride the Greyhound. At least he didn't mention he wanted to ride and I sure wasn't going to bring it up. That was one more thing to add to the list of reasons I loved him so much.

* * *

Over the past several weeks since Kyle and I had been dating I discovered he was a trivia buff and a movie freak. We saw every movie worth seeing, and some that weren't. A movie wasn't complete without a big box of popcorn and a large Coke, so Kyle got to know the concession stand workers on a first name basis.

One evening toward the end of October we went to a movie at the Thunderbird Drive-Inn. That particular night the feature movie was Cleopatra, with Elizabeth Taylor and Richard Burton, and it was an exceptionally long movie.

When Kyle came back from the concession stand his arms were loaded down with hotdogs, French fries, popcorn, and Cokes. It looked as if he were going to feed an army.

Throughout my life I was accused of having a thimble-sized bladder, and that night I ran a path between the car and the restroom. Normally that was embarrassing when I was on a date, but Kyle and I just laughed about it.

When we finished our junk-food feast, we sat quietly, engrossed in the drama of the movie. Kyle commented on the costumes and the amount of budget for the movie versus the gross profits. He always knew all those trivial facts, but since I didn't have the vaguest idea about it myself, he could have been feeding me a line of bull for all I knew.

I always felt so safe with him, not the least bit threatened. I snuggled closer when he coiled his arm around me. Those past several weeks it seemed I stayed tired, and I almost dozed off with my head on his shoulder.

But then I felt the sparks again. During what started as a simple kiss, our feelings began to get out of control. All our senses were lost to desire—the desire for our feelings to completely dominate our actions.

We were almost to the point of no return, when the memory of that awful night in August with Tommy flashed through my mind, and I felt the shame all over again. *He'll know I'm not a virgin. I can't let him know. He'll think I'm trash!*

I jumped up, tears rushing from my eyes, as I tried to explain, "I'm sorry. I just can't. I—I had a bad experience once."

That was all I needed to say. He didn't ask me to go into details. "Okay, it's all right. Don't cry."

I could discuss most anything with him, as a best friend, but I couldn't bring myself to discuss that bastard and what he did to me. I was too ashamed.

He was there to humor me when I needed it, and offer moral support when I needed that, too. So he accepted my explanation, however frustrated he might have been, revealing a side of him I really admired—a side of true compassion.

That night was awkward for both of us, and he never mentioned it again, but continued to accept and respect my feelings toward sex. He didn't rush the matter with me, and because there were no pressures, I felt comfortable knowing that we wouldn't have sex— not until I was ready. We both knew it was inevitable, but only when the timing was right.

* * *

With the warmer temperatures, indicative of the traditional Indian Summer that graces Georgia in the fall, I had been feeling somewhat sluggish. I attributed it to the few pounds I had gained since the end of the summer. I hadn't been as active, and I developed the habit of bringing candy bars back to my desk from breaks. And Kyle wasn't helping matters taking me out to eat all the time and the candy and popcorn at the movies.

Once I ate a pack of crackers and Coke in the morning the stomach queasiness would settle down. I became pre-occupied with my weight.

I went to a so-called "weight-loss specialist," to whom I paid sixty dollars for shots three days a week and a supply of diet pills. I became very nervous all the time—and nauseous.

The diet program made me feel so bad I thought I would just starve the weight off instead, alleviating the shots, diet pills, and expenses. I soon discovered that idea to be as dumb as it actually was when I almost passed out one afternoon at work that last week of October.

I spoke with one of the resident nurses at work ad she explained, "The weight gain may be caused by a female hormonal imbalance." She advised me to consult a gynecologist, so I flipped through the Yellow Pages and called a nearby gynecologist to schedule an appointment.

"Hello. O.B.G.Y.N.," the voice on the phone answered.

"Hello. I'd like to schedule an appointment with one of the doctors for a checkup," I said, hesitantly.

"Have you seen any of our doctors before?"

"No, ma'am."

"Do you think you're pregnant?" she inquired.

"Oh, no ma'am. I think I may have a hormonal imbalance," I responded positively. "I just haven't felt so good and I've been a little sluggish lately."

"Are you late?"

"Late?" I asked.

"Your period…is it late?"

I stopped and thought, *I've never been exactly twenty-eight to thirty days between menstrual cycles, but, now that she mentions it, I haven't had a period since the first week in August.* After I told her, she said, "We can probably work you in Friday afternoon, the 31st, at one-thirty. You'll be seeing Dr. Bradford."

I felt relieved to have scheduled the appointment so early. I only had to wait three days before getting to the bottom of the weight gain and rotten feeling.

* * *

I had some time off coming to me, so I left at lunch for my doctor's appointment and planned to take the remainder of the day off. I decided I needed the break.

When I walked into the doctor's office the clock on the wall said one-twenty-five. I was early for a change. The sign next to the receptionist's window instructed patients to *"Sign In Please."* I added my signature to the long list of names and the receptionist asked if I were a new patient, as she handed me a form to complete.

"Yes, I'm here to see Dr. Bradford."

I felt a little strange when, like the nurse on the phone she asked, "Miss James, are you pregnant?"

As I answered, "No ma'am," she gave me a paper cup with my last named taped on it and instructed me, "Please void in this and leave it on the shelf in the ladies room." Anticipating my next question, she then directed me, "It's the first door to the right."

I was amazed at the number of pregnant women in the office. Of course, the doctor was a female specialist so what should I have expected? But there were so many!

There was one young girl who was obviously close to delivery time. She had with her another child about eighteen months old. The child had a runny nose, encrusted dirty face, and a soiled diaper that stunk to high heaven, and was so heavy with moisture it drug down between his knees.

My first thought was *How pathetic for this little baby to be dependent on such a negligent mother.* Then I took a good look at the mother. Pregnant as she was, she couldn't be any older than I was at the time. A lump stuck in my throat.

When she was called into the office, I overheard a few of the remaining ladies talking about her as if she were dirt: "You know we support that baby, don't you?"

Another one chimed in, "That's right. As tax payers, part of our money goes to welfare to encourage such gutter babies as that. These young tramps who don't know any better than to mess around and get themselves in that shape—then it's up to us to support them."

And yet another added her two cents worth, "That's right. I think the government ought to take the babies away from such as

213

that and fix the girl so she can't have anymore. That kind breeds like rats in the street, you know."

I couldn't help noticing how well-dressed those ladies were, with their fine jewelry, fashionable clothes, and matching shoes and handbags—all coordinated like models in the maternity section of the Sears catalog.

How could they feel so cruel and insensitive about another woman? I overheard another of the ladies state the age of the girl as "sixteen." That would have made her only fourteen when her first child was born. *My Lord! How was she coping?*

It seemed that particular lady had befriended her one afternoon in the waiting room, and she had gathered the information from the young girl herself. That, together with the fact that the girl wasn't sure where the father is.

Another woman chimed in, "She probably meant she didn't know *who* the father is!"

When she came back out to get her diaper bag and things after the examination, the same lady who provided the pertinent gossip smiled one of those nauseously phony smiles and asked, "How did everything go, Sweetie?"

The young girl was so nice and looked so appreciative to have someone show concern, as she responded, "The doctor says any day now!"

As the office door closed behind the girl, the women looked at one another, shaking their heads in disgust.

I sat and waited for two full hours with nothing to do but read and observe—observe and read.

I couldn't believe it. The only magazines in the entire office had baby pictures on the front, with titles like "Baby Talk" or "Baby's World." My mind drifted while I flipped through those books with all the sweet little baby pictures, and imagined what Kyle's and my baby would look like when we got married.

In two hours time I had memorized all the pictures in the books, as well as all the shoes, handbags, jewelry, clothes, hairstyles, faces, and physical characteristics of every woman in the room...even down to the runs in their hose.

Curiosity became more than one of the ladies could stand, so she asked me, "Are *you* pregnant?"

"Oh, no," I assured her. "I—I think I have a hormonal imbalance. I've just been feeling a little sluggish and nauseous lately...and I've put on a few pounds since the summer."

"Ohh-h," she replied in a patronizing tone. She had the look and mannerisms of the proverbial sophisticated snob, from the so-called upper circles of society. The feeling of intimidation rushed over me, as the other ladies took a long glance in my direction. I had always looked younger than I actually was. And there I sat, in my baby-blue shirt-waist dress, navy cardigan sweater, and navy loafers. I knew what they were all thinking.

"Miss James," the nurse was waiting for me in the doorway, "This way, please."

I knew that I would become the new topic of conversation by those vultures back there in the waiting room, as they were sure to be speculating the worst about me.

I felt rescued and relieved to finally be in the examining room.

Once inside, the nurse instructed me, "Take off all you clothes and put this on, Miss James," as she presented me with one of those horrible backless, cotton gowns that tie at the neck.

I almost fainted when she drew blood from my arm. After she checked my temperature, blood pressure, and weight, she instructed me, "Lie up here on the examining table and place your feet in the stirrups. Dr Bradford will be right in."

I lay there in that awkward position for what seemed like hours before the doctor finally entered the room.

I had never before been given a pelvic examination. I thought I would go through the ceiling, as I couldn't decide what feeling to go with—the pain or the embarrassment. He pulled the light over closer and instructed, "Relax your legs to the side, Miss James." He pressed my abdomen, and made noises like "Uh-huh," and other grunts. I wasn't sure whether they were grunts of approval or disapproval.

He popped off the rubber surgical glove from his hand and tossed it into the trash, finalizing the examination then he instructed me, "Get dressed and step into my office, Miss James."

Upon entering his office, he invited me, "Have a seat, Miss James." He always placed the emphasis on the "Miss" when he said my name. "Now, let's see. When was your last menstrual period?"

"The first week in August."

"Hmm-m-m, it's too early to be absolutely certain without an early morning urine specimen, but I would say you're about two months along."

I gasped, "Along? What do you mean by *along*?"

"The examination reveals only slight evidence of early pregnancy, but the odds are that you are approximately two months pregnant."

My shock and dismay must have become obvious, so he asked, "Do you know who the father is?"

I envisioned that young, pregnant girl earlier, and recalled the unkind comments that were made in judgment of her. Tears welled up in my eyes and rolled down my face onto my lap.

He repeated the question, "Do you know who the father is?"

I whispered, "Yes, sir."

"Good. We'll need to know his blood type and, if possible, have him come in, so we can discuss what to expect in the upcoming months…"

I thought, *My Lord, he's assuming I love the guy! Love? My feeling for Tommy couldn't by farther from that of love! I hope he rots in hell!*

I interrupted, "I *can't* be pregnant! I mean—I don't *want* a baby!

Recognizing my distress and hysteria, he instructed me, "Now, Delaney, before you panic, bring your first morning urine specimen into the lab on Monday morning, and call the office after two-o'clock that afternoon for the test results. Get some rest over the weekend. I'm sure everything will be just fine."

He wished me a nice weekend as I left the office.

I was relieved that the waiting room was cleared of all the ladies I had gotten to know and hate. I walked out of the office, got on the elevator, and went to my car, without making eye contact with anyone.

How I hoped he was mistaken, as I thought and prayed all the way home. *Doctors do make mistakes, don't they? Dear Lord, please let this be one of those times. I can't believe this is happening to me. Monday—that's three days away—an entire weekend to live with the uncertainty. This weekend's gonna seem like an eternity!*

* * *

I was unusually quiet that evening with Kyle. He knew me well enough to know I had something on my mind. But no matter how often he asked, I said everything was "fine."

That weekend did seem like an eternity. I recalled the time when I thought I was pregnant at the age of thirteen, and prayed this would turn out to be the same—just a silly mistake.

I kept telling myself, *Doctors do make mistakes. Doctors **do** make mistakes. He could be wrong about this. I'll be so relieved when Monday afternoon comes and they tell me it was all a mistake.*

Ironically, there was a photo of Tommy and Michele alongside their wedding announcement in the Sunday Journal. I didn't know it at the time, but he was already engaged that evening he was out with me. I stared at their smiling faces and thought, *What a son-of-a-bitch.* I felt sorry for his new wife. *Michele doesn't deserve this bastard for a husband. They went steady all the way through high school, and now, three years after they graduated, they're getting married.* After going with someone for eight years, I supposed she knew what she was getting into.

I ought to call him and tell him about this. Better yet, I'll call her—ruin his marriage, the way he's ruining my life!

But no, it made me sick to even think about him. He disgusted me so. *God, I feel so ashamed and guilty. It's just not fair. He can go on with his life as if nothing ever happened, and yet I...I don't know what I'm going to do if Monday doesn't hurry up and get here.* I prayed, *Please God, make Monday afternoon hurry up and let the doctor be wrong!*

* * *

Monday, October 31st, was a damp, rainy day, when I drove downtown to the lab and dropped off my first morning specimen. I had so much on my mind I forgot it was Halloween, until one of the mailboys startled me. He had waited just inside the evaluation office door and grabbed me when I turned on the light. He wore a silly mask, the kind that covered his entire head, so I had no idea who he really was.

He apologized when he realized how much he had frightened me.

To change the subject, he asked about my weekend.   As a group, we would preview our weekend plans on Fridays, and then recap them on Mondays.   I didn't have much to say, so I excused myself, "I have a lot of catching up to do." All that day my only thoughts were, *two-o'clock...hurry up and let it be two-o'clock.* I was useless behind the typewriter. I ate lunch alone in the lounge and avoided my friends.

Had my watch stopped? It seemed like it had been one-thirty for hours!

I called the doctor's office at exactly two-o'clock.

"Good afternoon, O.B.G.Y.N.," the voice answered.

"Hello, I'm calling to get some test results," I said softly. I didn't want anyone in the office to overhear.

The voice asked my name and I answered, "Delaney James." My stomach felt sick, as she placed me on hold for what seemed to be forever.

"Yes, we have those results right here, and...congratulations, Miss James, the results were positive!"

"Positive?" I asked, "What does that mean?"

"Why, it means you're definitely pregnant! If you'll remain on the line, you can schedule your prenatal appointment. Please hold."

My heart felt as if it were in a vice, my face became flush, and I felt sick—really sick—sick all through my mind and body. I laid the receiver back in place—without waiting—then I stood and walked slowly to the restroom down the hall. *Oh, God, I'm going to be sick to my stomach!* And so I was. I made it to there just in time.

What am I going to do? I whispered aloud. *I need to talk to Kyle. I need to go home. I have to get out of here.* I told my bosses I had contracted a bug of some sort, and went home for the remainder of the day.

* * *

I thought being home would make me feel better, but I was wrong. I went the long way home, so it gave me time to sort things out.

It was always so relaxing to sit in front of the big gas heater in the living room. There I became mesmerized and lost my thoughts in the open flames. It brought back the childhood memories of when my mother would wrap a heated blacked around me as I got out of bed on the cold, winter mornings. I would have a slice of jelly toast and glass of milk for breakfast, there on the floor in front of a smaller but similar heater.

It all seemed so long ago, and then, it seemed like yesterday. How I longed for it to be that time again; when I didn't have a worry in the world—a time when everything in my life was so simple.

I couldn't tell anyone about the pregnancy. I wondered if Daddy knew what was going on with his little girl. I turned his picture facedown on the table, so he couldn't see my crying.

I sat there feeling so helpless, and thought how I'd love to be that little girl again, sitting on Daddy's lap. *Daddy could fix anything, but I don't think even he could fix the mess I've gotten myself into.* I squinted my eyes at the fire like I did when I was little, but no matter how hard I concentrated I couldn't see any pretty pictures in the flames. I was only reminded of the hell I was in.

It seemed that all my life I had wanted to be a woman—and for what? Everything that constituted being a woman was nothing but headaches, problems and pain!

Angrily, I thought, *I hate being a woman!* I imagined what was forming there within my abdomen as I examined the smooth flat surface that would soon be bulging with a bastard-child. *I hate this thing inside of me—it's not a baby—it's the devil's seed! I wish it would die! I wish I were dead!*

But no matter how hard I wished...I wasn't dead. I was very much alive, with the worst problem I had ever faced, and I couldn't afford to lose my thoughts in those flames. And there was no sense in getting caught up in the past. I was all alone in this, and I had to figure out a way to handle it—all by myself!

I had to make plans—plans for the future.

The skeleton from the trunk of the "Lost Chapter" had come back to haunt me. How appropriate it all was, with that day being Halloween. It all still seemed like a hideous nightmare.

Then, I remembered Donald, someone I had dated that summer. He was a counselor's assistant where I worked, and a much older guy, about twenty-five. I considered him to be a pretty good friend, although I hadn't known him that long when we were dating.

We had only dated about four weeks when one Sunday afternoon in July, he professed he loved me. He had already bought a ring and took me by to see a house on which he had already paid a deposit. It was a nice house, fairly new—brick—even had a fireplace, and it was vacant. He already had a key, so he led me inside to show me around. When we got to a room on the backside of the house, he said, "This will be our bedroom, with our own separate bathroom." That's where he proposed to me, right then and there.

I was impressed with the house. I had always dreamed of owning a brick house, and the fireplace made it extra special. The ring was a cluster of diamonds, similar to my sister's ring, although I was sure it wasn't nearly as expensive.

He had surely taken me by surprise, and I didn't know what to say. I didn't have those kinds of feelings about Donald. I reminded him that we hadn't really known each other but a couple of months, but he told me he knew I was the one from the moment he saw me.

I told him I really liked him as a friend, but I didn't love him, so I couldn't marry him, but I thanked him for asking.

Of course I couldn't marry anyone I didn't love; besides, I thought he was a little off his rocker and maybe he needed a little counseling, to think he loved me enough to marry me when we hadn't known each other that long. My Lord, I hadn't kissed him more than a half dozen times!

He avoided me after I declined his proposal. I supposed he was embarrassed. Too bad—he was such a nice guy.

But things had changed since that summer's day. My situation was different. I had to think of that damned baby. I could call and tell him I had reconsidered, and that I really did love him and wanted to get married as soon as possible. Then, I could just say I got pregnant on our wedding night, and the baby would be born prematurely at seven months.

I had that all worked out in my mind, when Kyle called. I had needed to talk with him all day. Now, that he was on the phone, what was I supposed to say to him?

If I married Donald, I would never be able to see Kyle again. I had to tell him by phone, right then. It would be too painful in person, and besides, it wouldn't have been fair to wait.

A definite tone of anger was in Kyle's voice, "That's *crazy!*"

I wished I hadn't told him over the telephone. I just didn't know if I could have told him to his face. *What is he thinking of me? How can all this be happening?"*

Kyle's tone changed as he reassured me, "Don't worry, Delaney. Everything's gonna be fine. I'll help you work it out. Just don't do anything stupid. I'm on my way."

For some reason I believed him. He had a way about him. He could soothe, even that most hysterical woman I had become.

* * *

When he came over that evening we just spent time together—not much talking—just quiet time together.

By the weekend I managed to push the pregnancy back into my subconscious. I pretended I wasn't pregnant. That it was all a mistake, and the tests had been mixed up. Besides, I felt better. I hadn't been nauseous for a couple of days.

I just wouldn't deal with it.

* * *

Wednesday evening, November 9th, Kyle and I went to the drive-in. On the way home he turned down the radio, placed his arm around my shoulder and pulled me closer to him. "Delaney, it makes me crazy to take you home at night. Damn it, I love you so much it hurts."

I couldn't believe it, he finally said it! I knew he loved me, he just hadn't told me. And, of course, I said, "I feel the same way. I love you, too." I felt so wonderful inside, and that everything would be fine, just like Kyle had said.

But where would we go from there? I thought, *Does that mean he wants to marry me? No, he didn't say that. I shouldn't jump the gun. Don't mess things up by mentioning marriage.* Of course, it would have solved all my problems—marriage, that is. After all, I

222

did love Kyle. I wouldn't let myself think about whether it was fair to him, or not.

* * *

That night I dreamed only on Kyle, reliving the evening and his words, "I love you, Delaney. I love you…"

I felt like Kyle was right and that things were going to pull together. I didn't think about how—but I just knew they would.

I fluffed my pillow and closed my eyes, with a whisper of prayer on my lips, *"Lord, please let Kyle be right. Amen."*

CHAPTER XVIII
WHO SENT THE DEAD ROSES?

The next morning the sun shone beautifully somewhere in the world, but not in Atlanta, Georgia, where it was windy and rainy. Nonetheless, I felt surrounded by the feeling of warm sunshine, as the memories of the previous night's tender moments with Kyle were fresh in my mind.

That day, Thursday, November 10th, was going to be great day—rain or shine—I could just feel it in my bones! The next day was Friday and I'd be with Kyle again.

Maybe I chose it for sentimental reasons, but that morning I wore the same olive-green, linen suit I had bought for my first date with Kyle. It fit a little snug, but it still looked fine.

Several at work told me I had a certain glow about me, and they hadn't seen me smile that big in a while. I wanted to tell everyone about the night before, but I just smiled a little wider to acknowledge their comments.

Kyle called at lunch. He was a pressman for a printing company, and he always waited until the presses were shut down, so it wasn't so noisy when he called.

I had lunch early and got a head start on my work with the counselor, upstairs on the main floor.

I was in the Unit I nurses' station, gathering the information to update the patients' progress report files for the counseling department.

Several of the nurse's aids were out with the flu so the Unit was short-staffed that day. It was lunch hour and there was only one nurse inside the station when I sat at the desk and started going through files.

The nurses' station was like an island surrounded by glass and it divided Unit I from the rest of the building's main floor. From where I sat in the station I had a clear view of the parking lot through the building's front doors, and I could see the torrential rain pounding on the pavement.

Double sliding glass doors that met in the middle were the only way in or out of the Unit. They were operated by green buttons--one in the hall on the outside of the Unit, and one just inside the station below a sliding window.

The nurse said, "Delaney, I need to run some errands in other parts of the building. How long will you be here?"

I said, "No problem—go ahead—I should be here a good while."

"Thanks. Anita will be back from lunch in a few minutes."

I was engrossed in the files and my work, so I didn't notice she had neglected to close the sliding glass window. I was facing the opposite direction, copying information from the charts, when I was distracted by a noise. I glanced over to see a hand reaching through and pressing the green button to open the doors.

"Oh, my God. Wait!" It was Diane, a seventeen-year-old, six months pregnant by a boy in her neighborhood. She was in her own fantasy world, and had convinced herself that the boy loved her as much as she loved him.

He denied even so much as liking her, and claimed he wasn't the only boy who had been to bed with her. He wouldn't even come to visit her there.

She had been in there about three months, where she remained in Unit I, showing no real signs of improvement. Her chart said she was suffering from paranoia and schizophrenia, with tendencies toward manic depression and capable of suicide. She blamed her parents along with the doctors there for not allowing her boyfriend to see her. She was convinced everyone was keeping them apart.

Diane wasn't in the least bit pretty. On the contrary, she was very plain, with long, unkempt hair, and she was extremely large— about five-ten, three-hundred and fifty pounds.

I shouted, "Diane, don't!" But I was too late. The doors flew open and she was in the hall, on her way to the parking lot.

I ran after her, not even thinking of danger. I had become familiar with Diane over the past months, and she had smiled and talked to me when she came to the counselor's office. I related to her problem—her pregnancy—and I was totally empathetic with her situation. She trusted me and I was sure I could talk to her until some aides could come to retrieve her. "Diane, wait! Calm down and let's talk about where you're going."

I didn't expect what happened next.

She stopped, turned around, and suddenly that Amazon-of-a-girl grabbed me. There was a sarcastic tone in her masculine voice, "Yeah, good idea, bitch. Let's *talk* about where *we're* going." She held me about the shoulders with one arm, while with the other hand she held to my jugular vein a metal letter opening she had filed and sharpened.

I didn't have to scream to get attention. The patients were inside the Unit, watching through the glass doors. They were frightened, yelling like caged monkeys at the zoo—pointing a screaming.

Two male aides approached, one from each side, but she warned them, "Don't come any closer or this one'll be dead!"

She continued to threaten, "I'm tired of this place! I'm going to see Josh, and *nobody's* gonna stop me! Anybody tries and you'll have to pick this bitch's head off the floor!" She waved the letter opener in the air, then I felt a sharp prick and its cold metal edge as she drug in across my throat to demonstrate, "See how easy it'd be? Now, let us go, or I *swear—I'll do it for real!*"

She was more than twice my size, as she dragged me along the hallway with her, stepping backwards all the way. My knees were so weak from nerves I couldn't support myself, but she didn't seem to notice as she drug me like a rag doll. She was enraged by the thought of anyone stopping her.

Once we were outside the door and in the parking lot, she pushed me away from her, and I fell face forward into a huge mud-puddle.

The marble-size hail stung my face and I could barely see the building through the sheets of rain, much less the person who was there to help me. "Here, Delaney, put your arm around me." It was Brad from Unit A. He helped me up and carried me back inside the building. "Man, that was a close one. Are you all right?"

"I don't know. I think so."

My arms and legs were sore from the bruises and my knees were raw as hamburger meat, from being drug on the pavement. I was in shock and didn't cry a tear, until I realized the rain and mud had ruined my favorite linen suit.

The ear-piercing, security alarm sounded and it reminded me of the fire drills in school—only louder and with a more pulsating tone.

Brad brought a blanket and wrapped it around me, while the nurse cleaned the mud off my face and arms and bandaged my knees. When the nurse dabbed my throat with the antiseptic-soaked cotton, I saw the blood and passed out for a few minutes.

* * *

After ten minutes or so, when I regained consciousness, my throat was bandaged and Diane had been brought back to the Unit. She never even got passed the front gate. She was pulling and yelling at the top of her lungs, and bucking like a wild bull. She was yanking her own hair out by the fists-full, and like a mad-dog, she was biting and spitting on the aides and security men.

With her fighting them all the way, they physically drug her into the last room on the right. That was the padded room. I had never actually seen inside the padded room, but I imagined it to be like those I had seen on television or in the movies, with the walls and floors covered in vinyl padding.

Even with the door closed, I could hear her screams, until the noises suddenly stopped. She had been given a shot to calm her down and make her sleep.

* * *

My nerves were shot and I was shaking like a leaf. I just couldn't take it any longer. It had gone far enough. The security wasn't the best in the world because the institute was so newly established. But I knew I could never feel safe there again.

That was the second time that a letter opener had been filed and sharpened on those premises, then used as a weapon against an employee.

I began having flashbacks of another afternoon back in late August. I was delivering some paperwork to Cottage A and I used the underground tunnel to avoid the rain.

The tunnel was well lit, but it was like a catacomb, a tomb where the silence was unnerving. The only sound, other than my footsteps, was the *drip-drip* noise of water trickling down the inside wall from a leak in the structure.

I was always afraid the lights would go out from a power failure, the locks on I the exit doors would jam, and I'd be trapped there, in that tomb of darkness.

I remembered how I felt the tunnel closing in on me that afternoon, when I suddenly heard the sound of footsteps, other than my own. It was one of the patients—a young male—who had been left unattended, walked out of Cottage B, and was roaming the tunnel.

He recognized me and called me by name. "Don't be afraid, Miss Delaney. Dave won't let nothing get you." His name was actually Daniel, but he always called himself Dave. Dave was his younger brother who was killed in a car accident on the way home from Daniel's 25th birthday party the previous year. Daniel was driving. "Dave's twenty years old now, Miss Delaney. Did you know that?" His eyes were kind, and his voice was soft, yet I felt threatened by the sense of unsettled nerves he displayed as he paced from side to side—like a caged animal, contemplating escape—or attack.

The alarm button was only a few yards down the corridor, but I wasn't sure I wanted to take the chance of provoking him.

Lord, the tunnel seemed like it went on forever, with no end.

"Dave, will you come with me to deliver these papers to Cottage A so I won't have to walk alone?"

"Sure, Miss Delaney. Dave'll help you. Don't be afraid." The aides greeted him with a stern reprimand, and the case was dropped.

I wanted to give those aides over in Cottage B a stern reprimand for leaving him unattended in the first place.

That afternoon in August I wasn't physically harmed, but I could have been. What if he had had one of those letter openers?

They knew I was only seventeen when I took that job. Why didn't they warn me that I'd be placed in those situations? How could I go on working under the pressures of not knowing when the next dangerous, life-threatening situation would arise?

The incident with Diane was a straw that would break any camel's back.

I would rather have worked at minimum wage in a department store than subject myself to that kind of danger. Besides, with my secretarial skills I could have any job I wanted.

So I quit.

Every ounce of my being was shaking, but I mustered up enough strength to march into the counselor's office and quit, right then and there. Who could blame me? It was unsafe there.

With Brad begging me not to leave in my condition, I ran out to my car through the driving rain. I needed to get as far away from that place—that city—as I could.

I stopped by my house and hastily threw some clothes in the red suitcase my sister gave me as a graduation gift. *God, that seems like years ago. So much has happened since then,* I thought, as I was leaning on it to force it closed.

I filled the Mustang with gas and I was on my way, to where, I wasn't sure, yet. I thought, *Just head south on Interstate 75 and go until I get to Florida.*

I had never seen so much rain in one afternoon. It was coming down so hard I could barely see the road, and I thought, *Maybe, just maybe, I'll have a wreck and be killed instantly. That would end my problems. The way it's looking, I don't have much of a life to look forward to, anyway.*

I can't explain why, but Kyle had not even entered my thoughts that afternoon.

I only got about thirty to forty miles south of Atlanta when I remembered I hadn't left Mama a note to say good-bye. I couldn't do her that way. I didn't want her to worry, so I turned around and headed back toward home to leave a note.

The rain was so heavy. I should have pulled over to the side of the road, but I was running out of daylight, so I ignored my better judgment and drove on.

My wipers were on the fastest speed, but they weren't clearing the windshield fast enough when, suddenly, I thought, *Are those brake lights ahead? Is that car stopping?*

There was a huge eighteen-wheeler to my left, and the building-size truck was throwing muddy slush on my windshield faster than the wipers could clear it away. I couldn't see a thing, but I thought the car in front was stopping, as I said aloud in a panic, "Are those brake lights?"

I stomped on my brakes and swerved on the pavement. The Mustang fish-tailed over so close to that truck I could have reached out and touched the side of it.

I lost control of the car and passed out behind the wheel. My foot fell off the brake and onto the accelerator and the car spun out, flipped into the air, made a 180 degree turn, and finally came to a stop about 50 feet from the road, embedded in a mud embankment. I was semi-conscious, but I do remember the driver's door wouldn't open because of the mud-wall. I unhooked the seatbelt and climbed over the console to try and get to the passenger side door.

Some witnesses stopped, pulled me from the car and placed me in theirs until the ambulance got there.

The ambulance took me to a small community hospital in Jonesboro. Still semi-conscious, I was lying on a table with a sheet covering me to my neck, and blinding overhead lights. I overheard a man's voice, obviously talking to someone on the phone, "Mrs. James, do you have a daughter by the name of Delaney?"

He went on to explain, identifying himself as a driver for Jackson's Funeral Home, and that they had her daughter… I thought, *My God! Am I dead? Is this what it's like to be dead?* I passed out completely, thinking, *I'm glad I'm dead, but I wish I had left Mama that note.*

* * *

I had no way of knowing at the time, but a week had passed before I was awakened by the uncomfortable feeling of someone or something squeezing my upper, right arm. I was barely conscious and extremely groggy, but I heard a woman's voice calling my name, "Miss James? Delaney, lie still so I can check your blood pressure."

The brightness of the woman's white clothes was no more than a blur through the slits of my squinting eyes. "Are you...an angel?"

She laughed and said, "No, but my mama thinks I am."

I groaned and asked, "Where am I?"

"Why, you're in the hospital, honey...Georgia Baptist Hospital."

"I...I thought I was dead. How'd I get...?"

"How'd you get here? Jonesboro Community transferred you to us a week ago. You got a pretty good lick on the head from the wreck, and you've been out ever since."

I later discovered Jackson Funeral Home provided ambulance service for the hospitals south of Atlanta. That explained the conversation I overheard the night of the accident.

I frowned when I reached up and discovered bandages covering the left side of my head.

She assured me, "Don't worry, honey—no permanent damage— only took of couple of stitches, and they're so far back in the hair you'll never even see it. You're mighty lucky though. That and a bruised kidney from where the seat belt was fastened are the main injuries. Of course, it looks like you got pretty scraped up, too."

Everything in the room was blurry, but I saw what looked like wilted flowers—roses—on the table at the foot of my bed, so I mumbled, "Who sent the dead roses?"

* * *

I later discovered Kyle had sent them. He had been there every day since the accident, and he had sent the dozen red, long-stemmed, American beauty roses the very first day. In the course of the week, sadly, they had wilted and became all shriveled. I left them there on the table until I went home. They were blackened and deader than the proverbial door-nail, but I still saw some beauty in them…and I knew roses didn't come cheap.

CHAPTER XIX
LOCK THE DOOR AND
THROW AWAY THE KEY

In the days ahead, as I lay in the hospital bed, I had nothing but time on my hands. Time to think—think about the future—a happy future with Kyle.

I didn't discuss the past with anyone, not even Kyle. I fought the thoughts of the past, but from day to day there were things that would trigger sudden flashbacks.

I might see a souped-up car on television or hear its loud engine racing, or I'd see a white dress, or red heels, and my body would suddenly jerk in a reflex, as one might react to a memory of intense pain. I was watching a movie on T.V. one evening, and I turned the channel because the main character's name was Tommy. Rainy days, Mondays, especially at 2:00 in the afternoon, or the sight of a young pregnant woman, even church and Sunday nights—all triggered memories I wanted so desperately to forget. Nightmarish memories I'd turn over in my head, then my mind jolted back to a fabricated reality when I convinced myself that none of it ever really happened.

* * *

My friends were great about cheering me up when they called and visited me at the hospital. We laughed at my vague recollections of the night I had the accident, as I recalled how I overheard the phone conversation between the driver and my mother, and how I thought I was dead. We imagined how funny it must have looked when one of the witnesses fished my drenched hairpiece out of the mud, and placed it beside me in the ambulance. It must have looked like a drowned rat—a dirty drowned rat.

* * *

After lunch one afternoon I was almost asleep when a man entered my room.

"Miss James? Do you remember me?"

I was drowsy and I hesitated because the man looked only vaguely familiar, "I—I don't know."

"I'm Dr. Bradford. I need to talk with you about the baby."

"What? What baby?"

He continued, "The accident did *not* cause you to miscarry… yet. But I'll need to examine you in a few days, just to make sure everything is fine."

I kept silent. I didn't understand why he was saying all those things. Didn't he know? I pretended all of that away. I wasn't dealing with what he was saying, so I didn't have to deal with him. I pretended I didn't hear him, as I turned my head away, without saying a word, directing my complete attention to the television.

I heard the door close several minutes later. It must have been him leaving, because he was gone when I looked where he had been standing. Or had I imagined him there? I turned back to the television while thinking *I probably dreamed he was in my room. I'll just pretend I dreamed he came in to see me. He still thinks I'm pregnant. No one ever told him of his mistake. No one told him I pretended that all away.*

* * *

Mama asked me who he was when she received a bill for his visit, so I told her he was a gynecologist I had seen about losing weight. After all, that was the truth, in part. I never knew if that doctor violated doctor-patient confidence, by telling her the whole truth.

I felt so sorry for Mama. It would have killed her or broken her heart to know that her baby girl was fighting the memories of such a horrible nightmare. I hurt so for her. She had sacrificed so much while raising me, she didn't deserve the pain of knowing the truth.

* * *

Mama couldn't afford to take time off work to stay home with me, so I convalesced at my sister's home in Kennesaw, north of Atlanta.

Sis had always been a great cook. Thanksgiving was only a few days away so she was busy making her specialties—fudge, cookies and cakes.

The bakeshop's cinnamon spice and chocolate aromas were unforgettable as they wafted from the kitchen and danced on the air throughout the house. The hands belonging to her three sons were continuously being slapped for snatching samples without permission. But who could blame them? I snatched my share of samples, too. I just didn't get caught.

Our entire family celebrated Thanksgiving at Sis and Bryan's home. I looked forward to having a home with Kyle one day—like hers—big enough to have my sister and all my brothers with their families over for Thanksgiving.

* * *

After a big Thanksgiving meal with my family, Kyle and I went to the Georgia vs. Georgia Tech game. Following the game we went to his house for dinner, and afterward, we went downtown for the traditional lighting of the Christmas tree atop Rich's department store. That always marked the official beginning of the Christmas season, and people came from miles around to see the giant evergreen and hear the choral groups.

Traffic was at a standstill, and the 007 car began to make its presence known to all, as it began to overheat with smoke bellowing out from underneath the hood. Combined with the usual smokescreen from the rear, it appeared as if it were about to become an exploding threat to the entire population of Atlanta. How embarrassing!

We left the car sitting there in the street and walked the rest of the way to the tree lighting. Afterward, it was a relief when Kyle got everything under control, and we were on our way home. I prayed all the way that the 007 would get us home safely, and so it did. However, that wouldn't always be the case.

* * *

One night Kyle and I went to a movie and stopped by a quiet spot on the side of a residential street to talk, and "be alone." When it came time for us to leave, Ole Faithful 007 coughed and choked and sputtered. It did everything but start. The battery had obviously gone to meet its Maker.

Once again, we were forced to get out of the car and walk—this time—several blocks to a pay phone, where we called his brother, Howard.

When he came to rescue us, he snickered and asked, "What were you guys doing all the way over here, anyway?" Howard was pretty wild and had a reputation with the girls, so Kyle and I both considered that a stupid question, coming from him.

Our answer, "Oh, nothing," befittingly confirmed that "a stupid question deserves a stupid answer."

* * *

One Friday evening in early December, Kyle and I were on our way home from a date. He pulled me over closer to him in the Mustang, and his kiss made me think, *God, I love this guy! White Christmas* was playing on the radio and everything was perfect, except I didn't want him to take me home and be away from him, even for the night. I gazed out the window at the houses all decked out and trimmed with their colored lights and window candles, thinking, *One day Kyle and I will have our own home to decorate for Christmas.*

It was such a clear night and the air was so fresh, the entire universe had a glow of infinite serenity. The full moon shone and the millions of brilliant stars sparkled like diamonds surrounding a huge pearl, all in a setting displayed to perfection against a rich, black velvet sky.

I had always heard that people react in different ways to a full moon. Lovers become more in love, the sane become insane, and the insane become even more insane. I'd like to blame the moon for what happened next, but I'm afraid I have to blame it on the fact that I was young, stupid, in love, and anxious.

For almost a month I had waited for Kyle to mention marriage. I sat next to him in the car with my head resting on his shoulder, his right arm around me, and I said, "I do love you so much, you know."

He responded, "I love you, too."

"Do you really love me?"

"You know I do."

"Well...how much do you love me?" I quizzed him.

"I never new I could love anyone this much. That's how much I love you."

Before I knew what happened, I blurted, "Well...then...are we gonna get married? Or what?" My immediate thoughts afterward were, *Oh God, me and my big mouth! Why can't I stop being so darned forward? Wait! Shut up! Listen to what he just said.* "What did you just say" I asked, hoping I heard him correctly.

He repeated, "Of course, I want to marry you. I just didn't know how to go about asking."

Relieved, I took a semi-deep breath and said, "Well, that's easy. You say, "I love you more than I've ever loved anyone. I can't live without you, and I want to spend the rest of my life with you. Will you marry me?"

By this time we were parked in the driveway at the front of my house.

He quickly said, "Okay, I love you more than I've ever loved anyone. I can't live without you…and I want to spend the rest of my life with you. Will you marry me?"

Coyly, I asked, "Are you asking me to marry you?"

Anxiously, he replied, "Yes!"

"Well, I don't know. I may have to think about this for a while."

He took a deep sigh of exasperation, and I could see his face by the moonlight as he looked at me out of the corner of his eyes. "Well…?"

I interrupted before he could get any further, "Okay. I've thought it through, and the answer is yes, *of course I'll marry you!*"

He leaned across and, this time when we kissed we knew we were sealing a commitment to one another, as he whispered, "You've made me so happy. I love you so much."

"Wait a minute. I said I'll marry you, but you'll have to ask my mother's permission, you know."

Only a few lights were on in the house, and the dim glow of the television shone through the Venetian blinds in the living room, so I suggested we go inside right then. In the back of my mind I was thinking, *Better strike while the iron is hot.* He wouldn't be able to change his mind after asking my mother's permission, and I had no doubt she would say "yes" since she was so crazy about Kyle.

We entered the living room where Mama sat in the green vinyl rocker, with her feet resting on the ottoman. The only sounds in the house were the television and her snoring, the latter being the louder of the two. She was in her pajamas, robe and terry slippers, and looked so peaceful, lounging cozily there in front of the gas heater.

The snoring stopped when we startled her, and she sat straight up in the chair.

Kyle sat next to Mama's feet on the ottoman and cleared his throat before he said, "Mrs. James. I'm sorry we woke you up, but I have something I really need to talk to you about."

"Is there something wrong?"

"No, ma'am. I—I just need to ask you something. We—I mean, Delaney and I—we really love each other, and…well, I just asked her to marry me and she said she would, but I'd have to come inside and ask you first. So…will you give us permission to get married?"

I could see a mist of motherly tears building in her dark eyes as she asked, in a soft but stern voice, "Are you two sure about this? Have you thought it through?"

He said, "Yes ma'am, we've thought about this for a long time." I nodded in agreement, all the while thinking, *We've thought about this for a long time? For crying out loud, Kyle, we've only known each other since September—that's only three months, anyway you look at it—so allowing the entire time couldn't exactly qualify as "a long time."* But who was I to argue? After all, I *had* been thinking about it for a long time—all my life—so that statement was half-true.

Mama swallowed and coughed, trying to rid the lump in her throat, finally to answer, "Well, if you've thought this all through and you really do love each other—then yes—you have my blessing."

Kyle kissed her on the cheek and promised to take care of me and make me happy, as that was a stipulation she had thrown into the agreement.

* * *

On Saturday, December 10th, Kyle presented me with a forty-karat diamond solitaire engagement ring. Actually, it was a little more than half-karat, but it couldn't have been more beautiful if it had been forty-karats.

That night, after he gave me the ring on our date, I left the hallway light on so I could lie in bed and admire the shine and sparkle of my beautiful new ring. I went into the bathroom and cut the surface of the mirror with the diamond as a way to check its authenticity. When it made a nice, clear cut, about an inch long in the mirror's glass, I thought, *What a relief! It's a genuine diamond. Of course, it's genuine. I never really had any doubts.* I went back to bed with total peace of mind.

I didn't tell Kyle about the diamond test, but I wondered what I would have done if it had failed the test?

* * *

Neither Kyle nor I ever brought up the reason we needed to marry so quickly, but we set the date for January 2nd, and planned an intimate wedding with family members in the pastor's study.

I nodded whenever Kyle asked me, "Does the doctor think everything's going all right?" He was unaware I had never even gone back to the doctor. Kyle wouldn't have understood. He didn't know me well enough to understand how well I could make unpleasant things go away,simply by pretending they weren't real and never happened.

* * *

The next Friday night, December 16th, we went to his sister's house to watch Star Trek. They had a color television, a real luxury item, and the only people I personally knew who owned one.

Kyle had spent all of his money on my ring, and with our wedding day fast approaching, we needed to pinch pennies, so it was nice to have a relative with a color T.V. set. It was the next best thing to going to the movies.

I had been having abdominal cramps and lower back pains all that afternoon. I thought the back pains were related to my accident, or my kidneys. I was prone to kidney infections.

When the pain became unbearable, I excused myself and went into the bathroom. I couldn't breathe without hurting. I wanted to scream from the excruciating pains in my back. My slacks were soaked and I was relieved when I realized they were soaked with blood. I thought God had answered my prayers, *Thank you, God. I knew the doctor was wrong. No wonder the cramps were so bad—I haven't had a period in four months.*

I took off my slacks and tried to wash the blood out with soap and water from the faucet, but another pain—more severe than the others—shot up my back and crescendoed in my abdomen. I splashed cold water on my face to keep from passing out.

I wet a washrag for my face and sat doubled over on the toilet, when one pain was followed by another. One pain didn't subside before another more excruciating one followed. I was nauseous at the sight of blood and clots in the toilet water. The bleeding was heavier and a brighter red than any menstruation I have ever before seen.

I couldn't conceal the groans within the confines of the bathroom walls. His sister knocked on the door and asked if I was all right.

"Yeah, I just have the most awful period cramps."

"There's some Midol in the medicine cabinet. You're welcome to as many as you need."

I said, "Thank you," but I was in so much pain I wasn't sure she understood me. It sounded like she had gone back into the den, and wasn't standing outside the door any longer, so that was a relief.

The sharpest pain suddenly rolled through my abdomen, like a steamroller. It was so intense it took my breath away. I began bleeding so profusely, I thought I was hemorrhaging.

I had never experienced anything that equaled the pain and I wondered, *Could this be it? Could I be having a miscarriage?* I prayed, *Oh please, Lord, please let it be a miscarriage.*

When I saw the hideous sight of an undeveloped 3 month fetus, floating there in the toilet, I was both nauseous *and* relieved at the same time. I couldn't stop crying tears of relief at the thought of that bastard's monster being out of me. I hated that thing floating there, and I was glad it was dead. *I wished it dead! I prayed for it to die!* And my wishes and prayers had come true.

I was in there for more than an hour. When the bleeding tapered off and the pain subsided enough for me to pull myself together, I placed one of her sanitary napkins inside my panties. I cleaned the bathroom so there were no traces of blood, and flushed the toilet several times to make sure the thing was gone forever.

His sister came to the door again and asked, "Are you all right in there?"

"I'm just having horrible cramps. Would you please tell Kyle I need to talk to him?"

When Kyle came to the door I asked, "Will you please take me home?"

"What's wrong?"

"I'll explain in the car." I couldn't believe I had miscarried in the bathroom—alone—without allowing anyone to know what was going on in there.

On the way home I was exhausted, so I simply said, "It's gone. I'm not pregnant anymore. Everything's fine now."

"Do you feel all right? Do you want me to take you to the hospital?"

"No. I feel fine. Everything's fine."

* * *

I wondered if Kyle pretended the whole episode away, the same as I did, because the subject of the pregnancy was never mentioned again.

I didn't go to the gynecologist, and I never discussed it with anyone.

I took the memories of all those bad things that happened in my life since August, and pushed them back into the attic of my mind. And to make sure they stayed there, I locked the door and threw away the key that night, as I pretended those times never happened at all.

Tears of pain subsided to happiness and my face broadened with a smile, "Now that there's no reason to rush, we can postpone our wedding until June. I've always wanted to be a June bride."

Kyle agreed with the change of plans and we set the new wedding date for June 2nd 1967, a little less than six months away.

My mother was relieved to hear about the postponement because it allowed more time for the preparations.

I was much more relieved about a lot of things. And I was happy—happy and thankful that God had remembered and smiled down on me, just when I was beginning to think He had forgotten me, altogether. *Thank you, Lord. Amen.*

THURSDAY AFTERNOON, SEPTEMBER 6, 1984: CHESTNUT, GEORGIA DR. ROBINSON'S OFFICE, OAKWOOD'S SATELLITE FACILITY

Dr. Robinson began our session by asking how things were going at home.

I explained, "The house is too quiet during the days since Keith and Clay have gone back to school. Mama and Sis have spent their share of time with me over the past months, but they have lives of their own. I've grown accustomed to someone being there all the time, and the hardest thing is being alone in that house. I keep the television's volume turned to maximum when I'm there by myself, so I won't hear the dog in the backyard. I rarely hear that dog unless I'm there alone. Mama, Kyle and the boys keep insisting there isn't a dog—that we no longer have one. But the incessant barking is too real to be my imagination, so the TV runs all the time, whether I'm watching it or not. It keeps me company."

* * *

My plastic surgery was the next topic of discussion on the doctor's agenda. "The surgeon did a wonderful job, Delaney. You can barely tell there was ever a scar there."

The plastic surgeon told me I was some of his best work. It had been only six weeks since Dr. Sims patched up the scar on my face, and there were still slight traces of the surgery, but he said, "Don't worry. You're coming along just fine. Give it six more weeks and it will be as smooth as the other side of your face. Continue to stay out of the sunlight as much as possible."

Staying out of the sunlight wasn't a problem since I never went out of the house except when I went to the doctor and to the movie on the weekend.

Learning to drive again was the problem. The first time I sat behind the wheel my palms were so wet from nervous perspiration, I had a hard time gripping the steering wheel. Kyle had made such a big deal about the Mercedes being so expensive because it was a foreign car, I was a little surprised when he traded it for a Toyota. I didn't care what kind it was, as long as it got me back and forth to the doctor.

* * *

The assignment had become my obsession, and I was engrossed with writing about the memories of meeting Kyle and falling in love. Those were such wonderful memories. I wished I only had to remember the good times. It never occurred to me that the lost chapter would rear its ugly head and come back to haunt me.

I went through so much hell because of that bastard Tommy. I considered him to be a more evil form of lowlife than the filthiest of roaches.

The memories of him and that awful time in my life stirred up new nightmares, in which I saw something floating on a pool of water. Everything was blurry and I couldn't make out what the object was or its color, because the dream was in black and white. I heard a child crying and repeatedly screaming, "Mommy! Help!" In the dream I couldn't see a child, but I could hear him. I covered my ears with my hands, but I could still hear the cries. The screams grew louder as I watched the object get drawn into a whirlpool and pulled beneath the water, beyond my reach and out of sight. A dog always started barking and the child's pleas faded along with the disappearance of the object.

I wondered, *Am I being haunted by the child the fetus would have become if I hadn't miscarried? Were the screams and cries for "MOMMY!" coming from Tommy's bastard-child? But why now, so many years later? Have I condemned myself to future guilt, as a woman who didn't want her own child and wished it dead? And is hell coming to claim my soul because I turned my back on one of my own? Should I have felt remorseful when I watched the thing flush down the toilet that night, eighteen years earlier at Kyle's sister's house?*

I was overwrought by grief and guilt, the tears flowing uncontrollably as I thought, *Of course. That has to be the child in my nightmares. I didn't realize until now, how I've carried this guilt around for all these years.*

With that conclusion came a sense of relief, and I was proud of myself to have figured it all out without the doctor's help. I consoled myself by saying, *If it had been Kyle's baby I would never have felt that way about it.* I supposed the child couldn't help who its father was, but it also had no way of knowing the pain Tommy had inflicted on me.

* * *

Doc Terri read the latest addition to my assignment, glancing up at me occasionally when she reached certain parts.

"Well, you've really gone through quite a lot, haven't you? I can only imagine the pain."

I nodded, wondering what she really must think of me, and if she ever had anything bad happen to her? I wanted to say, "Okay, Dr. Terri Robinson. Now it's your turn. I want you to open up and talk about *your* pain—*your* feelings!" If the truth be known, I bet she'd led a near-perfect and problem-free life, with no way in hell of even beginning to imagine my pain!

She continued, "It's been painful but you've endured it, and even wrapped it up on a positive note. I admire you for reliving that nightmare and dealing with it the way you are. Your memory is progressing so nicely. I know you've expressed how you wish you could only remember the good times, but the bad times are part of what makes you who you are today."

"You mean *crazy*? The bad times are what made me crazy?"

"Delaney, we've talked about this time and time again. You're not crazy now, and you've never been crazy. You just got off-centered when you endured some traumas back at the first part of the year…"

First part of the year? I was confused. *I thought I had everything figured out.*

"You're coming along fine. If your memory continues to progress, we'll be able to reduce the sessions to once a week before long."

I was looking forward to remembering some more good times. I considered my good memories as my reward for dealing with the nightmares.

* * *

"Delaney, you're a lucky woman to have met a man like Kyle, who loves you unconditionally, and stuck with you through all that."

If she'd ever been right about anything, she was right about that—one-hundred percent! And I was falling in love with Kyle all over again.

* * *

The good doctor directed my attention toward the mirror behind her desk. "Delaney, look at yourself—you're smiling! You're a very pretty lady, but you're gorgeous when you smile."

Sure enough, I was smiling, and I blushed when I thought of reliving my years together with Kyle.

Her next comment surprised me. "I can only wish that someday I'll be lucky enough to meet a man like your husband and fall in love."

I was even more surprised when I felt a sense of compassion for the young, little doctor with the auburn hair, and I hoped her wish came true.

CHAPTER XX
THE STAIRWAY TO PARADISE

Toward the end of December, a couple of weeks after the miscarriage, I scheduled a doctor's appointment with the urologist. The examination and tests revealed a problem requiring corrective surgery, which we scheduled for February.

Even though my secretarial skills were above average I had difficulty finding a job. When I went on interviews and they asked my condition of health, I felt obligated to tell them about my scheduled surgery. They were always very interested in me; however, I would be asked to check back with them after February.

I decided it would be simpler to work through a temporary job-placement company and postpone my search for a permanent position until after my surgery. That arrangement was just fine, until one week in the early part of January, when I was placed with a trucking company to do secretarial work.

I was the only female in the office, and I was a little intimidated by all the truck-drivers always hanging around the place. The manager was a real flirt, and apparently thought his vulgar jokes and off-color remarks were amusing.

I really hated it there, but it was conveniently located near my house. I kept reminding myself that the job assignment was only for four weeks, just long enough so that I could work right up until my surgery.

The office was a filthy little metal building. It reeked with the smell of grease, and the concrete floor was damp and gritty, in need of a good broom and mop. The furniture consisted of those old green metal desks, with Formica tops, that were all chipped and dented, and the desk chairs with broken rollers, so they sat crooked.

The files were kept in the back in a small room that doubled as a living quarters for the night watchman. There was a bed in the room that was always unmade, and the air carried a heavy stench from the empty liquor bottles that overflowed the trashcan. I always dreaded the times I needed something from the files.

One morning, I was pre-occupied in the back room, filing a stack of invoices. My thoughts were in wishing I were anywhere but there. I was imagining the kind of place I might be working after my surgery, when I would be employed on a permanent basis. Wherever it was, I hoped it would be in one of those professional buildings, nicely decorated with wooden furniture, where the floors were plushly carpeted and everything was spotless. Of course the typewriters would all be electric instead of the antiquated manual version I was using at that trucking place. And last, but certainly not least, a place where the lock on the restroom door wasn't broken, and I wouldn't be afraid someone would walk in on me when I was in there. And another thing—the men's and ladies' rooms would be separate, and sanitary.

I straightened up from putting a file in the bottom drawer, only to be startled to find that awful manager hovering over me, with his arms entrapping me against the file cabinet.

I tried to step to the side while nonchalantly asking, "Can I help you with something, sir?" All the while, I thought with disgust, *Ugh! 'Sir'? I can't believe I have to show this creep respect, just because he's my boss.* It wasn't even ten in the morning, and the smell of liquor on his breath almost knocked me over.

"You sure can, Delaney," as he grabbed my chin in his hand and attempted to kiss me. When I turned my head away, he grabbed the front of my blouse, but I pushed him away. When we heard one of the drivers call from the front office, it startled the old creep so that he lost his balance and fell onto the bed. He was laughing as though it had all been an amusing little joke.

I ran out of the back room, gathered my things, and announced I was going to lunch. My only thoughts were to get out of there as I slammed the door when I left, leaving the sound of their humiliating laughter behind.

I didn't go back after lunch and when the agency asked if there was a problem, I didn't hesitate telling the story.

The next week I applied with the Gas Company for a position in the secretarial pool. When they asked about my health I said it was fine, and they hired me on the spot. I didn't tell them about my surgery until a week before I was scheduled to go in the hospital.

I had a speedy recovery and was back on the job in no time after the surgery.

* * *

I went by Kyle's house every afternoon on the way home. Sometimes, we would go off in the Mustang, and sometimes he would just follow me over to my house in the 007 car.

Whenever he was following me I always felt safe enough to take the shortcut, through a rough neighborhood.

One particular Friday night, I lost sight of Kyle for a few blocks and decided to turn back, in case there was trouble.

There stood Kyle, leaning over the front of the car with its hood wide open, resembling the jaws of a giant red shark in the process of devouring him, leaving nothing but his legs and feet. He decided to leave it there and get it the next day when it was safer and we continued the rest of the way in my car.

Mama was working late and we had the house to ourselves. I made grilled-cheese sandwiches and tomato soup and as usual he complimented me on how great it was.

He drove my car to his house that night since the next morning wasn't a workday.

The phone rang about midnight. It was Kyle calling to let me know he made it safely. However, when he drove by ole 007, someone had completely stripped the car of its wheels, balding tires, brand new battery, radio—that didn't work half the time—and various other parts. The next morning he hired a tow service which placed the car on a flat-bed trailer and delivered it to the front of his mother's house in East Atlanta, where they left it on the street.

It was such a pathetic sight as it remained there growing rust, until Kyle sold it to a garage, which made it into a race car. The Lord works in mysterious ways, because Kyle was paid seventy-five dollars for the heap, and 007 had a chance at fame and glory on the racing circuit.

* * *

The Mustang was our only mode of transportation, so on Friday and Saturday nights Kyle took it home with him and brought it over early the next morning.

We always looked forward to Saturday mornings when he brought the car over because, with Mama at work, we had the house to ourselves. In fact, I think it would be fair to say that Saturday mornings were our very favorite times.

I always woke up about forty-five minutes before Kyle was expected so I could take a shower, brush my teeth, fix my hair, put on—just a little—makeup, and finish up with perfume and bath powder, to the create the perfect aroma. Topped off with a pair of cotton, baby-doll, shorty-pajamas, the most alluring sleepwear

I owned. I'd crawl back into bed, appearing as though I was still asleep when Kyle let himself in the back door with my key.

Kyle thought I woke up looking and smelling that good in the mornings. He was sure he had found his dream-girl.

* * *

June 2nd was only a few weeks away and my friends from school were giving my first bridal shower, so I wanted to look my best.

I had heard of an oil treatment for long hair that involved massaging mayonnaise into the roots and leaving the hair wrapped up in a towel for fifteen minutes. The people who told me about it said, "It will make your hair shine like a new copper penny."

I tried the treatment on Thursday evening, the night before the shower. I didn't have any mayonnaise so I used Miracle Whip Salad Dressing that was in the refrigerator. I used half a bottle of shampoo trying to get all of the gunk and gooey mess out of my hair. The next day the smell was still so strong, all the other girls in the office developed an unexplainable craving for lettuce and tomato, while I had a strong desire to stick my head in the refrigerator.

The treatment made my hair shine like a copper penny—a greasy copper penny that looked as if it hadn't been washed in a year.

I developed an intense headache and left work early, with the sole intentions of going straight home and washing my hair again and again until the odor was gone. However, it was about three more days and four more washings before that would be achieved. So, in the interim, I was forced to go to my party that night smelling like a tossed salad.

I said, "Y'all don't look at my hair…" and I went on to tell the whole story. That was to eliminate their thinking I wasn't aware how my hair looked and smelled. We all had a good laugh and the evening was a blast.

* * *

The phone rang about six-thirty one Wednesday evening about a week before our wedding night. I was shocked to hear Richard's voice and it stirred up some old feelings. His sister, Charlene, worked at Rich's with Mama so they kept in contact. That's how I knew he was discharged from the Army for medical reasons.

Richard went on to tell me that he was scheduled to go into the hospital, and asked if I would drop by his house the next afternoon on my way home.

When I drove up and parked on the street in front of his house, it brought back wonderful memories, as both his mother and father greeted me with hugs and kisses.

His father informed me, "The doctors aren't sure what's wrong with him, so he's going to be hospitalized for tests. He's waiting in his bedroom and he's so anxious to talk with you."

I entered his room and I was overcome by a very sad feeling and a surge of regret. Regret that things hadn't ended differently between us.

I was afraid I was still in love with Richard as I thought, *What will I do if I still love him?* He was lying flat on his back, unable to get up, so I sat on the chair beside the bed and held his hand. He was so weak. His six-foot three-inch tall body extended the full length of his bed, and showed such signs of frailty, the likes for which I was not prepared. *God, I do still feel for him. Now I'm confused. How can I still feel so strongly for him, while I'm so much in love with Kyle?*

He explained the reason he wanted me to stop by, "I want you to make sure you're marrying the right man. I've always regretted acting so much like children, the way we let our stupid pride get in the way."

I couldn't resist responding, "You're the one who acted like a child, with your petty jealousy."

"I know, and I'm sorry. But I'm asking you to wait. Don't marry this guy. Wait until I'm back on my feet again and give us another chance."

255

"But Richard, I'm in love with Kyle, and I know he's the right one for me." Our eyes met and we both read a sense of sadness in our looks. "I'm sorry, Richard."

I leaned over and kissed him on the forehead, "I have to go now, but I'll call you to see how the tests turned out."

He grabbed my arm and said, "You can do better than that!" I knew he wanted more of a kiss than just on the forehead.

I hesitated for a moment then I took a deep breath and leaned over the bed. When our lips met I anticipated fireworks, but I was relieved that the feeling was not as it had been two years earlier.

After offering my good-byes to him and his family, I walked out the door and drove away, without so much as looking back—not even in the rear view mirror.

* * *

Kyle and I were soon faced with the task of finding an apartment— an affordable apartment.

We found an upstairs duplex in one of those nice, older homes, located over in the Morningside district of Atlanta. It was a tan brick colonial style, with really high ceilings and hardwood floors, and it was loaded with charm. We had a private entrance on the side next to our very own walkway that led to the sidewalk at the front of the house. We wouldn't mind parking the Mustang on the street.

The rooms needed a coat of paint, but we would tackle that, together with Kyle's brothers. Other than that, it was perfect. All of the rooms were over-sized and it was conveniently located near Kyle's work at the printing company, and mine at the gas company. Carpeted living room with fireplace, bedroom with Oriental rug, kitchen, bathroom, and a hallway—all for eighty dollars a month.

The price was so attractive we certainly wouldn't mind climbing the eighteen stairs to get there. We were so much in love we considered those eighteen steps our Stairway to Paradise.

CHAPTER XXI
$8.63 INCLUDED THE BROOM

My wedding gown was beautiful, but I was disappointed because I didn't lose the extra pounds I had gained so it was a size twelve. I had always dreamed of being a slender, June bride of model proportions. Kyle repeatedly told me, "Don't be so hard on yourself, baby. I love you and I don't care what size you are." When he said that I always said to myself, *Have I found the perfect man, or what?*

The night of the wedding rehearsal I cried so hard, the pastor doubted I would make it through that night, much less for the real ceremony. He had grown accustomed to my high emotions, since he had been the pastor of our church for several years. Kyle and I had met with him for pre-marital counseling sessions, and I cried during all of them.

I especially cried when he told us, "Kyle and Delaney, you'll find that you won't have to actually say the words, "I love you," twenty-four hours a day. There will be times when you'll simply glance across the room at each other, and that certain look in your eyes will state your feelings."

* * *

Kyle's brothers were the ushers and my best friends at the time, Betty and Donna, were the bridesmaids. Kyle's sister, Karen, was the matron of honor and her husband Lloyd, was the best man. My sister's youngest son, Matthew, was the ring bearer. I could just image how beautiful the candlelight wedding was going to be. Kyle and I covered most of the expenses because Mama wasn't in the best shape, financially.

The wedding was to be at eight so the candlelight would be more effective. Randy's cousin was the photographer and he was taking pictures of me before the wedding. I was so nervous until Randy came in to help with the camera equipment, and he smiled at me.

He walked over, took my hand in his and led me to the side of the room, away from everyone. After he kissed my hand he gazed into my eyes for only a moment before he said softly, "My God, Delaney. You're Beautiful. Kyle's a lucky man." After he glanced around to make sure he wasn't overheard, he whispered, "I'd give anything if...if it were me instead of him tonight."

"Randy, what are you saying?"

"I'm saying I love you. Damn it to hell, Delaney, I've always been in love with you. There, I've said it. I know it doesn't make a damn bit of sense to tell you tonight, of all nights, but at least I got it off my chest, and if this guy doesn't treat you right, you just let me know."

I didn't know what to say, so I said, "Oh, Randy. I love you, too. You're my best friend in the whole world. You've always been there for me and I want you to know you can always count on me to be there for you. We don't have to stop being friends just because I'm marrying Kyle."

"If he suspects how I feel about you, we will."

I really cared for Randy as a friend, and I always assumed that was all he thought and felt toward me. How could I have been so blind and insensitive to overlook his feelings when they were right there in front of me? The answer was very simple—I wasn't looking. That night I felt as though I had lost the best friend a girl could ever have. I knew it would never be the same between us.

* * *

The nerve pills and aspirin I took didn't seem to have calmed me down, but by the time I was to walk down the aisle, I felt they had without doubt taken effect and I thought I had everything under control.

My oldest brother, Gene, looked so handsome in the front hall of the church, waiting to escort me down the aisle ad give me away. I loved my brother, but I couldn't help thinking, *Oh, Daddy, I wish you were the one here giving me away. It was always you in my dreams.*

The songs were so beautiful. Mary had been my Sunday school teacher for several years, and her voice always did send chills over me. We were taping the evening so our memories would be preserved.

A lump suddenly formed in my throat when I heard the organ strike the opening chord to begin the bridal march.

Gene looked at me as he offered his arm, winked, and whispered, "Well, little sister, are you ready?" When he kissed me on the cheek it was more like a fatherly kiss than a kiss from a brother.

I was all right for the most part and I think I would have made it, but then I saw Mama. Her eyes were filled with tears and the look on her face was of a mother, whose thoughts were that she was losing her baby girl. I was so thankful she had no idea of the hell I went through the previous fall, so her view of me as her baby was not skewed.

Standing next to the pastor was Kyle, looking even more handsome than I remembered, and I wondered if he was as scared and nervous as I was. I had horrors of tripping over my gown and falling flat on my face.

We were finally there together at the altar, and we were going to be so happy! Then why was I feeling as if I were going to be sick? That would have been worse than falling.

Delaney, you can't be sick, I told myself, *you should have eaten something for dinner.* Mama had warned me that I better eat and get something on my stomach or I'll be sick. What was it about her, anyway? Why did she always have to be right about everything? I'd go to pour a glass of tea or milk when I was a little girl and she'd say, "Delaney, now hold that pitcher with both hands or you'll spill it all over the table!" And I was always "so sorry" when I spilled it. I thought I could handle the pitcher with just one hand, despite her warning.

And then there were times she'd tell me to "tie your shoestrings or you'll trip and fall over on your head." I was amazed at how she could see into the future that way. A woman who for the past eight or nine years, I thought had no sense at all, had suddenly developed into one of the wisest women I knew. I wondered how anyone could get so smart all of a sudden?

* * *

Kyle and I both said, "I do," and the deed was done. The knot was tied.

The pastor's words, "I now pronounce you man and wife," were the words I had dreamed about for months. My sick feeling dissipated as the kiss to seal our vows ignited a surge of joy and happiness inside. We couldn't wait to get this marriage started as we ran back up the aisle.

His mother had arranged for us to stay that night in the honeymoon suite at the hotel in downtown Atlanta, where she worked—The Americana Hotel. We decided not to waste our money on an extravagant honeymoon. We would use our money more sensibly. Perhaps I should say we would have used our money more sensibly if we had any money. The truth was, we didn't have any money for a honeymoon, but that didn't bother us in the least.

The light mist of rain prevented our lowering the car's windows for air, and it became a little stuffy. In fact, the word "unbearable" comes to mind when I think of it. There was a smell that was a cross between my brother, Bud's, dirty socks, and Mr. Echols' fishing tackle box. We looked into one another's eyes, watering as they were, and before I knew what happened, I said it, "Did you bring your deodorant?"

He laughed and replied, "I know you're excited and anxious, but try not to spoil before we get to the hotel." I didn't understand what he meant but I laughed along with him. However, the fact still remained...something smelled fishy.

A can of sardines had been poured on the engine and, of course, when the car heated up, the smell was our companion all the way to the hotel.

* * *

We were about to shower and prepare for the night of our dreams when we discovered my suitcase was locked...and the key was on the same key-ring along with my car key...and the garage attendant currently had custody of those.

My white negligee and peignoir set Mama had given me for that special night was in that suitcase, and I simply had to wear it. Although Kyle was very convincing when he assured me that it really wouldn't matter. Nonetheless, it was imperative that I have that nightgown, so Kyle retrieved the keys from downstairs and the marriage began properly.

I wasn't crazy about the taste of champagne, but we opened the bottle, toasted to our future, and retired for the night...after I called Mama, of course.

It was exactly the way I had imagined it would be. We had a view of Atlanta that was exhilarating, but we were more interested in what was inside the room—and I don't mean the furniture.

When we made love it wasn't just the act of sex. There was a special closeness that was tender and exciting, simultaneously. There was a mutual feeling of serenity and reassurance to follow, as we lay in one another's arms breathing one another's air. Sharing silent thoughts of happiness, as this would be the growing foundation for our unconditional love.

* * *

I felt so safe with him I never wanted that night to end. But it did, and we awoke to a rainy Saturday morning. Of course, I called Mama first thing—almost first thing.

"How is everything?" she asked, with a degree of innocence in her voice.

"Everything's wonderful, Mama," I answered. I couldn't help but smile to myself as I thought, *How is everything? Everything couldn't be any better! Could Kyle be even better as a lover than he is a friend?* All evidence pointed in that direction, as I smiled even bigger, remembering, *And we're married, so it's legal—it's all perfectly legal! What a life!*

* * *

We couldn't wait to get our marriage officially started, so we checked out of the hotel and rushed to our little apartment.

We opened the door and stared up at the eighteen steps. Then we looked at each other and decided to forego the newlywed threshold tradition. We would put our energies to better use.

We didn't have a phone yet so I couldn't call Mama.

We admired our new furnishings and then decided to take a closer look at the bedroom. Exactly as we had suspected—it was "just right," as Goldie Locks said. The only problem was the noise factor, as the bedsprings seemed a bit loud. Kyle turned on the attic fan to drown out the noise. The attic fan was huge and sounded like a seven-forty-seven was flying overhead.

In love as we were, the reality hit that we had no food in the apartment.

As we donned our grocery-shopping clothes, we were off to conquer our first frontier together, that being the corner grocery store.

We made a list and shopped carefully because, as I mentioned earlier, we had limited funds. Our grocery list, June 3, 1967 consisted of: cleanser, salt, pepper, Miracle Whip, bacon, eggs, bread, hot dogs, buns, peanut butter, grape jelly, Velveeta cheese, margarine, tomato soup, chicken..."Chicken?" as I explained, "But, I don't know how to cook chicken."

Kyle laughed and replied, "Well, now's as good a time as any to learn," as he directed me, in addition, to buy flour and potatoes. Oh yes, and grits, ice cream, Coke, tea bags, sugar, and of course, toilet paper was also on the list.

Kyle came walking up the aisle with a broom tucked underneath his arm, and I made a corny crack about "here comes the groom carrying the broom."

The check we wrote for our first grocery supply amounted to $8.63, and we proclaimed upon leaving the store that, "If we have to put this much into groceries every week, we'd better be looking for second jobs" But then, I reminded Kyle that, "The $8.63 included the broom!"

We both sighed of relief and he said, "Well, then maybe we can make it after all."

* * *

Little did we know how rock bottom we were, as Kyle's checking account left a lot to be desired in the balancing department. We weren't aware until the following week, but the checks bounced that he wrote to the florist, as well as the pastor. We were so embarrassed, we avoided church the following two weeks, to give the checks time to clear.

* * *

That week I learned the art of frying chicken and mashing potatoes. The next weekend we had our first dinner guest—Mama. After she gave me her seal of approval by saying, "Delaney, baby, I'm so proud of you," we decided to invite guests over for dinner more often.

We first invited his mother and brother, then his sister and her husband, then his brother and his girl friend, then his friend and fiance, then another married couple, and so on.

Fried chicken, mashed potatoes, beans, salad, rolls and ice tea was the menu for each and every dinner party. We had eaten so much chicken by the end of the summer, it's a wonder we didn't start sprouting feathers and clucking.

* * *

I committed myself to a regimented diet and lost all the weight I wanted to lose, much to Kyle's pleasure. The only problem was that I saw Kyle become even more jealous than before. I didn't complain because I thought it was romantic.

* * *

Our little paradise upstairs from the rest of the world was where it all began. It marked the blissful beginning shared by best friends and lovers, who dreamed of a lifetime of tomorrows together.

CHAPTER XXII
THE CEMENT BLOCK PALACE

Life was perfect in every way! Our little newlywed corner of the world was brimming over with love, laughter, and everything to make our lives happy and complete.

However, something was missing--something that had been a big part of my life for the past decade.

It seemed as if we had been waiting for years, as I wondered, *How long could the waiting list be?* Not that Kyle's companionship wasn't more than sufficient, but woman does not live by shopping, love, and food alone—not necessarily in that order. Woman must have communication. At any rate, this woman needed communication with her mother on a daily basis, and at thirty-five cents per gallon, gasoline was much too expensive to drive across town to her house every afternoon.

So after many days—it was actually less than a week—the beautiful, basic-black was delivered. The telephone had arrived. Perched over on the table we had refinished, especially for the new member of the family, it looked as if it had always been there.

I stroked its clean, fingerprint-free, plastic case of shiny ebony, as I caressed the receiver in the perfect fit of my left hand and placed it to my ear. The sound of the dial tone brought about such a sensation. It wasn't like I had never been with a telephone before, but there was a certain thrill in knowing it was our very own, and Mama wouldn't be there to say, "Delaney, you've been on that phone long enough."

I placed my digit finger in the correct holes and spun the dial to make my first phone call. There was a nice, smooth sound to the spin, unlike Mama's that made a choppy, *click—click—click* noise when it was dialed.

Of course Mama was the first person I called, and then Sis, and then Diane, and so on and on. It wasn't long before Kyle referred to it as my umbilical chord.

I couldn't wait until the new telephone directories were delivered in the fall so we could see our names—correction, Kyle's name—listed.

After only one week Kyle threatened to have the phone taken out and I responded frantically, "But we need a telephone in case of an emergency."

"Emergency? I suppose it's an *emergency* to call your mother and talk for two hours about what you just cooked for dinner?"

What we had was the beginning of a problem in communication—too many communications over the telephone on my part—as we began to settle down to the more realistic routine of marriage.

* * *

I missed the comforts of home—meals prepared and on the table, my clothes washed and ironed, a clean house, all compliments of good ole Mama. She never *trusted* me in the kitchen; therefore, she prepared all the meals except for the grilled cheese sandwiches, tomato soup, and scrambled eggs, and who was I to argue? As far as the housework, when Mama said to clean the house, my favorite comeback was, "Aw, Mama, there's nothing wrong with the house. It just looks lived in." It's odd, how the "lived in" look took on an entirely different meaning when we had a place of our own.

* * *

Kyle had a built-in alarm clock set for five-fifteen every workday morning, so it wasn't necessary to own a regular alarm clock. He had his own special way of waking me on workday mornings, and it *wasn't* "Delaney...Delaney, get up...Delaney, come on, now... Delaney...," and on and on, the way Mama did every morning when I lived at home.

One might have concluded that, had I responded to her first, "Delaney, get up," the *'and on and ons'* wouldn't have been necessary. But an observer wouldn't have had anyway of knowing that Mama was always the kind who needed to feel needed, and mornings were my way of helping her feel that way. My lying there in the bed simply fulfilled her needs in that area, aside from my insatiable love of sleep. Nonetheless, the mornings back home could turn a person against her own mother.

* * *

A typical workday morning married to Kyle could be summed up with one word—rushed. He had to be at work at seven a.m., and I was relieved when he informed me he didn't like to eat breakfast so early in the morning. He said it made him sick to eat so early, and it made me sick to cook so early, so we were very compatible on that note.

* * *

Most afternoons the after-work hours found us at his mother's house. It was great to belong to such a close knit family...for a while. But by the end of the summer the novelty of the closeness wore off.

After dinner we'd draw our lawn chairs into a circle in the front yard for the evening's family discussion, which would always include at least one argument between Kyle and his mother. I had never seen a mother and son have so many differences of opinion about everything—politics, world problems, family affairs, inflation. She'd always find something to debate about: "We don't have any business in Vietnam. When is Johnson going to get us out of there?" Or "What's the sense in the country spending all these millions on rockets and space travel and such? And going to the moon? Ha! That'll never happen in our lifetime, and what are we going to do when we get there?" Or "the price of gas is more than forty cents! What's Johnson gonna do about it? Do you think President Johnson's gonna run for re-election next year?"

They weren't unlike my family, in that they told the same stories over and over again, and after a while, I knew them all by heart.

Pug, the family dog, stayed under our feet the entire time, which was usually until dark and the blood-sucking mosquitoes began their evening feasts. Pug wasn't so bad for a Heinz 57, mixed breed mutt. He was toothless from old age and harmless enough. But he was a pretty good watchdog—when he was awake. However, as soon as he growled and gritted his gums, I'm sure any intruder's fears would have subsided. He had survived being hit by so many cars, but arthritis from old age forced a limp from his rear leg. A run-in with a neighbor's cat left him blind in one eye, so he was a bit pitiful looking. But Pug had been with the Rutherfords since he was a puppy and he was part of the family.

Nonetheless, the army of fleas and gnats that accompanied him everywhere made me feel like they were all up my nose and in my eyes, as I sat there in the yard scratching right along with the dog. In fact, there were so many little pests hovering around him, it appeared as if they were carrying him, instead of the other way around.

* * *

To celebrate the Fourth of July and his brother, Ray's birthday, we had a family picnic at Lake Spivey.

I was embarrassed to be around his three brothers when I was wearing no more than a two-piece swimsuit. I wasn't bad looking in a two-piece, but I still considered myself a little under-developed up top, for a woman almost nineteen years old. Kyle always reassured me, "Anything over a handful is wasted." But that didn't make me feel less self-conscious.

To compensate for my less-than-womanly bust-line I safety pinned some foam helpers to the inside of the swimsuit top. I remembered how some of us girls in school stuffed toilet paper and Kleenex in their bras for the purpose of building a bustline underneath our sweaters. There was one girl the boys called "Pinky" because she used pink tissue.

The family had the brilliant idea to rent a ski ride on one of those boats we'd seen spinning around the lake.

When it was my turn I skied around like a semi-pro, but then a rush of anxiety came over me and I began to imagine falling into a bed of snakes. Before I knew it I was overcome by the fear of falling, and I was down like a flash. In the interim my swimsuit strap broke and I was floating strapless in the water waiting to be fished out. Quick thinker that I was, I remembered the safety pin that held the foam helpers in place, and I used that to secure the strap.

The only problem was that because they were no longer secured, the helpers completely disjoined themselves from me, and began to float on their way.

Before I had a chance to retrieve them, the boat was pulling up to retrieve me!

As we were pulling away, the white mini-mounds swirled and tossed about in the water, floating, bobbing up and down in the wake behind the boat. I was hoping the others in the boat would remain facing the front, and I cringed at the thought of them washing up to shore. Even worse, I could just imagine them washing up on the beach and someone walking up to me while holding them out in front and saying, "Excuse me, Miss, but I believe these are yours."

I wondered it the family noticed I looked a bit deflated in that area after the ski trip. And if they knew the real reason my face was so red…and that it wasn't from too much sun.

* * *

Later that first summer we all drove to Panama City—together. There was his mother, his sister, her husband and little girl, along with all three brothers. Kyle and I stayed in the motel room, while they all stayed together in a cottage.

We considered that to be our honeymoon since it was the first trip we had taken together on a vacation. With so many romantic plans we couldn't wait to get there.

The air conditioner in the motel room was a real luxury for us since we didn't have one in our apartment back in Atlanta.

But the motel was far from luxurious. The units were built of cement blocks and painted turquoise—pink—turquoise—pink, alternately, and it had a gaudy, flashing flamingo on the lighted neon sign in front of the office. It was one of those economic "cement block palaces," as we called them, so numerous in Panama City and most of Florida. We kept our suitcases sealed tightly at all times for fear we'd take a strange crawling insect home with us by mistake.

We rushed down to the beach as soon as we arrived there, and stayed in the sun all that day. There was always something about lying in the sun that made my hormones rage, so I couldn't wait until we got back to our motel room after dinner that night. Unfortunately, I had to learn to keep my raging hormones under control, as Kyle wasn't exactly in an affectionate mood.

I couldn't believe he sunburned so easily. Not only did we forego our romantic interludes that evening, I had to be careful not to bump up against him in the night.

I soon discovered just how stubborn my husband to be, as he repeated the sun ritual the next day, and the next.

By the end of the second day however, we had discovered zinc oxide, the white cream that all the life guards and full-time professional sunbathers smeared across their noses. The entire family smeared the cream in the most sun-sensitive areas, and we resembled aliens from God only knows where.

The tops of Kyle's feet were so sunburned they looked like red lobsters, so I encouraged him to smear some of it on the tops of his feet. What seemed like such a great idea wasn't so great after all.

The problem came when he tried walking across the beach. The sand stuck to his feet like iron ore to a magnet, and the burn was irritated even worse.

We could have stayed in the cottage with the rest of the family and saved a lot of money that trip. We did nothing during the entire week that the entire population of Panama City Beach couldn't have seen. What a waste!

Aside from all the agony of Kyle's sunburn pain, there are fond memories from the summer of 1967 and the time we spent on the beach and in the pool. Among those memories is room eleven of the Surf n Sand Motel. Or was it the Sand n Sea? Or, maybe it was the Sea n Surf? Whatever the name, we'll never forget that summer and the cement-block palace on Panama City Beach, Florida.

CHAPTER XXIII
WE'LL NEVER LIVE
THIS TIME AGAIN!

It was such a thrill when we received mail addressed to us—correction, to *Kyle*—even if they were bills. We had purchased our living and bedroom furniture on a convenient charge plan. Those payments, the electric and telephone bills, along with groceries and my car note were the extent of our commitments, so we considered ourselves doing all right financially.

We were able to go out for dinner once in a while, to the movies every weekend and buy clothes. What more could we possibly want?

I was shopping one afternoon on my lunch hour and ran across the perfect stereo—on "sale"—and they also had a credit plan. After persuading Kyle to go take a look, I convinced him it was only seven dollars a month and they delivered our beautiful new stereo the very next afternoon.

By the time Kyle's birthday rolled around on September 28th, we saved enough money to pay cash and bought our very own color TV. Color televisions were still considered luxury items—among our friends and relatives, at any rate. The old black-and-white TV we had bought from Diane for twenty-five dollars found a new home at the foot of our bed, and that was when a man named Johnny was first introduced to our bedroom. Kyle didn't like being kept awake late at night, but the real reason he hated the TV in there was because it was robbing him of quality time with his wife. "Not tonight, Kyle. Johnny Carson's gonna have Burt Reynolds on his show."

* * *

I couldn't believe it. I was only nineteen and Kyle was twenty-three, and we had it all—nice car, apartment, furniture, stereo, *two* televisions (one that was color), our very own telephone and of course, we had each other and were so much in love.

We socialized with only a few friends. We didn't need anyone else, and it seemed as if all of our married friends argued all the time, so we pretty much kept to ourselves.

* * *

I had a violent reaction to the birth control pills prescribed for me by the doctor, so he suggested other methods. One such method, for which Kyle and I developed a mutual dislike, was contraceptive foam that could be bought over the counter at the local drugstore.

There was no way we could afford a baby at that time, and we were ninety-eight percent safe with the foam.

However, there was a time that fall when my period was about six weeks late and we were sure the other two percent had caught up with us. My periods had never been very regular, but I was certain I was pregnant.

We had only been married four months, but we became excited about the prospect of starting our family.

I had nausea with morning sickness and all the symptoms of pregnancy. After a doctor's examination, he told me it was too soon to tell, then directed me to take an early morning urine specimen by the lab and call that afternoon for the test results. The feeling of deja vu came over me.

When I called I was so certain the test results would be positive, I requested the nurse to repeat herself when she said, "The results were negative, Mrs. Rutherford."

"But how can it be negative?" I later asked the doctor. "I have all the symptoms."

"Mrs. Rutherford, you are experiencing a 'pseudo' or false pregnancy. You apparently wanted to be pregnant so that you convinced yourself you were, and your body reacted by producing the symptoms. It's sometimes call psychological pregnancy."

It was difficult for us to understand at the time, but it was a true blessing that I wasn't pregnant. However false it was, the experience of being pregnant with Kyle's baby only made me want one for real. I enjoyed the warm feeling of closeness—that special bond Kyle and I shared for those few weeks. I was just barely nineteen years old, but I had already imagined having a little bundle to love, and then I was told it wasn't so.

* * *

That first Thanksgiving we were going to my sister's house for the traditional feast. I volunteered to bring potato salad and bake a cake. It was my first attempt at potato sale, but I used my mother's recipe, then I decorated the surface with a turkey I crated out of pickles, olives, and devilled eggs. I saved a spoonful for Kyle and I smiled at his reaction when he tasted it, then gave me a big kiss and said, "Mm-m, that's the best potato salad I've ever eaten!"

But I couldn't wait until my family saw the cake. I wanted it to be super-spectatularly special. Not a two or three-layer, but a *six* layer cake should do the trick, so I bought three boxes of cake mix from which I made six single layers. The eleven-inch total height of the cake was simply overwhelming. However, the chocolate icing between the layers caused cake-slides, similar to land-slides.

My quick thinking directed me to use toothpicks to reinforce the chocolate tower, holding it together so I could decorate the top with icing, in the creative design of a pilgrim's hat. I stood back to admire my creation and thought about my chronically critical sister-in-law, Jackie, and her digs about my cooking, *Hmm, this should make her eat cake.*

There were so many wooden mini-spikes in the scrumptious structure it was similar to eating a piece of bony fish, as Mama warned, "Everybody, look out for the bones when you're eating Delaney's cake!"

Nevertheless, the cake was a tremendous hit with my niece and nephews, as each single slice was the equivalent to three. Subsequently, Jackie was speechless.

I owed the pride of my baking career to Duncan Hines. Still, Kyle was so proud of me he took pictures from several angles, of both my contributions to that year's family Thanksgiving. We considered submitting the cake photos to *Ripley's Believe It or Not.*

* * *

Christmas was so exciting! We bought presents for everyone, sparing no expense. Within reason, of course.

The most exciting time of all was shopping for the tree. A fifteen-foot fir tree had to be altered about three feet, to fit in the twelve-foot ceiling of our living room.

Decorating the apartment was so much fun. In every room and everywhere you turned you saw Christmas. I was so cozy as I lay on the sofa in Kyle's arms. I squinted my eyes to make the tree's lights appear to have pretty colored halos around them, while I reminisced about Christmas' of my childhood.

That was our first Christmas together as husband and wife, as that morning we awoke to open our gifts, dressed, and ran to the family get-togethers for the day.

Christmas night I developed the sentimental sniffles, and that was the first time Kyle would see me cry and hear me blubber, "We'll *never* live this time again."

He wrapped his arms around me and tried to comfort me, "Don't cry, Baby. I promise you, the best are yet to come."

The tears of Christmas night were nothing compared to the tears of depression I displayed on the day we put the tree out for the trash pick-up. I felt so sad when I thought about the tree that brought us so much love and happiness, only to be cast aside.

* * *

Our first anniversary was another "We'll never live this night again" event.

I didn't know it at the time, but the end of every vacation, holiday, or special day of any kind would be marked as another "We'll never live this time again" event.

I couldn't help it if I was so sentimental. It's been said that Libras are that way, and I'm living proof.

CHAPTER XXIV
INVASTION OF THE
UNINVITED VISITORS

The day I turned twenty the fact that I was no longer a teenager dropped on my head like a lead balloon. I felt ancient, but Kyle did a good job of cheering me up. His family gave me a surprise birthday party. Of course they gave every family member a surprise birthday party, so after a while the surprise failed to be as effective.

Birthdays were just another reason for his family to get together—not that they needed a reason.

* * *

As nice as the apartment was, I wanted a house of our very own. Perhaps, I should emphasize the "I," in the preceding statement, as Kyle was perfectly content to remain in the apartment…forever. After all, it wasn't as though we had any children. We had more than enough room there, so whenever I mentioned the subject he always responded, "What's the rush?"

That was Kyle's theory, but I ignored him and began to think about what kind of house we could afford. After a lot of calculating, the magic figure of thirteen-thousand dollars was set as the limit for the purchase price, and we had only saved five-hundred dollars for a down payment. I always dreamed of owning a brick house. Sis had a brick house. Every time they had moved from one state to another, Sis and Bryan always managed to buy a brick house. Mama always used my sister as an example of the ideal American woman, "If you grow up to be as pretty as your sister, you'll be doing just fine." Or, "If you could grow up and marry a man like Bryan, you'll be doing great!" Or, "If you could teach yourself to sew like your sister," or "If you could learn to play the piano like Trish." I didn't realize it at the time, but it became a silent competition—me against my sister.

That fall as I looked at houses, I felt intimidated by the possibility of Mama comparing whatever house we bought to my sister's beautiful, brick home.

I scanned the newspapers on a regular basis and became obsessed with buying a house, an obsession which Kyle never shared.

* * *

It was just after midnight in November when I heard a noise in the kitchen—*flip—flop—flop*.

"Honey, did you hear that?" I whispered.

Then I heard it again—*Flip—flop—flop*—so I nudged Kyle and said, "There it is again. Did you hear it?"

We cautiously approached the kitchen and turned on the light. We didn't see a thing, but we heard a sudden scratching noise from inside the trash can. "Don't touch it!" I warned. Then I shrieked, "It sounds like a big rat in there!"

I jumped up and stood on a chair while Kyle bravely and courageously peered down into the darkened depths of the flip-top, plastic trash can. It startled me when he exclaimed, "There it is! I see it! Come over here and look at it—it's not gonna bother you."

I wouldn't get off the chair so Kyle brought the can over where I could look inside. There was an adorable little chipmunk, cowardly hovering down in the corner, looking ever so innocent as the light reflected in its beady, dark eyes when it peered up at me. It was entrapped there with a plea for mercy displayed through its petrified silence.

I felt so sad for it to be trapped like that so I told Kyle to "Let him go. We can't kill Chip or Dale." So Kyle emptied the little chipmunk outside the door and granted him his freedom, and we went back to bed.

It was only a few minutes later when we heard *flip—flop—flop*, once again. We discovered he was more than one, as Kyle repeated the trip to the door with can in hand. In fact, that became a regular course of action. They were running along the counter-top and jumping into the trash can, as if it were a game.

The fear of stepping on one of those little critter beasts was unnerving and thus hastened my search for a new house.

With the invasion of the uninvited visitors, the apartment no longer seemed as cozy as it once did. After all, one could run out and bite my toe in the night—and just what if it had rabies? Besides, if the chipmunks had found a way to sneak in, what's to keep other varmints from discovering the passageway? Kyle thought it was humorous, as he scoffed at me and said, "Delaney, you're acting like a typical woman. Those little things aren't gonna hurt you."

Kyle was working one particular night when I hysterically called the landlady's son and asked him to please come upstairs and empty one out of the trashcan. He came up wearing combat boots and carrying a baseball bat. I wondered if I was supposed to regard that as a "typical male reaction."

CHAPTER XXV
ANOTHER YEAR TOGETHER
AND DEEPER IN DEBT

After several weeks of dedicated searching, I found our dream house. It was not only brick, but as the real estate agent pointed out, it was "authentic antique brick."

The minute I stepped onto the chipped-tile floor of the portico extending along the front, and gazed through the full length, triple-wide window, I fell in love with the place. It had beautiful, hardwood floors, unique double-sided fireplace, dining room, two bedrooms, small den with genuine pine paneling, and not one, but *two* bedrooms. The built-in dishwasher and single car carport were just icing of the cake. Complete with an air-conditioner and a sun porch with a huge patio in the back, the house was all I ever imagined, and so much more.

At fourteen-thousand, it wouldn't be on the market for long, so I rushed Kyle over to see it that very evening. Reluctantly, he rode over with me, declaring, "That's more than we can afford!"

I kept saying, "But just wait 'til you see it!"

Unfortunately, it was totally dark by the time we arrived there and Kyle could barely see the house, so we shined the car lights on the outside and looked at the inside by flashlight. Kyle was impressed by what he saw—impressed enough that it would be our very first house, even if it did cost more than we planned to pay. We considered it our present to one another since Christmas was only a few weeks away.

I couldn't wait to call Mama and tell her all about it. I had no doubts the house would meet with her approval, with it being brick, having a fireplace, a dishwasher, and an air-conditioner, along with so many extras.

She was excited when she said, "I'm so proud for you, Baby." But then she cautioned, "Just don't get in over your heads." I thought, *For crying out loud, Mama, stop worrying.*

* * *

Kyle and I were disappointed when the final arrangements couldn't be made in time for us to move in prior to Christmas. It was just as well, because we both contracted the Hong Kong flu. We always did things together, but that was carrying it to the extreme!

Christmas was only a few days away, but sick as we were, I couldn't bear not having a decorated tree. Since I was almost over my flu, I went out to buy one while Kyle stayed home under a blanket on the sofa.

I promised Kyle before I left, "I'm just gonna get a small one to sit on top of the television," as I went out in the misting rain to find the perfect little tree.

I went to the Christmas tree lot in front of Sears on Ponce de Leon. With Christmas only two days away the trees were drastically reduced. In fact, all the trees were the same price of just $3.00. Logic told me, if they're all $3.00—no matter what size—the best bargain would be the biggest tree on the lot. I was so proud of myself as I handed the man my money. It towered over the others and I considered it to be the most beautiful tree on the lot.

The two men took the tree off the stake and said, "Okay little lady, where's your truck?"

"Oh, I don't have a truck. I'm in that Mustang over there."

They acted amazed and amused that I was going to take that tree home in the trunk of a Mustang. "Little lady, don't you want us to tie it to the top of the car for you?"

"Naw, I'm only going about four or five miles, tops. It'll be all right. Besides, I don't want to scratch the paint.

"Well, okay, but…this is a twenty-two-footer. Don't you want us to chop some off the bottom for ya?"

"No, thank you. Our ceilings are real high, (though I had no idea how high they really were), and I don't think it's that much bigger than the one we had last year. We may need to chop off a little bit, but my husband has a little saw, and he can do it when I get it back to the apartment. Besides, it's such a perfect tree I don't want to ruin its shape."

It began raining so they told me to get inside the car, out of the rain, which I did without argument. I didn't want the flu to turn into pneumonia.

They loaded the tree in the rear, and after they secured the trunk lid with a rope, they knocked on the back fender of the car and yelled, "Okay, she's ready to go!"

Everyone I passed on the streets stared in my direction. I could see their look of amazement and I thought they were admiring my beautiful tree. I smiled, thinking, *If they only knew how little I paid for it.*

I pulled up in front of the apartment and blew the horn while I parallel-parked on the street. Once I was parked, I glanced up and saw Kyle looking down from the window. He was shaking his head, side-to-side, and he had the same look of amazement as the people I passed on the road. I knew what he was thinking, "She said she was going to get a table top tree, and she comes back with the most gorgeous tree I've ever seen. My wife is *brilliant.*"

That's what I *thought* he was thinking, however, I was wrong. I was *very* wrong. What he was actually saying was more like, "What have you done? We'll never get that big damn thing in here!"

I got out of the car to get it out of the trunk and drag it up the walk-way, right up to the door to make it easy on Kyle. That way, he wouldn't have to get out in the rain, and he could get his little saw and cut some off, like he did last year.

I was heartbroken and shocked when I walked around to the back of my car and saw the awful sight that was hanging out—way out—of my trunk. I had no idea it was *that* big!

My mind was a little fuzzy from the cold medicine, and that's the only excuse I could come up with for buying such a huge tree. For some reason I was thinking our ceiling was eighteen feet high, instead of only twelve.

By the time I reached the apartment, the entire top of that beautiful, twenty-two foot tree had drug the street and left it as bald as Yul Brenner.

I had not only underestimated its size, but the weight of the tree. I couldn't budge it, so Kyle threw on some jeans and jacket, and came down to the car to get the thing.

"Delaney, you have done some stupid things since I've known you, but this tops it all. What in the world were you thinking?"

"I guess it just didn't look that big on the lot. The tree we got last year was big and it looked good after you cut some off. You're gonna have to cut the top off, anyway, and that's the only part that's bare. The man told me it was a twenty-two-footer, but I guess I just didn't realize twenty-two feet was that much bigger than the one we had last year. "I'm sorry," as I began sniffling and tears welled in my eyes.

"Aw, don't cry, I'll fix it," as he got his little saw and went on to cut ten feet off the top. The twelve foot tree remaining was so big around we had to move all the furniture to the opposite side of the room. Once it was in place, it gave the illusion that it went all the way up, through the ceiling and the roof. The best way to describe it would be to say it looked more like a giant Christmas *bush* than a tree.

Poor Kyle—he was so sick and yet he still managed to hang the lights on the tree for me.

After watching all the trouble my husband had to go through to alter the thing, I thought, *I should've stuck to my original idea of a table-top tree,* but that's why they call it "hind-sight."

* * *

January 22, 1969 was our first day in our new home. What more could a young couple want?

We had a fenced backyard, so in April we purchased a cute little black Scottie dog. After much deliberation on our part, we officially named him Dandy Duffy McTavish, and we called him Duffy. I had always wanted a little black Scottie dog, so now, together with our dream home, we had our dream dog, too.

We were so lucky, with our beautiful brick home, fireplace, washer, dryer, dishwasher, color TV, a nice car, *and now* a pure bred, pedigree dog. We were the epitome of a successful young married couple…thanks to credit.

* * *

Our plans were for me to continue working two years after we married and then start a family, so Friday, June 6, 1969 I bid farewell to my friends and co-workers at the gas company.

It wasn't a new house, so we weren't surprised when the hot water heater developed a leak and needed replacing, inconveniently timed only one week before my last day of work. So it wouldn't interfere with our plans for me to quit work, we conveniently added the heater to our Sears charge account and considered it our anniversary gift to one another.

I loved the idea of credit. It was nearly as good as not having to pay for things.

* * *

Kyle and I weren't getting any younger. I was almost twenty-one and Kyle was twenty-five, so we needed to start a family right away.

My first responsibility, however, was housebreaking the dog. It was extremely difficult to paper-train male Scottish terriers like Duffy because they have short legs and long stomach hair. There were times when he relieved himself on the floor and we wouldn't be the wiser until he moved from where he was standing. And sometimes he put his front legs on the paper and thought he was completely safe, but the uncovered floor beneath him took the brunt of his error in judgment.

His favorite place to leave a "surprise" was on the floor beside the bed—on Kyle's side—strategically placed, so when Kyle got up during the night it smooshed between his toes. It was so funny, but I didn't dare laugh. I reminded Kyle that Duffy was just a dumb animal and didn't know any better. But at those particular times, in the height of temper, he referred to the dog by every name in the book *but* Duffy.

* * *

When Friday night, June 6th finally arrived we went out to celebrate my retirement. We reviewed our two years together, and Kyle commented, "Yeah, another year together and deeper in debt."

I thought, *Deeper in debt? Maybe...but we're no different from everyone else in the country.*

After all, isn't that the American way?

CHAPTER XXVI
THE VERY BEST
CHRISTMAS GIFT EVER

I experienced several false pregnancies over the next year, and felt the devastation and disappointment each time. I began to reason that there must be something wrong with me, and I wondered if God was punishing me for the past.

The doctor prescribed some fertility pills and when Mama found out she said, "Delaney, I've read articles about those things causing multiple births—two, three, four, even five babies at once—like a litter of puppies. You don't want that. Get off the things before it's too late."

* * *

Despite her warnings, I continued taking them but I told her I had thrown them away, just to get her off my back about it. I followed the doctor's instructions to the tee, including checking my temperature every morning to verify time of ovulation…but still no pregnancy.

The doctor advised, "Find yourself a hobby and get your mind off becoming pregnant. You could be trying too hard."

Trying too hard? I thought, *I've never heard of that, but he could be right. We have been trying every chance we get. Maybe Kyle's sperms are just worn out from trying so hard.*

* * *

When I explained to Kyle how we needed to take a rest from trying for a while, and the idea about getting a hobby, he understood and suggested we buy a sewing machine—on credit, of course.

Within days the store delivered my new electric Singer, beautiful walnut-grain cabinet and all, and I began to teach myself to sew. To begin with, I whipped out a mean pair of kitchen curtains. Then I made some clothes, and even swimsuits, with built-in bras for padding, of course.

* * *

Duffy became our child replacement and we took him everywhere with us. I even bought a red doggie sweater for him, and we placed doggie toys and chew-sticks under the tree to surprise him Christmas morning. He was nonchalant about all of it and never developed the sparkle of Christmas morning in his eyes, but after all he *was* just a dog.

* * *

Duffy could never really take the place of a child. Whenever I sat on our back porch and watched the little two-year-old Maria play in the yard next door, I was sad at the possibility that we may never have a baby of our own playing in our backyard.

* * *

Our best friends, Ronald and Teresa Turner, came over to the house one Saturday evening to grill hamburgers outside. They brought along their horse-of-a Great Dane to play with Duffy. "Blue" was their only child, too.

The dog left our house in a wreck and ruined the screen doors. He scratched the paint off the outside of the doors and tore the screens when he jumped up on them.

I was running through the dining room to answer the phone in our kitchen when I slid about three feet, landing on my backside. I suddenly realized I was soaking wet. I wasn't even aware I *knew* the words I said next, when I discovered I was sitting in the middle of a lake-sized puddle of dog urine—from *their* dog.

Needless to say, they were never invited back—not with that dog, at any rate.

* * *

I felt so awful that spring of '70—tired and sluggish—just downright sick. That April, when I went in to see the doctor, I told myself I either had a case of the flue, or I was experiencing another false pregnancy. By that time I had realized that having all the symptoms did not a baby make.

I had grown so tired of the doctor saying, "It's too soon to tell. You'll have to bring an early morning urine specimen, etc." I really thought it was just a horrible case of the flu, or either I was dying, as Mama drove me over to the doctor's office that morning. Mama always drove with two feet, and she jerked the car so badly at the stop signs and lights that I was seasick by the time we reached the office.

When I called the next afternoon, and the nurse said, "Congratulations, the results were positive." I asked her to repeat it, and then make sure she had the right test results. Kyle was more excited than I was, if that were possible. It was estimated that we were about six weeks pregnant, and the news made that afternoon the happiest day in our lives.

* * *

The only foods I craved were soft ice cream from the Dairy Queen, and lime sour with cherry fountain drinks from the local drugstore.

I hadn't had a lime sour with cherry since I was in high school, when we'd all drop by Brown's drugstore after tennis, softball, or cheerleading practice.

I didn't gain much weight the first seven months. I was too sick to eat, and then I was too weight conscious, too. So that I would be tanned all over, I continued to sunbathe on our sun-porch, which had a wall around it and provided complete privacy.

The baby was due on November 6th. On Labor Day we went to a local swim area and I wore a two-piece swimsuit. Since my tummy was still flat and I wasn't showing yet, the two-piece wasn't unbecoming. I knew the lifeguard there and he didn't realize I was married, much less pregnant.

I only gained a total of eight pounds through September and I thought I had it made. November 6th took its own sweet time in getting there, but when it finally did roll around, there was no baby. November 7th, 8th, 9th…21st, 27th, November 30th, and still there was no baby. My nerves were on edge and the eating machine shifted into high gear.

Well meaning friends and relatives called daily, and I reached a point I dreaded answering the telephone to hear, "You mean you haven't gone *yet*?" "What's the problem?" "Did the doctor miscalculate?"

"No, I haven't gone yet." "I don't know what the problem is." And "I don't know if he miscalculated, or not…but it's looking that way."

Finally, in the early morning hours of December 5ᵗʰ, my contractions were only seven minutes apart so Kyle rushed me to the hospital. The afternoon of the 5ᵗʰ found me back home again… and *still* no baby. I was *beyond* frustration. I then knew the true meaning of the term "false labor."

* * *

On December 9ᵗʰ I decided I couldn't stand the thought of Christmas coming and us there without a tree. So I went out to get the prettiest shaped one on the lot. We adopted December 9ᵗʰ as our official traditional Christmas tree buying day for every year to come.

I decorated the tree and the house for the holidays, while thinking how wonderful it was going to be to have the baby with us for Christmas.

The backaches started in the night and continued through the morning hours. Kyle was supportive, loving, nervous, and excited, but he was apprehensive, afraid it was another false alarm, "Are you *sure* this time?"

"No, I'm not sure! But I'm sure it hurts like heck and I'm sure I don't want to take the chance that it's not the real thing this time. Now, let's go before I have it right here on the bedroom floor!"

It was difficult to explain the welcomed feeling of pain that I was experiencing. It was welcomed, in the sense that something I wanted more than life itself—a baby—would be coming because of the pain. A pain that was eased only by the visions of holding a beautiful baby in my arms when it was all over. The pain of childbirth is not an empty pain, but it's a blessed feeling that God is creating a miracle…and you're a very important part of it all.

A woman never forgets the pain from the birth of her child, creating a bond between the two that lasts a lifetime, and beyond.

* * *

After twenty-two hours of walking the halls of the hospital with Kyle and family members, as well as nose drops to induce labor, Keith Kyle Rutherford was born on December 14, 1970.

When I was awakened from the anesthetic, the nurse brought Keith and placed him in my arms. He was the most beautiful baby God had ever put breath into, weighing in at eight pounds, fourteen ounces and twenty-two inches long—an inch for every hour of labor. I was amazed that he had been inside of me—even though I had gained thirty-eight pounds.

A careful inventory confirmed all ten fingers and all ten toes were present and accounted for. Both his eyesight and hearing seemed normal, and there was no doubt about his lungs. The nurses said he had already begun exercising them, indicating he was hungry.

The expression on Kyle's face when he came into the room reflected that of tremendous love, pride, relief, and nerves—all in one look—as he kissed me on the cheek and whispered, "Thank you, Delaney baby, you did *great*. I love you so much."

To which I replied, "Well, thanks, honey. But I couldn't have done it without you."

* * *

We took our little bundle home a few days later and imagined he was excited to be there in his own "sunshine room." We had decorated the room in green and bright yellow—always safe colors for a nursery.

Even though I had thought I wanted a girl, we loved that beautiful little boy as much as a baby could possibly be loved as we imagined teaching him to do all the little things we took for granted.

* * *

That was the best Christmas of all, as Christmas morning I sat in the rocking chair with the baby in my arms while enjoying the warmth of the fireplace. Kyle sat on the fireplace hearth next to us and watched as I nursed our son. Our eyes met and I was reminded of what the pastor had told us three and a half years earlier, "There will be times when you'll simply glance at each other, and that certain look in your eyes will say "I love you" without saying a word." That was definitely one of those times. We loved one another more than life itself, and we agreed that the little one in my arms was the very best Christmas gift…ever!

With our new son to my breast, I was contented and feeling safe and loved, as I thought about how I was going to teach him to imagine pictures in the flames of the fire. Squinting my eyes at the tree lights, I envisioned Keith doing the same in the years to come. I admired how pretty his complexion was, reflecting the glow from the Christmas lights.

I wondered if Daddy could see his new grandson, and I wished so much that he was there.

* * *

Above and beyond all the feelings of happiness, I wondered if Kyle felt as apprehensive as I about the responsibility of this little boy in my arms—raising him to become a man in the years to come.

With that thought in mind, I said a silent prayer, *Dear Lord, we thank you for your gift of love. Please direct us to be good parents. We're brand new at this; but, then I don't have to tell you that.*

Amen.

TUESDAY AFTERNOON, OCTOBER 4, 1984: CHESTNUT, GEORGIA DR. ROBINSON'S OFFICE, OAKWOOD'S SATELLITE FACILITY

Doc Terri laughed and cried right along with me during the past month, as we discussed the memories of my first years with Kyle. I had forgotten what a sentimental fool I had always been, as I thought, *I must have inherited that trait from Mama.*

* * *

Words could never explain the euphoria I experienced during the birth of our son. I feared God had made me barren as a form of wrathful punishment. But, when I felt the movement of the child growing within me, and held Keith at my breast, I was exonerated with a resurgence of life.

I experienced the sense of relief all over again while reliving the memories of that time. I was so thankful God have not forgotten me, but had given Kyle and me this gift of love…and it weighed in at just less than nine pounds.

* * *

I thought, *God remembered me thirteen years ago. Maybe— just maybe—He'll remember me now. I pray He will allow my memories to continue progressing forward to the point where I'm a whole woman again—complete with my soul, love in my heart, and the rest of my mind.*

CHAPTER XXVII
PRACTICE PARENTHOOD?

All our dreams had come true. We had a nice home with all the conveniences, a new baby, and of course we still had the dog. We couldn't believe it was all coming true just the way we had planned. We had everything we ever wanted in life—everything money could buy, as well as things it couldn't.

When we got the pictures back from Christmas morning, we smiled at the one of Keith in his carrier seat, beneath the tree. We had stuck a red bow on his forehead, and his expression appeared as though he knew how ridiculous it made him look and he didn't appreciate it one bit.

He paid us back with a diaper full of surprise waiting for whoever was scheduled for the next diaper duty.

* * *

As we cleared the Christmas tree out and stored the decorations for the next year, I cried, as usual. However, I had a sense of reassurance that, just as Kyle had promised, "The best years are yet to come."

* * *

There came a time after a few weeks when Kyle went back to work and Mama went home, so I was left there all alone with Keith. That first day was the most frightening.

Keith went to sleep after his morning feeding so I laid him in his bassinet and just stood there, admiring him. I felt a chill in the room, and it seemed so natural when I adjusted the blanket to cover him up to his chin. I smiled because the motherly instinct was coming out in me so soon.

I realized there was much more to motherhood than pulling the covers over your child, as I thought, *Well son, ready or not. Until your Daddy gets home from work, it's just you and me—me and you—so we better get to know one another. I'll try my best to raise you right. All I ask is that you go easy on me...I don't know if you know it or not, but I'm new at this.*

* * *

With no detailed instructions to be found on the care of my new infant, I had to depend on Dr. Spock's Child Care book and the literature that was given me at the hospital, combined with maternal instincts.

I learned to check the diaper for moisture or mess by inserting my index finger just inside the leg opening, hoping not to "pull out a plum," so to speak. That procedure could often be eliminated by the mere process of "sniffing." If all was clear on the diaper front, then I assumed he was hungry.

That was easy enough to figure out—crying meant that he was either hungry or in need of a diaper change.

What was a new mother like me to do when the above tactics failed? A common back up plan was to caress the baby in my arms and proceed to the rocking chair.

Mama warned me, "Delaney, you have to be careful not to spoil him, so don't sit around holding him all day. You don't have to pick him up just because he's crying. He needs to cry some to exercise his lungs."

That was easy for her to say. She didn't have to listen to him. I wondered why God didn't design babies with built-in volume control buttons, or "On" and "Off" switches. Luckily, Keith was a good baby and slept a good bit of the time, so the back up plan wasn't required very often.

I was introduced to the "fountain of youth" after only a few days, when he lay on his back, kicking and looking ever so cute, and I failed to get his diaper on fast enough. He cooed and laughed as though he had intentionally aimed for my forehead, as I wiped away the warm wetness with a clean washcloth.

Once I got beyond the shock of being initiated into the "Mother of a Baby Boy" society, I proceeded with more caution the next time. Not to claim it never happened again, because it certainly did, and each time I was as stunned as the first.

* * *

For the first six weeks he was safe and sound in the bassinet beside our bed. He slept so quietly we made regular checks during the night to make certain he was still breathing.

We were fortunate in that Keith was very healthy, except for the time he ran an unexplained fever. I immediately called the doctor and left a message with his office.

While we were awaiting his call, I checked with the Dr. Spock Childcare manual, compared his symptoms with those described in the book, and I diagnosed him as having pneumonia.

Before allowing utter panic and hysteria to set in, I referred to the "witch doctor" book Mama had passed on to me. It was the so-called "medical book" she used to diagnose our chicken pox, measles, mumps, etc. when we were growing up, and with a copyright date of 1935, it wasn't exactly the most update in medical information. According to it I was convinced he had scarlet fever.

When Mama called I answered the phone in a fit of tears. I had checked his temperature with a rectal thermometer and it read one-hundred and three degrees.

As it turned out the "witch doctor" and Dr. Spock were both incorrect. He only had a little bug of some sort, for which we were thankful.

* * *

Keith was only a few weeks old when Richard's parents visited to admire the newest member of our family.

They told me that, after three years of testing and constantly in and out of the hospital, Richard's illness had finally been diagnosed as Multiple Sclerosis. They went on to tell me there was no known cure. The doctors didn't know much about it except that it was a disease of the nervous system and would gradually lead to complete paralysis.

I knew his illness certainly wasn't my fault, however a real sadness came over me and I felt guilty when I thought about his request not to marry Kyle. And how he had asked that I wait for him to get back on his feet.

He had married since then and I couldn't help but admire the girl. She obviously loved him very deeply to continue on with him, considering his illness.

I wondered if I was capable, if the need arose, to have that same strength and devotion to Kyle, as I recalled our wedding vow, "in sickness and in health." A sense of relief rushed over me that I didn't marry Richard, and once again, I felt guilty—this time for thinking so selfishly.

I still loved Richard's parents very much, and I continued to have feelings for him. I had those special feelings of friendship for the man who was now living an entirely different existence than he or I had ever imagined. While, at the same time, I was leading the life we had planned for "us"…except I was living it with Kyle.

I prayed that his future would be brighter. That a cure would be found to relieve him of the pain and break the chains of that horrible illness, freeing him and his wife to enjoy the sort of life Kyle and I were sharing.

* * *

A few days later Betty's parents visited. I was always proud to show Keith to visitors, especially Mr. And Mrs. Lowe. They commented how beautiful Keith was, and how happy they were for their number-two daughter. Mrs. Lowe said, "We're looking forward to the time when Betty gets married and has a little bundle of her own for us to spoil."

After they left I walked past the bathroom and detected the familiar scent where a match had been lit. It brought back memories as a child growing up when I visited their home. There was always a book of matches on the back of the toilet tank in their bathroom. The theory was that a lit match dissipated the odors whenever nature called, and so it acted as somewhat of an air freshener.

That afternoon my nose reminded me that the lit-match theory wasn't one-hundred percent fail proof.

I smiled at the fond memories of the Lowe household, as I wondered if a lit match would dissipate the scent coming from Keith's diaper.

* * *

One night several months later Kyle and I were standing over Keith as he lay asleep in the baby bed. He was so sweet and peaceful, I smiled and thought, *Hmm, parenthood's not so difficult—when the baby is as good as ours.*

The next morning we were awakened by a strange noise in the other part of the house. Keith had discovered the baby bed was escapable, and that was the beginning of true trouble.

At only eight months of age, he had found himself able to escape across the imprisoning boundaries of the baby bed, meaning there would be no more rest for his mother.

* * *

As Keith began to eat baby food, he developed his own taste-buds and definitely had his own opinions of the foods he like and disliked. The jaws of that nine-month-old little bugger were incomprehensibly strong, especially when he was determined not to open his mouth to receive the spoonful of food I was coaxing him to eat.

He especially hated strained spinach. He learned to recognize the difference between the green goo opposed to his favorite mixed fruit or strained bananas when he saw the spoon coming toward him.

I tried everything to entice him, including eating some myself. *Yuck!* It was hard for me to conceal the shiver that awful taste sent over me. There I was, twenty-two years old, sacrificing myself in such a way, eating one of the very foods I had always hated—spinach! That showed how much I loved the little squirt—I'd go to any length to make sure he was getting the proper nutrition. I felt pretty proud of myself for such an unselfish act, but after many attempts, I finally gave up.

I soon grew tired and realized that would be one of life's unselfish acts that would go unrewarded, because his little jaws remained tightly closed, as if they were a vise.

* * *

We were so excited when Keith took his first step and we thought it was so cute when he said his first word, "No."

His ability to walk alone was the beginning of that quality of independence that carried on to the breakfast table.

I wondered how many other mothers had ever been feeding their toddler, and when he refused to open his mouth, or he spit the food back out at them, they felt like turning the bowl of food up-side-down over onto his head?

Well, I did just that.

I had just had it with that kid, so I did it—with oatmeal! I turned the entire bowl up-side-down on his head and left it there as if it were a cap as I said, "There, take that, you little monster!"

The shocked look on his face became forever etched in my mind as I felt the distinct pleasure in winning the battle of the breakfast table that morning. He sat there afterward draped with oatmeal globs sliding down his face.

I said, "That'll show ya. From now on, you'll know who's running the show around here!"

Of course, I knew it would be my job to clean it up off the floor, the walls, the table, chair and him. But I thought, *Maybe next time you'll think twice before turning your nose up at another meal!*

Kyle's brother, Robert, was visiting that morning and witnessed the entire incident, for which I offered no apologies. He didn't say a word, but remained silent, I guess for fear I might do the same to him.

When the shocked expression on Keith's face subsided, he cried for only about thirty seconds. Then, he discovered it was fun to slap his hands in the mess on the tray and send bits of oatmeal sailing through the air, to attach themselves to the wall, table, floor…and his mother.

He continued to giggle while he watched his mother clean up the entire mess, both mine and his.

That's when I began to realize something very real and very scary!

I wasn't quite sure how to deal with that one-year-old child. He was becoming more than I had bargained for.

* * *

I hadn't expected him to be able to climb so well at such a young age. He scaled the four-foot high chain-link fence as if he had been specially trained for the sport. He had the agility of a cat, always landing on his feet, and he was afraid of nothing or no one…especially his mother.

* * *

That summer when Kyle's father and his wife visited, Mr. Rutherford told me, "Aw, Delaney, don't worry about the boy. He's just a normal, active child with a healthy sense of curiosity."

To which I responded, "Well, how do other parents deal with a normal, active child like Keith? And is there a cure for that healthy sense of curiosity?"

"I know how it is. Remember Kyle's mama and I raised *five* children."

Five! I thought, *My parents also raised five children, but I didn't know if any of them were like Keith.*

The term "terrible *twos*" sounded a bit witty and lyrical, however, we were talking serious business in Keith's case.

The child was beginning to feel the independence and freedom of walking by himself, talking a little, and eating by himself; thereby, giving him authority, (or so he thought), to dominate the family activities and rule the roost.

Under no circumstances would he stay in his bed, and if I even vaguely considered carrying on an intelligent, uninterrupted telephone conversation, I had better think again. The child entered the "Terrible *twos*" syndrome prematurely—the day he turned one year old. A more optimistic view of the situation would have been to say, "He was ahead of his time."

* * *

Diapers had become a big part of my life. When I wasn't changing them, I was washing or folding them.

I was extremely anxious to potty train the little angel, so I purchased a potty-chair and proceeded to practice all the tricks of the motherhood trade.

We sat for hours, me on the side of the tub, him on the potty as I read aloud. I turned on the water faucet, just enough that there was a slight trickling sound. That always worked for me. Unfortunately, the same wouldn't always hold true for Keith.

When he finally did something in the potty, he thought everyone wanted to see his accomplishment and so Kyle and I were his most enthusiastic cheerleaders.

* * *

On his second birthday we reviewed the previous two years, and decided that there was a lot more to parenthood than met the eye.

I wondered why God hadn't thought to give us experimental children. A child that would be for practice only—for a practice run—to prepare us for the real thing. After all, how could we be expected to be perfect parents without practice? In order to become perfect parents we needed practice before we're placed in the permanent position of parenthood!

I wondered if God might consider that concept if I could gather enough signatures on a petition. But then, I suppose the ones not interested in having children in the first place would've been unable to see the importance behind the concept. And of course, it would have been too late for those of us who already had a child.

So I resigned myself to the fact that Keith was to be our "practice run" and the "real thing," all wrapped up into one exhausting little ball of energy.

My daily prayer became, *Lord, we're counting on you. We're really going to need Your help all the way with this one.*

Amen.

CHAPTER XXIII
THE MAN IN THE WINDOW

After Keith was born I worked diligently to trim my figure to its previous size and shed the thirty-eight pounds I had gained during the pregnancy. I never seemed to stop from the time I awoke in the morning until I finally got Keith to bed at night, so there's no doubt my non-stop pace was helpful in my weight loss. Nonetheless, I was proud of myself from the results of my efforts.

* * *

To earn some extra spending money during the spring after Keith's first birthday, I fixed my friends' and relatives' hair in my home. I wasn't a licensed beautician, but I had worked in a friend's beauty salon during my junior and senior years of high school, and developed a flair for fixing hair.

Working with hair again reminded me of the time a lady came into the salon because she had burned the end of her hair when she gave herself a home permanent. Attempting to trim beyond the damage, she had cut her own hair to the point it was less than an inch long all over.

A friend told her to rub horse manure into the roots and wrap her head in plastic for fifteen minutes. That was supposed to be a sure-fire method of stimulating hair growth.

The Vincents swore manure was the best fertilizer for their garden, but I had never heard of it being used to make hair grow.

The horse manure didn't appear to have worked, so that theory turned out to be nothing but a line of bull manure. I wondered if her friend with the "miracle manure remedy" and my friend with the "mayonnaise treatment" knew one another.

I was given the task of shampooing her hair, and the stench that emanated from that woman's head opened my sinuses and closed my pores all at the same time!

* * *

Even though I was busy most of the day caring for Keith and working with hair, I found it difficult to wind down at night. I had always been a late-night person, and I found myself snacking while I was glued to the television, so a few extra pounds slipped back on before I realized it.

My gynecologist prescribed some diet pills that were extremely effective with my weight loss, and I had unlimited energy.

However, my nerves became as tight as twisted rubber bands and my personality began to change, drastically. Paranoia set in and I believed Mama and Kyle—the two people I loved most—were conspiring against me. I felt as though I could trust no one while my imagination began to run away with me.

One evening while I was washing dishes, the kitchen sink suddenly and for no reason began pulling away from the wall and the electric oven was in flames. I attempted to run out of the house, but stopped dead in my tracks when I saw a man watching me through the glass in the kitchen door.

There was no man, as Kyle tried to convince me I hallucinated about the entire series of events that evening. "But it seemed so real! Everything seemed so real!" I argued.

I was deeply disturbed by it all as I wondered, *Was I asleep? How could I have a nightmare like that when I wasn't asleep?* But no, I was awake—wide awake—so it must have been real! Kyle insisted it was my vivid imagination, and I finally said I believed him, even though I really didn't.

It was all part of Mama's and Kyle's conspiracy to make me think I was crazy. I didn't know why they wanted to drive me insane—I just knew they were.

* * *

Every night for that past two weeks—*every single night*—I had a recurring dream. It wasn't as if I had never dreamed it before, because I had many times when I was a child, and they even continued into my adolescence and early adulthood.

In my dream, my age was always twelve years old. I was alone in downtown Atlanta when I noticed a reflection in a storefront window. It was the reflection of a man standing across the street. When I turned around he was gone, but when I looked back at the window he was there, again. I watched his reflection in the window as he followed me up the street.

My sense of fear was overshadowed by confusion and curiosity as I boarded the bus to go home.

Shortly after I was inside the house and the bus pulled away I heard a knock on the door. I opened the door to see a man standing there—a man with a kind smile and tender, periwinkle blue eyes—a man I recognized immediately, "Daddy!"

The dream always seemed so real I could feel the warmth of his arms around me when we embraced, as he explained, "I couldn't stay away from my baby girl any longer." He told me he and Mama had decided to get a divorce, though I had never seen or heard them have harsh words between them. "Your mama felt a divorce would be too painful for you, so she told me to go far away and get out of your lives, forever. Then she faked my death." He went on to tell me, "Your Mama staged the funeral for your benefit. It wasn't me in that casket. It was just a dummy that looked like me."

In my dreams I sat on his lap, there in the green vinyl rocker in front of the gas heater, sharing its warmth, and cried tears of happiness that he was back with me. I hugged Daddy and said, "Don't worry. Nothing or *no one* will *ever* come between us, again!"

The thought of Mama's deceit and lies all those years aroused hatred and unmitigated anger toward her. When I awoke from the dreams and realized Daddy wasn't there, I was always overwhelmed by sadness and heart-breaking disappointment. Even though I knew it was only a dream, the anger toward Mama would always remain with me for a few hours after I awoke.

* * *

I had dreamed that exact same dream many times in the past, and each time, I dreamed it repetitiously over a series of nights. Sometimes two or three nights consecutively—sometimes a week or more—but every time it was the same.

That particular spring, the dream recurred every night for more than three weeks and each morning I continued to convince myself, *That was no dream—Daddy is alive!*

My anger toward Mama continued throughout the entire following day, every day during that three-week period. I was convinced Mama and Kyle were, indeed, conspiring against me—hiding the truth from me and keeping me from my father.

* * *

One night as I lay in bed beside Kyle, I began hearing music. I couldn't determine the songs but I recognized the guitars, drums, and horns—the works. Kyle swore he couldn't hear it, and I was on to his tricks, as I was determined, *He's not gonna get away with it this time. I'll find where the damned music's coming from and confront him with it.*

After several nights of my getting out of bed and investigating, I concluded that the music was coming from the air-conditioning window unit. But that didn't make sense as I attempted to rationalize the situation, *How could music be coming from an air-conditioning unit? Kyle must have rigged the electrical wiring to receive radio waves. It's all just another trick to drive me crazy!*

Keith became part of the conspiracy and wouldn't cooperate when I wanted him to go to sleep. It was all part of the plot to deprive me of my sleep.

My irrational thoughts ran rampant that spring, as I decided I couldn't stand anymore deceit. I could trust no one.

* * *

One morning Keith woke up before he was supposed to—once again, as part of the conspiracy to deprive me of my sleep. I wasn't ready to get up. It was just too early to start my day; besides, I hadn't gone to bed until around two-thirty because of all the music. I simply needed more sleep.

I didn't have any sleeping pills so I took the only thing I had in the house. The doctor had given me some pills to help ease some back pains after Keith was born. At that time I was afraid they would spoil my breast milk for Keith, so I had only taken a couple of the pills. There were still about ten remaining in the bottle.

I only meant to take a couple that morning, but I remembered they weren't very potent, so I took half dozen…and then, since there were only four remaining, I took those, too.

Keith's incessant crying grew louder with every minute I was awake, so I pulled the sheet up and rolled over onto my side with a pillow over my ears to muffle the noise.

It was heavenly as I began to feel the lightness of the room around me, and I drifted off to a completely different place. A quiet place without crying babies, where I could be all by myself—to rest, and sleep—without a care or responsibility in the world. And I could stay there as long as I wanted...

* * *

I felt something crawling on my face. If felt like thousands of tiny ants...or spiders. Then I felt a stinging sensation, as though something or someone were slapping me on the forehead, in the eyes, and on the cheeks.

When I awoke I was lying on my back with my head hanging off the side of the bed. Illuminated dust particles floated on the sunbeam as the rays shone through the window and gently caressed my chest. The room was a blur and I was disoriented as I tried to focus—everything appeared upside down. The slaps continued in rapid fashion and it startled me when I saw Keith's cherub-like face right up close to mine, "Ma-ma, Ma-ma..."

I don't know how long he had been standing there saying, "Mama, Mama," over and over again, while stroking my face and then slapping me in that playful way. But I do know when I managed to focus my eyes and read the clock, it was around noon, and I had taken those pills three and a half hours earlier.

When I realized how long he had been awake, alone in the house and unattended, I was thankful he was safe, as I scooped him up and held him in my arms. While rocking back and forth on the side of the bed, I hugged him like there was no tomorrow and kissed him all over his head and face. I cried and I couldn't stop saying, repeatedly, "I'm sorry, Baby. Mommy loves you. Mommy loves you so much!"

A sudden rush of nausea forced me to put him down on the floor and run into the bathroom to vomit. It was a good thing I was able to do that because it rid the remainder of the pills from my system.

The phone rang while I was in the bathroom and I ran to answer it. Mama's voice on the other end had a definite tone of panic, "Delaney, where in the world have you been? I've been calling you since nine-o'clock this morning! Is the baby all right? Are *you* all right?"

I snapped back with sarcasm, "Yes! The baby's all right. But *you* don't give a damn about *me*!'

My tone directed so much anger toward her she began to cry, "Honey, what's wrong with you? Why are you talking to me like that? You just haven't been yourself lately—have you called the doctor? Could it be those diet pills you're taking? If it is, *please* throw them *away*—flush them down the toilet!"

I resented her prying into my private life. She had no right. I wasn't a child anymore, and I didn't need her butting in and telling me what to do.

I never told her or Kyle about my taking all those pills that morning. In fact, I blamed my mother for not calling to wake me up in the first place, even though she told me she had tried since nine that morning. But I knew she was lying about that, too.

* * *

Within a week later I found myself completely out of my diet pills and my prescription had no more refills remaining. I tried to persuade the pharmacist to refill it, just that once, but he refused, "I'm sorry, Mrs. Rutherford. I can't refill amphetamines without a prescription. It's the law." I was forced to call the doctor's office.

The familiar voice on the phone said, "O.B.G.Y.N."

"This is Delaney Rutherford and I need for the doctor to refill my prescription."

"And what prescription is that, Mrs. Rutherford?"

I was antsy, "You know, my diet pills."

"Alright. I'll need to check your chart. Please hold."

I was on hold ten minutes, only to hear, "Delaney, I'm sorry, but you'll need to come in so the doctor can examine you before he'll issue a prescription for a refill. How about Friday morning?"

"But I don't have anyone to keep the baby that morning," I protested. "Couldn't he just do it over the phone...just this once? Please? I feel great! My weight's doing great! I only want to lose five more pounds!'

I only weighed one-hundred and fifteen pounds at that time and the doctor told me I didn't need to lose anymore. For the first time in my life I could have stood to gain a little. However, I still felt fat and I was obsessed with losing more weight.

"I'm sorry, Delaney. Rules are rules."

"Oh, all *right!*" I shouted, as I slammed the receiver down. I became enraged because it was only Monday afternoon and I was worried, *What if I gain back my weight before I get some more pills?*

Then it dawned on me. I knew what had happened. Mama had nosed into my business, called the doctor, and set up this whole thing! I began to scheme, *I'll fix her!* I won't talk to her when she calls on the phone and I won't let her see Keith. That should punish her for prying that way.

By Thursday morning, Mama knew something was very wrong, so she came over to the house. When I discovered it was her I wouldn't answer the door. That didn't stop her. She wouldn't go away, as she stood outside the front door, knocking and knocking, then banging with her fist!

Her persistence prevailed and I finally slung open the door. Enraged, I yelled, "All RIGHT! WHAT DO YOU WANT?!"

She scoped me up one side and down the other, then shook her head and demanded, "Delaney, get the baby and get in the car—right now! I'm taking you to the hospital!"

When I refused, she took Keith in her arms and started out the door, "I'm taking him with me, until you get some help!"

I began crying and begged her to stop conspiring against me. I reminded her I was her daughter and asked, "Don't you love me anymore? Why are you so mean to me?"

She responded with the same question, "Don't you love *me anymore?* Don't you know you're killing yourself, and you're killing Kyle and me right along with you? Delaney, for God's sake, get a grip on yourself—and think of this baby!"

I was so weak from not eating because I was afraid I would gain weight before I got my prescription on Friday. I fell to my knees right there in the living room floor, weeping and begging her, "Please help me, Mama. I don't know what's wrong with me. Please love me again. And please, please, don't take the baby away. I'll behave...I promise. I'll go to the doctor. I'm going tomorrow! I already have an appointment!"

"No, you're not! You're going *today*...right *now*! Now, dry your eyes, put some clothes and shoes on and get in the car."

* * *

How could all that have been happening? My thinking everyone I loved the dearest was involved in a conspiracy? I couldn't understand why.

I don't know what would have happened to me, my baby, or my marriage, if Mama hadn't come over that day and insisted I go to the doctor. She also insisted on going with me into the examination room so she could tell the doctor how I had been acting.

In later months it was discovered the diet pills had an unacceptable amphetamine content, and within a year the FDA banned such pills for weight loss.

After I stopped taking the pills I experienced the shakes, as if I were a common drug addict, which I was to a very real degree for those few months.

When I returned to normal it seemed as if I had been watching it all happen on television.

Once again, I could relax in my own bed, but more importantly, I could trust the ones I loved. That experience led me to be extremely cautious—cautious of any prescription drugs—and I promised Kyle, "Don't worry, Honey. I'll *never* take diet pills again!"

* * *

I never discussed those times with Kyle, Mama, or anyone else in my family. I didn't want my mother to feel hurt, and I was sure she would, to know I had those thoughts about her, even if they *were* provoked by the side effects of the diet pills.

The hallucinations stopped and the nightmares subsided. However, it wasn't the last time I saw my father in that same dream as the man in the window...the man with the kind smile and tender, periwinkle blue eyes.

CHAPTER XXIX
THE SIX WEEK LATE—
THREE DAY EARLY
BIRTHDAY PRESENT

The sauna-like heat and humidity drained every ounce of energy out of me, as the hot weather of 1972's summer drug into September.

I thought I was hemorrhaging when a neighbor rushed me to the hospital, where I aborted in the early weeks of pregnancy. I didn't even know I was pregnant. Though the doctor assured me the complications were from natural causes, I was worried that the amphetamine diet pills from the previous year had somehow induced the miscarriage.

We wanted another child very much and we were greatly disappointed by the news. I had been having quite a bit of trouble with my right ovary, and the doctor said that could have been the problem. He went on to say I would probably never complete another pregnancy full term, and suggested I have the ovary removed. I decided I wouldn't make such an important decision until after the holidays.

My depression was relieved *only* when I occupied my mind with other things.

* * *

Keith was at such a cute and mischievous age, and it was a full-time job just keeping up with his little fast-paced life. But I had other things on my mind, as well.

I decided we needed—correction—I *wanted* another house. We had lived there four years and it was time to move on to a bigger, nicer home. Of course, it had to be a *brick* house, and this time I wanted a basement, a *double* carport, three bedrooms plus two bathrooms, and a larger lot.

Unbeknownst to Kyle, I advertised our house for sale in the Sunday Journal and received several interested calls. Kyle was unaware I was reading about our own home when I read the ad to him, but he agreed the house sounded great. Needless to say, he was stunned when I informed him I had just described our place. When I told him my planned asking price, his response was predictably cynical, "If you can get that much for this place, be my guest! You'll *have* to get that much for us to be able to move!"

A week before Christmas I listed the house with a real estate agent. She advised us that ninety days was the average length of time to sell a house in our area of town.

Shortly after Christmas I contracted a flu bug, and it lingered on for several weeks. I felt downright awful. However, I wasn't too ill to go house shopping.

We found our dream home in a development located in Chestnut, north of Atlanta. The builder allowed us to choose the lot and style of our home to be built.

It would be everything I had ever dreamed: brick ranch, three bedrooms, two baths, living room with separate dining room, eat-in kitchen with laundry room off the kitchen, and den with a fireplace. All of that, plus luxurious wall-to-wall carpet, double carport and full basement, sitting on a three-quarter acre lot. For thirty-two thousand it was a bargain, even though we swallowed hard when we signed the contract, as it was more than we had planned to pay.

We signed the papers to build our dream home on January 22nd, 1973. As luck would have it, the very next day, January 23rd, we sold our other house for my asking price of twenty-eight thousand five-hundred dollars. We had lived in that house for only four years and more than *doubled* our investment.

We felt wonderful, with the anticipation of owning such a fine new home.

* * *

That flu bug was still causing me to feel awfully sluggish, so Kyle insisted I go in to see the doctor. I was shocked when the doctor said, "It's too soon to tell for sure, so you'll need to take an early morning urine specimen…"

"You mean you think I'm *pregnant*?" I asked, anxiously.

As he confirmed my question, I was on cloud nine. "But, I thought you said I couldn't…"

"It's possible to conceive with only one healthy ovary, but there could be certain dangers involved, if you are, indeed, pregnant."

The next afternoon it was confirmed. We were pregnant! And the baby was due around August 28th. What perfect timing! The builder told us the house would be completed by May, so that meant we could be all settled by the time the baby arrived.

The builders underestimated the time it would take for the completion, so we were forced to move into the "cave" on June 22nd. We called it the "cave" because we had no electricity, gas, water, or doors—the little things that make a cave into a home. Without those amenities we were faced with cave-dwelling for several weeks.

With no running water, luxury items such as a toilet and shower were non-existent.

Keith was extremely active and a typical two-and-a-half year old. Playing in the Georgia red clay mud seemed to be one of his favorite pastimes, so bath water was essential. The stove top served as the hot water heater for those weeks, while the neighbors provided the precious liquid for our baths and cooking. The builder went ahead and connected the gas line to the stove, even though the basement had not been poured, and the furnace hadn't yet been installed.

I was transferring some heated water from the kitchen to the tub one day in early July, when I slipped on a puddle in the floor and landed very hard on my hip.

That little accident would be the cause of much anxiety over the next few months. Both Kyle and I worried that the fall had damaged the precious baby inside of me. My water had broken at the time of the fall, and broke several times after that, so doctor's orders confined me to complete bed rest for several days.

* * *

The baby's due date of August 28th seemed as though it would never get there, but it did and with much anticipation. However, that day was just another date on the calendar, as there was no baby. Not that day, nor the next—not even two or three or four *weeks* later.

The usual, traditional phone calls from friends and relatives began and continued on a regular basis, right up until the actual delivery on Tuesday, October 9th, 1973.

As I lay in the labor room while they prepared me for delivery, I remembered how I had worried that we wouldn't—correction—*couldn't* love another child as much as we loved Keith. Kyle and I both had voiced that concern to one another.

I thought about how silly that was, and how much I had already begun loving this baby and I have never even *seen* it. I had read an article in a magazine which stated, "A mother's love for her child begins during pregnancy, and a very unique bond between her and her child continues throughout their lives." I thought how ironic it was that, not only had I been able to become pregnant and carry full term, but once again, I had carried six weeks *beyond* full term. I was so relieved the gynecologist had been wrong.

After eighteen hours of labor in the hospital, Clay Brandon Rutherford was born. He was the same length as Keith but he weighed more. In fact, he was the biggest baby in the newborn nursery for the first day. But I had gained so much weight during my pregnancy, I thought he would have weighed twice that much.

I had feared I would be disappointed if the baby wasn't a girl, but all I had to do was hold him in my arms and go through the traditional checklist to inventory fingers, toes, arms, legs, etc. I was in love with that beautiful little boy as if he were my very first child.

Kyle and I were so thankful Clay wasn't damaged by that fall on my hip during the summer.

I was amazed at how much love a heart is capable of feeling when it involves a mother and her children.

The third day in the hospital fell on my birthday, October 12th. I didn't know if I was crying from the postpartum blues, or the fact that I was twenty-five years old, as I thought, *A whole quarter of a century...I hope I'm not too old for motherhood.*

* * *

When Kyle and I arrived home with our brand new little bundle, Keith looked as though he had grown a foot, as he jumped up and down with such excitement about his new baby brother. It took a few hours before he realized he was no longer the complete center of attention, and the jealousy traits became more and more apparent. I knew how he felt remembering when I was a little girl and my niece invaded my territory when she and her parents moved in with us.

I felt safe and content as I rocked Clay that evening. But once again, the feelings of apprehension flowed through my veins—

apprehension about the responsibilities the future held. I prayed aloud, "Dear Lord. Please direct us with this child, too."

* * *

Time would bring us to discover that it was impossible to get enough practice at being parents, because every day and every child is different.

Keith and Clay were both fantastic babies, with similar good sleeping and eating habits, crying only when wet or hungry. Both were basically good natured, well-rounded, and active, with sweet personalities. I had heard that brothers often grew up to become very different from one another, and I wondered if that would be the case with our sons.

* * *

With the addition of Clay there were three Libras in the house—Kyle, me, and now him. I wondered what Libra traits he would possess? Would he be loving? Sensitive? Would he be easy going? Giving? Creative? Imaginative?

* * *

Once again, I thanked God for my perfect family and my perfect life, as our home was embraced by the presence of unlimited love.

CHAPTER XXX
A ST. BERNARD AND
FRENCH POODLES

For someone whose life was so perfect, what more could I have *possibly* wanted out of life?   I wanted to be *thin again!*   I had gained ninety-four pounds while pregnant with Clay, but I was dedicated and worked hard from October until April to lose every ounce—and *without* diet pills!

I was so proud of myself and I felt wonderful, but once again, my weight became an obsession. I vowed never to be heavy again, and to do that, I vowed never to put anything sweet or fattening to my lips again—ever!

I had lost the weight through a popular low-carbohydrate diet, and it was a fairly easy regimen to follow, so I decided it should be a breeze to maintain my weight. I was determined to avoid carbohydrates and starchy foods the rest of my life. I adopted the motto, "When in doubt, do without," along with "If it has a sweet taste, it goes straight to my waist," and "once it passes the lips, it goes straight to the hips."

All of the above were made extremely difficult by the damnable commercials on television. A law should have been passed a long time ago in this country, prohibiting those sinful commercials for Sara Lee and Hershey's chocolate. One minute they're pushing the low calorie soft drinks, with the sensually shaped and unrealistically perfect beautiful young women. The next minute they're presenting the scrumptious tempting full color close-ups of those fattening foods that prevent the average American women like me from looking like our above-mentioned counterparts.

We women can't patronize all those food commercials and expect to look like the models they present before us, too. Why can't they make up their minds? Do they want us to be slim and trim, or otherwise?

If they want us to be "otherwise," then take the blooming diet soft drink commercials off the air forever. On the other hand if they want us to be slim and trim, then discontinue the others.

Perhaps one of the reasons why we women suffer from so many headaches is simply that we're confused about which commercial line to follow—diet soft drinks or sugar drenched goodies.

It's easy to say, "You can't have your cake and eat it, too." But when the visions of chocolate and sweet things are drilled into your sub-conscious by the commercials, and at the same time, the grocery stores and drugstores insist on strategically placing the candy items right there at the check-out area, it's no wonder the temptations are far more than the average woman can resist.

As a new mother with a fresh new life in a youth-oriented neighborhood, I found myself too busy to watch television most of the day, so that helped get my mind off the allurements of food. However, I had a hard time resisting the temptation to sneak an occasional sweet taste of Gerber's Strained Fruit Dessert when I fed Clay—a spoonful for baby and a spoonful for me.

* * *

Life in the suburbs was not exactly as it's depiction on television, but similar. Magnolia Landing Estates, the new development where we lived, attracted a lot of other young couples and families whom we met in the course of the evening walk around the block. Everyone was working in their new yards, so it was easier to make friendship connections.

Another way for me to meet friends was through the local Garden Club; however, only a chosen few were admitted into the cliquish clan of women.

A prospective member first had to be sponsored—in writing— and co-sponsored by two other members, after which time she was then reviewed at the monthly board of officers meeting. If approved by the board, she was invited to visit a meeting in order to be sized up by the members.

If the members voted unanimously to accept her, she was congratulated as a new member of the Magnolia Garden Club of Magnolia Landing Estates.

Those of us among the fortunate few chosen, considered ourselves to carry a great deal of clout, but we probably impressed ourselves far more than we impressed others.

We weren't snobs in an extreme fashion. We only wanted to be known as the "elite," so we had to be careful. Otherwise, a woman who didn't drive a nice car, or didn't have her home decorated to look like *Better Homes and Gardens* magazine, a woman who yelled at her children, or possibly didn't wear name brand clothes, might slip into membership by mistake.

I couldn't afford to buy name-brand clothes either, so one time I sewed a name brand label into the lining of a jacket of lesser value. When the jacket was hung or stacked with the others, no one suspected it was a fake because the label was authentic. I transferred that same label from one garment to another, and then another, and so on.

We had all been out of high school for almost ten years, and should have outgrown the name-brand mentality. But peer pressure is peer pressure—at any age.

At the time, I wondered if I would have been accepted into the group, had I not been one of the charter members. I drove an eight-year-old Ford station wagon, I couldn't afford to buy authentic name-brand clothes, and I sometimes—no, make that *frequently*—yelled at my kids.

I saw the flower shows as a way in which to express myself artistically and creatively, and I especially enjoyed the recognition when I won first place ribbons.

One time I teamed up with Lauren to design a table-top arrangement for a competition. She and I were best of friends, and she shared a great deal in common, including "never being on time," and "procrastinating."

As to be expected we waited until the last minute and hustled to get things together the night before the show. We picked flowers from surrounding yards in the areas, but we forgot to put them in water so they were all wilted by the time the judges came around the next day at the show. We received "Honorable Mention." Of course, there were only three other entries in that category, with first, second, and third place prizes going to the others, so, in other words—we came in last. How humiliating that was.

I blamed Lauren for the less than admirable outcome of that competition. She was always the kind of friend that could be blamed for most anything that went wrong. She accepted the blame in that particular case, and we laughed about our sad looking arrangement.

Because of my victories in the other competitions I was elected to the honorable position of club vice-president and later to president. Having been elected to such prestigious positions, my nose was high in the sky, as I looked forward to Fridays.

Friday was grocery shopping day, and I was always assured of seeing at least two or three sister socialites at the new Food Giant in Chestnut. I always set aside at least two hours for grocery shopping—socializing—to allow for gossip update.

After less than four flourishing years, the group of perfect people disbanded as a club. That was a sad, sad day in Magnolia Landing Estates.

The acceptance by those women meant a lot to me, and the recognition and success in the competitions gave me a new insight for life outside the home. Life that included the responsibilities of leadership as well as the regained surge of healthy competition. Accomplishments for which I was praised, other than that of "Great biscuits, Baby," and competition, for which I was rewarded, as I learned to set goals to be a winner.

I was intrigued by the sorority pledging system used in the club membership process. I didn't feel comfortable with the plan, and I was relieved to be on the "inside" for once. "Inside"—a place I had never actually considered myself in high school, even though I was involved in cheerleading, sports, and a member of most of the clubs. But being a member of a club and "belonging" to a club are sometimes entirely different.

I wondered if I was actually on the "inside" with the garden club, or if I just had my foot in the door enough to qualify.

* * *

I suspected I probably wouldn't have been a member if it hadn't been for my next door neighbor Jeanette. She was the founder and president. Everyone looked up to her and respected her as an organizer and leader among the neighborhood women. Her home was uniquely and tastefully decorated, and she was admired for her decorating abilities.

Jeanette was only in her mid-twenties, like the rest of us, but she always looked and acted younger than her true age. She could have passed for late teens or early twenties.

When I first moved to Magnolia Landing she introduced me to the other women as her neighbor and friend, and I felt slightly more comfortable with her doing so.

I was intimidated by those slim, socially conscious suburban housewives at that time as my overly pregnant body made me feel like a Saint Bernard among slender French poodles. But that intimidation gave me the drive and incentive to lose my weight.

Despite how well-liked and respected by the group she once was, there came a time when the girls turned on Jeanette, avoiding her as if she were contagious. She had developed the dreaded disease of "divorce." A divorced woman had no place in a club where all the members were happily married, or so that's how some of the members reacted. Women can be vicious and needlessly cruel.

Jeanette was compelled to drop out of the club, as she confided in me, "I just don't fit in, and I don't feel comfortable around them any longer."

I was sad to lose her friendship in the club, and later as a neighbor when she and her two children moved to Marietta.

* * *

I questioned any pride I might have felt to be an insider among such a group. There was one woman, in particular, who was known to insight gossip—malicious gossip—wherever she went. Of course every neighborhood has at least one trouble-maker, and I knew she was one reason Jeanette dropped out.

There was another woman in the club who was sleeping around with her best friend's husband. Did everyone alienate her? The answer is "no," but for the life of me I never could understand the double standards.

The majority of the women were not at all like that—Regina, Ann, Carol, Jo, Peggy…

Peggy lived two houses down the street. She had a son the same age as Keith and she was a true friend. We met weekly at her home for a neighborhood Bible Study. She was always the special kind of woman who displayed a genuine interest in others and made them feel comfortable and good about themselves.

Despite the snobby reputation we had acquired among the neighborhood, it was women like Peggy, Regina, Lauren, etc. that made me proud to be a member of the Magnolia Garden Club.

We were women who shared a common bond with ideals, ideas, and insight for the proper ways. We were all at the same place and at the same point of time in our lives, desiring to be polished, flawless diamonds, when were all but chunks of coal. But of course a diamond is simply a chunk of coal that's put under great amounts of pressure. We were simply diamonds in the rough.

CHAPTER XXXI
ONE TENTH OF A CENTURY

The Rutherford household reached a point when we needed additional income, so I put my creative talents to work. I made crafts and bread-dough sculpture for local craft fairs, and placed them on consignment in gift shops. The unique art was molded and sculptured out of a bread-dough recipe consisting of salt, flour, and water, then slowly baked in the oven for approximately twenty-four hours, and finished with about six coats of marine spar varnish.

The later hours proved to be more productive because of Keith and Clay, and my projects often kept me working until three in the morning. The items sold for anywhere from twenty to two-hundred dollars. And since the investment was next to zero, I could turn a huge profit. However, considering the amount of time I invested in the items I probably only averaged about fifty cents an hour.

Nonetheless, I considered myself a true entrepreneur in the art world, and Kyle printed some business cards with my business name, "The ART ACT by Delaney."

I also scouted around for new shops and stores opening in the area and designed their logos, which I painted on their glass storefront windows. That led to designing flyers for the community's small businesses. I had a regular little marketing and promotions company going.

One of the store owners asked me if I painted murals. I replied with confidence, "Sure I do," even though I had never painted a mural in my life.

I completed the mural for her home, and before I knew it, I had several murals to do within her neighborhood. When I finished a mural on a nursery wall for one of my clients, she asked my decorating advice. She liked my suggestions so much she offered me the job of buying furniture and accessories, etc., and decorating her entire house. Her husband particularly liked the amount of money I saved them. So he told a friend who told a friend, and before I knew what hit me I had a full-fledged design business specializing in decorating on a shoestring budget.

Through the years that followed I attended art, decorating, and marketing courses at the local universities and colleges which helped tremendously in my newfound career.

* * *

I couldn't believe one-tenth of a century had passed since my graduation, as our high school class ten year reunion was scheduled for the night of June 19, 1976. As the only female among the senior class officers, I was left responsible for organizing the big event.

I was amazed how much telephone work was involved in such an undertaking. Kyle accused me of having an elongated yellow growth on the side of my head, coming out of my ear. The phone was yellow, of course, to match the kitchen décor.

I cooked, changed diapers, washed diapers, and did the laundry with this umbilical chord strapped to the side of my head. I understood how a caged lion must feel while pacing within the confines of a given space, as the thirteen-foot telephone cord only gave me a total pacing area of twenty-six feet.

I had to get out of the kitchen chair and pace the floor from time to time in order to give my behind a break from the foam, corduroy cushions. The word "cushion" was grossly overstated when referring to those orange pieces of material sewn together and stuffed with foam. They were supposed to be washable; however, once I washed them they took on the appearance of the moon's surface, with craters from the bunched up foam. After they were washed I decided it was my duty to sit on them and flatten them out so they wouldn't look so bad. They flattened out, all right—flatter than a quarter-inch thick, providing about as much padding as a pancake. I wondered if it would have made *that* much difference if I had unzipped the things and removed the foam before washing them.

Subsequently, the orange beauties found themselves in the next garage sale with a price of one dollar for the bunch. I was surprised when they sold the first day and I thought, *Maybe I should have priced them for two bucks.*

* * *

I busily contacted the alumni by telephone and was shocked at the number of people who considered *me* part of *"that crowd."* When asked to define their meaning of "that crowd," they went on to describe the people I had always considered as the *"in* crowd."

It was ten years later before I realized I had been recognized and considered by others as an "insider" all along. I wished I had known it in school. Maybe I wouldn't have felt so intimidated all the time. But it's probably a good thing I didn't know, because I would have probably been just as conceited as they were.

The peer pressure was awful in high school. The unsurpassed amount of emphasis placed on name-brand shoes, handbags, dresses, etc. Wejan? loafers, John Romaine? hand-bags, and Villager? dresses, just to mention a few. I placed question marks after those names because, not only had I never owned them, I wasn't even sure how to spell them!   We could never afford the real things, so I always had to settle for the imitations.

I imagined reaching a point in my life when I could afford the real things. My friends placed so much emphasis on material things and I didn't want to be considered different, so I couldn't see beyond the tangibles. How many times did I hear myself plea with my mother, "Mama, please. Everybody's wearing them!" Every time she turned around I was begging her to buy something we couldn't afford.

Mama tried to be good natured about it when she said, "Delaney, Sugar, put all your wants in one hand and spit in the other and see which hand gets full faster." I always hated when she said that because I didn't understand what she meant. I suppose her rationale was going to lead her next to say that if God had meant for me to have those things, I would have been born wearing them.

* * *

I talked on the phone to people I hadn't seen in ten years. I was saddened by several phone calls when I discovered we had lost a couple of classmates to the war in Vietnam.

When I contacted Clark's parents they told me he had shot himself in the head, about two years after we'd graduated. He had enrolled in a college in Central Georgia where the boys were very cruel. They called him a "queer" and refused to be roommates with him.

I supposed his mother just needed to talk to someone about it, as she began to cry when she told me of the suicide note. It read: "I've been ridiculed all my life because I'm different. I'm going to a place where being different doesn't matter."

I remembered the last time I had seen Clark. It was the night of graduation as we were all leaving the Atlanta Auditorium. I left with my date. Clark left with his mother. His father didn't attend the graduation. As a career army officer, he disowned his son because he was ashamed of him.

Instead of being embarrassed to be seen leaving with his mother, he smiled, threw up his hand at me and said, "Bye, Delaney! Have a Good One!"

* * *

After many calls and several meetings, everything was ready for the big night.

Kyle and I drove into Atlanta and checked into the hotel that Friday night, so we would be there to set things up the next day. Kyle's mother worked at the hotel so we were able to stay there free of charge.

We were so excited to be staying in a name brand hotel—and for free. The Dunfey was an upscale place, decorated in medieval fashion like a gigantic castle. And it had air conditioning, too. But, of course, a swanky place like that would be expected to have everything.

Kyle and I went to a dinner theatre that evening and someone stole his wallet containing two-hundred dollars. We were absolutely sick—that was more than an entire week's pay! We never found the wallet, but we—correction—I went on to have one of the best times I can remember. Kyle was never one to recover so easily. Aside from a slight hangover, I'm sure the thought of all that money gone up in smoke was part of the reason for the shade of green his face maintained that entire weekend.

* * *

As the primary coordinator of the extravaganza, I felt so important that weekend.

Kyle had helped me shop for my dress for the event. It was a black, spaghetti-strap, slinky and sensual, floor-length formal with matching shawl. One of the most exciting factors about the dress was that it was a size five. I was tempted to wear the size tag on the outside of the dress for all to see.

It came from Macy's and I was shocked when Kyle approved its ridiculously expensive price of seventy dollars. It was a little daring with a small opening strategically placed to emphasize my cleavage.

Oops, cleavage? Did I say "cleavage?" What was that? I knew what it was, but how could it be emphasized, when it wasn't there to begin with? The trusty foam helpers were called to action, once again. A visit to Frederick's of Hollywood in the mall, and a purchase of some falsies especially designed for the push-up effect should do the trick.

Alas the helpers did their job beautifully, and I felt as confident, attractive, and womanly shaped as anyone there. I may have been twenty-eight years old, but I felt like a young debutante that evening, as I floated and flirted around the room. After all, that's what you do at a reunion; mingle and reminisce—reminisce of times that were gone forever, stored away in our memory banks to be recalled for occasions just such as that night.

Most everyone from "that group" was there, and most all of them looked as gorgeous and handsome, if not more so than they had ten years earlier. Some were housewives, others were technicians, nurses, teachers, clerks, secretaries, mechanics, and carpenters. Not a doctor in the bunch, and the closest thing to an attorney was Lamar, the president of the student body and class valedictorian. Of all people he had lost his mortarboard right before graduation and had to accept his diploma bare-headed.

He was the class brain, destined to lead our country in Washington, D.C. His written profile in the alumni directory stated that he had lived in Washington D.C. for a year, although it didn't say for what reason. I supposed it was to be considered an honor and a privilege for a man of such accomplishments—having lived in Washington, D.C. and all—to be present among peons, such as ourselves. That must have been the reason, because he was always surrounded by everyone wanting to speak to him, and be spoken to by him, though it was near impossible for most to get close enough because of the crowd.

* * *

After ten years it was difficult to even recognize some, much less determine in which group they were in school. The reunion provided a melting pot where all seemed to get along famously. Not to claim there wasn't a definite point of separation between the groups, as they mingled mostly among their own.

* * *

Tracy, Carol, Mary Beth, Sharon, Peggy, Larry, Ronnie, Dave, and on and on. It was great seeing all of them. But where was Betty?

I hadn't seen her since my wedding. We had talked on the telephone but not in person. I couldn't wait to see her. After all, she had been my very closest friend all through school—we had been like sisters.

When she finally appeared, I hugged her almost as soon as she walked in the door. She greeted me in a pretentiously, cool manner, "Hi." I could count on my fingers the number of words she spoke to me the entire night. Why did I let that bother me so much? I guess it was that of all the people there she had changed the most, and I'm not just referring to her appearance. Her personality was different. Oh, many others noticed it, too. Her smiles were insincere, and for some reason I felt sorry for her—sorry she couldn't loosen up more with those of us who were married. She seemed to cling mostly to the single, career oriented women like herself and the men from the group of boys with which she ran around in school.

Kyle tried to convince me that I may have intimidated her because I was happily married with two beautiful sons and a lovely home. And all she had was her career. She didn't present that impression, but rather that simple housewives were beneath her...and I was a simple housewife.

The saying that "You can't go back home" is painfully true, especially when referring to someone for whom I felt so much love. So many of those with whom I had been so close during those years of school I now discovered to be distant. We talked and reminisced, but once the laughs and memories were shared, we found we had little more in common. Maybe that's how Betty felt about me—we had little in common.

I was at the punch-bowl when a really good-looking guy came up to me, smiled, and said, "Hi, Delaney. You look better than ever!"

I didn't recognize this guy right off, so I glanced at his name badge. It was Arnold—all trim and muscular, with a beautiful wife at his side. I was so glad to see him, and I couldn't stop going on about how great he looked. He was awarded the prize for the "Most Changed."

He and his wife owned an accounting firm. Whether or not anyone else there would admit it, he was probably the most successful alumni that night, and I was proud and happy for him.

* * *

Besides Betty's attitude, only one brief incident put a damper on my evening. We went downstairs for cocktails afterwards to catch up on gossip, when Lee Ann gasped, as if she had just remembered the hottest gossip of all, "Did you hear about Tommy Swanson? Michele divorced him because he knocked her around all the time."

Teresa was shocked, "You're kidding..."

Lee Ann continued, "No, really. Her sister said he'd always been rough with Michele, but when the doctors confirmed she couldn't get pregnant he became violent with her. When he was in Vietnam, a grenade went off close to his head and left bad burn-scars allover one side of his face and neck. They had to do surgery to insert a metal plate there at the skull. He went off the deep end—you know, not just right in the head."

Peggy said, "Yeah, and I heard he's not even working—he's just drawing disability from the service. He moved in with his sister and her husband, somewhere up there around Marietta or Smyrna. Who would've thought it, Tommy Swanson, the great football hero—nothing but a bum, living off his sister. What a shame—and he was so great-looking."

Carolyn chimed in, "Yeah, I had the biggest crush on him, but he was always going with Michele. Nobody else ever had a chance with him."

All that talk about Tommy was bringing back that awful, sick feeling of nausea. I solved that problem by taking a drink, and another—so much I could hardly remember my own name, much less Tommy's.

* * *

Ten years—one tenth of a century—an entire decade had passed and brought us to that night in June, 1976, as some of us made new friends of old and vowed not to wait another ten years for the next reunion. The candles died and the band departed, as we bid our farewells with hugs and kisses, while expressing sincere intentions, "Let's keep in touch, ya hear?" Some would care if they did…most would not.

* * *

As Kyle and I drove home that next evening we reviewed the weekend as I drilled him and solicited his opinions of the different people that were there.

My questions were endless, "How do you think it went?" "Do you think everything went okay?" "Do you think everyone enjoyed themselves?" Then I got more specific, "What'dya think about Mary Beth?" What about Lee Ann?" "Well, how about Caryolyn?" and so one. "Do you think they're pretty?"

Of course he responded with, "You were the most beautiful woman there, and you were wearing the prettiest dress. The others couldn't hold a candle to you."

That was all I needed to hear. As for Betty, he ascertained, "She's probably insecure because she's gained a few pounds and she's not married yet. She sees you all slender and looking good, and married to a great guy like me who loves you, with two wonderful sons and a beautiful home. She's jealous—that's all. Hell, I'd be jealous of you, too, if I was a woman."

I nodded in agreement, thinking, *He always knows exactly what I want to hear, whether it's completely true or not. But he* **is** *right about one thing—he* **is** *a great guy!*

* * *

I was anxious to get to our beautiful home and see those two wonderful sons of ours. I leaned my head back on the headrest and folded my arms across my chest, as I slid down in the seat to get more comfortable and listen to some soft, slow music on the radio.

I gazed out the window into the darkness of the night and continued to reflect on the weekend, thinking how quickly the last couple of days had flown. I had put so much time and work in the preparations, it seemed like it should have lasted longer. Why did it have to be over so fast? But then, why should that weekend be any different from the rest of the ten years that flew by so quickly?

* * *

We finally drove into the carport but before Kyle turned off the ignition he leaned over and kissed me, "I love you, baby. I'm so proud of you. You did a hell of a job this weekend."

We hadn't been home for two whole days so we were anxious to see our sons when we went inside, but Mama had already tucked the boys in and they were fast asleep.

We went into Keith's room and then Clay's and just stood over each of them, admiring how sweet they were. They were the most beautiful five and three-year-old boys I'd ever seen.

Kyle placed his arm around my waist and pulled me closer to him, whispering, "God, I love you so much, Delaney. Thank you for giving me two beautiful sons." Then he kissed me on the forehead, "You make me so happy. I'm a lucky man."

I wrapped both arms around that man and squeezed him like there was no tomorrow, "I love you, too, Honey." As my emotions rose to the surface, I began sniffling and tears of happiness streamed down my cheeks. Clay's Braves baseball night-light cast an ever-so-soft glow over the room and illuminated Kyle's face just enough that I detected a slight trace of mist in his eyes, too. It was one of those tender moments that made me think. *It just doesn't get any better than this!*

* * *

I considered womanhood and motherhood to be the very best place to be in the whole world. As a woman, I only wanted to be the most loving wife to my wonderful husband, and the very best mother for my two beautiful sons God had given us. I felt complete and abundantly blessed...and fortunate to be a woman.

My entire world revolved around—and in fact, *was* our family of four. My life was perfect in every way!

HAND ON MY SHOULDER
NOVEMBER 22, 1984:
MONDAY MORNING
BEFORE THANKSGIVING

The den was nice and warm from the cozy fire Kyle started before he went to work. I tossed another oak log in the fireplace, pulled the Boston rocker closer to the hearth and threw a blanket over my legs. I was ready to settle in for a quiet morning, beginning with a steaming cup of hot chocolate topped with marshmallows.

We were fast approaching the holiday season with Thanksgiving only a few days away. The little fluffs of white floating in my cup reminded me of holidays when I was a child sharing a cup of hot chocolate with Daddy as he gently rocked me in front of the big gas heater. I remembered the comfortable warmth generated by the flames of that old heater combined with my Daddy's love. How I longed to be that little girl again.

I wished Daddy was there with me that morning—just to talk. I envisioned his smile as I wondered what we would talk about. I imagined the things he might say: "How's ya Mama, Sweetpea?" "I really like that husband of yours. You got a good man there.

I couldn't have hand-picked a better for for ya." "My grandsons sure are good-looking boys—take after their mama. They're really growing. Looks like they're gonna be tall like their daddy."

I wondered if Daddy could look down from heaven and see what had been going on in his Sweetpea's life the past eleven months, as I thought, *If only he was here with me now, I'd gladly share my hot chocolate and marshmallows with him. I'd even let him sit in this big, old rocker...and I would sit beside him here on the floor.*

* * *

Sipping my chocolate, I thought about that last chapter of my assignment—about my class reunion. I finished typing it on the word processor the night before but I hadn't printed it out yet. That chapter made me feel extremely blessed, as though my life really was "perfect with my family of four."

It was a very happy chapter of my life and I couldn't wait to discuss it during the next day's appointment with Dr. Robinson. She told me how much she looked forward to our sessions so she could read what I had written. I had grown very fond of Terri and trusted her implicitly. She had become more to me than my psychiatrist or therapist. I considered her my friend.

I glanced back through the pages of the chapters I had written over the past months. I couldn't believe they had developed into a book and I thought, *My God, I've gone through some hell in my life, but there were some great times, too. More good times than my mind allowed me to remember in the beginning.*

The writing showed me that life goes on after traumas and tragedies. Life's dark hours of hell pass with time, just as the darkest of nights step aside to the beams of the morning sunlight.

I enjoyed writing about the memories as I relived them in my mind. I could never say I *enjoyed* reliving the *bad* memories, but it was necessary in order to get back to the *good* ones.

Terri knew what she was doing, and she was very smart to have given me the assignment as a form of therapy when I wasn't responding to anything else.

I looked forward to continuing the sessions with my new friend. After reading one of my chapters, she always responded in the same way, "Delaney, you are so smart to remember all of that. You're coming along beautifully and I'm so proud of you." I never got tired of hearing her say those things. They always made me feel good.

* * *

I shared Terri's sense of pride in what she and I had accomplished through my therapy, but a feeling came over me that, *There's something very unsettling about those words—"My life was perfect"* and especially the phrase, *"Family of four."* For some reason I felt incomplete and apprehensive in saying those things. Those seven words gnawed away at my mind and a gripping sense of anxiety rushed over me, such that I suddenly became hesitant to go forward with my writing…and my memories. The gut-wrenching feeling in the pit of my stomach reminded me of that night on the Greyhound.

As if my mind was back on that roller coaster, I pushed away the very thoughts of ghosts and monsters, afraid to open my eyes. It felt as though I were on pretty solid and level ground. But what if I were just on a long stretch of track that would plateau out just so far, only to drop out from under me like the Giant Crest?

* * *

I was deeply troubled by something I saw later that afternoon. I was going to replace Clay's last year school picture with the new one, and when I removed the frame's back…there it was. I had uncovered a puzzling photograph that stirred up many questions in my mind, beginning with, *Why don't I remember this?*

I recognized Kyle, but Keith and Clay had changed—they were a lot younger in the photo. My hair was as long as Doc Terri's, and in my arms I held an infant—a baby boy. He was wearing a while sailor suit with navy-blue trim and a red tie and matching booties. His eyes were the same vivid blue as Kyle's and Clay's, and his golden strands of hair, however sparse, were brushed to one side. He had the same cherubic face as Keith and Clay. The words, "Christmas, 1981" were printed on the back.

Clay was in the living room next to me on the piano bench, so I pointed to the baby in the photo and asked, "Who is that?"

He acted surprised that I didn't know, "You don't remember, Mom? That's Chris."

"Chris? Who's...?"

The phone rang and Keith yelled from the den, "Mom, telephone! It's for you! It's Grandmom!"

I handed the picture and frame to Clay and told him to put them back together, while I went to answer the phone. "Hello?"

"Hey, Dollbaby, how ya doin' today?"

I answered, "Oh, all right, I guess...Mama, who's Chris?"

After a brief silence, she asked, "Is Kyle working late tonight?"

I wondered why she avoided my question. Maybe she didn't hear me, so I repeated, "I said, "Who's Chris?""

"Baby, just wait 'til Kyle's home with you. He'll be home in another couple of hours. Talk to him about it. That'll be better."

* * *

Kyle wasn't anymore enlightening. He hesitated a few seconds before he answered, "Chris? Well, he was..." He paused, then continued stammering, "...he was a little boy. Do you remember?"

I thought, *Well, that's a stupid question. If I remembered, I wouldn't be asking.* "No. Who is he and where is...?"

He interrupted, "Baby, I think you need to talk this over with Dr. Robinson tomorrow. You do see her tomorrow, don't you?"

"Yes, but..."

He continued, "Well, I'll tell you what. We're not that busy at work, so I'll take the morning off and drive you to your appointment. Okay?"

I just shook my head, confused.

He quickly changed the subject. "Now, come give me a hug and let's eat dinner so we can get the kitchen cleaned up early. I went by and picked up some hamburgers so we won't have a big mess. And I've got a surprise for you. I rented a movie for tonight and it's one you'll like...it's a comedy. I know how much you love comedies."

* * *

After the movie I withdrew into my office, compelled to read over my last entry of the assignment before printing it for the next day's session with Terri. As I read those unsettling words, "My life was perfect," "family of four," the sensation of the air solidifying in my throat began to hinder my breathing. The reality hit me—I was still in the dark about so many things.

I knew the coming chapters of the assignment would uncover the mystery, but somehow I wasn't so sure I wanted to know. I wasn't certain I wanted to continue writing those chapters of my life. But I reminded myself, *Terri will be with me to see me through whatever horrifying memories might be ahead. After all, I'm thirty-five years old, and I was only twenty-eight at the time of the chapter about my class reunion. There's still seven more years to cover.*

* * *

By the time I waited for the chapter to finish printing I was exhausted. It had been an extremely long day. When I flipped the processor's off-switch I became mesmerized by the little dot on the screen, as it slowly faded away. It was later than I imagined and the room was totally dark, except for the fading dot of light.

The air in the room suddenly became very heavy and cold, and a chill ran up my spine and throughout my body.

As if time were on pause…and then fast-forwarding my memory banks, I began hearing sounds and seeing things I didn't want to hear or see. But they wouldn't go away! All my senses ran rampant as I tasted and smelled things so putrid I wanted to vomit!

A dog's incessant barking broke the dead of silence, and I saw sunlight reflecting off a pool of water. I thought, *My imagination is playing tricks on me again. But…wait!*

There's something floating in the pool. It's a ball, and a child's red and blue jacket—but it's not just an empty jacket. My heart raced out of utter panic and my hands were so cold—frozen—as if they were submerged in ice water.

Frantically I wailed, "No-o-o!"

I saw the child's face…so cold to the touch. His eyes were closed and no matter how hard I shook him, they wouldn't open.

The dog's barking grew louder.

The feeling of absolute helplessness was unbearable and the haunting sounds of my own repetitive screaming, "No! No-o-o!"… endless wailing—sobbing—all too real.

The barking grew even louder and the bone-chilling sirens were ear-piercing while people were all around. Horror and agonizing pain filled my heart so it nearly exploded, beating so hard and so loud in my head, it was deafening. I wanted it to stop and in a jolting reflex I covered my ears.

I pleaded again and again, "No…No!" But it wouldn't stop!

I was disoriented. The dog's barking faded, along with the terrifying vision of the child, and I was relieved it was finally over, but then…

My mind was drawn into another chaotic whirlwind of a different time and place where it was colder. The glaring sunlight stepped behind a heavy curtain of darkness and, once again, I couldn't see. My jaws ached when the forceful vise of something foul-smelling—like a hand—covered my mouth. I flinched when

343

the cold, metal surface of what felt like a gun was jabbed into the base of my neck. I was petrified when I felt and smelled the stench of someone's hot breath in my face. I couldn't move, as if weighted down—struggling—but I couldn't break free. There was immediate pain from a striking blow to the side of my face and blood poured from my cheek.

My own pleas echoed, begging, "No-o-o, Ple-ease Don't!"

Excruciating pain left me soiled within—forever unclean—and the intense humiliation of being violated shamed me so. I had experienced that feeling before.

My body jolted at the dull, solid "thud" of a heavy door slamming above me—a tight sound, like a lid—enclosing me in such a way I felt completely sealed off from the universe and entombed in total blackness. I couldn't sit or raise my head where I was—closed in—trapped in such a cramped space I became claustrophobic. Stripped of all my dignity, I was naked and forcibly lying in a fetal position... freezing.

There was so much confusion whirling around in my head as I begged aloud, "God, if this is a dream, please let me wake up!"

But God ignored my pleas.

My eyes squinted in reaction to sudden extreme brightness as the door opened above me, as if a lid had been raised.

There were more sirens and flashing lights...then more people.

The big white light overhead forced my eyes tightly shut. There was a cacophony of noises in my head and people talking—questioning—incessant talking, all at once. It was like the disturbing sound of a fifty-piece orchestra all playing different songs at the same time.

Then a child was screaming in sheer panic, "Mom-my!" growing louder, "MOM-MY!" and louder, to a deafening point. It was more than I could stand. "God, please make it all stop!"

But vile demons were making their presence known, and I was surrounded in such a way I couldn't breathe! Hanging on to sanity by a sole unraveling thread that was on the verge of breaking, I felt myself slipping into a dark abyss…

Drained of all my strength and overcome by the demons' visions, I was sobbing so my plea was weakened out of sheer desperation, "Oh, dear God, not again. Please save me from his hell…"

I suddenly felt a hand on my shoulder, as God had answered my prayer and sent my husband in to bring me back to the present. "Delaney, Baby, it's all right. I'm here, now."

My body was shaking as if electrical charges were pulsating rapidly throughout my entire being. Rocking back and forth with my arms tightly clasped across my chest, I was wringing wet with perspiration and I was extremely weak

Standing behind me he then leaned over and embraced my shoulders in such a loving, calming way that reassured me I was no longer in the land of nightmares, but at home in the safety of his arms.

I was so relieved God had sent Kyle to rescue me from the pit of hell I had fallen into. I broke into tears, as I knew deep down in my soul those *flashbacks* were merely previews of coming chapters— chapters I would be forced to face sooner or later…no matter how painful.

* * *

I followed Kyle into the bedroom, within the realms of safety, but before bed I wanted to take my nightly shower.

As I stood naked before the bathroom mirror, I noticed the bruises had faded with not so much as a trace remaining. Dr. Sims was right about the surgery's scar up the side of my face. It had healed to the point it was barely noticeable. I wondered if my heart would ever completely heal, and if there would come a time when there would be no more pain.

I closed my eyes and lightly caressed my face with both hands. Exploring every inch of the surface along the way, I directed my fingertips to glide across my eyelids, around the cheekbones, then down around the mouth and across the lips, over the chin and finally, the neck and throat.

The skin felt as smooth as that of a baby's. When I opened my eyes, the mirror reflected a complexion that appeared just as perfect and without so much as a trace of gray in my dark hair.

However, I was standing a few feet back away from the mirror and direct lighting, observing an image of myself as I must have appeared to others—to the naked eye.

I stepped closer and leaned forward to inspect my reflection under the brightness of the lights. The seemingly faded scar suddenly became more prominent. The slight crow's feet outside the eyes and laugh-lines at the corners of the mouth became obvious, while the brownish-black hair revealed an ever-so-slight hint of graying.

The brown eyes belonging to the image in the mirror were staring back into my own as I came to a startling realization. Even at close range and under the brightest of lights, the mirror didn't reflect my levels of pain, sensitivity and emotions, dwelling just beneath the surface.

I wondered just how much deeper into my mind Terri and I would be required to explore in order to rediscover the real Delaney and restore my freedom. I reminded myself that I wasn't so unlike other women, and that people are rarely as they appear to others.

Some are destined to enjoy reasonably trouble-free lives. While others are sentenced to endure a certain course of hell-like happenings that leave deep, ugly scars beneath the skin...far beyond the naked eye's range of vision.

I turned away from my reflection and stepped into the shower where the hot water was downright therapeutic, as it ran over my stiffened shoulders and down my rigid back. I became so relaxed my knees almost buckled. I couldn't wait to dry off and crawl in beneath the covers next to Kyle.

* * *

While I lay in my husband's arms he kissed me on the cheek and then on the lips. He whispered softly, "That's better, Baby. You know I love you, don't you?" With a gentle squeeze and one last kiss, "Now relax and get some sleep. It'll be morning and the sun will be up before you know it." He began stroking my forehead, knowing full well that normally put me to sleep within minutes.

I felt so safe in his arms—secure and loved—truly loved. We'd been together nineteen years and his touch still sent the sensation of love and adoration throughout me. A calming warm feeling replaced the cold I had felt earlier.

My eyes welled with tears, as the questions rolled over and over in my mind, repeating like a broken record, *Who is Chris? Where is Chris? Who is...? Where is...?*

Teardrops flowed onto my pillow.

Thanksgiving was only three days away. I thanked God for my sons, and I was so thankful to have my husband and Terri to help me get through the next chapters of the assignment. I didn't know what I would do without the both of them to be there with me.

I wished I could remain in the past, especially the chapter about my class reunion. Those were such happy times. But I realized I couldn't live in the past, just as I knew in my heart that the emotional roller coaster of my life was no different from the Greyhound. It didn't matter if my eyes were opened or remained tightly shut—ready or not—I was fast approaching the Giant Crest with the inevitable, heart-stopping Break soon to follow.

I shuddered from that chilling thought as I bit my bottom lip in a nervous reaction. The sickening rush of anxiety made me consider relaxation as an absolute impossibility...until my yellowbird took flight with me on its wings.

I rolled over onto my side and lay my head on my freshly fluffed pillow. *Hmmm, soft as a cloud,* I thought, as I took a deep breath, closed my exhausted eyes, and with a sigh I was flown away to the peaceful land of sleep.

My last thought of the night was, *I'll deal with the break of the crest when my memory allows...and Dear Lord, when I do, please give me the strength to get through it.*

Amen.

Printed in the United States
83566LV00004B/25-36/A